The

DASTARDLY
MISS LIZZIE

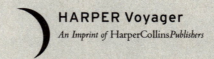

HARPER Voyager

An Imprint of HarperCollins*Publishers*

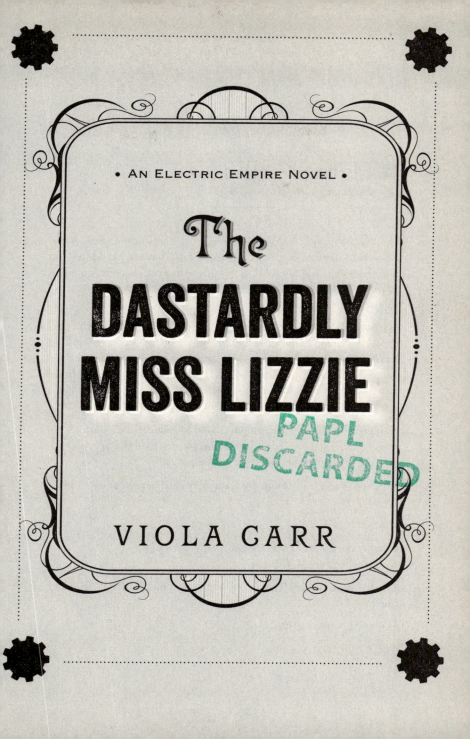

· An Electric Empire Novel ·

The
DASTARDLY
MISS LIZZIE

VIOLA CARR

HarperCollins
PUBLISHERS
Since 1817

HarperCollins books may be purchased for educational, business, or sales promotional use. For information, please email the Special Markets Department at SPsales@harpercollins.com.

Harper Voyager and design are trademarks of HarperCollins Publishers LLC.

FIRST EDITION

Chapter opener art © Flat Design/Shutterstock.com
Designed by Janet M. Evans

Library of Congress Cataloging-in-Publication Data has been applied for.

ISBN 978-0-06-236312-1

17 18 19 20 21 DIX/LSC 10 9 8 7 6 5 4 3 2 1

The Dastardly Miss Lizzie

a Delectable Tale of Murderous Mayhem!

STARRING

DR. ELIZA JEKYLL

intrepid practitioner of legal medicine,
also appearing as the bold adventuress

MISS LIZZIE HYDE

AND FEATURING

CAPTAIN REMY LAFAYETTE

clever Imperial Spy and lycanthropic prodigy

The eccentric alchemist **MARCELLUS FINCH**
dabbler in unorthodox medicinals

LA BELLE, a wicked warmonger,

with the bloodthirsty henchman **LA BÊTE**

and the fabled and sizeable **MR. JACK DAWKINS**
famously named **THE ARTFUL DODGER**

ALSO ONSTAGE, in various haunts and dreadful guises:

PROFESSOR EPHRONIA CRANE

Inventor of astounding Electrical Marvels

The singular Philosopher, **SIR ISAAC NEWTON**
Regent for mad **KING EDWARD VII**

MR. MALACHI TODD, a Homicidal Lunatic,
escaped or not from burned Newgate;

and **MR. EDWARD HYDE,** the insane and inimitable

KING OF RATS

As Always, the Splendid Scenery, Machinery, and Effects
produced by **MISS VIOLA CARR**

The

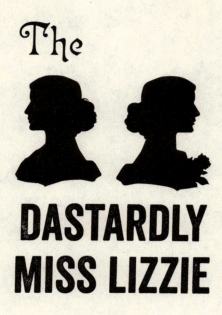

DASTARDLY
MISS LIZZIE

AN ELECTROMAGNETIC
DISTURBANCE

GO AWAY, LIZZIE, I'M WORKING."

Eliza Jekyll prodded the dead inventor's burned face with her scalpel, shivering in the damp chill. The laboratory's coal fire had long since died, and drizzling rain shrouded the outside world in grim gray mist.

The inventor was slumped in the desk chair, cheek against an ink-stained ledger, dried blood crusting her mouth. A pen was clutched in her stiff fingers. On the page, in the victim's blood, her murderer had scrawled the word *WHORE*.

Lizzie Hyde peered into the dead face, grinning like a ghoul in her lurid red dress. "Ooh-er. Nothing like a juicy dead'un first thing in the morning, eh?"

"Have some respect," hissed Eliza, shoving Lizzie's translucent apparition aside with a gray-skirted hip. Around her, uniformed police constables milled, searching crammed bookshelves and rooting through electrical equipment. "This poor woman deserves justice, not a bad circus act."

"Say again?" Inspector Harley Griffin shot Eliza an odd look as he examined a clockwork centipede that marched across the ledger, its tiny feet clacking. The impeccable detective's dark hair was neat, suit and necktie immaculate. Not even this filthy weather could ruffle him. But her nerves ratcheted tighter. Lizzie's specter was imaginary. Harley couldn't see or hear her. Eliza was safe. No one would find out.

That didn't make the prospect of going insane at a crime scene any more appealing.

"Never mind," she muttered. Now Lizzie was poking a gleeful finger into the corpse's ear. Exasperated, Eliza held her scalpel alongside the woman's blue bodice. *Thwock!* The blade jumped, attaching itself like a magnet to the metal corset bones within. "Killed by the action of electricity. Not a gunflash. A sustained application of a much larger current."

Griffin consulted his leather-bound notebook. "Miss Antoinette de Percy, twenty-nine, inventor of electrical gadgets and visiting research fellow at the Royal Institution. Last seen alive by the maid at six last evening. A social butterfly, I'm told. Held a kind of salon here. Intellectuals, poets, drawing room radicals. Specialty something called 'aether-fluid dynamics,' under a professor named Crane."

"Pah." Lizzie tossed ghostly mahogany curls. "All that book-reading never kept her breathing. Brain the size of Bloomsbury and still just some bastard's *whore*."

Eliza eyed the red-smeared message with distaste. Lizzie was right. Such a clever scientist, written off in this hateful fashion. Always a man's wife, daughter, lover. Never just herself. "Poor girl. Hardly a crime of passion."

Griffin stroked his luxuriant mustache that was the envy of the Metropolitan force, and likely the City of London police as well. "You don't think finger-painting *whore* in her blood indicates a crime of passion?"

"I'd have expected a stabbing, or similar. Not a rearward attack from such impersonal distance." She sidestepped a brass anteater that snuffled its nose across the floor, in hot pursuit of a metal mouse. Her own clockwork assistant, Hippocrates, bounced on his long hinged legs, trying to reach a surly mechanical cat that glared down from a high shelf.

"*Felis catus,*" trumpeted Hipp in his little electric voice. "Playtime. Make greater speed."

Griffin covered a smile. "Seems unlikely Miss de Percy was struck by lightning."

A brass caterpillar crawled laboriously along the windowsill. Lizzie poked it. It fell off onto the floor, where it wriggled faster, trying to escape. "Oi! Come 'ere, you little rotter."

"How adorable," exclaimed Eliza hastily. "What amazing engineering! Perhaps one of these creatures did it, in a fit of electric jealousy. Hipp, stop that, she's twice your size."

"Clearly Puss is the gang's mastermind." An electric blackbird swooped above Griffin's head, and he ducked to avoid gleaming gunmetal wings. "So, if not a pistol—what?"

"Good question. If one of these malfunctioned badly enough to kill, you'd expect more spectacular wreckage. Let's see." Eliza tilted her optical down over her spectacles. An array of lenses and spectrics that detected all manner of substances and invisible forces, the optical wasn't strictly legal— but orthodox science couldn't always provide answers.

"Boo!" Lizzie's dark eye loomed, magnified. Eliza jerked back, and Lizzie guffawed. "Gotcha! Teach you to mess about

with Henry Jekyll's dodgy contraptions. Them Royal Society
goons will fry your saucy backside, Captain Lafayette or no."

Surreptitiously, Eliza glared back. Since her engagement
to a Royal Society investigator, the prospect of being sum-
marily arrested for scientific heresy and tossed in a dank
electrified cell at the Tower worried her a little less. But only
a little.

She slotted in a thick aether-reactive lens. Starry white-
ness flared, dazzling. "Ouch!" She tore the optical away. "The
aether excitation in here is extraordinary. Energized by these
creatures, no doubt." She rubbed aching temples. "A shame.
I'd hoped for a more conclusive pattern."

Lizzie squinted at the smudged blackboard. "'The boy
stood on the burning deck with a pocket full of crackers,'" she
read. "'One fell down his trouser leg and blew off all his—'
Clear off, I'm learning here." She swiped at the swooping
blackbird as it cackled and pecked.

Eliza resisted the urge to wring Lizzie's neck and convince
Harley once and for all that she'd lost her marbles. She sliced
off a sliver of the victim's scorched flesh and slipped it into a
glass tube, then took a blood sample.

Eagerly, Lizzie plonked her satin-flounced rear on the
desk, leering like a freak-show spectator. "About time we got
to the gory part," she announced. "Slice away!"

"Last seen alive at six, you say?" Smiling sweetly, Eliza
bumped Lizzie off the desk with a casual sweep of hip—but
inwardly, she cringed. Lizzie's spectral skirts flopped dangerously close to where Griffin stood. What would happen if Lizzie touched him?

She slipped a glass thermometer inside Miss de Percy's

tight collar. "The body has cooled several degrees," she reported, swatting aside Lizzie's meddling hand. "Skin bluish, arm stiff. Full rigor takes around twelve hours to set in. Granted, it's cold in here, but I'd say she died no later than eight last evening."

Griffin shifted aside a red glass vase and slid the splintered wooden shaft from the corpse's hand. "Pen's broken," he noted. "Was she writing when attacked?"

Thoughtfully, Eliza examined it. "Scribble, scribble, the killer creeps up, and *boom!* Her fingers convulse, the pen snaps. And she falls forwards, onto whatever she was writing!"

Lizzie cheered, waving her skirts. "Hooray! Better than a circus, this gaff."

Together, Eliza and Griffin forced the body into a sitting position. Limbs stiff, neck rigid. And beneath where she'd lain . . .

"It's blank." Griffin examined the ledger, flipping back one bloodstained page. "Yesterday's diary entries. 'One: team meeting,' it says, at noon. Perhaps with this Professor Crane? But nothing for today."

"Mmm." Absorbed, Eliza inspected the corpse's face. Miss de Percy's eyelids were half-closed, mouth bruised black, skin mottled—but across her left cheek was the smudged imprint of handwriting.

"Aha!" Triumphantly, Eliza copied the letters onto a scrap of paper, reversed from left to right.

but then $\nabla \times H = 1/c$ (

$- \nabla^2 B = 0$ in $\mathbb{R}_4$! It's im

what to do. Please h

Lizzie snorted. "What in green hell does that mean?"

"Logical," bubbled Hippocrates, whirring excited cogs. "Curl of magnetic field equals one over speed of light multiplied by—"

"Very instructive, Hipp," cut in Eliza, elbowing Lizzie aside. Her head throbbed with memories of torturous mathematics lessons, her patient tutor demonstrating algebraic matrices and cross products while her adolescent wits boggled. Fluents, gradients, rates of change . . .

"Gradient squared," muttered Hipp indignantly. "Zero. Implications unclear."

"You can say that again." Griffin studied the ledger once more. "But where's the original? Nothing like it in the book."

"A separate letter? But why would the killer take it?"

"Perhaps his name was on it."

"'Here's a bunch of equations, and so-and-so just came to kill me'? Not very likely."

"No," admitted Griffin. "Our man contrives this mysterious murder weapon just to confound us, scribbles his insults to make it easier for us to catch him, then makes off with a letter full of equations? What's his motive: wasting police time?"

"Inspector Griffin, sir!" A young female police officer hurried up. Her dark blue uniform frock was spotless, silver buttons polished to mirrors, and she'd combed her thick dark hair into London's neatest bun. Even her boots were impossibly free from mud. "This is Mr. Locke, sir," she reported, dragging forth a bedraggled fellow in an ill-fitting gray suit. "He discovered the body when he called this morning."

Eliza had to wonder why Constable Perkins even wanted

to be a police officer. There were few enough female constables, fewer still who lasted more than a month or two. She
glanced at her own creased skirts and carelessly pushed-up
sleeves, and sighed. Once, she'd been as keen as Perkins. Perhaps she was getting old and jaded. Perhaps they all were.

"Excellent," said Griffin briskly. "Anyone see anything, or
hear a racket last night?"

"Nothing so far, sir." Perkins cast her lashes down.

"No curious servants? Not a single irate neighbor or nosy
passer-by? So many upstanding citizens roaming about, yet
no one notices a high-voltage explosion. Extraordinary."

"No, sir." Perkins turned pink. "I mean, yes, sir. I'll keep
asking, sir."

Griffin clapped her shoulder. "Good man. Persistence
pays. See to it."

Bushy-tailed with importance, Perkins bustled away. It
was clear that she idolized Harley—clear to everyone, that
was, except the eminent detective.

Griffin caught Eliza's smile. "What?" he said artlessly.
"She's a good officer. She deserves a chance."

"Tell that to our charming Chief Inspector." Eliza studied the new arrival—Mr. Locke—with interest, trying to
ignore Lizzie, who was grinning into the fellow's face from
a distance of three inches. Locke was young, fair-skinned,
with damp blond hair that kept falling in his face. Too long
for a proper gentleman's. More like a university student. "I'm
Dr. Eliza Jekyll. Might we ask you a few questions?"

The fellow blew his nose, stuffed his handkerchief into his
pocket, and swiped back his hair before shaking her hand.
"Jekyll, did you say? A famous name. Seymour Q. Locke,

engineer's assistant." His tones were polished with Oxbridge *ennui,* but retained a disarming hint of west-country farm boy. "Antoinette is my dear friend and colleague. Was, that is." His eyes glittered hard, as if he held back tears.

Her chest ached with swift sympathy. But still, a cruel diamond shard twinkled in her heart, icy with impatience. What was the point of hysterics? Grief didn't bring back the slain.

"May I ask when last you saw her?" Finally, Lizzie had vanished. It didn't make Eliza feel safer.

"Last evening, around five." Locke shivered, rubbing damp hands. Mournful as a dog left out in the rain. "We were to meet this morning for our daily walk—"

"In this weather?" interrupted Griffin.

"Walk!" piped up Hipp hopefully, his blue *happy* light flashing. "Walk?"

Locke smiled weakly. "She's invented an aether-powered rain shelter that hovers overhead as you proceed. Antoinette wouldn't let a few showers stop her. She doesn't let anything get in her way."

"That's the second time you've used her given name, Mr. Locke." Griffin didn't let his gaze slip. "She must have been a *very* dear friend."

"Indeed." Locke cracked his knuckles, fidgeting. "As you say. Well, I don't suppose it matters now, Seymour old thing. You might as well come clean, as they say in the police gazettes. She and I are secretly engaged, you see," he confided, with a flash of white teeth. "No one is to know. I'm practically bursting with the news, you can imagine, but Antoinette will have her way." His mouth trembled. "Oh, dear. Who'll care for her menagerie now?"

Eliza exchanged glances with Griffin. "Forgive me, but I must ask: Do you know why someone might scribble this word on her diary?" She showed Locke the page.

He averted his eyes, his face green. "You're a professional woman, Doctor. You're familiar with what *that's* about. Some people don't like a lady to be accomplished and independent. They'll spread filthy lies to keep her in her place. None of them are friends of mine."

"Lies? What kind?"

"Antoinette isn't independently wealthy. You can imagine how they say she affords all this." He waved to encompass the laboratory. "The neighbors shout across the street at me, you know. Apparently we shall burn in hell for eternity. I tried to explain that the laws of thermodynamics don't allow for a fire that never extinguishes, but there's no reasoning with religious thickheads, is there? I suppose it's not their fault," he added ungraciously. "Indoctrination rots their brains. I'll be glad when the Philosopher finally outlaws the whole idiotic business. Not before time."

"And how would you describe Miss de Percy's mood last evening?"

Locke stared, doubtful. "Agitated, now that you mention it. She'd a bruise on her face, as you see. Mentioned an accident with some laboratory equipment. And in the afternoon she'd received a caller who'd upset her. Wouldn't say who. Bade me forget it, said she had work to do. So I wished her good night and departed."

"At five o'clock," murmured Griffin.

"Or thereabouts."

"In the rain?"

Locke looked confused. "I suppose so. I tend not to notice such things."

"And you live . . . ?"

"On Tottenham Court Road."

"Quite a walk, then."

Locke's gaze frosted. "Not really."

"Don't tell me: you were home alone all evening," guessed Griffin stoutly. "Convenient for you."

A chilly smile that made Eliza flinch. "Perhaps you weren't listening, Inspector. In your eagerness to make insinuations, I mean. I didn't say I went home."

To his credit, Griffin didn't blink. "Where, then?"

Sighing, Locke rubbed his eyes, as if his head ached. "If you must know, I spent the evening at the Royal Institution on Albemarle Street. There's to be a demonstration of Professor Crane's miniaturized aether engine at the RI tomorrow. As I said, I'm the assistant. I've many arrangements to make and I stayed until quite late. You can ask the professor."

"And *then* you went home?" persisted Griffin.

"Assuredly. But first I crept back here and murdered the woman I love." Locke reproached him with reddened eyes. "It was two in the morning, I was exhausted, I had the most frightful headache and I was due to meet Antoinette at nine. Of course I went home, idiot. Where else would I go, Piccadilly Circus?"

Coolly, Eliza proffered the scrap of paper. "Since you're

not an idiot, Mr. Locke, might you tell me to what these figures refer?"

Locke gave it only a perfunctory glance. "Sadly, I'm but a lowly assistant. I purchase materials, set up the equipment, adjust levels, take readings, that sort of thing. Antoinette's physics is quite beyond me."

"But you know that this *is* physics," persisted Eliza. "Not pure mathematics, for instance."

Again, he looked blank. "Advanced aether physics is her field. I assumed it was to do with the new miniature engine. Is it important?"

A tiny clockwork opossum climbed down from the overhanging light into Locke's hair, blinking solemnly. Eliza tried not to stare. "That's a very fine clockwork. Did Miss de Percy build it?"

Locke extracted the opossum and reattached it to the light. "It's not clockwork. Fully electric. No winding necessary."

"Surely it's far too tiny for an autonomous power cell."

"Attend our demonstration if you don't believe me," said Locke impatiently. "I did say *advanced* aether physics. You people really ought to listen harder." He made a defiant show of checking his watch, clicking his tongue at the time. "Satisfied, Inspector? May I go?"

Griffin opened his mouth to answer—but a scuffle in the hall cut him off. The door slammed, boots banged in the corridor—and in burst a short, ruddy-faced man in an unkempt brown suit, chewing on a cigar.

Griffin sighed. Eliza groaned—and Lizzie bristled into

view like an irate scarlet hedgehog and started snarling curses.

"Griffin," exclaimed Chief Inspector Reeve with an insolent smile. "Just the man. You remember General Sir Stamford Owen?"

"Ahh. Griffin, is it?" The ancient Commissioner of Police squinted down at Griffin through an enormous monocle, leaning on a spindly cane that creaked under his weight. He had a drooping mustache of pure white and a moth-eaten top hat, and his coat gleamed with dusty campaign jewels dating back to the Peninsular Wars. "Banged up that Slasher chap yet? Can't be an Englishman. No decent public school chap would slice a fellow up so rudely. Dirty Froggie spy, says I. One of Boney's men!"

Eliza winced. Reeve was angling for promotion again, and had put Griffin in charge of a particularly gruesome set of murders in Soho that were proving stubbornly impenetrable. It was the impossible case, with no evidence and no witnesses—just a rising body count. And with each new grisly discovery, Reeve gleefully made sure everyone knew exactly who had failed to stop the killer.

Griffin smiled faintly. "We're doing everything we can, Commissioner."

"Shitsmear!" Lizzie paced around Reeve, a ball of frothing scarlet rage. "Gropenoddle! Wormstained green shagbollock . . ."

"Takes me back to Waterloo," declared Sir Stamford, oblivious. "Damned Froggies all over the shop. Horses screaming, cannonballs whistling by, men running to and fro with their arms torn off. The fog of war!" He waved his cane heartily, sending the electric light swinging, and the opossum clambered dolefully for cover.

Griffin steadied the old fellow's arm. "Glad you're keeping on top of things, sir."

"Ahh," said Sir Stamford again, jamming on his dislodged hat. "Excellent. First rate. But who's doing something about it, eh?" he added, suddenly fierce. "Shopkeepers closing early, ladies of the night staying off the streets in Haymarket and raising their prices, by God. Why, a man needs a guinea just to get himself a good rogering! It's scandalous!"

"That's the spirit, Commissioner." Reeve looked the victim over, chewing his cigar, equally oblivious to Lizzie's tirade. "What have we here?"

"Dead scientist, sir," said Griffin crisply. "Weapon some kind of electrical equipment."

"Ahh." The Commissioner nodded solemnly. "Why, I once saw a man's torso blown to smithereens by an enemy capacitor! Hidden in a barrel of Dutch gin, by God. Innards all over the campaign tent, eyeballs in the ice bucket. Loyal toast quite ruined. Never saw a gin and tonic in quite the same light after that." He peered at Griffin's mustache. "I say, they're shiny. Do you use whale oil?"

Reeve flicked through the ledger, snorting. "'Whore,' is it? Having a bit on the side, I'll warrant, and got taught a lesson. These radical floozies get their leg over with anything in trousers."

Seymour Locke flushed. "Now look here—"

"Naturally," snapped Eliza, ears burning from Lizzie's creative invective. "A single woman of education and intelligence simply *must* be lifting her skirts to all and sundry. And what business of anyone's if she is? Heaven forbid one should seek out entertaining conversation that isn't about hairstyles and babies."

"Exactly right," said Reeve, utterly without irony. "All this science is unhealthy. If she'd had a husband to protect her, this wouldn't have happened." He studied Locke insolently, earning a sharp-frosted glare. "Who's the pretty boy?"

"The victim's intended," said Griffin. "He found the body."

Reeve tucked thumbs into tartan braces, cigar clamped between his teeth. "Book 'im."

"Is your act meant to be funny?" snapped Locke. "I thought this Griffin character was the police force's village idiot. Apparently he's just the warm-up."

Griffin cleared his throat. "Sir, the man has a checkable alibi."

Reeve chortled. "I'll bet he does! It's always the lover, Griffin. Police work doesn't get more basic than that. Book the snotty brat and be done."

"Ahh!" Sir Stamford's rheumy eyes gleamed. "Excellent job, Reeve old boy. Just the sort of man we need to win this war." He flourished his cane like a saber. "Charge for the guns, men! We'll have Boney in chains by nightfall!"

Eliza's heart sank. "But there's no evidence."

Reeve grinned. "Then find some. Isn't that what you're for? Or have you forgotten how?"

She opened her mouth to retort, but her failure in the Slasher case burned bitter on her tongue. Flushing, she said nothing.

Smugly, Reeve beckoned to a pair of Griffin's officers, ignoring Constable Perkins, who'd waited eagerly to be called upon and now deflated visibly. "Bow Street, lads, quick as you like. Griffin can do the paperwork. Not too busy, are you, Griffin?"

The two blue-coated men grabbed Locke, one arm each. Locke shook them off, prickly as a thistle. "Leave off, half-wits. This is a waste of time," he added over his shoulder as they led him away. "You'll see."

"Don't worry, Mr. Locke," she called after him, glaring at Reeve. "We'll check the *facts* at once. We shan't trouble you for more than an hour or two."

"Facts," grumbled Hippocrates, scratching disconsolately at the carpet, where a brass snake slithered, its forked copper tongue flickering. "Evidence negligible. Does not compute."

Satisfied, Reeve chewed his cigar. "Job done for you again, Griffin. No wonder you're getting nowhere on the Slasher case. Perhaps it's time we had fresh eyes on that."

"Indeed, sir!" Sir Stamford prodded Griffin in the chest with his cane. "Put some effort in, lad! Hunt that Froggie interloper down, or we'll find someone who will!"

"You heard him, Inspector." Reeve smirked. "Better come up with some leads. Shame if we had to replace you."

"Screw you, weedbrain," retorted Lizzie, steaming in a fit of scarlet pique. "Don't see you down there getting your hands dirty."

Eliza gritted her teeth, her own anger fresh. As if Reeve knew anything about real detective work, as opposed to thrashing suspects into false confessions and cultivating corrupt informants who'd say anything for a price. "But—"

"Not a word, missy," snapped Reeve. "I've told you before: police work is no job for a girl. Don't you have a wedding to plan?"

Lizzie hopped like a dervish, shaking her fists. "I'll plan *you*, fartstain! I'll wring your greasy neck until your god-rotted eyes bulge!" Dizziness overcame Eliza, hard and fast like a blow to the head. Scarlet mist descended, and she swooned . . .

"Oi!" Reeve leapt backwards, swearing. "What the devil are you doing, you crazy twat?"

"Eh?" Eliza jerked, startled.

Griffin and Reeve gaped at her. Hipp boinged sheepish springs and muttered, "Sorry. Sorry."

That red glass vase lay smashed on the hearth, shards glittering.

She'd hurled it at Reeve. Or rather, Lizzie had.

The Commissioner peered through his monocle at a patch of empty air. "I say, who's the saucy minx in the red skirts?"

Oh, bother.

Eliza scrabbled up her things and ran.

A WOMAN'S PLACE

OUT INTO THE DRIZZLE, RAINDROPS A STINGING SO-lace on her burning cheeks. She clutched the wrought-iron fence, panting for breath. Her stomach lurched. This was it. Reeve's taunts had finally gotten under her skin. This time, he'd have her job for certain. Her career was over. Not to mention having to explain to Harley.

She fumbled in her satchel for her bottle of remedy, the medicine that was *supposed* to keep Lizzie at bay, and swallowed a big gulp. Reproachful sweetness burned her throat. *Get rid of me, will you?* hissed Lizzie's disembodied voice in her ear. *The lackwit deserved it. You want me to stand by and listen to that? Poor Eliza, too chicken-shit to speak up.*

Her vision whirled, a disorienting blur, and she barely registered the constables stretchering the corpse out, Reeve and the Commissioner climbing into their carriage and rattling off into the distance. Sir Stamford's voice drifted back on a chill breeze of fear. "I tell you, sir! Brunette in a red dress, giving me the saucy eye . . ."

A hand gripped Eliza's shoulder. She jerked, ready to run.

"Easy, Eliza." Swiftly, Griffin helped her loosen her tight collar. "Breathe. That's it. And again. You can do it."

Gratefully, she gasped, the world spiraling. "It's all right, Harley . . . thank you. Just some . . . medication I'm taking . . . I get a little confused." Gradually, the swirling slowed, and she caught her breath. "Forgive me. This is frightfully embarrassing. Hush, Hipp," she added, as the little brass fellow tried to climb her skirts, squawking like a hurt kitten.

Griffin looked dubious. "That charlatan pharmacist of yours is nothing but trouble. Are you seeing things? We should fetch another doctor—"

"I'm fine," she announced shakily. "You ought to get along with the case. I suppose Reeve fired me at last?" Her nerves grated. The idea of losing her job drained her of hope. *Seeing things? Oh, only an apparition of my imaginary other self, who apparently mad old men can see. Nothing to worry about.* Griffin would call her crazy, send her packing . . .

Griffin just helped her put on her wet mantle. "No such satisfaction. I made some remark about women's problems and letting ladies have their hobbies, and Reeve chortled it off." He looked faintly shamefaced. "It got us another chance. I hope you don't mind."

Gratitude washed her thin. As if Griffin didn't have enough problems. "You're a good friend, Harley."

Gruffly, he brushed raindrops from his mustache. "Back to the case, eh? We must get poor Mr. Locke out of the Bow Street lock-up before Reeve wrings out a false confession and thrashes him to an irate pink pulp."

She adjusted her hat, wriggling tired shoulders with a

sigh. The remedy was working, for now. Lizzie felt distant, just a warm undercurrent in her blood, biding her time. But Eliza's own cowardice galled her. Hurling that vase at Reeve hadn't felt shameful, or an embarrassing overreaction. It had felt *good*.

"If Locke's guilty, I'd have expected less bad temper and a better alibi," she said hurriedly, to cover her distraction. "A little harsh on him, weren't you? He did just lose his future bride."

"Are you sure?" Griffin shrugged. "Ill-fitting suit, untidy hair, wanders around in the rain instead of paying for cabs. And he sets up other people's experiments for a living. Doubt he's ever been blessed with an original thought."

"So?"

"So, he's hardly Remy Lafayette, is he? D'you really think an accomplished young lady like Miss de Percy would marry a man like that? Would you?"

She stared. "You think Locke could be inventing their engagement?"

"He could be inventing the whole thing," said Griffin. "That mysterious afternoon caller, the lab accident, his walk to Albemarle Street."

"Hmm. The bruise on Antoinette's face is real enough. The maid sees her alive at six, but Locke returns unseen afterwards. They fight, he strikes her, it ends in murder . . ." She shook her head. "Call me sentimental, but I rather thought Locke's grief to be genuine."

"No accounting for love." Griffin jammed on his tall hat. "Share a cab? I'm back to Bow Street. Our friend the Slasher awaits." He sounded tired, dispirited. It wasn't like him.

Hipp bounced eagerly. "Raining. Forty-five degrees. Make greater speed."

"I'm headed to Finch's Pharmacy," she admitted. "Rather in the opposite direction."

Darkly, Griffin shook his head. "I wish you wouldn't put so much faith in that swindler. He's worked you nothing but trouble."

A pang of guilt stabbed. Griffin's wife had perished of a wasting disease, her condition exacerbated by idiot apothecaries and haughty physicians who cared more for honoring the mystic traditions of Galen and Aristotle than for treatments that actually worked. Eliza had tried to help, but too late. Mrs. Griffin had faded away, a ghost of the vivacious lady who'd been so delighted when Harley took on a female physician as his crime scene expert.

"He tries, Harley," she murmured. She'd told Griffin her medication was for headaches, and he'd believed her. Not for much longer, if Lizzie kept hurling vases and flirting with the Commissioner.

"So does Chief Inspector Reeve, and he's still an accident waiting to happen. D'you know, I had his wife in my office again yesterday, complaining I wasn't doing enough to further her husband's career."

Eliza winced. Despite her dislike for the Chief Inspector, she envied no man a partner so demanding as Mrs. Reeve. "There's gratitude for you."

"On that subject, did you see the *Illustrated News*?" Griffin offered a folded edition. REGENT AND CABINET AT LOGGERHEADS OVER WAR POLICY, read one headline. ENFORCERS

CLASH WITH SUFFRAGETTE PROTESTERS. IS THE SOHO SLASHER FROM OUTER SPACE? "Another Slasher suspect beaten to within an inch of his life," said Griffin, showing her an article entitled ARMED CITIZENS UNITE AGAINST BUTCHERS' GUILD. "Poor fellow, in the wrong place at the wrong time. And to top it off . . ."

"Oh, no." Her heart sank. "My post-mortem report again?"

"In full bloodcurdling detail." Griffin gritted his teeth. "Damned if I know where the pilfering lice are getting them. I swear, everything's kept under lock and key."

"Hardly your fault. Some greedy fool of a constable must be taking money from those disgusting vultures at the *News*." She shook raindrops from the paper. "'Slasher still at large,'" she read. "'Police fail again. Once more the myopic incompetence of our so-called law enforcement officers is an expensive and embarrassing scandal for the Home Office.' Honestly, it makes one wish poor Mr. Temple back again. At least his sordid penny dreadfuls were works of honest fiction—"

"Where are the po-*LICE*?" demanded a shrill voice, and across the wet road stalked a hatchet-faced lady. Her black mourning gown was twenty years out of date, skirts swishing like a street sweeper's broom, and she brandished a pair of brass opera glasses in one crow-like hand. "I have *information*! I demand to be heard!"

Constable Perkins came splashing after her. "A witness, sir," she panted triumphantly. "This is Lady Redstoat. She lives at number thirty-six."

"Told you so, Perkins," murmured Griffin, earning a blush and a pleased smile.

Lady Redstoat waved her glasses. "I told her! I told that brazen hussy what would happen if she didn't repent. And now she's swimming in the lake of fire!"

"A dread fate indeed, my lady," said Eliza, winking at Perkins. "What can you tell us about Miss de Percy?"

Lady Redstoat's fanatical gaze burned. "A sinner! Pride, lust, gluttony, taking the Lord's name in vain with her evil so-called experiments. Consorting with the devil!"

"I see. And did Satan call in person, or did he send messengers?"

The lady stabbed her on a sharp-nosed scowl. "Scoff if you will. Callers at all hours, day or night. These 'scientists' and 'intellectuals' and 'poets.' Hmph. Fornicators, the lot of them. The shame!"

Griffin coughed politely. "And did these, er, fornicators attend yesterday?"

"I watch for them, you know, through my drawing room window." Lady Redstoat glared fiercely through the opera glasses. "I know exactly who they are. I have the names and times written down. A sin ledger, sir!" She extracted a matchbox-sized notebook from her reticule, and flicked feverishly through. "Yes. That's them, the degenerates! A pair of her so-called scientists at twelve o'clock, that disgusting Locke creature and his one-eyed accomplice. Then that *professor*"—she spat the title like a bad-tasting morsel—"and the old gray-haired pervert at a quarter past."

Eliza nodded. The team meeting. "And after?"

"A man on his own at a quarter to three. And then Locke again at four. For an hour!" She fanned herself, perspiring. "Imagine the debaucheries! Ohh!"

"Perhaps imagining a little less vividly would help," murmured Eliza dryly. "A different man at a quarter to three, you say? Not Mr. Locke or the others?"

A disgusted wrinkle of nose. "That vile boy curses at me with the devil's tongue. I would have recognized *him*. No, this was some long-haired reprobate in a top hat, with a dirty overcoat and a blue scarf. Never seen him before. A fresh recruit for Satan! He idled about in the street for ten minutes before going inside. For the world to see!"

"But no one called later than five?"

"No one." Haughty certainty.

"Did you hear anything unusual last night? Loud noises, anything like that?"

"From this dreadful house? Constantly! Groans and booms and screeches at all hours. The devil himself, laughing as they carouse!" She wagged a bony finger. "This hussy and her coven will burn in hell, mark my words."

"I see. Thank heavens you were here, Lady Redstoat. You've been most diligent in rooting out the sinners."

Satisfied, the good lady snapped her book closed. "If I were you, madam, I should vacate this loathsome cavern of depravity immediately. We know not the hour!" And she gathered her black skirts and huffed away.

Eliza eyed Griffin expectantly. "See the devil on your way in, perchance?"

"Afraid not. But this corroborates Locke's tale of the afternoon caller," said Griffin. "And if you include our killer, Lady Redstoat is the second person we've met today who doesn't approve of Miss de Percy's lifestyle. Perkins, did you get all that?"

"Yes, sir." Perkins finished scribbling and looked up expectantly.

"Good man. You questioned the footman. Did he mention these same visitors?"

Perkins dutifully consulted her notes. "The four scientists around noon, then Mr. Locke at four. But no mention of the caller at a quarter to three!" Her face shone. "He didn't mention the fellow in the blue scarf. I'm sure of it!"

"Excellent work. What should we do about it?"

"Um. Question him again?"

"Top marks, Perkins. What are you waiting for?" Griffin watched her rush off. "A mysterious visitor. How droll."

"A long-haired man in a blue scarf," mused Eliza, "who wasn't at the team meeting—and who lingers outside for ten minutes. Waiting for the footman to absent himself, so Miss de Percy would admit him personally?"

"If it's that easy to arrive unnoticed, he could have returned after six to kill her. So could Locke, for that matter. Or any of them."

"Or," added Eliza, inspired, "Blue Scarf remained the entire time! Damn. I should've asked Lady Redstoat if she noticed him leaving."

Griffin grinned. "Perhaps Blue Scarf is a fiction, too, and Locke and Lady Redstoat are in cahoots. Fabricated the entire story to hide their sordid affair, and even now bemoan the failure of their scheme to elope to the wilds of Mongolia."

"Foiled by the village idiot. How embarrassing. Still, one thing's certain: not much here is what it seems. And that includes Seymour Locke, engineer's lowly assistant."

But uneasily, she recalled Lady Redstoat's exhortation:

This hussy and her coven will burn in hell. Locke's angry riposte: *They'll spread filthy lies to keep her in her place.* The scrawled accusation on the ledger: *WHORE.*

Miss de Percy had lived as she pleased, with no care for opinions or scandal. And someone had killed her for it. Scorched electricity through her body until she died in agony.

But was it Seymour Locke, jealous of a secret lover? Or someone else? Someone who loathed independent women. Who thought a "lady" ought to be just that and nothing more.

Who assumed any woman who entertained male visitors must be a whore—and that whores deserved to die.

Either way, this killer merited no mercy. She would root him out, and give him his due justice. Sobered, she managed a smile. "Meanwhile, back to the Slasher, yes? Before Reeve fires us both and the Met never solves a murder case again?"

Griffin straightened his already perfect hat. "Four days since the last victim. Perhaps our nemesis has fallen under a convenient train."

"One can always hope." She opened her umbrella, eyeing the blackening sky. "I might take you up on that cab after all. I've no wish to swim all the way to Mr. Finch's."

MARVELS AND MIRACLES

ELIZA JUMPED FROM THE CAB AT NEW BOND STREET into a splash of dirty water, and struggled to open her umbrella in torrential rain as she bade Inspector Griffin good day.

"God rot it," announced spectral Lizzie at the top of her voice, hopping down beside Eliza and swiping ghostly mud from her skirts, "won't this poxy rain never piss off?"

The cab clopped away into the traffic, and Eliza rounded on Lizzie with clenched teeth. The remedy hadn't lasted but a few minutes before Lizzie was upon her again like a red-skirted barnacle. "What were you doing, mooching around in that cab like a sixpenny whore? I honestly didn't know where to look. Harley must think I'm quite insane."

Passers-by also, apparently, because they sidled past, shielded by their umbrellas, not meeting Eliza's gaze. A campaign huckster with a bowler hat and a dripping sandwich board—STOP THE LANDSLIDE! VOTE LIBERAL!—giggled at her and winked, hair plastered down his cheeks. From the corner, a pair of Royal Society Enforcers studied her with solemn electric-red eyes, their brass skeletons speckled with raindrops. Since the old queen's assassination, there seemed to be more of them every week.

She smiled weakly and turned away. Talking to herself in the street again. Excellent way to get arrested, or worse. And what if those Enforcers glimpsed Lizzie, as Sir Stamford had done?

"Just gettin' comfortable," said Lizzie loftily.

"You were trying to sit in his lap!"

"He needed cheering up. What'll he do, send us to the nut house? Harley's your *friend*." Merrily, Lizzie danced a polka, a scarlet splash of gaiety against the dull gray day, and she didn't seem to mind the downpour. For a moment, Eliza's envy was so rich, it choked her.

"I'll send *you* to the nut house, as you so charmingly call it." She dashed for Finch's Pharmacy, Hippocrates doing his best to trip her up, and ducked shivering beneath the porch. "We agreed, Lizzie. Monday, Wednesday, Friday, and Saturday nights. It's not your turn until eight o'clock."

"Aye, and I'm makin' sure I get my share. Mayhap I can't trust you to quaff that elixir when my time comes."

"We've been over this. Eight o'clock, and not a minute sooner."

Lizzie glared. Eliza glared back, shaking rainwater from her umbrella. They'd developed a timeshare arrangement, and for the moment it was working. It stopped the writhing skin, the blistering need for elixir, the creeping agony of a monster bursting out.

Yes, it was working. Right until Lizzie decided it wasn't.

The bell tinkled as Eliza entered Finch's Pharmacy. Blessed warmth greeted her, the familiar scents of an apothecary's ingredients. She inhaled, letting the soothing ambience wash over her. The sheaves of drying herbs, the gleaming counter, the shelves of rainbow liquids and towers of drawers with copperplate labels in Latin.

Finch's was a good place, filled with pleasant memories. Midnight chemistry sessions in his strange-smelling laboratory, arcane potions bubbling. Odd fellows with strange spectacles or artificial limbs, mathematicians and alchemists, botanists and physicists, bringing wild ideas and esoteric inventions. Endless shelves of books filled with bizarre diagrams and meticulously labeled figures that sparkled in her young imagination like fairy tales.

She'd made up stories about them. Much better than those dull morality plays about princesses (and what had these silly girls done to deserve the title?) holed up in desolate towers, waiting to be rescued by equally dreary and inexplicable princes on horseback. Horses were stupid animals, anyway, and fairy-tale princes always seemed more interested in kissing than in thrilling escapades.

Rather, Eliza's bold adventuresses flung themselves into the sky by means of Mr. Newton's centripetal forces, explored leagues beneath the ocean's surface in unorthodox phlogiston-powered submersibles, operated on beating hearts with the new anesthetics to discover the secrets of life itself. And one day she'd read about Dr. Jenner, a vicar's son from Gloucestershire who'd saved the world from the horrors of smallpox, and she'd known exactly what she wanted to be when she grew up.

As for Mr. Finch, he'd never chided her for dressing late

for dinner, or insisted she finish her embroidery. He just re-laxed in his armchair in that purple smoking jacket, a book in his lap, puffing a pipe of fragrant (and probably overly me-dicinal) herbs. "Eh? Translate that into Latin, my dear," he'd say, or "No, child, that's a *non*-organic compound," or "Finish your Pythagoras, say what, and you can help me decant my new mosquito repellent before supper."

An odd childhood, to be sure. In her father's absence, Mr. Finch had done the best job he could, and mostly Eliza thought it a good thing. What would life have been like as Edward Hyde's daughter?

Hippocrates hunkered before the little coal fire, grinding contented cogs. She cornered her umbrella and peeled off wet gloves. "Mr. Finch?"

Finch's head bounced up behind the counter like a jack-in-the-box, his white hair bristling beneath a crumpled cone of silvery metal. "Shhh! They'll hear!"

"What? Who? I say, are you wearing a tinfoil hat?"

Suspiciously, Finch peered left and right, his pince-nez gleaming. "Sorcerers! Invisible mind-reading waves, say what? Stinking pressure machines that suck your thoughts into the aether. Frenchmen, you know. Republicans! No one's safe!"

"Marcellus," said Eliza gently, "didn't we agree telepathy is impossible? The brain uses too much energy for thought transference to be practicable."

"Gadzooks! You don't say? I suppose the calorific would be astronomical." Reluctantly, he emerged, dusting off his apron and shirtsleeves. "Doesn't mean they *can't* do it," he muttered, glaring out at the rain-soaked sky. "Vigilance, say what? High alert! Ask that furry Royal Society captain of yours. He'll know all about it!" He winked. "I expect you'll be all about the wedding now. No time for lonesome Marcellus and his hare-brained schemes. Housekeeping and babies, eh?"

"Naturally. My usefulness as a human being shall immediately come to an end. Shouldn't be surprised if my brain stops functioning the moment we say 'I do.'"

The thought of her upcoming wedding made her smile—but then her eye caught on Lizzie outside the bay window, making frightful faces at a passing trio of high-born ladies. Splashing through puddles and throwing mud, for heaven's sake. Eliza's skin shrank cold, all the old fears thundering back. How could she ever have an ordinary life? Surely before long she'd be exposed. Arrested as a sorcerer, locked away in the Tower to be interrogated by merciless Enforcers.

She shuddered. Her fears were unfounded. The apparition plaguing her wasn't real. Just a dream . . .

"Marcellus, I'm going mad." The words rushed out, unstoppable.

"Ha ha! Not possible, dear girl. Sanest person I know."

"My remedy doesn't work anymore." Her dry throat stung. "I see her everywhere. She *moves* things, *touches* people. This morning she threw a vase at Chief Inspector Reeve. I practically had to drag her off Harley Griffin on the way here. We fight, Marcellus, she's always in my face and no matter how hard I try she's never satisfied. I want her gone!"

It echoed dully in her mind, an impossible dream. *Gone . . . gone . . . gone . . .*

Anxiously, Finch ruffled his white hair. "But that's the

thing, dear girl. She can't *be* gone. You know that. Not the way the remedy works, eh?"

She stared, hope draining. "But can't we change the dose, or alter the ingredients? I can't go on like this."

"Already at the edge of efficacy, say what? Anything more or less and it'll be lolly water. Afraid it'll have to do, old thing." He patted her hand fondly. "You'll pull through. Always do, eh?"

Easy tears prickled the back of her nose, and angrily she sniffed them away.

"Luckily," added Finch, seeing her distress, "I've revisited a few old angles on the elixir itself. Bleeding-edge alchemy, all that." He plonked two black glass bottles onto the counter. "This should make for, shall we say, a more intense experience? Better satisfaction all round. Keep her quieter when it's your turn. Henry swore by it, back in the day. Until, well, you know, he didn't."

Inside the bottles, her elixir shifted, whispering, possessed of a ghostly life of its own. The salty smell watered her mouth, disgusting yet seductive, and the rough twin fists of her addiction yanked in opposite directions, stretching her guts like rubber. Hurl the horrid stuff into the fire, watch it explode. Gulp the whole thing down, peel off her skin like a shedding snake and let Lizzie crawl out . . .

"—strengthening the active ingredients." Finch's rambles cut into her fantasies. "The dose was getting ridiculously large. Increases the side effects, eh? Only so much one can guzzle down before one explodes. Guts everywhere, alchemy spilling onto the street. Dead before they can arrest you! How embarrassing."

She stuffed the bottles into her satchel. It'd have to do. "Any luck with those samples I sent you, from the Soho Slasher cases?"

Finch brightened. "I do enjoy a gruesome murder. From a distance, of course. Reminiscent of that Razor Jack, eh, though without that artistic flair. Blood on the walls, hysterical ladies screaming, missing body parts, ahoy!" He waved his arms. "What's he *doing* with all those kidneys and gallbladders and things? That's what I'd like to know."

"Marcellus, this is serious." The Slasher was an animal. The victims were beaten, torn, abused by a maniac with no more human sensibility than a beast taunting its prey.

Not like Razor Jack at all.

Besides, Malachi Todd had to be dead. Killed in the fire that gutted Newgate in the riots that followed the old queen's assassination. No trace, then or since, and Mr. Todd tended to lead a conspicuously bloody lifestyle. She shivered, imagining the bleak hellhole of a cell she'd consigned him to after he'd saved her life. In her nightmares, he'd died horribly in flames, screaming vengeance upon her—not to mention the ghosts of his victims, all those dead she'd failed to save or avenge. They'd haunt her always.

Sheepishly, Finch grinned. "Forgive my enthusiasm, eh? Justice for the slain, all that. But I'm afraid I've nothing for you."

She checked a sigh. This Slasher hunted in streets notorious for brothels and liquor-fueled revelry, populated with nameless girls, drunken criminals, and gentlemen in disguise satisfying forbidden lusts. The perfect haunt for anyone wishing to go unnoticed and unrecognized. So far, her precious science had yielded nothing helpful at all.

Her uselessness galled her. If she could catch this Slasher, would it make up for her failure with Razor Jack? Hardly. But it was a start. "Can we hurry it along? It's rather urgent."

"You don't understand." Finch looked grave. "I tested everything, same as you. No commonalities, eh? No matching blood or hair, not even a fingerprint that looks the same. For what it'd be worth," he added gloomily, "with no proper records for comparison. Your Slasher is giving us precisely zero. Not a sausage! Dastardly clever chap, say what?"

"Very." She bristled to think of that mean-spirited, jealous, puffed-up turkey Reeve, handing Harley an impossible case and then crowing about it when he didn't uncover any evidence. Distorted images swirled, of mangled bodies, clotting blood, gin-soaked laughter. The itch to become Lizzie and take her vengeance scrabbled at her bones like a hungry rat. Reeve bore a grudge against anyone who'd had the easy misfortune to make him look foolish. He'd long wanted to destroy Griffin's career. His troubled marital life didn't excuse that. With that muddle-headed Commissioner in his pocket and the superintendent's job up for grabs, it seemed Reeve would at last get his way.

The bell tinkled, and she whirled, dizzy with dread. Ghost-Lizzie would burst in, a howling harpy in drenched red skirts. *It's my turn, Eliza. Give me my TURN or I'll throttle you in your sleep, I'll grab your intestines from the inside and squeeze until they BURST . . .*

A gentleman strode in, flourishing a brass-topped cane.

He wore a bottle-green coat, a tall hat, and gold-rimmed glasses, one lens clear and one dark blue—for his left eye was sightless, milky like mother-of-pearl.

"Finch, you madman," he exclaimed, "whatever's that on your head?"

Finch whipped off the tinfoil cone and tossed it over his shoulder. "What? Don't mumble, old bean. Can't hear a word you're on about."

Hipp scampered up, blue light flashing hopefully. The stranger bent to pet him. Smooth dark locks ended with a flick at his chin. A sprig of jasmine gleamed in his buttonhole.

"Mr. Starling?" Eliza stared, incredulous. Her schoolroom, those difficult mathematics lessons—and her tutor, an awkward young Cambridge scholar in a threadbare coat with white flowers, who'd taught her Euclid and Descartes and the epic *Principia*.

Recognition dawned as a sunny smile. "Miss Jekyll! Well, I never. How you've grown up!" He shook her hand warmly. Still an unfashionable burr of Lancashire in his voice. "And even more beautiful than I remembered."

"Oh, stop it. You haven't aged a day." Almost true. He still had the same dramatic dark hair, although it was shorter now. Quite the romantic poet type. Her adolescent self had been rather sweet on him. "D'you know, only this morning I was thinking about you?"

An odd asymmetrical wink. "Pleasant memories, I hope."

Finch scratched his head. "Byron, you perplexing old peanut, do you know each other?"

Eliza laughed. "Don't you remember? Mr. Starling had the ill fortune to tutor me in mathematics. I was fifteen, and my limp wits quite exhausted his patience. I never did master those fluxions." For years, Mr. Hyde had posed as her anonymous "guardian," paying for her expenses and education, first in Henry's rambling house at Cavendish Square, and when she grew older, at her own house in Russell Square. Curiosity warmed her. How much did Byron Starling know about the man who'd hired him years ago?

Starling chuckled. "Who does, my dear? I imagine you've never cared about rates of change since."

Outside in the street, Lizzie leered in, her nose and lips squashed to the fogged window. Eliza tried to ignore her. "Only at school, happily. I'm a physician now, for the Metropolitan Police."

He grinned, enchanted. "Always knew you'd go far, fluxions or no. I did show you mercy, as I recall," he added, "under doctor's orders. Whilst you were so ill."

Eliza shook her head, bemused. Starling might be absent-minded, but he knew perfectly well she'd never been seriously ill. "Not I, sir. You must be thinking of someone else."

Starling's spectacles flashed. "Indeed," he corrected with a laugh. "My mistake. A mere student myself in those days. Still wanted to be a physicist, God knows why. Like the Philosopher himself, I suppose. You used to say he'd made vector calculus difficult on purpose."

"One rather suspects he did." Eliza eyed the obligatory Royal Society portraits on the wall—Halley with his long white wig, proud and prickly Robert Hooke, a supremely arrogant Newton at the height of his powers—and her stomach jittered. Since her days with Starling, she'd learned a lot that wasn't pleasant about the scientific method. *Nullius in verba,* insisted the Royal Society motto. *See for yourself*—but in these days of fear and witch-burnings, it was far from that simple.

"And a good job, too," announced Finch, "otherwise we'd all be experts, and who'd want that, eh? Nothing worse than smarty-noses who bang on about quaternions while you're trying to read. Henry had an assistant like that. Insufferable show-off. Quentin, Henry would say, fetch me that crucible, and off the lad would go, spouting about covalent bonds and molecular decay until one's eyes glazed over." He rubbed his hands. "Well, Byron, you crusty old tortoise, what can I do you for? Ague? Piles? A touch of the old gout? I've invented a wonderful prophylactic. Arsenic and the flesh-eating curare! Have the offending appendage off in no time, say what?"

Starling shared an amused glance. His blind eye glinted, iridescent amidst white scars. He'd had two good eyes when she'd known him. "I visited last week, remember? You were to hunt out some books from your collection."

"Eh?" Finch looked befuddled. "Not making sense, old chap."

Shyly, Starling tapped his cane on the floor. "Well, I'm sure you're right. I'll return when it's more convenient."

Eliza laughed. "I assure you, I've not aligned with the forces of darkness. I'm quite familiar with Mr. Finch's 'collection.'"

A sheepish smile. "Oh. Well, one can never be too careful." He dropped into a whisper. "You know, Marcellus: *Michael's* books?"

"Why didn't you say so?" Finch rummaged under the counter, herbs and pill packets flying left and right, and thumped a moth-eaten book onto the wood in a cloud of dust. "The Royal burned most of Faraday's things when he was arrested. But was crafty Marcellus foiled by dullard metalheads? I think not."

Reverently, Starling stroked the cracked leather binding. "Excellent. This will do nicely."

Eliza's curiosity itched, and inwardly she groaned. The Royal had burned poor Faraday for his unorthodox ideas, his insistence that aether was a fantasy, that light required no medium and invisible lines of force held the world together. What was Starling's interest in such a book?

What was hers? Aether science wasn't even her field—but she couldn't quench this burning desire to *know*. To see what others could not. It was Henry Jekyll's curse, too, this dangerous fascination for the bleeding edge, and it had brought him only trouble.

Still, her anticipation sparkled. Fresh knowledge awaited. What could be more exciting?

Finch brushed dust from the book's cover, and sneezed. "This is his more theoretical work. Can't make head nor tail of it myself," he added gloomily. "Michael, I'd say, Michael, you boneheaded old moose, you must put this drivel into language they *understand*. You need to *flatter* people. Make them feel like idiots, and it'll be questions and insinuations and hot needles under your fingernails, and next thing you know it's build up the fire and burn him to a crisp." He scratched his fluffy head. "But did he listen to wise Marcellus? Of course he didn't! Smoke everywhere, people choking and covering their noses. The smell was dreadful."

"You needn't fear on that score." Briskly, Starling wrapped

the book in a calico bag he extracted from his pocket. "The Royal Institution is all in favor of flattery these days. Aether engine efficiency is a touchy subject down at the Tower. I'm hoping Mr. Faraday's musings will shed alternative light on some issues I'm having controlling the electromagnetic potential. A very particular conundrum."

Eliza's ears pricked. "Is that Professor Crane's project, perchance?"

"Our fame spreads." Starling gave an ironic wink, and she recalled Lady Redstoat at the murder scene: *Locke and his one-eyed accomplice.* Starling's eyes had been lovely, back in the day, of melting dark brown. "Where did you hear of us?"

"Under less than pleasant circumstances, I'm afraid. I'm sorry to report that Miss de Percy has been murdered."

Starling's face drained. "Whatever do you . . . oh, no. What awful news." Removing his glasses, he mopped his face with a handkerchief. "This is terrible. Who'd do such a thing? When?"

"Last evening. Was she a close friend?"

"Not as such," he admitted, still crestfallen. "An extremely clever young woman. We collaborated on this project, but I confess she thought me rather a bore. What a tragic loss."

"Can you tell me what she was working on?"

"Apart from this engine? A doctoral thesis. Something to do with electrodynamic deconstruction of matter. I never enquired. As I say, we weren't friendly."

She dug into her satchel for the scrap of paper from the crime scene. "Any idea what this means?"

He studied it, frowning. "These are magnetic wave equations. Regarding the propagation of light via different media.

Not my field, I'm afraid. You might ask Professor Crane. She's the true expert." He flashed an unsettlingly wide smile. "Attend our demonstration at the RI, if you like. See our miniature engine for yourself. I'd love to see you there."

"Perhaps," she murmured. Another invitation to this famous demonstration. How curious. "I don't suppose you were helping set up, late last night?"

"Matter of fact, I was."

"Was a fellow named Locke there?"

A snort. "So you've met his highness, have you? Yes, he was picking my brains about advanced waveforms until at least one o'clock."

Ha. Take that, Chief Inspector! A lucky meeting. She'd telegraph Bow Street immediately. "Did no one wonder where Antoinette was?"

He grimaced. "I hate to say it, but Miss de Percy disliked getting her hands dirty. We'd have wondered more if she did arrive to help." He tucked Faraday's book under his arm. "Sadly, I must be on my way. Marcellus, my friend, I shall take good care of this. Delightful to see you again, Miss Jekyll. *Enchanté.*"

"Doctor," she reminded with a smile. "I'm a physician now."

"Of course. Old habits. Do attend our demonstration, if you've an eye for the marvels of aether physics. It'll be quite something." And with a tinkle of doorbell, he was gone.

Eliza watched him go, absorbed. "That was unexpected."

Finch scowled. "Byron's never unexpected. Always does exactly what you think he will, which is mostly get in the way and ask irritating questions. Can't imagine why Eddie hired him."

"He was a good teacher," reminded Eliza absently, still thinking about Miss de Percy. Magnetic wave equations . . .

"So was Socrates, and what good did it do him? Blasphemy trials and hemlock tea with his biscuits, that's what. Starling just wants to piggyback on my experiments without doing the work himself. Gave me some fascinating particles to test. Said he can alter their refractive indices with the right advanced energization. Poppycock, naturally, but hooray for science, eh? *Nullius in verba,* all that."

"I see." She didn't see at all. "What exactly was in that book?"

"Haven't the foggiest." Finch beamed. "Faraday was a bookbinder's apprentice, you know. Wasn't much for maths. Never learned his *Principia* like a good boy should, and thank heavens for that, come to think of it, but he'd insist on putting in pages of diagrams that were just as incomprehensible. 'Oh,' he'd say, 'these are magnetic flux surfaces, and here are lines of force, and those are the imaginary inverse twin-dimensional co-efficient differential ratio thing-umy-bobs of the whosy-whatsit,' and so forth. But who could fathom what he was babbling about? No one, that's who. Except the Philosopher," he finished glumly, "and we all know how *that* ended."

"Maybe Starling and his Professor Crane will make some sense of it, for their engine project."

"Doubt it, dear girl. There was a second volume, as I recall. Michael was always lurching about with it tucked under his arm, muttering about getting his lady friend to look his new theory over before he submitted it to the Royal. She knew a thing or two about transforming an equation, they say.

But I'm damned if I could locate the moldy old tome." Finch scratched his head. "Perhaps the Royal burned it after all."

Eliza shouldered her bag. "Well, I've Slasher work to do. If you think of any other tests we could run on those samples, let me know. And it's Lizzie's turn tonight, so I'll report on the new elixir."

Finch was already shredding a pile of piquant-smelling herbs, mixing in what looked like fingernail clippings. "Oh, this is fabulously fetid! Fearsomely ferocious! Wart removal, say what? Doubles as a tonic for dropsy."

She retrieved her umbrella, and casually turned back. "I meant to ask. Who was the doctor I saw?"

"Eh?"

"When I was ill as a child."

"Oh, that." Finch chopped his herbs with vim. "Henry, of course. Physician, wasn't he? 'Twas nothing. Just a fever."

Swift disappointment jabbed her throat. "Marcellus, I was fifteen when Mr. Starling was my tutor. Henry disappeared when I was seven."

Finch reddened. But before he could speak, she quietly walked out into the rain.

Chill raindrops stung her cheeks, the bruised clouds reflecting her mood as she turned left towards Oxford Street. Hipp dashed after her, splashing in muddy puddles, and she kicked at the splatter, frustrated. Why had Marcellus lied? Couldn't she be trusted with the truth?

She sighed, adjusting her satchel. "Hipp, run along and telegraph Inspector Griffin. Tell him Seymour Locke's alibi is confirmed. At least that's good news."

Eagerly, Hipp whirred his cogs and galloped away.

"Good boy— Oh! I say." She nearly collided with Byron Starling, who'd waited for her on the corner, calico-wrapped book clutched under one arm.

"Dr. Jekyll. Forgive me. I was wondering . . . that is, I thought . . ." He fidgeted, tapping his cane. "Listen to me, stammering like an idiot. Never could string two words together, could I?"

She cleared her throat, self-conscious. "Mr. Starling, I'm afraid I must be going—"

"Byron, please. Enough with formality." He edged closer, raindrops glinting on his mismatched lenses. He smelled of jasmine and dry paper, a faint bouquet of distant memory. "I hope I'll see you at our demonstration. Perhaps, one day soon, I might call on you? We might take a walk together. Catch up on old times. Renew our acquaintance."

Oh, dear. Inwardly she cringed. Across the street, Lizzie was clutching her ribs, miming fits of laughter. Eliza laid her hand on Starling's sleeve, making sure her sapphire ring was clearly visible. "I'd enjoy that very much. But I shouldn't like to misrepresent the situation. As you see."

"Oh." He had the grace to blush. "My apologies. I meant no insult."

"Perhaps we might take that walk in any case," she offered politely. "I should like us to be friends."

"Indeed." His smile shone, a little too bright. "Congratulations, my dear. Whoever he is, he's a lucky man." He bowed, and strode away, cane tapping on the stones.

Eliza watched him go, curious. Antoinette de Percy's colleague on this arcane science project. Lady Redstoat's "one-eyed accomplice." Who just happened to show up at Finch's the day after Antoinette was murdered, asking for Faraday's forbidden books.

Just a chance meeting. Coincidence. Nothing to do with anything.

Across New Bond Street, by Asprey jewelers, Lizzie danced a mocking jig. "Eliza and Byron, up in a tree, K-I-S-S-I-N-G!"

Anticipation twinkled like starlight. "I always enjoy a good hard science demonstration, don't you? Lizzie, I believe we have a date."

MY SCIENTIFIC HERESIES

IN EARLY EVENING, ELIZA SLOSHED HOME TO RUSSELL Square, skirts flopping through puddles and rotting leaves. The rain had ceased for now, but the park's sodden grass still oozed, and no birds sang. Along Southampton Row, Enforcers marched in pairs, electric pistols glinting, their heavy brass tread sinking deep into the mire.

She'd spent an exhausting afternoon with Harley Griffin, examining the Slasher case files until her brain ached for respite. She'd also presented Starling's alibi evidence to Reeve. The Chief Inspector had snorted in disgust, muttering about hysterical doctors giving themselves airs, but grudgingly he'd released an apparently bulletproof Seymour Locke, who'd flung Reeve a sarcastic smile and asked for cab fare home.

Eliza grinned, recalling Griffin's glee. Small victories. But she couldn't shed the unsettling suspicion that Reeve didn't care. He'd scored his point with the Commissioner. Locke's usefulness to him had ended. He'd just chewed smugly on his cigar, and given them three days to come up with a lead in the Slasher case or be replaced.

Three days. After all these weeks with nothing but dead ends.

An old-fashioned coach clattered by, drawn by two iron-shod horses, the driver huddling in his waterlogged coat. Brass-legged omnibuses and electric hansoms vied for space with jogging clockwork servants and those like her who were unlucky enough to slog along on foot, soaked from hatbands to boot heels.

Eliza picked her way across the street, accompanied by a dancing ghost-Lizzie, who splashed gaily along without a care, sending sheets of water flying. No one seemed to notice—but they all noticed crazy Eliza, dodging to escape an invisible deluge. Mrs. Bistlethwaite from number twenty-five strutted by with a disparaging yet gleeful sniff. According to that good lady's endless store of gossip fodder, Eliza was already a radical and secret suffragette who'd entrapped an unsuspecting gentleman into marriage with unorthodox scientific tricks. Now, she'd be insane to boot. Excellent.

"Will you stop that?" she whispered fiercely, jumping to avoid another torrent. "You're embarrassing me!"

"You're just sore because you and Inspector Goody Two-Shoes didn't save the world today." Lizzie slapped a passing horse's rump, sending beast and rider careering into the crowd. "When will that Slasher grab another 'un, d'you think?"

"Shame on you." Eliza stomped up the filthy steps to her dripping porch. Her brass shingle—ELIZA JEKYLL M.D., the engraving announced politely—was water-stained, and the electric light buzzed and spat. "Those unfortunate women deserve as much respect as you."

"What they deserve is not to be slaughtered in their beds." Lizzie pretended to ravish the wrought-iron fence, translucent red skirts bouncing around her knees. "Or out of 'em. A girl can't turn a decent trick without getting dismembered. Worse than your Razor Jack, this Slasher cove. At least Todd kept it tidy."

Eliza let herself into the warm hall, gritting her teeth on a mean retort. She didn't like to be reminded of Malachi Todd. He was dead to her. Dead in real life, with any luck.

Gratefully, she divested herself of umbrella and wet gloves. Her consulting room door was ajar, and the fire inside threw welcoming shadows. The scent of roasting meat watered her mouth. Hipp sprinted eagerly inside, spraying rainwater over the rich red carpet. "Calm down, idiot," she scolded. "Mrs. Poole, that smells delightful—oh!"

She'd bumped into her housemaid. Pretty Molly had her simple brown coat buttoned to the throat, a bonnet jammed tightly over her golden hair. "Sorry, Doctor. Didn't know you'd be home."

Eliza raised teasing eyebrows. "Walking out on such a rough night?"

"Aye, well, we can't all be courted by carriage folk," said Molly stoutly, a vision of her future as a double of the redoubtable Mrs. Poole. "No doubt the chill will improve my color."

From the first-floor landing, Lizzie wolf-whistled, making lewd faces. Eliza had suspected for a couple of weeks that Molly had formed a new acquaintance. She wished the girl well, but it did seem odd. Molly had never been one for flirting and fellows. "Here, take my umbrella, or you'll be drowned in minutes."

"Thank you, Doctor." Molly grinned, and the door clicked shut behind her.

Eliza started after her, and halted, bereft. As if she ought to be saying something about "mind how you go" and not stooping to pick up nothing. Some medical advice on contraception, perhaps? She snorted. Molly was a sensible girl, and in any case, a servant's life was different, with fewer appearances to keep up. Molly likely had more first-hand knowledge of such matters than Eliza.

"Ho-ho-ho!" Now Lizzie stuck her head out from under the stairs, chortling. "Not for want of his honor trying."

"That isn't true," she protested, though the memory of certain unguarded occasions made her blush and smile. "Captain Lafayette is a perfect gentleman."

"Right. Buggered off to Paris this last month, ain't he? Wouldn't be because waiting for the wedding is sending him bonkers. Foreign Office business, my arse. Handsome soldier lad like him, pawed at by all them sex-crazed mademoiselles and keepin' it in his trousers? Not bloody likely."

Eliza rolled her eyes. "More likely he crossed the Channel just to get away from you."

"Aye, well," said Lizzie loftily, "you can always take up with your old friend Byron. He's keen for another round."

"That's quite enough out of you." Eliza had to laugh. But her stomach squirmed. They hadn't yet set a wedding date, and with Remy's work keeping him abroad most of the time, she'd been content to wait.

What if Remy thought *she* was dissembling?

She sighed, dejected. This wedding planning business was fraught with more danger than she'd anticipated. The fuss

with dresses and flowers was nothing compared to the pernicious permutations of awkwardness the idea of co-habiting
might present. But if Remy had concerns, he'd say so. He was
that kind of man.

Wasn't he? What if it turned out they didn't really know
each other? They'd always been thrown together in times of
crisis, investigating murders and saving lives. What if, without all that excitement, they simply had nothing to talk about?

"Molly, dear, here's your tea." Little Mrs. Poole bustled in
from the kitchen, splashing a brimming teacup over Hippocrates, who whimpered and dived under the hall table. "Oh.
Gone, has she? Disobedient child."

Eliza took the teacup and slurped a mouthful. "For me?
You shouldn't have."

"Tea." Hipp shook himself, hot droplets flying. "Two hundred and twelve degrees. Danger."

The housekeeper's steel-gray hair bristled indignantly beneath her cap. "Have you met this *friend* of hers? He could be
an axe murderer. Or a Roman Catholic! Talk sense into her,
can't you?"

Lizzie guffawed. Now she was hanging by her knees from
the first-floor landing rail, skirts tumbling to reveal stockinged legs with lace garters. "Never kiss up to a killer, eh?
Grand advice, coming from you."

Eliza gritted her teeth. "Molly's the most sensible girl I
know," she soothed. "Any lad she has eyes for will surely be
the finest in London."

Mrs. Poole sniffed. "Know a lot of London lads, do you?"

"I know a few. Anyway, who says she's taken up with anyone? She could be sneaking off to a secret gathering of suf-

fragettes, or attending a symposium on how to contribute to the war effort."

"That's an improvement, is it?" muttered Mrs. Poole. "What if she's cavorting in a public house with those extreme radicals your Captain Lafayette's forever moaning about? Running around Westminster, defacing Richard the Lionheart and taking pot-shots at members of Parliament? No loss, come to think of it." She proffered the silver tray. "Here's your post, Doctor. Skipping dinner again, I suppose, and wasting my nice veal roast?"

"A tray at my desk would be lovely, please. Not another word," added Eliza sternly. "I don't wish to hear about it. Until I actually do work myself into an early grave just like my father, and then you can be the first to say 'I told you so.'" A thought struck her. "Mrs. Poole, was I ever ill? As a schoolgirl, I mean."

"Never a day. Excepting the chicken pox, and head lice, and once or twice the Black Death, usually when you didn't want to do your lessons. Why? Planning on self-medicating?"

"No reason. Just . . . don't you think it's odd?"

"Odd? You? Never." And Mrs. Poole waddled away, unruffled.

Eliza's smile faded. Would she be keeping Mrs. Poole and Molly on after she married? A household could sustain only so many staff. Doubtless Remy had people who deserved loyalty, too. Where would the Pooles find work?

Wearily, she climbed to her first-floor study, Hipp snuffling at her heels. Inside, the reddish firelight gleamed over bookshelves in the smells of damp straw and alchemy. Thick drapes hung, redolent with memories. Many a late evening

Eliza had spent here, wrapped in her best silk and pearls, awaiting her mysterious guardian. The man behind the curtain, a velvet laugh and a shadow on the wall. Here, Hyde had first given her the warm, bitter drink that set Lizzie free.

"And a fine thing, too." Lizzie plopped her red-skirted behind in the chair and propped her boots on the desk. "What about my cabinet, eh? All our potions and secret malarkey. What's to become o' that when you piss off to get married?"

"Didn't I ask you to leave me alone?" But she knew this house wasn't large enough for two. Remy had several far more suited to his social standing. Could she relinquish this place, with its years of history, its walls and floorboards steeped in ghostly reminiscences? Fact was, the house would no longer be hers, like it or not. Once they married, all her rights and property passed to him. Remy was a wonderful man. That didn't make the legal inequities any less humiliating.

The mantel clock struck six. Hipp settled by the fire, muttering sleepily. "Rat . . . Rat-rat-rat . . ." She dropped the mail on her desk and switched on the electric lamp. *Pop!* Shadows leapt, unveiling a trestle table upon which she'd erected a crucible and a pair of gas burners. Flasks steamed, iridescent liquids hissing and silvery solids subliming. She checked the beakers, adjusted a flow valve, tapped the glass walls of a precipitating tube. These reactions were uncannily self-sustaining, seeming to make their own decisions about when to activate and when to remain stubbornly inert.

As if they were alive.

On the table, a book lay open, filled with the rambling handwriting of a madman. Evil, rapacious scribbling, chewing up the page with reams of ugly text, alchemical equations, and molecular diagrams. It recalled legends of grimoires penned by demons, tomes so terrible that if you read them, you lost your mind.

She'd filched it from the awful laboratory on Piccadilly where François Lafayette had perished. It had belonged to the devil who'd named himself Moriarty Quick. His dark alchemy had achieved something hideous yet wonderful: he'd separated one person into two entities. Pure scientific blasphemy, but it offered the hope of a miracle: a cure for Remy's dreadful affliction. If Quick could extract a person's soul, why not their monster?

For weeks, the book had lurked in her desk drawer, unopened. What of Quick's appalling specimen jars, those fleshy remnants of tortured souls? Could she in good conscience use his results, gained at such terrible cost?

Yes, she'd decided. Quick's victims would not have died in vain. She'd defeat Remy's creature, whatever it took. Her niggling conscience seemed a small price.

In four small cages, white mice whickered, rubbing their whiskers. Each cage was carefully labeled with type of alchemical preparation administered, dosage, and time. Alongside this row of cages sat another—and inside, pale, fleshy, hairless *things* slobbered and oozed. Nasty, evil-tempered things she'd *grown*—and as they grew, their furry white twins stayed calm and serene.

She cooed softly to them, moved by pity. She didn't like experimenting on animals any more than she liked dark alchemy. But what choice?

"Keep telling yerself that," called Lizzie from the desk chair, where she'd helped herself to a ghostly glass of claret and a cigarette. "It's me you really want rid of. Just you try it, missy."

"Don't be ridiculous." Eliza waved away impossible smoke. But the thought tugged at her, a sly hand thieving her good intentions. What if Quick's methods could "cure" Lizzie, too?

Eliza picked up a soft-bristled brush and stroked one of the hairless mouse-things. It snarled, baring sharp teeth, and its corresponding furry white mouse startled and chased its own tail. She sighed. Still inextricably connected. For the cure to work, she'd need complete severance.

She made a note in her journal, and tried the next mouse-thing. Its counterpart squeaked and dashed shivering into the corner. Same with the next.

Inexorably, the clock chimed half past six. *"Hickory, dickory, dock,"* sang Lizzie, swinging in the chair, *"the mouse ran up the clock. The clock struck eight, and fuck me, we're late! Hickory, dickory, dock!"*

"I'm well aware of the time." Eliza poked the brush at the last hairless blob.

Its brother mouse didn't react.

She tried again. The furry mouse just sat there, washing its little face.

Her heart skipped. Surely it was sleepy, or had ceased to care for her proddings. Or the fleshy thing had developed a nerve problem and hadn't felt anything.

She reached through the bars and tweaked the fleshy thing's nose. It reared, snapping, and she snatched her hand away.

The furry mouse just pensively scratched its ear, and returned to its dinner.

A grin split Eliza's face. "It's working!"

"Great," muttered Lizzie, quaffing her imaginary claret. "Squeeze me out into a fat Lizzie-shaped blob, will you? Nice. After all I've done for you."

Eliza jotted eagerly in her journal. "Don't be ridiculous," she repeated absently, her mind racing ahead. Repeat the experiment. More mice, same dosage, controlled conditions. She'd ask Mr. Finch to supervise her methods, weigh the ingredients, check the seals on her flasks, ensure the alchemical products were exactly as before.

"Plotting against me, that's what. Say it ain't true."

"Mmm." Eliza scribbled faster, but an icy finger prodded her spine. Was it vanity to think she could cure this *creature,* when everything Remy had tried—potions, talismans, even witchcraft—had failed? Memories taunted her, of a crimson-haired killer whom she'd foolishly imagined could be cured of his madness. How wrong she'd been—and how costly her weakness.

But her determination firmed. Remy wasn't Todd. Remy's disease was real, and science must hold the answer . . .

"God rot it, you never *listen* to me!" Lizzie hurled her glass away, and it hit the hearth and smashed, shards glittering like jewels. "I won't be carved up like a friggin' Christmas ham. If you even *think* about boiling up that mouse-fucking hellbrew for me, I swear to God—"

"Dinner," announced Mrs. Poole cheerfully, entering with a steaming tray.

Pop! Lizzie vanished. As if she'd never been.

Mrs. Poole arranged the tray on the desk, glancing at the broken crystal. "Clumsy fingers, eh? I'll have Molly clean it up later."

"Er, no. Don't bother her. I'll get it. Silly me." Eliza ushered Mrs. Poole out, soothing her protests, and closed the door.

Silence.

The empty chill made her shiver. Holding her breath, she turned. "Lizzie? Are you there?"

But Lizzie didn't appear.

Woodenly, Eliza picked up the broken crystal, sat, attended to her meal. But her appetite withered. The fine food suddenly seemed impossibly rich. Surely she couldn't keep down a single morsel. Her skin itched, as if infected with a virulent fungus. She wanted to peel off her clothes, scratch until she bled.

Dutifully, she picked at the meal, a bite of potato, a sliver of slick warm meat. The flavors sickened her, corrupted, as if she ate with some other woman's mouth. *Lizzie's mouth,* she thought crazily. Dare she touch her face, find Lizzie squeezing out in misshapen lumps of flesh, a half-changed grotesque? Hysterical laughter escaped her, but it was her own, twisted into a mockery. Her own face under her fingers, clammy with frightened sweat.

She was losing her mind.

Ting! The clock struck again, making her jump. Only a quarter past seven. Was this night to be interminable, like Sisyphus forever rolling his rock up the same hill? She poured a shaky glass of wine, and forced herself to sip. It coated her mouth like fish oil.

Listlessly, she flicked through her mail. Advertisements for a new triple-bolted front door and an upgraded clockwork servant promised to *Keep Your Home Safe from Sorcer-*

ers and *No More Squeaky Joints!* A flyer entitled BE VIGILANT! assured her that *Spies are everywhere—even in your HOME!* An account from her book-seller for a recent order, another from her dressmaker. Nothing she'd have trouble paying on time.

It was nice to have money again, she reflected dimly. Nice to know her job was secure, even if it did mean pandering to a prehistoric woman-hater like Reeve. Smiling in the face of his chauvinistic insults while she labored at yet another murdered woman's crime scene. Standing obediently by while he ruined Harley Griffin's career for the sake of petty jealousy. Lizzie would never stand for such abuse. She'd speak her mind and damn the consequences.

Nice. What a suffocating little word.

Next was a note, typed in black, a sprig of white jasmine tucked into the envelope.

```
Dr. Jekyll,
I cannot describe my pleasure at seeing
you again after all these years, your
charm and cleverness undiminished.
I trust I haven't alarmed you with
the ardency of my desire to renew our
acquaintance. Always, I have thought of
you fondly, and I hope we shall be seeing
more of each other before long.

     Your servant,

     Byron.
```

P.S. Should you care to call, my office at
the RI will always be open.

She snorted, amused. *Charm and cleverness,* indeed. Still,
something in Starling's manner seemed odd. An air of supe-
rior memory. As if he knew something she didn't.

The next was on parchment paper, penned in a confident
scrawl that elicited a thrill of pleasure.

My dearest Eliza,

*I'm sorry this is a letter, and not me in person, but I hope
soon to be free of this place and fly back to you. Paris is grim
and freezing and it hasn't stopped raining since Friday, which
renders it even more wretched than can be accounted for by the
customary misery and ill cheer of Parisians in these heady days
of liberty. Anyone would think the common people objected to
slave ghettos and pogroms and public human sacrifices—but
please, don't be alarmed, as I am quite safe.*

*Except perhaps from tedium, and ghastly French coffee,
upon the endurance of which my eye aches for a smile and my
ear for a light-hearted witticism, which only makes me wish for
you all the harder. Which is all to say that if our parting hasn't
rendered you as abjectly miserable as yours truly for every second
of these past weeks—or at least for a minute or two—I shall
never forgive you.*

*I'm finally getting to the heart of F.'s labyrinthine affairs,
you'll be relieved to hear, and I hope to settle matters soon. If
the Foreign Secretary calls, you can tell him I've done what he
asked, and could he kindly stop inundating me with his soporific*

missives, as I'm already more than adequately supplied with
kindling by his honor at the Royal Society. Oh, and if _he_ calls,
tell him I'm busy with the Foreign Office.

Anyway, enough about my glittering career in espionage. I
long to hear your news. I trust this finds you (and Hippocrates)
in the best of health, neck-deep in some obligingly intriguing
murder case, and as desperate to see me as I am to see you.

All my love

Remy.

P.S. I've something to show you on my return, by which I
fully intend to render you speechless with the ludicrous depths
of my devotion and your stellar luck in bewitching me. Don't
claim you weren't fairly warned.

She smiled, touching the parchment's edge to her lips. But
dark doubts stirred. Remy had taken François's death—the
manner of it—hard. The revelation that his brother had kept
so many terrible secrets had forced Remy to doubt his own
judgment in everything. What did he mean, "settle matters"?
What exactly had the Foreign Secretary asked for?

Remy hadn't mentioned the recent full moon. Nor the
wedding, exactly. Did that mean . . . ?

Firmly, she shook her head. It didn't mean anything. Remy
had written, and he was safe. That was reason for good cheer.
Upon his return, they'd talk and she'd put her uneasiness to
rest for good.

Simple.

She picked up the last letter . . . and her bones jittered at that
silver seal with its singular coat of arms, the lion and the unicorn.

Dr. Jekyll:

Kindly attend on His Majesty The King tomorrow, at your earliest. Bring your medicine.

Is. Newton, Regent, &c.

The Philosopher's swift, legible cursive somehow made even her name into a sneer. She dropped the paper, squirming at her own double-dealing. An urge gripped her to write back and refuse. *Tell him I'm busy with the Foreign Office.*

She'd sworn she'd have nothing to do with the immortal scientist—responsible for the once-great Royal Society's corruption and hypocrisy, not to mention forcing her to spy on her own father. But a few weeks ago, without warning, he'd offered her the job of physician to seventeen-year-old King Edward—and she'd accepted.

She gritted her teeth, vanity bitter in her mouth. The king was a pitiable fellow, a drooling half-wit who sometimes smeared the walls with his own excrement, far from fit to deal with the conniving politicians and sycophants who surrounded him. Her heart had gone out to the poor child. Just a motherless boy.

But the new Regent had flattered her, too. Lauded her innovation as an alienist, though what eccentric skills she possessed were rusty, since her ill-fated tenure at Bethlem Asylum had ended so spectacularly.

And she'd fallen for it. Dared to believe her star could rise. Tending the dead was no route to medical fame. A rich, influential future awaited whichever physician was sufficiently erudite—or lucky—to cure the king.

Truth was, the Philosopher had manipulated her merci-lessly. She still stood in awe of the mighty force of nature that was Isaac Newton. To defy him seemed as impossible—and as perilous—as defying gravity.

She relapsed into her chair, that awful wine swimming laps in her stomach like an eel driven mad. Her limbs ached dis-tantly. Too hot. A fever? Or merely her awakening need for the elixir? The coals crackled, hypnotic like a demon's laughter. Her eyelids drooped. She'd rest her eyes, just for a moment . . .

Icy water slapped her face. She choked, splutter-ing for air. Light dazzled, brighter than the sun. Her wrists were bound. Her wet dress glued to her body. Her head pounded. Instinctively she struggled. What was happening?

"Easy." A male voice soothed her senses, a hand stroking her hair. "Easy, now. Get a move on, Fairfax, she's waking up. If he sees her like this . . ."

Blinded, Eliza fought. Fairfax? A surgeon, her erstwhile mentor at Bethlem, once a friend of Henry Jekyll's. But Fairfax was long months dead.

"Where am I?" she tried to cry. Fingers gripped her chin, holding her mouth open. Something rough and scaly forced down her throat. A tube. God help her. She gagged, cold slimy liquid spluttering. But the awful stuff kept coming, glug-glug-glug, and she retched and choked and finally swallowed . . .

A smack in the face jerked Eliza awake.

She gasped blessedly clean air. Not bound. Not tortured. No tube choking her. Still in her chair, the study clock's final chime dying. Eight o'clock.

"Up, slug-a-bed!" cried Lizzie, eyes alight with impatience. "Eight o'clock, by God! It's my turn!"

Bewildered, Eliza staggered up. The fire was black and cold, her rain-dampened dress clammy. She reeled, dizzy from that awful dream. "What happened? Did I fall asleep?"

"You was yowling fit to wake the dead." Lizzie shoved her scornfully. "Don't think you can get out of it by faking you're off your rocker."

Eliza shivered, that dream-man's voice echoing. A burr of Lancashire. *She's wakin' oop . . .*

Warm relief swamped her. Of course. The mind played strange games. Somehow her unexpected encounter with Byron Starling had stuck with her, recycling itself into fitful dark fantasy. Yes. That was it.

But Starling's odd remarks this morning stung like half-healed burns. *When you were so ill. Doctor's orders.* When she'd quizzed him, he'd denied everything—and Marcellus had told a clumsy lie. Her tongue burned, itching to ask Lizzie what she knew, but she swallowed the question unformed. A nightmare, brought on by fatigue and Lizzie's mind games. Nothing more.

But she couldn't shake the memory of Starling's expression, in the split second *before* he'd first smiled at her in Finch's shop. Not confusion, exactly.

More like terror.

"Leave me out of it, whatever 'twas. Elixir time for you."

Lizzie grabbed the bag containing the fresh elixir and frog-marched Eliza upstairs.

Warm darkness shrouded her bedroom. Firelit shadows tugged at the curtained bed, her washstand, her wardrobe. The carriage clock on the mantel ticked crookedly, a monster's limping footsteps. *Click-CLOCK, click-CLOCK . . .* By the draped window stood a tailor's mannequin, swathed in pale dream-like fabric, a sinister fairy-woman shape in the dark.

Her unfinished wedding dress. It seemed a foolish conceit, the hollow shell of some other woman's life. She'd as well have married in secret. A Fleet wedding, if such things still existed, or an elopement to Gretna Green, as was done in days of old by defiant heiresses with unsuitable *beaux*. But Remy's mother had insisted, and to keep peace with that formidable matriarch, Eliza had agreed—and that meant a new dress. She'd only one suitable piece, and that was tainted with too many unpleasant memories.

Dr. Eliza Lafayette. It rang strange discord in her ears. False, like a carnival mirror's warped reflection of reality. Truth was, she didn't want a wedding. She wanted Remy— but to have one without the other? She recalled nosy, judgmental Mrs. Bistlethwaite, and shuddered. It'd be scandalous. Impossible. Unforgivable.

Fatigue clawed at her. She longed for nothing more than to creep under the covers and sleep forever, free of dreams.

But this was Lizzie's time. Eight o'clock until dawn, four nights a week. She'd promised.

Fumbling, she yanked on the sconce above the fire, and with a seductive *click!* Lizzie's cabinet door swung open.

What a mess. Lizzie's red dresses scattered the place, one draped over the mirror, another tossed over the shelves holding Eliza's most secret and unorthodox books. Lizzie's swordstick leaned against the wall, its silver-plated dragon head leering, next to a man's lime-green frock coat stuffed into a shelf.

Beside it, a rolled canvas poked out, its end unfurling. A half-finished oil painting. Her gaze kept slipping back to it, compelled by those startling, corrosive colors. Velvet skirts the color of dark blood tumbled from a green velvet chaise, unfinished edges blurring to empty canvas. A smooth cheek, a fall of pale hair shining like an angel's.

Eliza shoved the picture out of sight. A toxic love letter, the exquisite ravings of a lunatic. An excruciating reminder of how close her vanity had dragged her to ruin.

So why don't you throw it away?

She didn't answer.

The black bottle of fresh elixir hissed, glowing with its own secret warmth. She thumbed the cork—darkly reminiscent of her dream, that sour-tasting tube filling her with poison—and gulped the dreaded brew down.

A DEAL TOO ARTFUL

I SCREECH, AND SLITHER OUT LIKE A SNAKE. OUR bones crackle, bright agony. Our reflection in the mirror contorts, our eyes darkening, *me-her-me-her-me*. Our cheekbones jut, my chin sharpens, our lips swell in a saucy cherry pout. My hair bursts from its pins, no longer blond but rich dark mahogany.

"Why, hello, Miss Lizzie!" I wastes no time in tossing away her stupid spectacles—I can see just fine, thanks—and wriggling out of Eliza's wet clothes. I kick her dull gray dress aside, break out of her corset with its stupid flat chest. Even her chemise is wet and moldy-smelling. *My* set's much more accommodating, and thank bleeding Christ for that. A woman's allowed to have boobs. I push 'em up real nice and yank the laces tight.

Urgent claws rip at me, desperate for pleasure. This new elixir's got a punch, all right. Everything's louder, stronger, brighter, and I'm thirsty for flavor, famished for every dark sensation. But despite my craving, bright relief staggers me. I can't breathe in your uptight body, Eliza. Like Newgate's foul cells in there, it is, rusted bars and stenches and ugly darkness. If I lose my marbles, like you're always saying—*mad like Eddie Hyde, Lizzie, and you'll be the end of us, boo hoo!*—it'll be no one to blame but yourself.

I shake out a gown of magenta satin, all fancy-like, and pull it on, buttoning down the side and hooking up the frillage at my thighs. Stockings, aye, and little black garters, and button boots with pointed toes. I coil an ostrich feather into my hair. Hmm. Blade or umbrella? Better wet than dead. I grab my dragon swordstick, throw that fairy-lime frock coat around my shoulders, and I'm ready.

Hell, Lizzie's always ready. Ha ha! And I've business at the Rats' Castle tonight. Sultry gin-soaked business, if I gets my way, and I've a fine fey-fingered gent down at Seven Dials who'll gladly oblige me. This is my life, this tiny glimmer in the gloom, and I intend on living it to the full. But first, I need to see my father. He's been acting odd lately.

Down my twisting back stair, out to the narrow lane. I spear a baleful glare up at her domain. So safe and sheltered, hiding her stubborn face from *my* concerns. What about me, eh? Where am I to go, once she marries her fancy captain? We've always *shared,* she and I, and it's worked well enough, a few famous hiccups notwithstanding. But soon this cozy love nest will be ours no more, for since his elder brother passed, Remy Lafayette is lucred to the hilt with Froggie blood money and has villas and grand houses to burn.

I inhale fresh frosty air and stalk out onto Southampton Row, splashing up mud and horse dung. Storm clouds scoot across coal-smoked stars, chill wind a-stinging, and my nose tingles with the vibrant scent of thunder. A wild night ahead, ha ha!

Only a loping clockwork servant's abroad, a box tucked under its arm. "How do, brassbrain!" cries I, and skip a stone in its direction, *ping!* It jumps and lurches on, its white plaster face emotionless. Like Eliza's face, showing naught but politeness while we're seething inside.

I kick at rotting leaves. Don't take me wrong, I like Remy well enough. A more dashing, able, god-rotted *honest* devil you never did meet, and for the longest time, I wanted what Eliza had.

But no longer. He's hers, not mine, and a life designed for Captain and Missus Lafayette (ha! Imagine it, Eliza giving up her own self) leaves precious little room for me.

Besides, I tried to steal him and he wouldn't have it. Never say Miss Lizzie don't take the initiative.

Swinging my cane, I stride onto New Oxford Street, where electric lights glimmer and intrepid shoppers and late-running commuters huddle in the rain. A hairy-nosed Welsh boy waving a late-edition broadsheet dances a jig, his puppy ears flopping. "Crowds riot at Duke of Wellington's funeral!" he shouts in his sing-song accent. "Last week of general election polls, Tory majority tipped to rise!"

I flip him a penny, take a copy, toss it into the mud and stomp on it. Good riddance to the crusty old bastard, by all accounts a living corpse in his electric breathing machine for years before now. And screw the election, too, for women and working men can't vote, and not the late duke nor the lords nor them inbred land-owning goat-fuckers in the Commons ever gave a flingin' shit for ordinary folk like me.

The shops are still open, their windows spattered with dirt. In the drapers, a shopman's team of lackeys offer roll after roll to a cross-eyed lady in a ribboned crinoline, bowing as if she's the Queen of friggin' Sheba. My silver dragon hisses, resentment burning. As if I'd want Eliza's prissy life anyway. Never saying what you please, forever acting like your turds don't stink and knowing your goddamn *place,* Miss Lizzie, just who do you think you are?

Her scolded child, that's who. Her meek and obedient pet. Her *prisoner,* behind rusted bars of fear.

But tonight, I'll go to hell by my own road. "Fuck it," mutters I, to the consternation of a lady and her gentleman companion. I wave my dragon on high as they hurry by. "Fuck it!"

Gaslights flicker as I sashay down to Drury Lane, where bright-lit theaters and gin palaces rise like mirages amidst a desert of darkness and filth. Music drags to and fro on the wind, rippling piano and twanging banjo accompanying drunken song. Gaily dressed whores and their fancy men promenade, and the dazzling colors water my eyes. I feel stronger, my blood sparkling, my skin a riot of sensation. The smells sting my nose harder, the sounds a raw delight. Oho! This new elixir's a right bit of fun, and I can't help but wonder exactly what sneaky Marcellus had in mind when he gave it to us. The last time he tried something new, it didn't go well.

Exotic smoke drifts, opium mixed with stranger fey-struck delights. At my feet, a dwarf staggers, blind. A sly Ottoman with gold plaited into his luxuriant beard proffers a green-smoking pipe, dark eyes seductive beneath his hood. "A pleasure for the lady?"

"No thanks, handsome." Tempting, but I wave it away. I need to see Eddie before I waste my night away. Beneath the bright sensations, strange foreboding plagues me, an itch I can't scratch. As if I'll need all my wits tonight.

I turn down the laneway towards the Rats' Castle, that cracked doorway with the dim blue light, and bang on the door with my dragon. "Open up, warty-face!"

But it ain't the usual door-keep. It's some sweaty thug with a broken nose and greasy yellow hair. He leers, gin-soaked. "Whassaword?"

"How 'bout, who the fuck are you?" But my stomach twists. Something ain't right.

"Nope, ain't it. But giss a kiss, pretty." He opens his arms, a flood of moldy stink. Jesus, how long since them armpits seen daylight?

I ram my knee into his nuts. He wilts, gasping, and I step over him and in.

I hurry along the black corridor, nerves firing like flint-locks. Fusty darkness mumbles and groans. Ordinarily, it smells of fairy dust and incense, a sparkling enchantment to lure you on. Tonight, all I smell is shit and dust.

I sweep aside the cracked leather curtain, and instinctively brace for noise, light, heat. Screams, howls, the stinking press of bodies, colors to boggle your wits.

Instead, I shiver in uncanny quiet. The atrium yawns, a cavernous hole, but the tiered balconies is usually crammed to bursting with fey folk, oddball creatures what don't fit in nowhere else. Tonight, I barely need to turn sideways. Still a crowd, for sure. I'm jostled by a hairy-faced lady in an orange gossamer gown who's chasing a greasy pig, fighting off a raw-boned bloke with green tentacles for hands. By the railing, a troupe of drunken dwarves form an unsteady pyramid, one atop the other. One passes out, and the whole thing tumbles, short blokes rolling like marbles and shouting curses.

But it's like a circus big top where no punters turned up— and the air, usually rich with sweet-drugged haze, instead contorts in pain, groaning with evil dreams. No bonfires, no crackers to whistle and pop. Listless folk linger in shadow, dull eyes fearful, hands leaping to weapons at the slightest noise. Everyone's sullen as a cheated whore.

No one's having *fun*. And at that, my elixir-warm blood crackles cold.

My dragon snarls, his forked tongue spitting sparks. That's right, handsome. Something's rotten here. Where the hell's my Johnny when I need him?

I fight my way down a ladder, through a troupe of drunken quadrille dancers, into a roped basket what lowers me down a few more floors, counterweight whistling. Something scaly— someone?—slithers by my ankles. A man with a hound's drooping ears thrusts a goblet into my hand. My mouth waters for rich oblivion, but I hurl the bubbling black muck away. No time for debauchery now.

At last, I skid down a rusted slippery slide, and stumble out at the atrium's bottom. Eddie's carnival, gay and bright, light and music and strange electric joy—but the carousel spins drunkenly, its plaster creatures cracked, that broken melody tinkling off key. Acrobats stumble and slip, their cheap costumes rotting, and a stinking miasma of mold and decay palls at eye level. The hurdy-gurdy man's face is green, weeping with sores, and on his shoulder, his monkey slumps, dead.

Distant lights swirl, an enchanted waltz luring me on, but

somehow I know 'em for a sham. They're candles in the windows of the tower of death, worthless paste jewels in a monstrous crown. *You're losing your mind, Lizzie,* hisses Eliza in my ear, an unexpected challenge. *Always said you would. Give up and let me back in . . .*

I feel my way into dank gloom. "Johnny? You there?"

Dark eyes follow me dourly from the sidelines. A skinny cove picks his nose and wipes the snot on his trousers, tracking me with one rolling glass eye. A sweaty-faced prat in a pastel pink coat chews wet fingers and laughs, over and over, *A-hee-hee! A-hee-hee-hee!* like a cracked phonograph.

An uncomfortable finger prods my spine. Not fey, these malingerers. Not Rats' Castle folk. Common thugs. Interlopers. They shouldn't be here.

I flip 'em the finger and stride on, but my nerves crackle. Drunken dancers fight and lurch. The fire-eater's flames roar like hellfire, and she laughs, her mouth full of rotting teeth. A clown staggers up, red nose bleeding black, waving a broken vanity mirror. Even the knuckle-fighting ring is brooding and watchful as the two big warty blokes duel grimly. Uncannily quiet, just the smack of flesh, rattling teeth, the dull ring of coin listlessly changing hands.

"Ring-a-ring o' roses . . . a pocket full o' posies . . ." A throaty song catches my ear. Behind the carousel, in the dark, lurks an iron cage, six-foot-square by four high. Inside, a chain clatters, dragging across stone. I smell rotting skin, the fleshy decay of madness. Eddie's pet. He calls him *Sunshine.* Sort of a stray dog what followed him home one day, in a manner of speaking, and Sunshine has cooled his heels in that cage for a good couple of months now. He's singing, his voice rasp-

ing, snatches of an old rhyme. *"Atishoo, atishoo, we all fall down . . ."*

I shiver, but his song is strange comfort in the clinging mist. A whisper of normality, sinister yet sweet. At least *he's* still here.

Eddie's twisted metal throne is empty, coated in a week's worth of dust. Where the hell is everyone? Impatient, I stretch on tiptoes, and *squish!* I collide with a meaty body.

Grotesquely fat, this cove, his stretched suit splitting at the armpits and straining around thunderous thighs. Deep in his doughy face, his eyes glint, evil pinpricks buried like jewels.

"Lizzie Hyde, m'dear, as I live and breathe." With sausage fingers, he doffs a dented black topper. Kinked, it is, as if a rampsman thwacked him over the noggin and he never beat it out.

A famous hat, that. Almost as famous as the name what wears it.

"Dodger," announces I breezily, though the smell of his sin-soaked flesh makes my guts slime cold. If there's one filthy fuck I never thought to lay eyes on in my father's kingdom, it's Jack friggin' Dawkins. "Never heard the sewer overflowed today."

"And what a pretty bird floated to the top." The Dodger grins, showing blackened stumps. Jowls wobble under greasy brown elflocks what ain't seen soap in my lifetime. This cove can barely move, let alone dip your hard-earned in fancy rig with the swellest of the swell mob, but sometimes a man's name outlasts him. No one's called this whale-man Artful in decades and meant it.

Behind him, his shit-witted disciples line up. The nose-picker with the glass eye, whose name I forget. Charley Tee-Hee Bates in his faded pink coat, the one who laughs. Flash Toby, scraggly red hair around a shiny pate, a traitorous whore what'd ream his grandmother for thrippence and sell her bony carcass to the pie man for a few pennies more. Amongst others.

The Dodger's gang. Never did see a sorrier lot of grimy ne'er-do-wells.

I back off, casting a side-eye. What in hell's going on? Everyone knows Eddie and Jack Dawkins had a falling out, back when the Dodger's name were still well-earned and Eddie were fresh and fiery, carving out his slice with no regard for reputation. Some tale about a stolen snuffbox and a sneaky tip-off and seven years in the black-rotting hell called Van Diemen's Land. The finest thief in London, transported for a ten-penny trinket—after which the Dodger slinks back to Blighty a broken man, nerves shot and hands a-shaking, jumping at every shadow.

He's harbored a grand cockstand for Eddie's guts ever since. *You ruined me, Eddie. All your doing, Eddie. Coulda been someone, Eddie, if it weren't for you.*

So where the fuck *is* Eddie?

I fix my face into a sneer. "Even dumber than you look, showing your carcass around here. If Eddie sees you first—"

"No need for hostility, m'dear." The Dodger laughs, clutching his weighty belly as if he fears it might burst, and Charley Tee-Hee joins in. I can smell the Dodger's breath, stale beer and vomit. "You're a comely lass, notwithstanding your father's grim outlook on my freedom. I understand you've a name yourself these days. Can't we be chums?"

"Oh, aye?" I swagger closer, leaning on my cane to fling him an eyeful. Never hurts to distract your enemy. "Came all this way just to see me, did you?"

"Could've done," says Dodger loftily, his beady gaze licking at my swelling chest. "Or maybe we was just passing through. Wasn't we, Charley?"

The laughing one spurts his load again, his silly high voice squeaking like a greased rat. "A-hee-hee! That's right, Artful. Passing through. A-hee-hee-hee!"

"Then pass on out again, like the turd you are." My dragon hisses, and I yank him open a foot and jam the blade two-handed under the Dodger's jowly chin. "Get out of my castle before I have your guts for sausages, you weasel-dick cock-sucker."

Dodger just grins like a shark, rubbing his sweaty bulk against me. "Don't play hard to get," he purrs, and fuck me if that ain't a hard-on pokin' my thigh. "If it's cock-sucking you crave, why not just say so? I'll gladly oblige."

Charley nearly dies laughing. "A-hee-hee! Why don't she just say so, Artful? A-hee-hee!"

My rage explodes, and I shove the blade in tighter. Just another man who looks at a woman and sees trash, to be tossed away once he's had his fun. "You stinky vomit-bucket—"

"Kill me, you rot-crotch slut?" Dodger's stinking spit flecks my cheek. "You wouldn't dare—"

"Peace, Lizzie." It's Johnny, long fey fingers gripping my arm, his lean shadow falling on Dodger's face. "Don't want no oceans of whale blood drowning us."

Hell for timing, Johnny.

I slam my blade away, cheeks afire. Easy mark, Lizzie Hyde. Shame on you.

"Mr. Dodger was just leaving. Wasn't you, Artful?" Johnny's mismatched eyes glint like cold jet, firelight crackling in his velvety black hair. He's always had a name, my fancy man, but he's flaunted new confidence of late, and though Johnny's sporting a coat the color of mustard and a green necktie like a lurid six-foot leprechaun, Dodger takes an involuntary step back.

But he hides his mistake with a sloppy smile. "A simple misunderstanding, John. I present myself for palaver with the sinister, singular, and spectacular Mr. Hyde. Take me to him."

"Like Eddie wants to talk to you," mutters I, still smarting. "He shopped you once. Don't imagine he'll blink for twice, you chicken-arse shitstain."

"You can palaver with me." Johnny draws up to his full lean height—nigh as the Dodger is wide, then—and folds his arms. In the shadows, I spy Eddie's people, a loose collection of thieves and fakers. Handsome Tom o' Nine Lives and his suave offsider Jimmy, Three-Tot Polly with her buxom scowl, the cove with the flippers called Fishy Dolittle.

Dodger's wobbling face falls. "'Twon't do, m'dear. Can't deal with the help. 'Twon't do at all." He sighs like a melodrama heroine. "Suppose we'll have to linger 'til Eddie comes back. Won't we, lads?"

Jeers and curses from his gang. "A-hee-hee! Suppose we will, Artful. A-hee-hee-hee!"

And Dodger waddles over, hitches up his straining trousers, and plonks his flabby fundament on Eddie's throne.

And that's it. I charge at him, sword drawn. "Get off my father's chair, you greedy bumwipe."

But already his lads are shouting insults and dragging me off him, and Johnny's men pile into the fight. *Oof!* A fist across the temple. I stagger, stars floating, my limbs weak. My dragon's lost. Around me, punches and kicks and curses fly.

"Topsy tart." Charley Tee-Hee guffaws at his own poetry and hurls me to the floor. "Topsy friggin' tart. A-hee-hee!"

Umph! A boot slams my ribs. I grit my teeth, and fling myself at Charley. *Crunch!* "Ha! Ain't laughing now, dicksqueeze."

He howls, blood streaming down his face. "You broke by dose, you topsy tart!"

My own laughter splits my aching ribs, and it feels good. "That the best you've got? Ha ha! You ain't half the man Eddie is, Jack Dawkins. Won't never be king, not in a thousand years."

I laugh more, tears flowing, and brace for a slating. Worth it to see the look on the ugly turd's face. But Johnny's dragging me up, warding off the Dodger's boys with my sword. He whistles, *tooo-whit!* and his lads fall back, melting into shadow. "Another day, Artful," snarls Johnny over his shoulder. "Count on it."

He and I stumble away with as much grace as we can muster. I shake my head to clear it. Johnny slants me the greasy eyeball—and then he laughs, too, cuffing my shoulder. "Jesus, Lizzie."

I shove him back, ribs still smarting. "Someone had to try 'im."

"Aye." He hands me my swordstick, and I grab it with a grin. He's a sight, my Johnny, all luminous skin and crushed-velvet hair. I want to sink my hands into it, pull his mouth to mine. Get gloriously drunk, lose us both in gin and sorrow and honest desire.

But hot confusion makes my head throb. A crowd of would-be revelers engulfs us, gaunt faces and lank corpse hair. They're sick, skin peeling, drool frothing from slackened lips. The room swirls, the carousel's animals dancing around me in mocking circles. *Ring-a-ring o' roses, a pocket full o' posies . . .*

I stumble against Johnny's shoulder, my guts roiling. Fuck, did I just spit up a little on his coat? He's so wonderfully strong and warm, his flowery scent suddenly all I've got to hold on to in this awful field of death. The sneezes from the rhyme grate my eardrums, a rough strep in my throat. *Atishoo! Atishoo! We all fall DOWN . . .*

The Rats' Castle is poisoned. Dying. Rotting from the inside. And only Eddie can save it.

The carousel whirls on, singing its mournful dirge. I eye the spinning animals suspiciously. Spy on me, will you, poxy traitors?

But they ain't listening no more. No magic left in 'em. Just plaster corpses with glassy eyes.

I pull Johnny into a hidden corner, where mirrors lurk and giggle. Inside that iron cage, Sunshine sighs and stretches, his chain rattling. His skin makes a crackling sound, like a centipede crawling through parched leaves. I find I'm clawing my hair, searching for pins, and I yank my hands away.

"Johnny, where's Eddie? How long's this been going on?" He and Eddie's thick as thieves (ha!) since Johnny's flash house burned down in an Enforcers' raid and Eddie decided he needed a new henchman, the kind of sharp and shifty cove who can patter flash and put up a lay double-time and don't ask the wrong questions.

"Few weeks."

"Why didn't you tell me, you glocky sot?" But my soul burns with acid guilt.

Because you're never around, Lizzie. Because you spend half your time swanning about in an Eliza-suit, toffing it up in Russell Square and the Bow Street crushers' shop, sniffing around murdered folks and trying on six hundred god-rotted wedding dresses, for fuck's sake.

Because you're never here, with me, where you belong.

What I'll do when Johnny finds out ain't an idea I cherish. My charming fey dolly-boy might be many things unsavory— pickpocket, fence, bent innkeeper, and upon-occasion thuggish brute—but thick-witted he certainly ain't. Surely, he wonders where I vanish to, *pop!,* like a ghost, only to return days later, bright and breezy as if nothing's amiss.

Or maybe he simply don't care. Johnny's never been a man to seek out reasons why sommat can't be done. Thinking things through is not his strong point.

"Eddie's never here no more," says he. "The longer he stays away . . ." He waves at what's around us. The dusty, faded carnival, its dimming light and stink of mold, the decaying wood and rotting clothes.

My swallow hurts my throat, and I don't voice the darkest fear in my heart. That Eddie's not sick, but *mad.* Lost it.

Gone . . . and the Rats' is gone, too. Without Eddie, none of this can be. And without the Rats', where will all the fey folk go? What's to keep 'em from destitution and murder and the Royal's dank dungeons?

Johnny folds his fingers between mine. Fine fingers for thieving, lithe and quick with a few more knuckles than they've any right to, and curse it if his touch don't feel *safe*.

Har-de-har, and get on with you, Lizzie Hyde. If I've learned one thing about being half a person, it's that there ain't no such thing as *safe*.

"So take me to him," says I, gripping his hand. "I'll talk some sense. Where is he?"

"Soho, most like. Mrs. Fletcher's—"

Leathery fingers latch onto my ankle and yank sideways.

My knee buckles, pain bolting up my leg. My hand rips free. *Doingg!* My head hits the carousel, dizzying me. "Argh! What the shit—"

Ping-whizzz!! Metal ricochets, directly above my head.

A bullet. Right where my dumb skull would've been.

Heart pounding, I scan the crowd for the assassin, but there's only a sea of sick faces, receding into stinking gloom. And then I spy a brassy glint, a puff of smoke, and the gleam of dirty red ringlets disappearing into the dark. "Flash Toby," accuses I, scrambling up. "Fucking Dodger."

A blackened hand in a filthy linen sleeve creaks back into shadow. "We all fall down," Sunshine whispers, and laughs. Save my life, will you? Ain't irony a killer?

Was Toby aiming for me, or Johnny? It don't matter. "We need to un-fuck this, John, and fast. Take me to Eddie."

Johnny's crooked fairy gaze darts into the darkness, where

the creature's sing-song still floats like dry leaves. "That's one we could bring with us, y'know."

I shudder. *Sunshine,* Eddie calls him. Blood and roses, cognac and absinthe, the sting of steel and a hot crimson splash . . .

"No!" My voice lurches, too loud. Suddenly, I don't want to stay in this rotting tomb one misbegotten moment more.

"Eddie likes 'im," offers Johnny. "He could help. S'worth a look—"

"No," I says again, calm-like, "he stays where he is," and I grab Johnny and pull him towards the light.

CHIEF OF SINNERS

AN HOUR LATER, WE'RE AT MRS. FLETCHER'S, A higher class of whorehouse in a gaslit Soho street teeming with swells and lushes and sly-eyed girls on the game. The wooden porch is freshly painted, blue picked out in expensive fools' gold. Prospective customers eye the place off. I push past a richly dressed gent with his hair in a rain-spattered blond pigtail, who lounges against the porch and glances at his jewel-chained watch, casual-like, as if it ain't clear as balls on a greyhound what he came for.

I guffaws. "Jump in and get your rocks off, sir. Looks like you can afford the best."

The cove just ignores me, his face oddly blank. Hmph. Hoity folks got no sense of humor.

Letitia Fletcher herself greets us in the hall. She's wearing a showy green off-the-shoulder gown, her elaborate ringlets dyed black to hide the fact she's on the desperate side of forty. Tawny skin, swan-like neck, almond-shaped eyes lengthened with kohl like a harem girl's. A striking beauty in her day. The most sought-after courtesan at Whitehall, some say, while others mutter about whips and spikes and the Hellfire Club.

Me, I'll have a quid each way. Making lily-arsed lords squeal with a silken cat o' nine seems just the sort of playtime this frost-hearted madam would enjoy.

Still, you can rely on her love of cold hard cash. Many's the time Eddie's caroused here, drowning in drink and girls and sweet-smelling smoke. Shattered windows, holes punched in plaster, bruises and tears and nightmares. Such is the cost of Eddie's recreation—but he always pays for the damage in full, or madam penny-pincher here wouldn't have hide nor hair of him.

Ho-ho! *Hyde nor hair,* by God. Miss Lizzie should've been on the stage.

"How can I serve you this evening? Something for couples?" Fletcher favors me and Johnny with a glacial glare. We ain't good for business, partly because we don't need no help to get our rocks off, thanks very much, but mostly because we care what Eddie gets up to and don't want him friggin' his life away on whores and rotgut gin.

"His Majesty in?" Johnny kisses her hand, flipping her a grin that'd charm any warm-blooded woman's corset off no trouble. It hits Lady Frostheart and bounces right off. She scowls, but lets us pass.

We trot up the stairs. The usual zoo—yelling, moaning, the smack of joining flesh—rattles along the velvet-draped corridor. On the landing, twin blue-eyed girls in skimpy silks recline, puffing on long-stemmed pipes. A client smokes with 'em, a baby-faced youngster with sweat in his ragged mud-brown locks and a hungry glaze over his eyes. The right-hand twin flips his trousers open, licking her lips. With a leery wink in my direction, Baby-Face pulls her head down, staring at me as she goes to.

I hurry by, wrinkling my nose at his queer animal stink. Rather your mouth than mine, darlin'. Wouldn't be a whore for quids, and that's quids more than this sorry sister will get for her trouble.

We head for the first door in a long line. Naught but the finest for King Eddie.

The place is a riot. Broken furniture, flowers strewn amidst smashed porcelain vases. Drapes torn from the window, broken glass like jewels on the firelit carpet. Greenish smoke drifts from a glowing brazier. Someone's kicked a hole in one wall. The curtained bed is unmade, torn and twisted sheets showing signs of harsh use.

And here's my father, slouched in a wing-backed chair. Trousers still on, thank Christ. His shirt's open, stained with wine. A blond-pigtailed girl wearing white silk stockings and not much else straddles his lap, trickling a bottle of gin over plump pink nipples.

It's Rose, his favorite for the now. I met her some weeks back when I were investigating one of Eliza's murder cases. A nice enough lass, if mercenary. A professional . . . but real affection glistens in her gaze, that expert red pout softened with tenderness.

I shiver. Poor Rose, besotted with the devil himself.

Eddie's singing at the top of his lungs. *"Maggie, Maggie Mayyy . . . they've taken you awayyy . . . 'n' you'll never walk down Lime Street anymore . . .* Ha! Taken you away, by God. To the crows with you, my fine thieving wench, and rot your skinny arse on a gibbet!" He slurps gin from Rose's breasts. "Ha ha! A fine medicinal distillation, my duchess. Bleeding Christ, your tits are spectacular."

"Sir?" I approach, careful-like, in case he springs into a rage.

"Lizzie, m'darling, how the hell are you?" He stumbles up, setting Rose carefully aside in the manner of a practiced drunk, and wraps me in a crooked hug.

I kiss his stubbled cheek, smooth his grizzled hair. He smells of gin and alchemy, that dark-spiced perfume that makes me long for years gone by. Young Eliza in the study at midnight, awaiting her rough-mannered guardian, that tipsy-gallant stranger what never shows her his face. Just a hunchbacked shadow on the wall, his husky voice liquor-rich, that same edgy scent of not-quite-gentleman.

Innocent Eliza, fascinated and repelled and a little bit in love. How the world warps beneath us while we're gazing at the stars.

"Let me look at you." My father holds me at arm's length. His shoulders are lopsided, and he waddles like a nut-drunk squirrel, but for all that, he's possessed of oddwise elegance fit for any society ballroom. His face—Henry's-that-was—is a thing of beauty warped, his smile a kinked leer. Disgusting, in his way—but then that screw-it-all glint ignites in his storm-gray eyes, and you're thinking wild and wicked thoughts and wondering if the devil put 'em there. Kicked aside many a broken heart, has Edward Hyde. "You're a beauty, Lizzie mine."

His praise glows on my skin like sunlight, and for one glittering instant, I hate him with all the ferocity of hell.

Ain't because I love him despite all his faults. Ain't even that he loves Eliza better, though the knowledge flays me raw.

It's that I'll forgive him. I always do. He's my father, for fuck's sake.

I work up a smile. "What's the story, Papa? We've just been to the Rats' and Jack bloody Dawkins is there. The Dodger, Eddie. In your friggin' chair."

"Eh? Don't bother me with trifles. This is a party!" He laughs, spreading his arms wide, and my blood chills. When Eddie laughs, stars fall. But not tonight. His mirth bounces hollowly from the walls, an empty clang of desperation. That stain on his shirt ain't wine. It's something crusted and thick.

He claps Johnny's shoulder, sending him sprawling. "Avast, lovebirds, let's play cards. Eddie Hyde feels lucky to-night! Where's my Rose? Rose!" he bawls, before he realizes she's still there, and grabs her waist, dancing a few steps of a half-remembered gavotte. "Ring-a-ring o' Rose, eh? My Rose is special. Just you wait and see."

Rose kisses him fondly, *smack!*—aye, see what I mean?— and dances on.

Johnny twists his velvety hair. "Eddie, let's have serious palaver, aye? Spare your skirt for shagging."

Rose simpers. "Blow me, Wild, ya lousy twist."

Swift as a serpent, my father drops the girl and grabs Johnny's throat. "Belay your cheek, son," he snarls into his face, "or you'll find your fairy arse ain't so pretty that I won't flay your skin to bake me a Johnny pie." He flings him away. "Rose is my duchess," he announces drunkenly to the world. "Not a word against her, men. I've been busy, s'all. Occupied, by God! Vital imperative busy-ness, ha ha!"

Johnny fingers his throat, where Eddie's dirty nails have dug red crescents.

I grip Eddie's arm. "C'mon, I'll shout you a tot at the Ten Bells. I need some air."

Eddie bares white teeth. "Air? This is the land of mud and shit, my girl, where they quaff misery like ale and bake starvation into cakes. But now you mention it, I've a thing to show you, Rose. Such a pretty thing. Let's be off, we've a date to keep."

And he jams on his hat and crooks his arm, as if he's forgotten he's half-dressed with blood splashed down his shirt like a nosebleed.

But Rose—a kind heart for all her dirty job—shoots me a glance, jerking her chin towards the door. "Can't we stay, sir?" she purrs. "I've an idea for a game." She nuzzles his ear, hands busy, and then they're kissing and in a minute or two, he's forgotten all about Johnny's fairy arse and cakes and his *pretty thing*. He's panting, sweating, glazed eyes fixed on her mouth. As if he's a hungry wolf, and she's food.

"Come, *duchessa*." A growl, beastly undercurrents of need. "You'll earn your crown tonight."

This is Eddie the lover, and no one's idea of Prince Charming.

I toss a few sovereigns on the dresser, *clang-clang!* She'll keep my father out of trouble 'til morning, and deserves an extra quid or two. Brave girl. But impotent rage stirs a wasp's nest in my chest. Naught I can do but watch, as Eddie and Rose fall onto the bed, and he starts doing what he does. Sheets rip, limbs stretch, muscles glisten and ache, the sound of edgy sighs and sensation.

Rose is making little squeals, *oh! oh!*—delight or terror?—and I walk out, leaving 'em to it. The Rats' Castle is dying, rotting to ruin around us, and Eddie don't give a damn. Contented as a pig in shit.

On the landing, the blue-eyed twins are gone, apparently used up. Baby-Face slurps his bee-stung lips at me. Coat off, necktie unraveled, dirty hair awry. "Care to play, madam? I do enjoy these games. That young lady swallowed everything. I wager you'd like that." He tosses a moist arm around my shoulders. "Five sovereigns for a nice hard suck. I'm good for it. Ask anyone."

His peculiar goaty-gin stink oils my tongue. The little squeezer seems familiar—gleaming eyes, tinny voice, affected little laugh—and I wring my brains, but nothing oozes out. Maybe one of Dodger's slop-brained gang, for all his toffy West End tones. "Not for all your gold, dickbrain." Disgusted, I shove him away and sweep down the stairs. Johnny scrambles to keep up.

Mrs. Fletcher's waiting by the door, frosty glare full-force. "For Eddie's recreation," says I, tossing her my purse—God help us if he breaks a girl, too—and I storm out, slamming the door. *Bang!* The window rattles. It don't make me feel better.

We jump down and head off into the muddy street. Colors glare, a cruel-bright rainbow. Voices and laughter spike my ears to throbbing, and I can't scour out that image of Dodger at the Rats', making like he owns the place. His pimply arse in Eddie's *chair,* for God's sake. And Eddie just slobbers gin and ruts with his duchess. If I were Eliza, telling him to scrape up his horseshit and listen, would he ignore me then?

Johnny shrugs listlessly, gaslight dancing in his hair. "He's getting old, Lizzie. He's tired of it all."

"I don't give a fuck if he's five hundred on crutches, Johnny. What about the fey? Where they gonna go if the Rats' Castle dies? Think Dodger will give a spit for them, once his flabby twat's on that throne for real?"

I don't even say the obvious, which is *what about us?* How long will Johnny and me last if Dodger gets his way? The sad, lonely creatures of London have a home at the Rats', safe from witch-burnings and pitchfork-wielding pogroms and the Royal Society's torture cells . . .

My spine tingles.

The Royal.

Did the Philosopher put Dodger up to this? Heaven knows, that greedy old skeleton would be cackling like a witch at the prospect of the Rats' Castle reduced to a moldy hole and Eddie a rotting corpse at the bottom.

Eliza should know. She *works* for the rusty-hearted bastard, and ain't she about to marry one of their own? Captain Lafayette might be one of us when the full moon comes, his furry wolf-creature a bristling bundle of *wrong*. But he still works for the god-rotted enemy, and she'll *marry* him and ruin my life. Fuck me raw, why can't she piss off and leave me be?

My fury erupts, and I punch the nearest thing, which is a fat iron lamppost. *Crrunch!* Pain spikes my knuckles and now I'm even angrier because part of me knows I'm just seething green. For Eliza and Remy, for Eddie and Rose and their thrice-damned happiness. For this whole benighted world and all those other people in it who always get their way.

"Fuck it," announces I, for about the tenth time this evening, "let's get drunk. Take me to the gin."

"Happy to oblige, madam." Johnny filches a bunch of pink dahlias from a flower-seller's cart and presents them to me with a roguish grin, tilting his hat over one wonky eye. "For my ruby princess."

The blooms smell of him, sweet and alive. I smile like a sloppy idiot—such a charmer, Johnny, damn your eyes—and tuck a flower into my hair, and we set off. Arc-lights flicker, shadows dancing over the crowd of drunkards and revelers. Food-sellers yell their wares, the scents of fish and roasting chestnuts floating. I sidestep a tiny pickpocket who's fanning my skirts. "'Ere, watch it, squirt."

Johnny smacks the child over his tousled sconce. "Clear off, ya clumsy shitweed," he growls, but he's smiling, too, and the little wrongful laughs as he darts away.

"The mouths of babes." Grumbling, I check my pockets. Good thing I already gave Letitia my money. "Little sprat's only just been born."

"The class of these here miniature practitioners leaves much to be desired. I'd have had your garters at that age, and more besides."

"More besides," I agrees with a wink. He blushes, and it's adorable, though like any good swell mobsman Johnny can blush on cue and it don't mean dog shit.

He were eleven the night we met, half-starved and precocious, his big black eyes shining with bigger dreams. My first night of freedom, when Eddie first came to Eliza's with a bottle of bitter-hot delight. What a night we'd had, little Johnny

and newborn Lizzie Hyde. We'd thieved, fought, laughed ourselves silly, fled from angry crushers, and swallowed more gin
than our tiny bodies could handle. At the end of it, he'd stolen
a kiss—and a long history of rotten decisions, worse timing,
and awkward *oh-shit* moments were born.

I wrap his lime-green coat tighter in the chill, my grumpy
mood persisting like a lingering fart. "I tell you, Johnny, Eddie's the king and that's that. Who the fuck does Dawkins
think he is?"

"He thinks he's a name with a loyal gang o' lads, and he's
right." Johnny's words slur a little, as if he's wearing thin. In
contrast to my sharpened senses, his dark eyes are dulled, his
sparking hair snuffed out like a failing enchantment. When
the hell did we get old, Johnny? "All the topside thugs who
hate us will take his side. Eddie's king because he acts like it,
no other reason. If he don't take charge . . ."

I pull my cane, revealing a foot of shining steel, and my
dragon breathes fire. This is *my* magic, Artful, you cockless
bastard, and it ain't going nowhere. "Then let's murder the
Dodger and be done."

"Ha! It's been tried. You'll never get close, not now you've
flashed your hand like a dimwit sharper."

"Piss on you," mutters I, but he's right. "Ambush, then."

"Eddie's people know me, but I ain't the man himself. We
can't throw Dodger over alone. His muscle will tear us apart.
Fifty of the bastards at least," he adds grimly, before I can
protest that I don't give a fuck.

I shakes it off, irritated. "Well?"

"I can get the gang onside." He shrugs. "It'll take time, and
coin."

"How much?"

"More than you'll make before closing time, sweet ruby Lizzie. I'd a few lays in waiting, but . . ." He shoves his hat back, a rueful flop of black velvet hair. "Ain't easy making an honest living right now. With the brass-arse Royals stinging up the fey, and the crushers and the regiments a-Froggie-hunting, London's coopered from Tothill Fields to Rother-hithe."

"Is it, now?" An idea sparkles, a dark poisoned jewel. "Reckon I knows a crib. A deadlurk, too, rich pickings."

"Plate or coin?"

"Coin. Your hand still in for a locked window, or is you too old and all?"

A deft ripple of knuckles, nary a shake. "Never."

"Us two should manage it, then. Your usual cut, o' course," I adds, for Johnny has a name to protect and don't so much as drag his fairy arse out o' the pub without proper compensation for his valuable time. *Anything free is shit,* he likes to say. Just because we're shacked up don't mean he'll work for nothing.

"Aye." He don't look convinced. "What's the catch?"

"The catch, my comely twist, is that I knows where it is and you doesn't." I tweak his nose. "You'll pay a fair price for the good oil, too."

He grabs my rear and pulls me against him, unleashing that grin I were mentioning. "Princess, all I have is yours."

Oi. A fair amount he's got, too. He kisses me, gin and desire and glassy desperation. He's a good man, my Johnny. A grand man, with the truest heart alive, for all his rascal's games, and for a moment I let myself believe I can stay. Just him and me, and to hell with Eliza and her god-rotted *better life*.

"Jesus, keep that thing under control." I shove him away. I'm due back at Eliza's by first light. That's our agreement, for all it's a tough break, and while she keeps her end, I must keep mine. Never say Miss Lizzie was first to break her word. "Let's do it, then. Fine night for a ruckus, my good fellow."

"'Tis indeed."

Hours later, in the darkness before dawn, I fall back warm and dizzy in our firelit bed, catching my stolen breath. Beside me, Johnny stretches, satisfied, his body glistening, a lean shock of beauty.

Christ, he's a sight, his black hair mussed and his crooked fey eyes a-smolder with our love. Pleased with himself, too, his cocky smile curling, and so he ought to be, for we're fed and warm and rich and in love and what more can decent folk ask?

Our little room ain't much, but it's ours and that's what matters. A small coal fire crackles in a real chimney. The roof don't leak, and there's even a glass window we've covered with a blanket to keep out the cold. These cushions are cozy, the quilt kicked aside for lack of need, and our clothes lie where we dropped 'em on the splinterwood floor.

Damn, but I don't miss the way it was. All that lying and sneaking about, pretending we don't care. Johnny and me's done our share o' cheating and slyfuckery over the years, and

I'm right sorry for it. Hearts got broken. People died. And he and I missed out on this.

A finger of chilly disdain prods between my shoulder blades. *Really, Lizzie. It's not very clean. What's that smell? At least get some furniture. And as for him . . . well, he's handsome, I grant you, but surely even you can do better than a third-rate thief?*

My mouth tightens. Don't judge me, Eliza. You've no right. And Johnny's thieving is fucking first-rate, thank you very much.

But the damage is done. I can't help but see my life through *her* eyes, the dirt, the squalor, the lower-class stench. God rot it, why's she got to be so much *BETTER* than me?

I shift onto my back, trying to forget her. Johnny trickles silver coins through his witchy fingers, and I giggle as they drop on my belly and roll away. Money ought to be cold, on such a raw night, but these coins is warm. The pillow-sack we fetched 'em in lies limp beside me, spilling its hoard like a pirate's treasure chest.

A rich haul, more'n enough to pay off Johnny's gang, and never you mind whence it came. Miss Lizzie knows carriage folk, so she does. An army captain with a wolfish reason not to involve the authorities, who I happen to know is out of town this week, raising revolutionary hell in gay Par-ee. Must have a word to Remy about his window locks, because in Johnny's flash hands they ain't worth a damn.

Sorry, Remy, but I know you can spare the cash. Likely wheedled it from some dirty enemy Froggies anyway. And we're in genuine need.

Johnny drops open-mouthed kisses on my throat, my breasts. "That's forty quid so far." His hot tongue plays sultry games on my nipple. "Is my debt settled, my princess? Might be I can find . . . something else . . ."

I squirm, sighing as he moves lower. "At a tenner a go? Manage again, good sir, and my fortune is yours. Consider me compensated . . . wait. Oh. Changed me mind. I'll take another . . . ah, sweet God, Johnny." And in short order I'm all dizzy and breathless again and when I'm finished he's kissing me and wrapping me in his arms and stroking my hair and God rot it, Eliza, how can you marry another man when *this* is happening?

For the longest time, I wanted what Eliza had. But no longer. I want what's mine. My own future, right here. Lizzie's already got her man; and she don't want no other. Don't need no poxy wedding to prove it.

"Shh, you'll wake the baby," whispers Johnny, winking towards the hearth, where Jacky Spring-Heels is curled up like a kitten in his dirty underwear, his wild white hair stuffed into his mouth.

Johnny takes care of him now, with the Cockatrice burned down and Jacky having nowhere else to go. I don't mind. Jacky's what you might call a cog short of the full clockwork. He likes to hide in the bushes at night and leap out at passers-by, hollering fit to split as he larrups off down the street in his knickers.

The lurid penny papers call him the Terror of Limehouse! but Jacky don't mean no harm. He just thinks it's funny as a ha'penny privy to watch 'em shit their britches. But if it weren't for us, he'd only get his shrieking carcass arrested, and they'd bang him up in the Steel with dog-fuckers and kiddie-rapers and next day there'd be a pink smear in the exercise yard and a new dreadful on the book-seller's cart entitled THE STICKY END OF JACKY SPRING-HEELS.

I blink sleepily. "That baby wouldn't care if you rogered me up the arse with a cactus." Though how the hell Jacky can sleep through the racket we're making is beyond me.

Johnny giggles. "Try it and see?"

I whack him. "More'n your life, you fairy-arse twat." I roll a sovereign's ridged edge along Johnny's collarbone. They say 'twas the Philosopher himself put that edge inscription on there, back in his day as the Mint's hired help, to stop fakers and smashers clipping off the gold. *Decus et tutamen,* it says, which far as I can figure means *It's pretty, but don't try kicking its arse.* "This enough? To save Eddie, I mean."

Johnny rolls onto his back in a flop of wild black hair. "Tom o' Nine-Lives, Fishy Dolittle, Three-Tot Polly." He counts off allies on long fingers. It's mesmerizing, considering what they've recently been about. "Twenty quid for them and their lads. Add the Sultan's gang—"

"The Sultan's put in lavender," I remind him. "No one knows where he is."

"Newgate," says Johnny loftily, "what luckily for us is burned. The Sultan ain't in lavender no longer."

"Ah." I'm impressed. "The Sultan's got a gang, so he has. What odds Tasty Mick at the dockside?"

"Already talked to Tasty Mick." Johnny rests his head on one loose-jointed arm. "In all, fifty-five pound ten and nine-pence, done and dusted and screw you very much. Ain't you delighted your swell gent's so clever?"

By the fire, Jacky mutters, scratching his buttoned back-side. Discomfited, I rise and go to the window, lifting the blanket to peer into the unlit Soho street. Rain patters the glass. Still black as pitch, only a feeble yellowish crescent struggling through clogging clouds. The new elixir bubbles, restless and strong in my heart. Still my time. But for how much longer?

Out in the rain, folks is still abroad, for life nor limb don't wait for sunlight. A fat cove waddles along wrapped in a horse blanket. A one-legged beggar in a moldy green coat hunches in a doorway, shovel hat jammed low, shivering fit to shatter. Remind me to drop him a few pennies, for he looks like he could use it.

A pair of gents hoofs it across the street towards this very tenement. The tall one's holding his coat over his head to stay dry, but the little one's dancing in puddles and laughing at the moon. Seems the Terror of Limehouse ain't the only simpleton in these parts. Rain spatters his cheeks, drenching his long ragged hair like wet silver.

It's Baby-Face. The oral enthusiast from Mrs. Fletcher's. My neighbors, eh? Fancy that. Thought he looked familiar.

I'm still wearing my garters, and absently I flex one knee and stroke my stockings smooth. "Fifty-five quid? Friends don't come cheap."

Johnny watches me, enthralled. "Don't come easy, neither, not averse the Artful Dodger. Lizzie, for the love of Christ, your legs will be the death of me."

But uneasy needles squirm deeper into my flesh. "What if they betray us?"

"They won't. Come back to my bed, princess."

"Why won't they? The Dodger's got coin, too."

"'Cause they's fey and the Dodger ain't, and 'cause the Dodger ain't pulled a decent lay since he shot the lag, and 'cause they know what hurt and foul ignominy awaits 'em if they piss me off. Stand there unclothed much longer, sweet ruby Lizzie, and I can't be held responsible for the tenner you'll owe me."

"And what then?" I pick moodily at a stitched patch on the blanket. "Say we manage to turn off the Dodger, along with Tee-Hee and Toby and all his hard men. What if . . . ?" I bite my trembling lip.

What if Eddie don't never come right? What if he's lost his marbles for good?

A world where Eddie can be king is a world where Lizzie can be free. Without him . . . that's no world at all.

Cold resolve burns my heart. *I'll be rid of you, Dodger, mark my words. Eddie will be well, and the Castle will be bright and gay, and all will be as it were before.*

My throat aches, and swiftly I turn away.

But Johnny comes to me, light on his feet as any fairy prince. He tilts up my chin, kisses a loose curl from my cheek.

Viciously I blink my eyes clear. "S'nothing," I mutter. "Get on with you."

He just smiles, and for a while we hold each other.

By inches, the dark window turns gray, the threat of approaching dawn.

I don't move. He's warm against my side, and my head about fits under his chin. When did he get tall, that cocky lad of eleven what stole a kiss in the rain? Tall, sleek, clever as a clockwork fox. When did we all grow up?

His heartbeat makes me feel safe. We're warm and fed and in love. I should be happy, by God. *Happy.* Imagine that . . . but crackling hatred ignites in my belly, consuming me as surely as any carnal lust.

This is mine, Eliza. *Mine,* hear me? And you can fuck me in the arse with a cactus before you'll take it from me.

Johnny shifts in my arms. "S'late."

But I barely hear. I'm starting to shake. I'm burning up. My anger's clean, pure as any hand in fire. I'm being violated. Ripped asunder, with no more care than a child tearing the wings from a fly.

I grab his lovely hair and kiss him, hard. Our teeth collide, a twinge of copper as my lip slices. I don't care. Tonight, I feel everything more, want it more, and it ain't only tonight that's in danger, but the rest of my life. I push him against the window, fighting for his tongue, raking my hands over his body. My nails dig in, and he grunts in surprised desire. I drop to my knees, and he tastes of *us,* of sugar and heat and the exotic mixture of our sweat.

He groans, helpless not to want. "Don't do that . . . Shit. You trying to kill me, woman? Don't you have to go?"

He knows.

My heart flips, and I glance up.

But he just strokes my hair, breathing hard. "You're always leaving me, Lizzie."

"Not this time." I push him back onto the cushions, in a fall of rich black hair and luminous fey skin. Such a sight, Johnny. I devour him, lips and hands and body, his scent tingling all over me, an irresistible fairy spell, and as I slide him into me, he sighs and whispers some rot-brained tripe about *love* and *forever,* and my tears sting and I whisper it back and I don't care.

Johnny's ten quid in silver clinks to the floorboards as we make love. Mine, Eliza. *Mine,* and to moldy green hell with you and yours. The rain outside can't touch us. The chill can't harm us. There's only him and me, and Jacky murmuring sleepy nonsense by the dying fire—*Atishoo,* he whispers in a scratchy voice like dry leaves, *we all fall down*—but before long, morning creeps in like a bright-cloaked thief to steal it all.

HYPOTHESES NON FINGO

WITH A START OF PURE DISMAY, ELIZA LURCHED awake.

She was trapped. Immobile. A hot smothering prison, no light, no air . . .

Gasping, she forced sticky eyes open. Gray daylight leaked in the window of a small wooden room. Cushions hugged her body, and a coarse quilt exuded the sweet fey scent of flowers. She was in bed. Warm and safe, wrapped in strong arms.

A man's arms. Naked.

Oh, Lizzie. Eliza's skin burned. She held her breath. Didn't dare move.

No reaction. So far, so good. Now what?

Carefully, she extricated herself. Unclasped a set of fingers—uncommonly long ones, with one too many knuckles, and how was that possible?—and inch by inch, eased the man's arm from her body.

He just murmured, contented. Didn't move. Didn't awaken.

She exhaled and sat up, sliding her bare legs from beneath the quilt. Lizzie's gentleman friend—Jonathan, she remembered, a crooked-eyed fellow who seemed a pleasant sort, when he wasn't housebreaking or picking pockets—just snuggled deeper, black hair spilling over the pillow.

She crept to her feet in a shaft of light, and wobbled, dizzy. Dark-mirror images swirled and shattered, shards of a lurid nightmare. *A knife cold in her hand, stabbing down, the squelch of popping flesh, a scream* . . . Her stomach felt as if it had been scoured out with sandpaper—*drinking again, Lizzie?*—and her skin broke out in bumps where moments ago she'd cradled that warm body. Something sticky bothered her between her thighs, and she spared a moment's thanks for whatever magic lurked in the elixir that *undid* such things.

The coal fire had died, and the chill soaked rapidly into her bones. Weariness washed her thin. It was long past dawn. She'd be late to the Palace. Worse, she'd be forced to walk the street in Lizzie's clothes again. Exposed. Nowhere to hide.

Coins littered the floor. The place smelled of breath, sweat, and intimacy, and that flowery scent clung to her loose hair. At least she still wore stockings. Lizzie's corset lay tossed over a chair, her chemise on the floor. Shivering, Eliza struggled into first one and then the other, fumbling with clips and laces. At least Lizzie's larger, um, dimensions made it easy . . .

Breathless, she halted in mid-pull.

A scraggy lad in dirty unmentionables gaped at her from his mat before the cold grate. Ashes crusted his white hair. "Pretty," he whispered, wide-eyed. "Pretty lady."

Carefully, Eliza lifted a finger to her lips. *Shh!*

The lad giggled and copied her. "Shh!"

She smiled and made a show of tiptoeing to the door, where Lizzie's satin skirts lay discarded.

"Shh," whispered the lad, entranced, "Jacky shh," and started to sing under his breath. *"Ring-a-ring o' roses . . ."*

Hurriedly, Eliza fastened her bodice, skipping buttons in her haste. Her hair was a disaster, the dress creased. Her mouth tasted foul, of gin and this strong new elixir and stale saliva that didn't belong to her.

She swallowed a curse. *Lizzie, why today?* She couldn't meet the Philosopher like this. She'd need to go home and clean up. *At her earliest,* indeed. It'd be midday before she arrived.

Finally, she yanked on Lizzie's boots, grabbed the first coat to hand (a voluminous thief's frock in mustard yellow) and crept out onto the dirty landing, closing the door on Jacky's rambling melody. *"We all fall down . . ."*

Out in the street, the rain had thinned to a drizzling mist that rinsed everything gray, as if overnight all the color had leached from the world. Dull-eyed folk hurried by in grim apparel, splashing drab mud. Even the electric coils of passing carts seemed subdued, their bright purple dimmed by the fog.

Eliza splashed across the road, huddling in her yellow coat. She felt wrung out, exhausted. Her throat burned, as if she'd swallowed too much gin or spent the night shouting— probably both—and her lips felt chapped from ill use. But that was impossible. The change healed all wounds, didn't it? Still, in this gloom no one would see anyone. She'd remain anonymous.

For now.

Frustration bit at her fingers. She'd kept her end of the

bargain, but Lizzie wasn't honoring hers. *We can't go on like this, Lizzie. How can I trust you?*

But no sharp retort came. Just silence. As if Lizzie slumbered, sated after her night's exertions, that bright new elixir drained away, leaving her soul empty.

Where was this? Soho, she supposed, or Seven Dials, though she recognized nothing. It could be Spitalfields or Bethnal Green. Her memory clogged like a scab, and every time she tried to peel back the surface, it stung and bled.

A ragged costermonger couple dragged their sodden vegetable cart through squelching mud. In the gutter, dirty children shivered. Under a darkened gin palace's window slept an old woman, her soaked dress dripping. Boarded-up shops moped, forlorn.

She reached a tiny crossroads. Courts and lanes led off every which way into a maze of dark passages that looked identical. The gray sky gave no hint of the sun's angle. Soon, she'd be lost. Her impatience prickled. She'd no time for this.

A filthy-dressed woman stumbled by, rolling her eyes and tearing at seaweed-like hair. Eliza approached her. "Excuse me, can you tell me which way to Oxford Street?"

The woman cackled, pointing—but towards what?

She'd no choice. Gathering her skirts, Eliza set off. The street narrowed. Drunken buildings lurched, ready to fall. No electrics or gaslight here, nothing that smacked of prosperity, only rotting wood and mud and starved groans. *Misery like ale, and starvation into cakes.* The dimming light threatened, its shadowy hands coveting her.

Eliza hurried on. Stinking mud sucked at her boots. A

sweaty fellow in a faded pink coat chortled unpleasantly, baring rotted teeth. "A-hee-hee! Topsy tart! A-hee-hee-hee!"

Shivering, she broke into a trot. Taunting voices followed her. *Run, you topsy tart. Where's your sister? You don't belong here.* She stumbled, caught herself with stinging palms. *Splink! Splink!* Footsteps approached. She flung a glance over her shoulder. Just a shadow, a crazed giggle.

A House of Correction loomed, its brick wall topped with electrified wire. Frightful wails echoed from within. A hound snarled, guarding a lump of gristle. Down some steps, through a darkened court, around a bend. A whore spat at her. Hungry children fought in the mud. Another dog—or was it the same?

Panic clawed her throat. She was going in circles. She'd never get out of here.

"Lost, my lady? Let me guide you." That chortling fellow lurched at her from nowhere. His breath slimed her cheek, and sharp metal pricked her waistline. "The Dodger says how-do. A-hee-hee!"

She swung her boot hard at his shins, and ran.

Whoosh! A carriage thundered by three feet away, drenching her with freezing puddle slop. She skidded to a stop, heart galloping. Rain-spattered windows, rushing vehicles, scurrying pedestrians huddled beneath umbrellas. Oxford Street.

And the laughing fellow was gone.

Shaken, Eliza hurried home. It took an hour to wash, dress, and choke down a cup of tea, and by the time she arrived at the electrified gate to Buckingham Palace, armed with doctor's bag and umbrella—and dosed to the gills with her remedy to keep Lizzie at bay—she was soaked, her head was pounding, and it was a quarter of eleven o'clock.

A pair of armed Enforcers confronted her beneath the gilded iron archway. Hulking brass brutes with grotesque flesh-and-plaster faces, electric eyes glinting red. One had a dead gray human hand grafted onto one arm. These machines weren't made for beauty or grace. Rather, to engender fear and obedience, and they performed their purpose pitilessly.

She proffered the Regent's crumpled letter. Hippocrates swaggered alongside her, a clicking bundle of self-importance. She hadn't had time to polish him, and dirt streaked his little face. "Entry," he squeaked proudly. "Palace business. Make greater speed."

The Enforcer digested the letter's contents, and pointed to her bag with its fleshy hand. The skin was rotting at the edges. It didn't smell good.

She clutched her bag close. She had medicines in there. Unorthodox ones. "I say, no need for that—"

The machine's hand snapped to its electric pistol, red eyes dilating black.

"Fine." She handed the bag over with ill grace, only partly feigned. "You can explain to your Philosopher why I'm late."

The Enforcer just walked its fingers through the bag—searching for what? Weapons? *Aqua vitae*? Mistakes in her arithmetic? Next time she'd hide an electric eel in there—and lingered over her phials, opening one to sniff the contents. Did Enforcers have a sense of smell? Some electrical sensor for explosives and noxious fumes? With anarchists and anti-sorcery vigilantes blowing up buildings and railway lines all over the city, the Palace couldn't be too careful.

Still, her nerves wriggled. Her private things. Her remedies. Alchemy. Good God, the thing would shoot her on the spot.

But it handed the bag back, and waved her through.

Breathless, she trotted across the wide gravel yard to the service door. A clockwork footman in black and gold livery admitted her, marching her through bustling corridors and busy stewards' rooms, the preparations for the king's birthday party in full swing.

"I say," she called, running to match its scything brass stride, "why am I summoned? Has His Majesty fallen ill?"

But the impassive servant didn't speak. She followed it up the back stairs, dodging equerries, liveried stewards, and hall boys, until they reached the exquisitely plastered *piano nobile,* where all was empty and silent.

Eliza shivered under the towering painted ceiling, feeling like a miniature Eliza who'd strayed into a giant's world. Hipp dashed ahead, raindrops flying. "Down, Hipp," she snapped, and he skidded into a sheepish tiptoe.

Portraits gazed sternly down, ladies in court finery and gentlemen in archaic military uniforms. Spotless red-and-gilt couches lined the corridor. Not a mote of dust invaded. The floorboards didn't creak. No drapes flapped, no servants whispered. Even the electric lights kept their hum and crackle to a minimum. The only sounds were raindrops pattering on the curved glass clerestory, and the soft *thud-thud* of the footman's brass feet on the carpet.

His Majesty's study door was shut. The footman knocked twice. No answer. It knocked again, louder.

Inside, furniture crashed—a chair hurled across the floor?—and the door yanked open.

"God's blood, what *is* it?" Sharp colorless eyes stabbed her from a flurry of unkempt hair, and lit up. "Dr. Jekyll! Excellent! Come and look at this." A thin hand shot out and dragged her inside, and the door slammed shut, leaving the hapless servant—and Hippocrates—languishing in the corridor.

The room was dark, gilt-rich plaster receding into gloom. The fire had died, and the tall bay window was shrouded in velvet drapes. Somewhere two clocks ticked, an unsettling fraction out of phase. The only illumination remained a cardboard-covered electric lamp on the desk, from which emanated a steady, horizontal beam of white.

"See here," insisted the Philosopher, plonking down a flat triangular prism the size of a dinner plate and adjusting it with a twist of his wrist, so the light beam shot into the prism, turned about, and splashed back onto his ink-stained hand. "Total internal reflection," he pronounced. "It's in my *Opticks*. No doubt you read of it in school."

Eliza couldn't help a smile. This was the Philosopher at his most endearing. His brocaded coat was missing, his shirtsleeves smudged, as if he hadn't changed for a day or two. His long hair hung loose and unbrushed, his eyes glittering with excitement. One almost forgave him a hundred years of hypocrisy and lies. "The critical angle of incidence," she recited, "beyond which all light is reflected and no light passes through—"

"Yes, yes. But look! I position this like so." He grabbed a

convex lens and set it behind the prism, so they touched—
and a second beam sprang out, slicing through the lens to
stab into the curtains across the room. "And egad! Now light
is passing through." He shot her a sidelong glance. No cynicism. Just pure scientific excitement. "Fascinating, yes?"

Eliza faltered. As per usual in his presence, she felt slow,
stupid, the dullest girl in class. "I'm afraid I don't see."

"Whence that light, Doctor?" An impatient edge sliced his
tone. "Have I created it from nothing? *Total* internal reflection, it appears, is no such thing—but only when I place this
lens like so, creating a tiny air gap. Without it, I get nothing."

"Oh." She frowned. "That does seem odd."

"It's positively diverting." His delighted smile subtracted
years of cynicism from his face. "I've thought about this off
and on for decades. Imagine your bedroom window at night,
wherein no doubt you admire your pretty reflection in the
candlelight." A disconcerting chuckle, as if he'd observed her
doing just that and was preparing to prosecute. "But an observer outside can still see in. Why do some corpuscles re-
flect, and some pass through? Why, Doctor? Do you imagine
each corpuscle *knows* what to do? Is it even conceivable that
these phenomena are based purely on chance?"

"I—"

"And even *if*," he stressed, returning to his prism and lens
without missing a beat, "light were acting as a waveform—
and *if* there's nothing but aether in that gap there . . ." He
tapped his teeth with a thoughtful fingernail. "I built a larger-
scale one of these down at Greenwich. I measured how long
it takes the light to move from one end to the other. To the

best of experimental error, of course. It's quite a surprising result."

"I see." She didn't see at all. She fidgeted, that scrap of paper crumpled at the bottom of her bag suddenly wriggling to be noticed. If anyone could make sense of Miss de Percy's fragmented equations—but what if the science were forbidden? She didn't want Mr. Starling—or this Professor Crane, for that matter—in trouble with the Royal. Eliza's credit with Sir Isaac took her only so far.

He chuckled at her bewilderment. "Never mind. I merely make the observation. Whatever isn't forbidden is inevitable. There is doubtless some fundamental law of the universe requiring light to behave in such bizarre fashion. But I do not hypothesize as to what it is." He pulled on his charcoal tailcoat and heaved the curtain aside, squinting into wintery gray glare. "Morning, is it? How time flies when one's having such excellent fun. You're late, Dr. Jekyll," he added sharply, and whirled on his heel.

And to that, she had nothing to say as she meekly followed him through the door into the king's inner audience chamber.

A merry fire crackled in a marble hearth beneath a glittering electric chandelier. Somewhere, a multi-phonic music box tinkled, an aria from Mozart's *Die Zauberflöte*. A silver tray of tea and cream cakes sat on a side table. In the corner, a liveried nurse bobbed a curtsey to the Philosopher. A low hubbub of conversation filtered in through the closed doors from the main chamber. Important people, no doubt, politicians and lords waiting to see the Regent and the king.

The young man sat cross-legged on the floor, rolling his

toy train over the thick red carpet. Someone—the nurse?—had dressed him painstakingly in a beautiful morning suit, white collar and cuffs and iron-gray coat. No mourning band for his mother, of course. One didn't mention death and the sovereign in the same sentence. But cream splattered down his front, the clips torn from his cuffs. He nodded compulsively, fair hair bobbing, and drool slipped down his chin.

Edward VII was seventeen with the mind of a six-year-old. He looked far too big to be playing with trains. Rumor whispered that the Philosopher addled his brain with poisons to keep him under control. But Eliza had examined the boy, and found no evidence of drugs, medical or alchemical. The king was simply absent, his mind locked away where no one, not even he, could find it.

At his side bent a thin fellow in a drab suit, all knees and elbows like a stick insect. He wore iron-rimmed spectacles with a retractable metal magnifier attached. Sweat dampened his sparse gray hair. On the floor, his hinged leather bag held brass calipers, screws, bellows, and a vile-looking funnel.

Eliza's guts churned. That tube from her nightmare, wriggling down her throat with cold medicine spurting forth. This fellow was an alienist of the worst sort. Was she being fired?

"Your Majesty." Sir Isaac bowed curtly. "Dr. Jekyll is here."

Eliza did her best curtsey. The king made no sign. Just kept rolling his wooden train back and forth.

"At last." From the window seat rose a lady in a vivid blue brocade gown, hair pinned under a hat of curled white lace. Victoria, the Princess Royal, elder to the king by five years. A capable young woman, who would have been king if she'd been born a boy. She motioned Eliza aside, her face dark with concern. "His Majesty is worse, I'm afraid, since last you came. That medication you prescribed was promising, but it's run out. Bertie, stop that, dear. You're spilling it."

The king giggled, gleefully banging his train into his cake plate. The nurse ran to the rescue, wiping up cream and retrieving broken china.

"Sorry to hear that, ma'am." Eliza kept her expression grim, but inside she brightened. If her medication was working even a little, that was progress.

"This alienist is a lunatic," whispered Victoria, out of the Philosopher's earshot. Suddenly she looked ten years older, a sister fearful for her brother's welfare—or his life. "I humor him for my late mother's sake, but . . . can't you do something? It's Bertie's birthday this week and he must appear at the banquet. And the Foreign Secretary is outside. I don't want that reptile to see my brother like this." She glared at the sweating stick-insect fellow, and raised her voice. "Dr. Savage here seems to regard His Majesty as a species of wild beast to be tamed."

Dr. Savage—a physician, then, not a surgeon or apothecary—gave a rotten-toothed smile and took a tin of evil-looking green snuff from his box. "Just the ticket for this type of mania, ma'am." He applied the snuff to the king's nose. The child sneezed violently half a dozen times and began to hiccup and weep, his nose turning purple.

Crestfallen, Savage squinted at the king through his magnifier. "The acid seems to have stung Your Majesty's eyes. How unexpected." From his bag he took a pair of sharp-edged steel handcuffs chained to a spiked collar. "Here we are, sir. We'll soon have you cured."

The Regent made a moue of disgust. "Savage, your interpretation of the term 'natural philosophy' makes one shudder. I ought to have reasoned her late Majesty's favorite would be an idiot."

"But restraint, Sir Isaac. That's what's required." Savage rattled the horrid cuffs. "It's the only treatment for these feeble-minded recalcitrants, when the strongest drugs don't work."

Politely, Eliza cleared her throat. "Forgive my presumption, sir, but perhaps Dr. Savage is confusing His Majesty's state with violent mania. I've found that if the heavier narcotics are left off, in cases of sullen dementia the patient eventually awakens into a state of calm, whereupon more specific treatments can be attempted without any restraints at all."

Savage scowled. Not at her, oh no. Heaven forbid he should inadvertently acknowledge she existed. "In inferior institutions such as Bethlem Hospital, Sir Isaac, the most wretched medieval quackery was perpetrated by so-called doctors in the guise of honest medicine. We can only be grateful that antediluvian relic burned to the ground."

She smiled sharply. "Did you ever actually *visit* Bethlem, Dr. Savage? If you'd bothered, you'd know that Mr. Fairfax was a fine surgeon and his treatments—"

"If your honor would allow me," cut in Savage loudly, "to transport His Majesty to my new state-of-the-art facility, where we can chain him securely and commence regular beatings."

Sir Isaac's eyes flashed stormy warning. "That will be all, Savage."

"But we must whip him, sir! Flog him! Release those troublesome choleric humors! It's the only way—"

"Out, fool." The Regent's voice sliced like a guillotine blade through fog. "Before I lose my temper and turn that whip on you."

Savage lost no time in grabbing his bag and marching for the door. "Mark my words, *Doctor,*" he muttered as he passed. "Leave that one unchained and you'll regret it."

Eliza checked a sigh. Surely professionals ought to be able to co-consult without jealous sniping? Had she unwittingly made another enemy?

But she shivered, too, recalling her nightmare, the manacles, that horrid tube. She hadn't liked the look of Savage's treatments. *When you finally drive me mad, Lizzie, let's hope we don't end up in Savage's "facility."*

Princess Victoria gave a satisfied *humph*. "What a perfect idiot. On that, Regent, at least we can agree."

"Such a pity your opinion troubles me none." Pointedly, Sir Isaac referred to some letters on the desk. "Proceed, Dr. Jekyll. I do have other appointments."

Eliza knelt by the king's side, setting down her bag. The music box finished its melody and began again, slower. "Your Majesty?" She stroked back his fair hair. A pleasant young face, if slack. "Sir, how are you feeling?"

He just stared dully, without recognition.

She made swift mental notes, needles stabbing into her back as Sir Isaac watched her with hawkish interest while he pretended to read. *Low fever. Eyes glassy, pupils dilated. Pallor exaggerated. Saliva clear.* "What's he eaten today?"

The nurse curtseyed again. "Cake, ma'am. I couldn't get the porridge down."

The clockwork music box wound down, its final chord fading. "Try again, if you please," said Eliza. "He won't improve if he doesn't eat . . . I say, whatever's the matter?"

The king clawed at his face, wheezing for breath. "Murder!" His eyes gleamed like poisoned darts, no longer vacant but afire. "Murder! They're trying to kill me. Run for your lives!"

Princess Victoria ran to wind up the music box. *Crink! Crank!* The melody started again. The boy was weeping now, rocking back and forth, blood oozing from scratched cheeks. "There, Bertie," soothed Victoria, "it's playing again now. He really does like his Mozart."

As always, his condition twanged loose wires in Eliza's memory. Sometimes a docile child, taking his supper and playing his little mandolin for hours on end. On other occasions, his rage lapsed into cunning, and he tore the wings from flies and twisted the fat Palace cat's tail until it yowled. Yet others, he rolled wet eyes at her with what she could only describe as a thoroughly lascivious grin.

Not unlike the polar states of another unstable fellow of her acquaintance. Almost a *transcendental* identity.

Sympathy tugged at her heart. He ought to be out playing polo, hunting, flirting with heiresses, all the things titled young gentlemen did. Not languishing here, trapped in his own mind, playing with a train set while others carried on his kingdom's business without him.

Her courage quailed. She'd never treated the king in the Philosopher's presence before. Was her dangerous choice of remedies justified? She hoped so, for the king's sake—and for her own.

From her bag, she took a glass phial. Inside, the medicine she'd developed—with Mr. Finch's assistance, naturally—bubbled and sang, a thick grassy color. Its bitter smell drifted, reminiscent of her elixir, and inside her, Lizzie thrashed like a trapped serpent. This wasn't the elixir itself. Merely some of the same ingredients. *Lux ex tenebris:* to make light from darkness. Scientific heresy, of course, but she'd judged it worth the risk. A patient like Bertie had forbidden corridors in his mind, locked rooms he couldn't open. If she could encourage those locks to break . . .

Ha! yelled Lizzie in her head, a bright shock. *I'll break you, my pretty Eliza. Dissolve you, like Eddie did Henry. Transparent like god-rotted glass. See how you like it!*

The liquid splashed over Eliza's hand, icy and burning.

Victoria eyed the bottle, abruptly suspicious. "What's that?"

"Similar to last week, ma'am. A tonic I've developed." Casually, she wiped away the spillage.

"Ah." A glimmer of interest. "What exactly does it do?"

"It should calm his jittery nerves, and encourage him to, er, communicate more lucidly. I've had some success with it with similar patients in institutions—"

"Madhouses, you mean." Victoria's mouth set hard. "My brother is not a lunatic, Dr. Jekyll."

"Of course not—"

"And I won't have it put about that he is. Do you hear me?"

"I assure you, ma'am, I keep the strictest patient confidentiality—"

"You doctors are all the same. Think you know everything." Victoria worked herself into a rage, skirts swirling as she paced. "You're not the first quack to attend on His Majesty's affliction, and I promise you shan't be the last."

Nothing to do but keep her eyes down. But the word *quack* stung Eliza's skin like an angry wasp. A moment ago the princess had practically begged her for help. How had she disappointed? Numbly, she waited for Victoria to dismiss her for good. So much for her opportunity to shine.

"Give me that." Victoria swiped the phial from Eliza's fist. "I'll have it tested by my own *reputable* physicians before he drinks a single drop. Think you can feed my brother whatever snake oil takes your fancy? I shan't allow it!"

Sir Isaac stepped deliberately into Victoria's path, oozing lean menace. "I'll decide what we shall and shan't allow, ma'am. I have studied such things. You have not. Dr. Jekyll's *medicinals* are of the finest efficacious quality."

Eliza felt faint. Was he being sarcastic? Playing with her, a sleek gray cat batting about its favorite timid mouse? A guilty mouse who could summon no legal defense. A mouse who, if he chose, was as good as dead.

Victoria's face suffused. "I am a princess of this realm, sir, and you are a farmer's son. Dare you presume—"

"Must we go over this again?" Sir Isaac's rain-gray eyes threatened murder. "I am Regent. The king is in *my* charge. Dr. Jekyll has my full confidence, and you are an irrelevance standing in my way." He beckoned sharply. "Now hand that over, if you please."

Victoria fumed, outraged—but with ill grace, she thrust out the phial.

He snatched it, cut her a razor-sharp smile, and turned away. At his feet, King Edward nodded and drooled, silent once more.

"You haven't heard the last of this." Victoria flung open the double doors and stalked out into the main audience chamber. Unseen deferential murmurs from the petitioners—*your royal highness, princess, ma'am*—rippled down the hall and faded into the distance.

Eliza waited, sick and shuddering.

The Philosopher held Eliza's phial to the light. Inside, the tell-tale green liquid bubbled and hummed. "Ah," he said lightly, "the famous medication. My curiosity knows no bounds."

Surely the stuff reeked of alchemy. Sir Isaac would tire of his games, dismiss her in disgrace. Worse, summon his Enforcers to drag her to the Tower, where a dank electrified cell awaited her, complete with rusted electrodes and agony. She might never be released. Day after day, locked up without elixir, enduring Lizzie's writhings and screamings to be free. And when she could endure the turmoil no longer . . .

He popped the cork, and sniffed. Frowned. Sniffed again. "Egad," he remarked dryly, "how peculiar. What's in it?"

She smiled weakly. "Numerous ingredients. I hardly know. As I say, I've had success with small doses in the more tractable lun— Er, patients at Bethlem."

"Extraordinary. One would almost say *transcendental*?" He tipped a drop onto his thumb. Rubbed it. Touched it to the tip of his tongue.

She nearly retched. "I'm afraid I don't—"

"Don't insult me, Dr. Jekyll. I've been preparing *aqua vitae* for a century or more. I know alchemy when I see it." A cold smile stretched his lips. "My, my. A shame if your unorthodox dabblings should offend me somehow. If the king's condition should improve too drastically, for instance. Do you understand?"

Her stomach knotted, cold slimy terror. So that was it. The Philosopher didn't want the king *cured*. He wanted him kept useless and pliable. Under control.

What part was she expected to play in this charade? Poison the king, keep him witless and drooling?

Or just . . . do nothing? *Primum non nocere,* said the ancient physicians' creed. *First, do no harm.* But how could she justify withholding treatment when she knew it helped? Didn't it?

Thump! The doors flew open, and Hipp barreled in and hurled himself eagerly at her skirts. She stumbled to her knees against the gilded red sofa. Footsteps slipped over the carpet, a sudden forest of legs. "Hipp, for heaven's sake—"

"Foreign Secretary," said Sir Isaac blandly, and in a twinkling hid her incriminating phial behind his back. "Good of you to come, my lord."

Hurriedly, Eliza gathered Hipp in, glancing up with trepidation at the Secretary and his entourage—into sparkling eyes of clear electric blue.

Remy Lafayette winked at her, his scarlet-and-gold cavalry officer's coat dazzling as ever. It only made his chestnut hair glisten harder, if that were even possible, and his eyes glow deeper.

She couldn't smother her delighted grin. She'd imagined

from his letter that he wasn't returning for weeks. Just like him to want to surprise her.

Languidly, the Foreign Secretary—namely the 1st Earl of Beaconsfield—sat. Dark and sardonic with a neat goatee, a green coat, and striped yellow trousers. Fastidiously, he crossed his legs, arranging himself to best advantage, draping one hand over a glittering diamond-headed cane. "Regent. Good of you to see me." His tone was dry, as if he didn't mean it in the slightest and didn't care who knew.

Eliza—still kneeling on the floor—couldn't help a curious stare. With Parliament dissolved on the old queen's assassination, and the general election halfway done, the papers said this vain, provocative little man would be the next Prime Minister. A career politician, and raised from the Commons to boot, his title newly minted by the late, besotted queen. Doubly disturbing to the establishment.

That reptile, Princess Victoria had called him. Certainly his eyes were narrow and heavy-lidded, his thin mouth perennially mocking. Not a man to be trusted.

But she couldn't concentrate on that now. Not with Remy's gaze on her, coaxing away her every glimmer of attention. Was it only that she'd missed him, or did he look even more unreasonably spectacular than usual?

"—your man here informs me the Paris sorcerers are deploying mesmerism and mind control to suppress their unruly citizens," Lord Beaconsfield was saying in his exaggeratedly bored drawl. "*Mind* control. I mean, *really.* Their Committee of Public Safety have gone certifiably insane." He fluttered a limp hand. "And apparently the incumbent set of lunatics are about to be stabbed in the back by an even more rot-brained outfit, who want nothing less than outright *anarchy*. Com-*mo*-tion, sir. Pure chaos. It's 1794 all over again."

The Regent smiled sharply. "Heaven forbid. This group *Liberté du Sang*—"

"*La Belle et la Bête,* their two leaders call themselves. Beauty and the Beast. Villains from an overwrought Italian opera, if you ask me. 'Liberty of blood,' indeed. What does that even *mean*?" Beaconsfield sniffed, dabbing his nose with a scarlet handkerchief. "*Shape*shifters, Sir Isaac. It's in*suffer*able. One almost wishes that half-wit Louis Philippe back again. At least he knew the value of an honest war."

The king crawled under the Regent's chair, and absently Sir Isaac stroked his hair, shushing him as one might a nervous puppy. "And the meeting with our envoys?"

Behind the Foreign Secretary, Remy cleared his throat. "All arranged, sir. Security is in hand. *La Bête* is a coward, but I think he might be persuaded."

Beaconsfield arched his manicured eyebrows at the Regent. "Good fellow, your Lafayette. When he does as he's told, which isn't often. Supposed to be spying on them, my boy, not joining their ranks."

Remy didn't flicker. "Only way to gain their trust, my lord."

"I'm sure," said the Regent dryly. "And what of their agitators in London?"

Beaconsfield sniffed. "Damned radicals. This government of ours may indeed be an organized hypocrisy, but at least it *is* organized. I hear they want women's suffrage and no income tax. Democracy," he declared with a delicate shudder, "is a perfect drain on parliamentary resources. What an abject bore."

Newton yawned. "His Majesty will receive your reports, I suppose?"

"Naturally." Beaconsfield admired the sparkling diamond-studded unicorn atop his cane. "Lafayette, be a darling, do. Just remember you're writing for royalty. They live to be flattered, my boy. Make 'em think they're the smartest person in the room. None of your damned regimental straightforwardness."

Remy bowed. "I'll lay it on with a trowel, my lord."

"Good man." The earl waved languidly. "Off you go, leave the adults to talk. We'll discuss your other matter later. At the Carlton, of course. Proper Tory stronghold. One can't use the privy at Whitehall these days without spies bursting in."

Eliza rose, taking up her bag. "Regent, may I also be excused?"

The Foreign Secretary stared archly at her interjection. Perhaps he'd imagined her a servant. But Sir Isaac winked conspiratorially at her—a disconcerting experience—and placed her phial on the desk. "Be on your way, Doctor. I'll administer this curious medicinal as per your instructions. What were your instructions, precisely?"

She forced a smile. "A drachm now, and another before supper, sir."

"Bated breath, I'm sure. Good day."

"I say," drawled Beaconsfield, "young madam, are you a physician? Is that allowed?" His heavy-lidded eyes were lazy on her face, but interest smoldered, too, as if she'd offered him some delicacy that watered his mocking mouth.

As if he'd imagined a tantalizing use for her, and intended on putting his plan into practice without delay. This man was no foppish idiot. Far from it.

Flustered, she curtseyed to the king and hurried out, Hipp galloping at her side. She pushed through the crush of grandees and civil servants, searching for Remy. "Oh, there you are—"

"And there *you* are." He flashed that ridiculously brilliant smile. "Hello, Dr. Jekyll. Did you miss me?"

She laughed, drinking in the sight of him. Irrational, how her pulse fluttered. Most unscientific. For once, she didn't mind. "I might have noticed you were gone. Dare I hope Paris has improved your manners?"

"Glad to disappoint." He tucked his hands behind his back, and bent closer to whisper. "Imagine I'm kissing you."

"Oh?" She inhaled, closing her eyes. "Hmm. I see."

"Yes. And again, you fascinating woman. Do you feel it? You can barely breathe. It's perfectly scandalous. You're practically fainting in my arms."

She popped her eyes open, grinning. She wanted to grab his hair, draw his mouth to hers for real. "Stop that, you pirate. People will stare."

"Let them." As usual, his ridiculously blue eyes undid her. Nothing but truth. "Let them marvel at how beautiful you are."

"Ha! If you'd only written ahead, I'd have had my hair done." She resisted the need to tidy imaginarily disheveled skirts. "I hardly expected you back so soon. Whatever will my husband say?"

"The wind was good, and I have ways of traveling swiftly." A mysterious wink. "I wanted to surprise you."

His presence made her ache, both sweet and bitter. She

wanted to laugh in bliss, but a darker, more shameful mood seized her, too. Living alone was so much simpler. Only herself to care for, only her own affairs to worry about.

But that was a joke, wasn't it? Since he'd left for Paris weeks ago, she'd struggled to fall asleep each night, fearing for his safety. Imagining all the horrible things that could be happening to him. And always, like a wicked worm coiled in the blackest depths of her heart, there lurked the creeping certainty that she'd be found out, slammed down, stripped of her illicit joy.

She sighed. Was this love, then? Because it came burdened with cartloads of unpleasant baggage that no one ever spoke about. Hmph. Those sonnet writers had a lot to answer for.

Remy touched her chin. "You look as if someone stabbed your ghost in the heart. Did I say something wrong?"

She smiled sweetly. "Given your usual addle-mouthed antics? I expect irate antagonists are scattered in your wake all the way from the *place de la révolution*. No wonder we're on the brink of war."

An unreasonably charming smile. "Is it wrong that I just swooned a little? Madam, if forced to trade away either your kiss or your wit, I'd be in agonies of indecision."

"The former, I should hope. Ought I to agree with your every idiotic remark, and surrender to your un-gentleman-like ravishment without a blink? Imagine how vain and indolent you'd become."

A gleeful glint of eye. "Imagine."

Hipp dashed up, blue light blinking madly and cogs whizzing. "Ee-e-e-e-e-EH!" he shouted, too excited to make any sense.

Remy petted Hipp's boxy head. "As eager as I."

"And even more articulate." She edged towards the exit, eager to leave this suffocating hall where they were public property. Where they couldn't touch or share confidences or be themselves. "I got your letter. How was Paris?"

He made a face. "Awful. A bloodbath. I still can't get the stink of sorcery out of my clothes. I'm only surprised the Philosopher didn't arrest me on the spot."

"And the mission goes well?" She kept her voice light, though she desperately wanted information. What was his mission, anyway? For whom was he working—the Royal, or this unsettling Lord Beaconsfield?

"Swimmingly. The Philosopher has me ferreting out crackpot scientists all over Paris. Wants to catalogue their contribution to the French war effort. Truly, it's mind-numbingly dull and I don't understand the half of it."

Uneasily, she recalled Mr. Finch's tinfoil hat. "Do they really have mind control machines?"

"It would explain a lot. You wouldn't credit the nonsense these people believe."

"And the Foreign Office? What do they want?"

"Oh, you know," he said cheerfully as they picked their way down the stairs through a forest of servants and petitioners. "Political machinations, Machiavellian plots, bloody *coups d'états* in the Tuileries. Up to our necks in it. Oh, I almost forgot. I've a present for you." He handed her a feathered cockade. Black edged with scarlet, the colors of *Liberté du Sang*.

She whisked it out of sight. "Put that away, you anarchist. Are you trying to get us arrested?"

An irreverent blue twinkle. "What? It's what they're all wearing in Paris this season."

"Honestly, do you take nothing seriously?" But she couldn't help laughing. He didn't. Never had. "How you ever succeed as a covert agent is a mystery. It's a wonder your tragic sense of humor doesn't give you away as soon as you open your mouth."

"Doubtless it would, my petal, if they didn't already know exactly who I am. All part of the fun." At her expression, he sobered. "It was inevitable, my sweet. This appalling fellow *la Bête* knows François was my brother. That's the whole point. It's a double game. Perhaps I, too, can be lured to the ways of darkness."

He said it lightly, but she knew that even the mention of François's treachery still hurt him deeply. The brothers Lafayette had both fought wars for the Empire, spilled too much blood—their own and others'—in the service of the late queen. The notion that François, a decorated Royal Navy captain, had thrown it all away for nothing was too much for Remy to bear. He was convinced François had been turned. Warped into a traitor by sorcerers' lies.

They emerged into the wet gray courtyard, where flower-beds ran sodden and puddles ringed the ornate memorial to the dead Prince Consort, who'd supposedly been poisoned by sorcerers. "And are you well? With the, er, moon phases, I mean."

"Well enough. I've barely time to worry about it." He shrugged, unconcerned. "Don't fret, my sweet. There are worse things than a night spent in a cage."

"It's only that I've made some progress with my cure,

and . . . no, let's not speak of it," she finished hurriedly, seeing his expression. "No doubt you'll be leaving again soon. Let's just enjoy each other?"

"Perfectly." His eyes glowed, and he kissed her gloved hand, warm and safe. "Tell me everything that's happened. You and Griffin making short work of that Soho Slasher business?"

"Not yet, sadly. But I do have another interesting matter." She explained about Antoinette de Percy's murder, the defaced ledger, the inexplicable equations. "There's a demonstration this afternoon of the new aether engine. I'd like to meet this Professor Crane, see what kind of people these scientists are. I don't suppose you can spare the time?"

"For you, I can spare *all* the time." A vintage Lafayette smile. "Lunch first?"

"Shirker. What of your reports for that ghastly Foreign Secretary?"

"As if he'll read them anyway. Too busy stabbing hapless Tories in the back on his way up the greasy pole."

"What a dreadful man. I thought he *was* a Tory."

"Precisely why they never see him coming. If they don't cover their flank, he'll be Prime Minister once the polling's in. Then those bunglers down at Horse Guards will see some action."

She smiled uneasily. If it came to war, Remy might return to his regiment. Leave her behind, helpless along with all the other women. The army needed doctors, surely. Would she be allowed to go? "But surely the Empire wouldn't risk such a shattering defeat. The French coalition army is too vast. Seems reasonable to build up our military capability first.

Rebuild the skyship fleet, that sort of thing." Immediately she winced at her carelessness. The skyship fleet had been François's project, terminated in a hail of flame and treason.

But Remy just shrugged. "Reason rarely comes into it, my love. They say this mysterious *la Belle* character is a double agent, a man with influence at the War Office. Perhaps we're all doomed. But you needn't worry your pretty head about unladylike politics," he added airily. "Leave the voting to the men. We're *so* much cleverer."

She swatted him, earning a strange look from the Enforcer at the gate as Remy collected his weapons: sword and electric pistol, both polished to perfection. "I liked you better when you were just an arrogant Royal Society investigator. This civil service nonsense is giving you airs."

"Oh, I'm still an arrogant Royal Society investigator. I'm just sharing my talents. Seeing as I've so many to go around."

"Don't spread them too thinly, Captain." She eyed him sternly as they crossed the wide avenue and turned towards Hyde Park Corner. "I should be disappointed if none remained for me."

A METHOD OF FLUXIONS

IN EARLY AFTERNOON, REMY HANDED ELIZA DOWN from their electric cab onto rain-splashed Albemarle Street. The Royal Institution loomed, a massive twelve-columned edifice in imitation of a Greek temple. Hipp jumped down after, and the cab clattered off into the traffic, brassy feet sloshing through the mud. It bumped into a rickety horse-drawn cart, eliciting shouts from the indignant driver. The popularity of the RI's demonstrations made for so many traffic snarls and accidents that the northern end of Albemarle Street was closed to entry, making it the only official one-way street in London.

Remy held her umbrella for her. "What are we here to see, again?"

Eliza pointed at the canvas banner above the door.

PROFESSOR CRANE'S
NEW MINIATURE AETHERIC GENERATOR
THE FUTURE OF ELECTRICAL POWER

He looked impressed. "I read something about this in the Royal's files. They say it's a fraction of the size and weight of the current models. What a fantastical modern age we live in."

She stifled an unladylike burp. Their lunch in Hyde Park had been glorious, despite the dull sky, and if her stomach now creaked, uncomfortably stuffed with smoked salmon sandwiches, strawberries, and ice cream, it was small payment for a wonderful time. To think she'd worried they'd have nothing to talk about.

Call that a conversation? whispered Lizzie sarcastically in her ear. She'd been quiet all morning, just a breathy warmth in Eliza's belly. *All that grinning and gazing into each other's eyes. I'm snoring over here.*

Casually, Eliza pulled out her flask of remedy and sipped. *My time, Lizzie. Don't interfere.* "So they've submitted for the Royal's approval?"

"Submitted, if not yet certified. Does that surprise you?"

"It doesn't seem like the kind of device the Philosopher would countenance." They wormed through a knot of protesters waving pasteboard placards and shouting slogans. Eliza nodded towards a banner that read ENERGY IS PRECIOUS— PRESERVE OUR AETHER. "Dare one hope he's mellowing in his dotage?"

"With Beaconsfield chewing his ear day and night about new technology for the war effort? 'Mellow' isn't the word I'd use. Given half a chance, he'd burn his lordship for unauthorized sexual ambiguity and be done."

"Down with progress!" yelled a man. "Jobs, not volts!"

A woman shook a NO ELECTRIC AUTOMOBILES! sign in

Eliza's face. "Science is sorcery! String up the sorcerers! Wring their Froggie necks!"

At her skirt hem, Hippocrates buzzed indignantly. "String. Breaking strain insufficient. Does not compute."

Eliza snorted. "By all means, blame the French for everything we don't like. Next this pestilent rain will be their fault."

"Didn't you know? English weather has been a French conspiracy since Agincourt." Remy held the door for her. "I suppose it hasn't occurred to these shouting buffoons that science has weaved their clothes and grown their food for the last two hundred years? Clearly Crane's engine is stirring up the common prejudice against good sense."

"Mmm. Still, tell that to a man whose children starve because an electrical generator rendered his job superfluous. It's not all onwards and upwards."

"I say," he remarked as they crossed the carpeted hall and entered the little theater, "am I marrying a Luddite? Smash the generators, tear down the looms, set the factories on fire?"

"Hardly. But progress ought to feed the poor as well as entertain the middle classes, or what good is it?"

Remy smiled. "You have my vote, madam."

"Well, I'd take it, but . . ." She frowned, patting her skirts. "No trouser pockets to put it in. Oh, well. Back to my embroidery."

A high gallery ringed the stage on three sides, seats receding into the gloom. Beneath it, gaslights illuminated more rows of steeply raked seats, all but filled. Well-dressed ladies and dapper gentlemen mixed with businessmen and scruffy students gripping notepads, as well as a few plain, ordinary people nearer the back.

On a table onstage sat the engine, a cubic frame about a foot square containing a bundle of wire-wrapped magnetic components. Long coiling wires connected the engine to a rack of heat sinks and capacitors, thermometers and barometers and aetherometers, their crystalline kernels glowing. Inside the engine burned a tiny electrical coil, just the size of her finger, shining too brightly to behold.

Her skin tingled with anticipation. Truly a marvel of modern science. But she recalled irascible Seymour Locke's jibe—*I did say advanced aether physics*—and her heart sank, prepared for disappointment. In all likelihood, the device didn't work. Just a flim-flam, pursued by careless researchers with more enthusiasm than ability.

In the front row sat Princess Victoria, fanning herself impatiently in the warm electric-smelling air, surrounded by bored-looking courtiers. She rose. "Dr. Jekyll," she called, "a moment."

Eliza rolled her eyes at Remy's delighted chuckle—she'd always been the one needling him for hobnobbing with the upper classes, entertaining Baroness Whoever or Lord So-and-so—and hurried over to make her curtsey. Hipp copied, executing a jaunty bob of brass knees.

"I trust you took no offense this morning." Victoria had the grace to look chastened. Gloveless hands, Eliza noticed, strong and capable like her own. "His Majesty's condition, that frightful Dr. Savage . . . I fear for what will become of us all."

"Don't mention it, ma'am." But her skin wriggled. *Don't mention it,* mocked Lizzie's voice in her ear. *The hell you say. Rude cow. Who's she think she is, eh?*

"You seem more sensible." Victoria studied her coolly. "I daresay you're used to imbeciles who assume they know better just because they wear trousers instead of a skirt."

"So you've met the Fellows of the Royal College of Physicians? Uncanny."

Victoria smiled, for once unguarded. Beautiful, if severe. The picture of her mother as a young woman, still sane and unfettered by grief. "I was rather thinking of His Majesty's privy councilors."

"The same, ma'am, I'm sure." She waited for Victoria to wave her away. What did the woman want? She felt dowdy and ill-dressed in her plain dove-gray working attire, and she hated it.

But the princess lingered, finery glaring in the gaslight like an exotic bird's plumage. "I couldn't help noticing you appeared on good terms with the Regent."

So now we're getting to it. "Sir Isaac has employed me in the past. In his capacity at the Royal Society, ma'am."

Another studious stare. "The Regent's a busy man. He can't always keep me appraised of His Majesty's affairs."

"I see."

"I'd be grateful for any assistance. Any tidbits you might happen to overhear." A polite smile. "Just a courtesy, understand. To spare the Regent's valuable time."

Eliza faltered. She was already supposed to be spying for both Sir Isaac and Mr. Hyde. How many sides could she be on? "I'll see what I can do, ma'am."

"Excellent." The princess glanced at Remy, who'd wandered insouciantly over. "And who's this?"

"Oh. May I present Captain Remy Lafayette, of—"

"I recall." Victoria's gaze smoldered with contempt. "Lord Beaconsfield's lackey. A baby reptile."

Remy executed a smart bow. "Your Royal Highness is doubtless thinking of my brother. Easy mistake. I'm the Philosopher's lackey, actually. Mind if I borrow the good doctor, ma'am? I should hate her to be party to a plot against him."

Victoria smiled sharply, and retired in a whisk of rich skirts and outrage.

Eliza chuckled as she and Remy found a pair of empty seats in the back. She settled, Hipp jumping into her lap. "Honestly, Captain, have you no care?"

Remy arranged himself beside her with a careless flick of scarlet coattails. "What? She started it."

"She's a princess. She can start whatever she likes. You ought to tread more carefully."

"You saw the Philosopher's attitude. Perhaps the day is finally coming when actions will count for more than accidents of birth." He eyed the crowd with interest. "Quite a society gathering. Look, there's Mr. Paxton from the North-Western Railway." He nodded towards a distinguished-looking old man a few rows below. "Nerves of steel even coming here, I'd have thought. Spying on his competitors?"

Eliza pointed to a young woman in a blue dress who watched the stage intently, her back to Eliza, dark hair in a severe bun. "Isn't that Miss Burton, your admirer from the Royal?"

"No longer, if ever she was." Remy grimaced. "An unpleasant disagreement over the best use of force in interrogations. That's what metal modifications will do for you."

"Oh, no." Eliza felt sick. Burton had lodged with her for a time. They'd never really gotten along. "Not one of the Philosopher's awful new special agents?"

"Mmm. Eager to please, I suppose. She's taken to asking sharp questions about Lady Lovelace and what happened that night at the Tower." He tossed her a grin. "You know. When you rescued me from my despicable captors against insurmountable odds, and spirited me away to be your concubine?"

She'd put an end to the clockwork-hearted countess in order to free Remy from her evil experiments. It had been self-defense, and she wasn't one whit sorry. "Is that what happened? I rather recall you staggering about drugged to the eyeballs and declaring undying love before passing out at my feet."

"Worked, didn't it?"

"Don't count your chickens, Captain. We're not married yet." Eliza slipped a pair of dark goggles over her spectacles. "Look, the professor's nearly ready."

Professor Crane—a tall, middle-aged woman in a dark brown dress and rubber apron—was on the stage, tinkering with her device. Thick reddish hair streaked with gray was knotted at her nape. She wore dark goggles, too, and long rubber gloves, and she wielded the twin prongs of an electrical meter like a conductor virtuosa with her baton.

Above the stage hung a vast glass sphere with a central electrode, suspended from a bulky metal scaffold. Eliza waved at Byron Starling, who was measuring aether levels, dark hair tied back and mismatched spectacles shining. He smiled, with a rueful glance at Remy beside her. She smiled back. At least he had a sense of humor.

In the wings, an older man with soft gray hair read from an instrument panel, scribbling figures in a notebook. And behind the table, fiddling with the testing wires . . .

"That's Seymour Locke," whispered Eliza with satisfaction. His flyaway blond curls were oiled down severely, which only emphasized his pale, pointed face. He looked like a cartoon mourner, with his bleak untidy suit and reddened eyes. "The murdered girl's unlucky *fiancé*. Reeve arrested him, but . . . oh, she's about to start!"

"Typically, aether electricity is inefficient," Professor Crane began, in her broad Edinburgh accent. "Energy is wasted via noise, and the incomplete reaction leaves the black smoke and residue you're all familiar with. This engine is designed to eliminate that wastage by de-phlogisticating the aether with close to perfect efficiency. Eighty-nine percent," she added with emphasis, "the best we've yet achieved."

Not a few people applauded, including Locke. Even the railway man Paxton looked impressed.

"A captive audience," whispered Remy in Eliza's ear. "She's quite the celebrity."

"Science is popular," she whispered back. "The public have a growing appetite for new gadgets, as well as for learning the science that drives them. The revolution is on its way, Captain. Doesn't bode well for the Philosopher's rule."

Remy shrugged, unconcerned. "Believe me, the Empire could do a lot worse."

Part of her longed to bite back her words. Remy had his

reasons for keeping his Royal Society commission. He knew their "rules" were mercurial, corrupt, and self-serving. He'd defied them for years, hiding his arcane curse behind his investigator's iron badge.

She shifted awkwardly in her seat. Was Remy working right now? Surveying this new invention for the Royal, reporting back to Sir Isaac? Scoping it out on the Foreign Secretary's behalf for the war effort?

Or merely spending a pleasant afternoon with her?

"With current technology, our hovering devices must be constantly recharged, or tethered to a ground-based generator," continued Professor Crane, tightening one last connection with her spanner. "This unit is small and light enough to be self-contained. And the efficient de-phlogistication means cleaner operation, with minimal noxious fumes, fewer health problems for workers, and increased productivity. Everyone wins." She unveiled an unnecessarily large red button on the machine's side. "Ladies and gentlemen, please do not look directly at the coil. Mr. Locke, in your own time."

Locke tugged down his own dark lenses, flicked a series of switches and levers, and stepped back. "Ready, Professor."

With a flourish, Crane hit the button.

A high-pitched magnetic whine emerged, barely audible at first, then growing. The glowing coil juddered, brightening until it hurt the eyes. The stormy taste of aether thickened. It was hard to breathe. The air shimmered and sparkled, the field energizing, and the suspended electrode began to crackle and hum with lightning forks of power.

Crrackk! The glass globe exploded, a rain of glittering shards.

Livid blue current hurtled back down the wires. *Boom!* The engine exploded, flash and fire like thunder, knocking Crane and the gray-haired man flat and staggering Locke back against his instruments in a cloud of smoke.

Hipp squealed and disappeared under Eliza's chair. Mr. Paxton jumped up, clutching his hat and shouting "Fire! Everyone out!" People screamed, running in all directions, trampling the seats and each other in their haste to escape. The princess's entourage leapt into action, forming a tight circle. "Make way! Make way!" Efficiently, they whisked Victoria out the side door into the street.

Dismayed, Eliza pulled off her dark glasses, fighting in the jostle to see what was happening. "Oh, dear. I don't think it was intended to blow up . . . Whatever are you doing?"

"That wasn't an explosion." Remy jumped onto his chair, bright eyes sweeping the gallery above. "That was a gunshot. There, stop that fellow!"

A dark shape darted along the shadowy gallery. Remy leapt for the railing, dragged himself over, and sprinted off in pursuit.

Eliza fought her way towards the glass-littered stage. Why on earth would someone shoot at Crane's demonstration? A protester from outside, trying to PRESERVE OUR AETHER? The crowd cleared rapidly, leaving her and the scientists alone. "Is everyone all right?" she called. "Can I help?"

Byron Starling had flung his coat over the burning engine's wreck to smother the flames. His lenses reflected rainbows. "Dr. Jekyll, what a dreadful shock. I trust you're safe?"

"What happened? Was it a malfunction?"

"What a brilliant deduction." A disheveled, dust-clogged Seymour Locke helped the professor to her feet.

Crane was a giant of a woman, towering over Eliza by a full foot, her skirts spattered with broken glass. Her hair had unraveled down her back, and a cut on her chin oozed. She batted Locke away. "That's enough, Seymour."

"You're bleeding," said Locke harshly. "Are you—"

"Perfectly." Crane shook herself. "Don't fuss."

Eliza pulled a swab and alcohol from her bag. "Allow me. I'm a physician."

Politely, Crane fended her off. "I'm quite well . . . I say, Ormonde, are you all right?"

The gray-haired fellow—the fourth scientist observed by Lady Redstoat?—had hit the stage's edge hard, and lay still. Crane rushed to his side. Ormonde murmured, half-conscious, blood trickling from his scalp.

Eliza joined her, examining the wound. "Struck by debris," she reported, pressing her swab over the gash. "Perhaps a minor concussion. Someone ought to take Mr. Ormonde home and watch him."

Crane waved at a pair of hovering servants. "You," she ordered, "find something to carry him on. Careful, mind."

One darted off to search. "Hold here," Eliza instructed the other, "it'll stop the bleeding." The man smiled condescendingly, and she sighed. "I'm a physician," she repeated impatiently. "Do as you're told." She pushed his hand onto the swab and left him, with a twinge of anger. Why were people so stubborn? Did she not seem competent? Were her words somehow nonsense because she wore a skirt?

Locke was trying to dust off Crane's clothes. The professor pushed him away. "Never mind that, laddie. Look at this mess! Months of work wasted! My calculations must be made all over again. Not to mention having to explain to . . ." She blew out her cheeks, an angry puff, but in her eyes lurked shadowy fear.

"How did this happen?" Locke stared at the wreckage, pushing his goggles up. A graze across his dusty cheek trickled scarlet. "I arranged it precisely. I checked a dozen times. Everything was perfect."

"So you say." Starling glared at him, still thumping out flames. "This configuration was your idea, Locke. Knew we should never have trusted you."

"That's not fair," retorted Locke, flushing. "You're the one who adjusted the coil. 'Just like so,' you said. 'It'll work better than yours,' you said—"

"Enough, gentlemen." Crane's sharp eyes flashed. "Time is pressing! We must rebuild, repair, discover what caused the overload."

"Here's your cause, madam." Remy appeared at Eliza's side, a little out of breath. He hefted an old-fashioned gunpowder revolver. "A single bullet fired. I'm afraid the miscreant eluded me. Why might someone shoot at your engine, Professor?"

Crane studied him coolly from her statuesque height. At the sight of his polished weapons and iron badge, her lip curled. Singularly unimpressed. "Who are you, sir?"

"Captain Remy Lafayette, Royal Society." He tossed off an elegant bow. "Have you met my colleague, Dr. Eliza Jekyll, police physician extraordinaire? Perhaps we can help."

Crane's frosty stare didn't melt. "I doubt it, if you're in the habit of letting revolver-toting vandals escape so easily."

"Madam, you skewer me." Remy fired a double-barreled smile. "Perhaps Dr. Jekyll can help, then. I'll just stand around looking dashing and dull-witted, shall I?"

"She's the one I told you about," put in Locke coldly. "From Antoinette's yesterday. I don't know who *he* is. Get rid of them, can't you, and we can get on with—"

"Seymour, please. We must assist our *dear* friends any way we can." The professor ignored Remy, offering her rubber-gloved hand to Eliza. "Ephronia Crane, Professor of Aether Physics at Trinity College. No relation to the late Henry Jekyll, I suppose?"

Eliza smiled faintly. Always the same question. "He was my father."

"Ah. I attended his classes years ago. Clever man." Crane sighed. "A police physician, you say? Poor Antoinette. I still can't believe it."

"My condolences. And I'm sorry about your engine, too. Is it badly ruined?"

Crane shook her head, morose. "Why would they shoot at us? Why?"

"Did any of you notice anyone in the gallery?"

Locke tossed his head impatiently. "We were concentrating on the equipment, not gazing at the sky."

"Can you think of anyone who might wish to upset your demonstration?"

Still rummaging through wreckage, Starling snorted a laugh. Crane shot him a sidelong scowl. "I can't imagine—"

"Everyone's jealous." Starling tossed aside a scorched capacitor in disgust. "At Cambridge, in London. They all want our invention for themselves."

"Why?" asked Remy pleasantly. "What are its applications?"

Starling muttered something under his breath. But Crane shrugged coolly. "Household items, mostly. As I said, it's more efficient. Which means quieter, and also cleaner, due to the reduced oxide by-products."

"You mean the burned aether." Remy gave another stubbornly charming smile. "I believe 'de-phlogistication' is the orthodox term. Not to quibble between friends."

"Naturally." Crane sent him a *you-don't-impress-me-idiot* glare that made Eliza hide a laugh. She'd made the same mistake the day she'd met Captain Lafayette. Imagined him a fool and a show-off, that a man with such confidence and verve couldn't possibly live up to it. How wrong she'd been.

"It makes any such machine ideal for indoor use," the professor went on grudgingly. "The domestic applications are endless."

"And lucrative. You're a clever scientist, Professor Crane, I daresay far cleverer than I." Suddenly, Remy's bright blue gaze wasn't so innocent. "Yet you honestly can't think of anyone who might want to put a stop to such a project?"

Crane's eyes flashed, and she opened her mouth to answer.

"What a mess!" An old snowy-haired fellow rushed up to the ruined apparatus, wringing plump hands. His buff suit was creased, his once-white scarf stained yellow. "What a mess, what a frightful muddle! Can anything be salvaged?"

"Speak of the devil," said Locke, with an unpleasant smile. "Clear off, Wyverne, there's a good lunatic. This is physics, not extra-dimensional chemistry for crackpots. And Antoinette's gone, didn't you hear? No need to lurk about making puppy-dog eyes any longer. Starling's doing quite enough of that."

Mr. Wyverne—what an odd name—wiped his damp forehead with his scarf, and Eliza realized with a start that he wasn't old. Barely thirty, in fact. His hair wasn't white, but colorless, and his skin held the same translucent hue, as if afflicted with achromatosis. He blinked, nose twitching like a squirrel who'd lost his way—but his red-rimmed eyes glinted, cunning. "You do me grave injustice. Grave! I have skills, sir. Talents, sir! Professor, might I—?"

"No," snapped Crane, dismissing him with a flick of skirts. "Mr. Starling's right," she admitted to Eliza and Remy. "Some of our colleagues resent our potential commercial success."

"And our scientific acumen." Starling shoved aside hapless Wyverne, who'd started poking at the burned fragments. "Money isn't everything."

"But science isn't free, either," said Eliza. "How are you funding this project? Isn't it difficult to find sponsors for experimental work?"

A cold smile from Crane. "We manage."

"Come, Professor, modesty doesn't suit. The market for such a marvelous engine must be competitive."

"No doubt there'd be interested parties. I hadn't given it much thought." Crane tried to feign carelessness, but her edgy gaze betrayed her.

"Interested in its failure, also? Investors in coal, for example, might lose a fortune if this technology became widely available. So might the railway men."

"If you say so."

"If we say so?" Remy cocked an incredulous eyebrow. "You

still can't think of anyone who might wish to sabotage your demonstration? I'm disappointed. Perhaps you're not as clever as I thought."

Crane sniffed, unmoved. Locke watched with a sardonic smile.

"Look here, sir," cut in Wyverne, dropping a scrap of charred iron with an indignant clang, "you are far too direct with your insults. What's your authority here? What's your expertise?" He shook his stained scarf, threatening. "Clearly you've no understanding of finer scientific minds—"

"What the professor means to say," interrupted Starling, again shoving Wyverne aside, "is that we're not interested in making money. We're scientists, not mercenaries. Have a care what you insinuate."

His comment earned a snort from Locke. Eliza touched Starling's arm. "Of course. We only wish to unravel what happened."

"Fabulous technology, though." Idly, Remy studied a blackened sliver of glass. "Could it be used for vehicles?"

Crane and Locke exchanged glances. Wyverne giggled. Starling cleared his throat. "That's confidential," he said.

Remy cut a sharp smile. "Not from me, it isn't."

Crane sighed. "Yes, we're developing a prototype for an automobile."

"Ships? Hovercraft? Service automata?"

"Certainly." Her voice had softened strangely.

Remy flicked invisible dust from his sword hilt. "Sky-ships?"

"Oh, for God's sake," snapped Locke, unable to contain himself any longer. "Go catch some real criminals, can't you?

It's strictly orthodox, if that's what you're fishing for, even if you're too stupid to understand the documentation. Have you any idea how many hours all your bloody paperwork soaks up? Why can't you vultures leave us alone?"

"Ah, the bereaved lover." Remy's eyes lit with fresh interest. "So sorry for your loss, Mr. Locke."

"No, you aren't." Insolently, Locke stared him down. "I imagine you're glad. Another genius dying young, taking her ideas to the grave. Just what you parasites at the Royal want."

"Oh." Remy blinked, perplexed. "But wasn't this engine Miss de Percy's doctoral thesis? A matter of public record. So her ideas shan't be buried, shall they? Unless there's more, that is, which you haven't documented."

Locke didn't flinch. He just grinned, flinty with challenge. Eager. And Remy grinned back.

Eliza rolled her eyes. "Gentlemen, please. All Captain Lafayette means to say is that the nature of your work is key to discovering Miss de Percy's murderer and the identity of the saboteur, and whether the two events are linked. We must follow every lead."

"Thank you," said Crane briskly. "Do let us know if the *police* have any more questions—"

"Professor Crane?" Mr. Paxton approached, white whiskers gleaming, straight-backed despite his advanced years. Finely tailored suit, gold watch chain, diamond tie-pin. The North-Western Railway Company was evidently making him a fine living. "What a dreadful accident. I trust no one was badly hurt?"

Crane acknowledged him coldly. "I'm sorry you weren't able to view the full demonstration, sir. Perhaps if you had, you'd stop spreading lies about my engine being dangerous."

"It did just blow up, madam," said Paxton reasonably. "Fair comment, that's all it is. When you're tendering for Empire contracts, the public have a right to know."

"Clear off, Paxton," cut in Locke rudely. "Go back to your cave and set fire to some coal, or whatever it is you do when you're not scarring the landscape with railway tracks and starving navvies to death. We don't need your gloating here."

Paxton reddened, and he bowed curtly and strode out.

Eliza exchanged glances with Remy, and hurried after Paxton into the street. "Mr. Paxton, sir! Wait!"

"Another time, madam, I've a meeting to attend." At the roadside, Paxton waved for his carriage. Thankfully, the rain had eased, and bleak afternoon sunshine swept the damp pavement. Protesters still waved their placards uncertainly, unsure what had happened inside.

"What's your opinion of the demonstration, sir? I'm a student of science, and—"

"Then you ought to know the aether is a precious, unstable resource." Paxton pointed at the PRESERVE OUR AETHER sign. "Why waste it on dangerous, pointless machines? Curse it, where is that coachman?"

"Why develop a competitor to your railway, you mean, that might usurp your government contracts?"

He regarded her coldly. "You have me at a disadvantage, madam."

"Dr. Eliza Jekyll, Metropolitan Police." Smoothly she extended her hand. "I was wondering if you knew of anyone interested in having that demonstration fail."

Stiffly, Paxton drew himself to his full height. "My railway technology is thoroughly tested and our safety record impeccable. We carry thousands of passengers and employ hundreds of men. What will happen to those families if their jobs disappear? Not to mention the new research—of which I'm sure you're aware, being a woman of science—that shows alarming instabilities in the aether due to over-zealous exploitation without care for conservation. If Professor Crane's reckless rabble imagine their *engine*"—disgust sharpened the word—"to be progress in the right direction, they can think again."

She faltered. "Research? I've heard of no such thing."

Paxton's open carriage rattled up to the curb, the horses champing. "As for the failed demonstration," he continued, eyeing her sharply, "I'm only relieved no one was badly hurt. She's already killed one researcher with her prototypes, let alone poor Ormonde in there. That device is a deathtrap even when it's working properly. Frankly, madam, I resent your inferences, and if you repeat any such slander I'll drag you into court to answer for it. Good day." Coldly, he tipped his hat.

"But, sir—"

"Ah, Miss Burton!" Paxton was already ignoring Eliza. "Are you for the meeting at Horse Guards? Care to ride with me?"

Miss Burton accepted his hand up into the carriage. Jerkily, she seated herself, smoothed her blue skirts, and turned stiffly to Eliza. Her Royal Society badge gleamed like gunmetal on her bodice. "Lovely to see you again, Dr. Jekyll. We must catch up for tea."

Eliza retreated, off-balance. Veronica Burton's pretty face had changed. A steel plate marred her forehead, the skin punched with rivets. Over her bright brown eyes, an ugly metal visor had been screwed, just an empty black slot. Not even a red gleam.

The same type of metal modifications as Lady Lovelace. The zealous late countess had a clockwork heart, and electrical components wired into her brain. How far had Veronica gone to emulate her? And for heaven's sake, why?

The girl's lips stretched into a cold smile. No emotion. She'd no eyes to show any.

"Er, yes," offered Eliza belatedly, "tea would be lovely . . ." But the carriage clip-clopped away.

An anti-aether railway tycoon and a Royal Society agent, off to a meeting at the War Office. What could they possibly have to talk about?

Remy emerged, Hipp trotting at his heels. "I say, did you accuse Paxton of criminal damage? I'm sorry I missed it."

"You missed him threatening me with a writ for slander, too. Must be your unlucky day." Eliza turned her face to the sun, enjoying the rare warmth. "Well, that *was* an interesting visit."

"Wasn't it? I've rarely met a bunch of such appalling liars." Remy jammed on his hat, and together they walked towards busy Piccadilly, Hipp gamboling ahead to chase a butterfly.

Eliza sidled around a lad who pedaled a tricycle at top speed, trailing a pennant that read STOP THE ROT! VOTE RADICAL! "Your touch wasn't exactly light, Captain."

"Believe me, Doctor, I've questioned a lot of scientists, and when they start giving me nonsense about 'domestic applications' I immediately know they're onto something big." Remy flashed her a glowing glance. "Did you see Crane's face when I asked about skyships? Dissembling, every one."

She laughed. "D'you think so? It's a marvel we extracted a single sensible word. You forget how you intimidate people. This is a murder investigation, not one of your Royal Society persecution parties."

Remy blinked sheepishly. "I confess, these militant science types raise my hackles. Think they're so revolutionary, with their little secrets and subterfuges. Likely they haven't the foggiest idea what they're messing with."

"The Philosopher's man, indeed," remarked Eliza, surprised. "You sound like Paxton. Surely experimentation can but lead to progress. *Nullius in verba,* all that."

"Do you really believe that, after all you've seen? That all progress is positive? The motto means *see for yourself*, not *try any insane thing and hope it works*."

A vision flashed, of contorted flesh stuffed into Moriarty Quick's jars, eyeballs blinking, deformed tendons stretching in a vain attempt to escape. Perhaps not all science was worth the price. "Still, that engine concept is amazing. Crane's crew might yet change the world."

"Every witless rebel with an idea thinks he can change the world. When they succeed, it's rarely for the better."

"And you used to be such a cheerful witless rebel, too. Don't tell me the Foreign Secretary has converted you into a raging Conservative behind my back."

A laugh. "Wouldn't my mother be delighted? She always fancied me as MP for Nepotism-on-Thames, or wherever. I ought to introduce them. With luck, the cunning old fox will marry her and I needn't talk to either of them again." Storm clouds darkened his gaze. "No, my sweet. But I do believe that some revolutions cost more than they're worth. A month spent swimming in Parisian blood will do that to you."

Awkwardly, she smiled. "I didn't mean—"

"Not at all. Please, don't let my morose mood spoil your afternoon." He watched a mechanical horse plod by, twitching its wiry tail. "That fellow Locke is a plucky piece of work. I almost thought he'd try me, badge and all. Is he still a suspect?"

"For Antoinette's murder? Not really. And he was on the stage today when the shooting happened." Absently, she sidestepped a woman in an enormous crinoline with a fat orange cat tucked under each arm. "But surely . . . hmm."

"Ah. The sound of you thinking. Ominous indeed."

"At least I *do* think, instead of just loitering about, gleaming like a table ornament and scandalizing irate professors with my come-hither smile. May I see the shooter's pistol, Captain?"

He grinned, and flipped it from his belt, offering it grip first. "Ugly contraption. Electrics are so much more civilized."

"Civilized," muttered Hipp dolefully at her heels. "Electricity. Boom."

She turned the pistol over, thoughtful. "So why did our saboteur choose this? Would an electric weapon malfunction in the rarefied air of that demonstration?"

"More than likely. Over-voltage on a handgun isn't pretty. The prize for most creative demonstration of the word *back-fire* is not one I'd want to win."

"Revolver-toting vandals, eh?" She squinted along the rusted barrel, visualizing the scene in her mind. "We have Crane stage front, Locke and Starling maybe ten feet upstage, Ormonde towards the wings. How far would you judge it from that gallery to where the professor was standing?"

"Fifty, sixty feet."

"And the range of this firearm?"

"If I may?" He took it and flicked open the cylinder, tipping the metal-shelled cartridges into his palm. "An odd model. Strange material. I've never seen one like it. I'd say a hundred yards, but you won't hit anything at more than about thirty. Twenty, if it's smaller than an elephant." He snapped the cylinder closed, thumbed the hammer, pulled the trigger with a *snap!*, and handed the weapon back empty. "I believe I see where you're going with this."

"Yes. Professor Crane assumed an act of sabotage that injured Ormonde by ill-fortune . . ."

". . . conveniently ignoring the possibility that said saboteur wasn't aiming for the engine at all . . ."

". . . but instead took a shot at Professor Crane herself— and missed." She smiled. "An assassination attempt. How dramatic."

"And not one of those Oxbridge geniuses thought of this." Remy cocked an eyebrow. "Extraordinary how their massive brains judder to a halt at the sight of a Royal Society badge."

"First Antoinette de Percy, then Professor Crane." She

tucked the pistol into her satchel. "Perhaps someone has a problem with female scientists. Ought I to worry?"

"It could still have been Paxton's man, taking aim at a competitor. I gather there's some friction amongst the Brotherhood of Brilliance about the nexus between commerce and science."

"But surely a shrewd businessman would cut off Crane's funding, or threaten her with some legal problem, or malign her in the press as he's already been doing. It's a big step from commercial rivalry to murder."

"As big as the pile of money he stands to lose if this engine succeeds," reminded Remy. "We mustn't discard the possibility that de Percy's murderer and the shooter are accomplices in some dastardly conspiracy." He rubbed his hands. "This gets better by the minute."

Eliza nodded. "So we can't eliminate anyone just because they were on the stage."

"Still, it does rather count out the swashbuckling Mr. Locke. If his motive is sexual jealousy, why fire at Crane? The fellow seemed rather in awe of her."

"I agree. He did claim someone else called upon Antoinette that day. A mysterious visitor who upset her, possibly fought with her. Perhaps that's our man."

"Speak of the devil," said Remy suddenly.

"Hmm?"

"Your blushing beau, Starling. He mentioned rival scientists. 'Speak of the devil,' Locke said. Right when that fellow Wyverne showed up."

She thought about it. "'Why did they shoot at us,' Crane said. Not *someone*. *They*."

"As if she'd an inkling who *they* might be." Remy gave a delighted laugh. "Told you they were all liars."

She grinned. "I declare, we'll make a proper investigator of you yet. Harley would be proud."

"Starling was practically bursting with secrets, too." A sly glint lit his eye. "You ought to flutter your lashes in his direction. I rather thought him hoping to resurrect a schoolgirl crush."

"Ha! Missed his chance. I gave up on witty romantics with dashing good looks long ago."

"Good decision. Look what you ended up with."

They halted at the corner of Piccadilly, where richly dressed shoppers promenaded and shop windows glistened amongst a cacophony of advertising hoardings. No doubt swell mobsmen worked the crowd, thieves disguised in fine clothes, picking pockets and swiping reticules.

Remy helped her clear a path across the street. Steam hissed from a vent in the paving stones, the Electric Underground rumbling beneath. People trotted down the steps to catch the next train, clutching umbrellas, briefcases, and shopping parcels. A man in a green Sikh turban operated a clockwork juggler, red and yellow balls popping mechanically into the air from tiny brass hands.

Eliza dodged a flower-seller's cart piled with crimson carnations. "Paxton and Veronica Burton certainly seemed chummy. What's her interest in the engine, if it's already submitted for certification? Picking out which scientific miscreant to burn next?" She shot him a side-eye glance. "Or was that your job?"

Jauntily, Remy tilted his sword, his scarlet coat gleaming.

"Madam, the man before you is enjoying an edifying day out with his alluring yet pitiless *fiancée*. In fact, consider it my day off. Beaconsfield's reports can wait. I've something to show you, remember?"

"I recall the word *speechless*," she conceded airily, "which seems at best highly improbable. I do hope you're not planning some hideous surprise party."

"You must wait and see." He handed her onto the curb, where a row of cabs waited. This one was an old-fashioned hansom type, with a real horse that snorted at his approach. "In you get, my love. Not a moment to lose." She bunched her skirts and jumped into the forwards-facing seat. He murmured something to the driver and hopped up beside her. "You must promise not to peek until we get there."

"Really, Remy—"

"Promise, or I shall need to use force." A fiery blue twinkle. "And then we'll be here all day."

Sighing, Eliza leaned back and closed her eyes. "Satisfied?"

"Tantalized, but it'll do for now." A flick of the driver's whip, and the cab rattled off.

Hipp snuffled in her lap, grinding his cogs. The leather seat cushioned her comfortably after what suddenly seemed a very long day. The memory of awakening in Lizzie's room—in Lizzie's *bed*, for heaven's sake—made Eliza's cheeks burn . . . and reality crushed in on her.

She and Remy needed to talk. About the wedding, the servants, the house, her medical practice. And Lizzie. Every awkward, unpleasant issue she'd been avoiding like poison.

Familiar sickness churned in her guts, her oversweet remedy repeating on her like Lizzie's ghostly laughter. Always, it was like this. Whenever Remy returned from France, sunlight would bathe her world, and for a few precious hours, everything would be perfect.

And then she'd remember, and all over again, her heart would break.

A DEAL WITH THE DEVIL

TWENTY MINUTES OF RAIN-SPATTERED TRAFFIC later, the cab lurched to a halt. Eliza jiggled, eyes squeezed shut. "Can I open yet?"

"Not yet." Remy's hand closed on hers, and she jumped down. Her boots landed on clean cobbles amidst the smell of wet grass and flowers. *Clank-clunk!* Hipp leapt down—none the worse for his ordeal at the theater—and hared off, *clitter-clatter* along the street. A bird whistled, a horse whinnied. Electric-warm breeze puffed her skirts, an omnibus or a carriage whisking by.

"This way." He tugged, and she followed, laughing. He led her across a street, up some steps. A door creaked, and closed again behind them.

A familiar, dusty scent assailed her, waxed furniture and a coal fire. Soft footsteps brushed the carpet. A third person.

Curiosity itched. "Who's that? Where are we?"

"Patience, my petal." Remy led her (and the unknown third followed in a faint odor of cloves) along a wooden corridor and out into a graveled yard. Up more stairs, and inside again, into a room smelling of old books and chemicals.

Eliza's recollection stirred, a sleeping giant. "Remy, what is this place?"

He held her in front of him, covering her eyes. "Charles, the lights, if you please." Electrics crackled, the smell of hot aether. "Surprise," he murmured, and let his fingers slip away.

She blinked, dazzled. Pale sunlight shafted through a frosted-glass skylight to illuminate . . . an anatomy theater. A marble dissection table, ringed by tiered wooden seats. The central hanging light was dark, but warm electric light flickered from sconces lining the distant walls.

Her vision frosted, smearing into memories of old. Dim gaslights, low murmurs of wonder, surgical bowls and specimen jars passed from hand to hand. Stern men in high collars, authoritative voices lecturing on the nervous system or blood circulation or the operation of valves in the heart. Henry Jekyll's earnest, insistent speeches, that way he had of *knowing* the truth, irrevocably committed, and his impulse to .tell everyone, for good or ill . . .

"This is our old house," she exclaimed. "In Cavendish Square, where we lived when I was a child. Before . . . oh, my."

Remy grinned. "I've had Brigham here cleaning it up. Still enough dust to smother an elephant," he added carelessly. "Hurry it up, can't you, Charles? The decade's end is nigh."

Charles Brigham gave her a cautious smile. A handsome lad, short in stature, with jet-black curls and startling dark-lashed eyes. His immaculate butler's attire gleamed. "Good evening, Doctor. Do please excuse the mess."

Eliza stared. She'd met Brigham a few months ago, when his previous employer had been murdered. One of Remy's pet spies, but a decent fellow for all that. "I-I don't understand."

" 'Twas the least I could do." Remy threw Brigham a wink, earning a blushing eye-roll. "Kept threatening him with a job, didn't I?"

"Oh. I mean, certainly. Hello, Mr. Brigham . . . but Remy, why are we here? Are the owners allowing visitors?"

"That'll be up to you."

She goggled. "What?"

"I bought it. For you. Us, I mean. I just inherited rather a lot of money, so . . . . Presumptuous, I know," he added quickly, taken aback at her surely undignified expression. "But I didn't want you to give up your working rooms, and my house on Berkley Square is too small. Seriously, this place is enormous, isn't it? This theater, the laboratory downstairs, the museum, the library, and that drawing room in the front can be your consulting room. Classrooms, too. We've space for an army of assistants, if that's what you'd like. Of course, we'll need your Mrs. Poole and Molly to help Brigham run the place. And there's that odd locked room for Lizzie's things, and . . . good God, Eliza, whatever did I say?"

She choked back tears, overcome. All her fears—for her house, her servants, her medical practice—seemed so foolish. Because he'd solved them, hadn't he, with a single elegant gesture like the impossible magician he was.

For a moment, her glittering good fortune blinded her. She didn't deserve it. Surely, she'd imagined it all, a wishful day-dream of heaven.

But Remy Lafayette was no dream. He was solidly, unde-niably real.

She swallowed another tearful laugh. He was *fidgeting*, so anxious was he to please her. Her gallant soldier, who feared little in this world and shrank from even less, talking over himself as if he mustn't stop lest it break some spell and she'd vanish.

She wiped her eyes beneath misted spectacles. "Captain Lafayette, I do believe you're nervous."

"Terrified." His blue eyes shone, brighter than the lamps. "Tell me if you don't like it. It's no trouble. I can always—"

"Stop it." She walked up to him, still dazzled that he'd read her so well. Touched that he'd even think of it. Frightened by how completely he *knew*. "I give up. You win."

A brilliant smile. "Speechless?"

"For all sensible purposes? Utterly dumbstruck."

He kissed her fingertips. "It's all right, then?" he whispered.

For a moment, a tiny sting of resentment spoiled her euphoria. She felt trapped. Swept along by forces beyond her control. Helpless . . . but her own ingratitude pricked like thorns under her nails, and she forced a smile. "It's perfect, you ridiculous man. *You're* perfect."

"No more than you deserve." A sparkling wink. "Well, maybe a little more."

She swatted him, and he caught her and kissed her and for long moments the world dissolved. Warmth twinkled over her, sinking deep, and she pressed closer and let him steal her breath. His mouth, his warmth, the scent of steel and aether she'd come to know so well. The deeply pleasant sensation of his strong body moving against her . . . and the catch in his throat, that tiny sound deep in his chest, the stretch and yawn of something *other*, stirring.

Politely, the butler cleared his throat.

"Oh." Rattled, Eliza stepped back. Her corset seemed damnably tight, a nuisance. "Right. It's getting late. Won't you join me for dinner, Captain?"

"Love to, Doctor, but I can't stay. Lord Beaconsfield at the Carlton Club, remember? And I'm for Paris tonight. How singularly inconvenient." Remy fingered his bottom lip, a sultry glow in his eyes. His chestnut curls were adorably disheveled, and she suppressed a dissatisfied sigh. Weddings were such silly affairs. She wanted theirs over with. Wanted to be married, so they could . . .

She flushed again. Desire had always seemed so foolish and unscientific. Not measurable, unfit to be analyzed. A disease that rendered the rational mind treacherous, the kind of eager insanity that had once led her up a dark stairway at midnight to a killer's lurid boudoir.

It didn't seem foolish with Remy. It seemed urgent. Irresistible. Inevitable.

Wouldn't be because waiting for the wedding is sending him bonkers . . . A rush of Lizzie-rich blood staggered her. Suddenly the conventions of wedding and marriage—and *waiting*—seemed so stupid and pointless. Inept, like buckling a straitjacket on an incorrigible lunatic. Not only a betrayal of principle. An abject waste of effort.

Images poured in, garish scenes through Lizzie's eyes, that rainbow of sensations and emotions, always more potent and painful than Eliza could bear. Remy, the way Lizzie had seen him, that one night in Regent's Park when she'd taken her way and had him in a pile of straw and breathless promises.

A glory of damp hair and taut skin, the scents of sweat and tainted blood. *Think you own this, Eliza? Think this is yours now? You won't ever be free of me . . .*

The illicit pleasure—even from a distance, warped through a dark prism of denial—stunned her. Lizzie had enjoyed herself, that was evident. And so had Remy.

How was she supposed to erase that?

Blindly, Eliza fought to hurl those fevered dreams away. She didn't want Lizzie's memories, bittersweet with jealousy. She wanted her own, at a time and place of *her* choosing.

You've got your life, Lizzie? Well, I've got mine. I won't let you spoil this for us.

"Hmm?" She groaned as Remy's words sank in. "Must you go back already?"

Remy wrinkled his nose. "The price of popularity, sadly. This meeting between *Liberté du Sang* and our envoys must go off without a hitch." He sobered. "This *la Bête* is the most dangerous man I've ever met, and they say *la Belle* is worse. If he stops trusting me for even an instant, my gruesome demise will be the least of our problems."

She bit her lip. Remy was capable and clever. He deserved a confident smile and a *go-with-God*. Not this fishing for guilt, her selfish fretting and *what-about-me*.

"You know I wish I could tell you more—"

"Don't." She stopped him with a light kiss—and her fingers brushed something cold and hard beneath his loosened shirt. It was a polished black stone on a chain, inlaid with a silver half-moon. She stroked it curiously. "What's this?"

"*La Bête* gave it to me. For the creature." Gently, he eased her hand away. As if he didn't like her touching it.

That sly mirrored gloss made her squirm. As if it were dishonest, somehow. *I've barely time to worry about it,* he'd said. Sparing her the ghastly details? Or merely avoiding her questions? "Is it witchcraft?"

A smile. "Just a precaution."

"Against what?"

"Eliza, I must go along with their ways." He tucked a stray lock behind her ear. "I'm so close to finding the truth about François. And this amulet . . . it's changing everything for me."

"Is it a cure?" She barely dared hope. A charm to keep the creature in. A version of her own remedy for Lizzie, except it *worked.*

"More of a peace offering."

He didn't elaborate. She didn't want to demand answers. "Are you sure it's a good idea? I thought we'd made progress."

"It's a means to an end, nothing more." Another brilliant smile, but shadows had crept in.

He didn't trust himself, she realized with dismay. Since François, he'd doubted everything. "Remy," she said softly, "what happened with François was . . . no, don't." She caught his hand as he turned. "Listen. Your brother made his choices. It wasn't your fault. You must let it go."

Remy folded her fingers in his. "Forgive me, but you didn't know him. My brother loved the Navy and he loved the Empire. These sorcerers poisoned his mind and they'll answer for it."

"But your mandate for the Foreign Office—"

"As I say: a means to an end." A steely edge to his voice alarmed her. "They did it because of me, don't you see? They destroyed the finest man I ever knew for no better reason than to get my attention. Well, they've gotten what they wished for, and I swear, they'll regret it."

For a moment, her courage quailed. François had craved Remy's curse, the key to that wild-hearted creature that killed by pure instinct. He'd betrayed his country, his family, everything he'd once believed in. But was Remy searching for answers? Or something more visceral?

"Just be safe, then. For my sake." She hesitated. "About the wedding. I wasn't putting it off. It's only that with you spending so much time in Paris, and my work, and—"

A surprised laugh. "Of course. I feared you'd think *I* was. Putting it off, that is." He kissed her hair. "One way or another, this next trip will be the end. I promise. When I return, we can try whatever marvels of medicine you like, and I'll marry you, Eliza Jekyll. Just you try to stop me."

She frowned. "Well, I would, but it seems you've given me a house. I can hardly jilt you now. The breach of promise action alone would bankrupt me."

"My villainous scheme unmasked. It's me or Chancery, I fear."

"And you know how I detest lawyers." She entwined their fingers, palm to palm. Her engagement ring glittered, brilliant blue. She drifted closer, enjoying that piquant scent she loved.

Inside her, Lizzie swelled, those malicious dream images waiting . . . but firmly, Eliza pushed her aside. *This is mine, Lizzie. Leave us be.* "Mr. Brigham, I'm about to embarrass you again. Give us a moment, will you?"

* * *

Too soon, Remy was gone, and she closed the front door on a darkling, mist-clogged Cavendish Square. A few weeks more, his mission would be done, and all this messing about and doubting herself would be over.

Hippocrates had dashed in from the park, scattering wet leaves as he hurtled down the corridor. "Rat-rat-rat!" he yelled in his tinny little voice. "Rat!"

"Be careful," she called. "You never know what bizarre inventions you might unearth around here." She lingered in the hall, inhaling the woody scent. The grand staircase swept upwards, a river of polished mahogany. It inundated her with dusty memories, disconcerting images of her childhood, like a box of old daguerreotypes years unopened. *Running along empty halls after a fat white cat, her tiny feet pattering . . . Mrs. Poole dabbing a cloth at Eliza's aching temples. There, little miss, it's all done, don't cry . . . Henry by the big steel laboratory door, swinging her high, her baby skirts flying. Who's the birthday girl? A magic number for my little lady . . .*

She shook herself. The past was gone. This, here, now, was the future. Never mind Lizzie's sneaky intrusions. Remy would complete his mission, they'd get the wedding over with, and life would be back to normal.

"Normal, ha!" Lizzie's apparition sprang into view, dangling her stockinged legs over the staircase railing in a lather of red skirts. "The part where you do as you please and I get the scraps? We ain't normal, Eliza. You don't *get* normal."

"Don't interfere," snapped Eliza waspishly. A malicious

headache hacked at her temples, and that new, intense elixir bubbled up in her throat, bringing memories of dazzling rainbow sights, swooning flavors, exquisite sensations. Her remedy was useless. She couldn't keep Lizzie away, not anymore. "I'll thank you to stay out of my head from now on."

"Interfere, my arse. Will we really live here, in Henry's god-rotted house? With *him*?"

"There's space for you, if that's what you're worried about. But you don't remember Henry's cabinet, do you? Because you weren't here!"

Lizzie slid down the bannister side-saddle and landed at Eliza's feet. "Space? That what you call it? One tiny pissant cellar out of a friggin' palace?"

Agitated, Eliza raked her already loosened hair. Pins clattered to the floor, bringing to mind a dim asylum cell, the smell of damp parchment and roses . . . "I hide your things where they're safe," she said tightly, trying to check her temper—but her skin wriggled like worms, as if the *change* lurked beneath, a hairsbreadth from erupting. "You know that's how it must be. We could all still get arrested by the Royal, Remy's commission notwithstanding."

"Easy for you to say. A tinsy-winsy corner for poor Lizzie, and the rest is yours." Lizzie stuck fists on hips. "You're all fine with your poxy *sharing* until you don't get everything you want. Well, I won't have it. Both of youse can go to hell."

Eliza folded her arms. "I see. And *your* place has so much room for *me*. That smelly garret in which I so inconveniently awoke this morning, in the bed of your"—she fought for a description that didn't involve the word *naked*—"*soiled* gentleman friend?"

Lizzie's face darkened. "Johnny's a good man."

"He's a thief, Lizzie," she hissed, fever suffusing her in a rush. "A criminal who preys on decent people like me for his living. Such as *that* is, if the condition of your filthy love den is any indication. Don't imagine he'll end anywhere but the gallows."

Immediately, she longed to suck her words back. Her guts churned. "I'm sorry. That was cruel. I didn't mean—"

"You'd like that, wouldn't you?" Lizzie shoved her, sending her staggering back onto the ancient hall rug with its pattern of olive leaves. "Johnny dead and me all alone. Screw you, Eliza."

"I said I didn't mean—"

"You don't want me, you don't need me, everything's my damn fault." Lizzie's dark eyes flashed. "Don't think I'll stand meekly by while you ruin me, missy. I wish you joy of this place, and of your god-rotted wedding, too. D'you think your fine captain's forgotten me?"

"He hasn't." Eliza smiled, poisoned sweetness. "He's just moved on. Sorry. So sad."

Lizzie gave an ugly laugh. "We'll see. When you finally condescend to have him, d'you imagine he won't be thinking of me?"

Eliza's guts clenched. "Don't be so petty!"

"Will you take Henry's room?" Lizzie danced a mocking two-step on the rug. Beneath it, half-hidden, a guilty stain darkened the floorboards. "Our mother *died* in there. Little Eliza, shitting her nightdress while Mummy bled out. Mayhap that's why you got on so famously with Razor Jack. Hot for the sight of blood! Ha ha!"

That monstrous staircase shuddered and threatened,

carved balustrades writhing like snakes. Edward Hyde had murdered Madeleine Jekyll on these stairs. Hurled her down in a fit of jealous rage, left her to die with shattered bones and a broken heart. And Henry and Marcellus had covered up his crime.

Lizzie's laughter tore at her, flaying her skin like knives. Eliza slammed her hands over her ears. "Get out of my head! If your life's so wonderful, why must you ruin mine?"

"Dr. Jekyll?" A hand on her arm.

She whirled, breathless.

Just Brigham, his long-lashed eyes brimming with concern. "I heard shouting," he explained.

The staircase was silent, unmoving, the rich wood welcoming once more. Lizzie had vanished. Of course she had. Never there to begin with. "It's nothing. Just . . . I'm fine."

But Lizzie's insults festered, a rotten itch. *Hot for the sight of blood.* After Razor Jack had been recaptured—no thanks to Eliza—she'd agonized into many a long night over why she'd acted like such an irrational idiot over a bloodthirsty murderer. Certainly, Mr. Todd was handsome, charming, talented. The world was full of handsome men with charm and talent to burn. There had to be something more. Was she, too, drawn to darkness, mesmerized by that last shuddering sigh between light and oblivion?

But in the darkest hour, she knew. Edward Hyde had killed her mother. Killed Henry, too, in a stranger, blacker way. Eliza was the daughter of a monster. She couldn't escape the truth: murder ran in her blood.

She forced a quick smile, fumbling to re-pin her hair. "So, Mr. Brigham, how do you like your new employment?"

"Very much. But there's a lot of cleaning." He grinned. An angelic face, for sure, perhaps too much so for his own good. At his previous job, for a baronet and his haughty socialite wife, Brigham had suffered for it, and for rescuing him, Remy had earned his undying devotion. He bent to pet Hipp, who'd rushed into the hall at his heels and was trying to climb his leg. "Hello, boy. Remember me?"

"Tell me, is the captain . . ." Her stomach squirmed. Sneaking about, asking questions behind Remy's back. Could she trust Brigham not to use her secrets against her? She sighed. "I haven't time to dance around it. I gather he's briefed you on his particular problem."

Brigham just nodded.

Her hands twisted. "Did he suffer greatly last month? It's only that I'm preparing a cure, and I thought everything was going well, but he seems . . . distracted."

"Couldn't say, madam. The captain's spent the recent full moon in France. Apparently these Froggie sorcerers know all about it. Says he's learned a lot."

"I see." Her throat hurt. Unconscious pride had warmed Brigham's tone. He admired Remy to a fault. A clever seducer, that Captain Lafayette of the Royal.

The same who'd just told her he'd passed the full moon in London.

Or had she assumed? *Worse things than a night spent in a cage.* He hadn't said where, or at whose bidding. What was he up to with these sorcerers?

"That setup at Waterloo Bridge, with the locks and bars?" added Brigham helpfully. "We've installed one similar here, just in case, but you needn't worry. He said he'll be spending most moons abroad from now on. More convenient that way."

"Oh." Her voice sounded small. She'd thought they were making progress. That soon the cage would no longer be needed.

But this didn't sound like the behavior of a man who wanted to be cured.

Her fingers recoiled, that strange glossy amulet an unpleasant memory, like touching a maggot. Her cure, however unsavory, was at least based on repeatable scientific results. It wouldn't be the first time Remy had tried witchcraft to counter his curse, even if he'd investigated too many greedy charlatans who exploited the gullible to really believe in it. Still, she knew how it was to be so desperate for relief that you'd try anything. If this amulet was helping him, oughtn't she give it a chance?

But this *Liberté du Sang,* as Lizzie might say, were a whole 'nother bucket of eels. Bent on destruction and murder. Evil.

Her skull swelled, suffused with the frightful stories she'd heard. Horrid spidery spells, candles and incantations, blood rites, the eating of human flesh, the flaying of skin and breaking of bone . . .

Rat-tat! Eliza jumped. Just the knocker. *Damn it.*

Molly strode in and smacked a kiss onto Brigham's cheek. "Charlie, you handsome rascal . . . oh." She flushed tomato-red, and bobbed a curtsey, damp hair curling under her bonnet. "Sorry, Doctor."

Eliza grinned, glad to change the subject. "Aha! The culprit uncovered! Shame on you, Charles Brigham. To think we imagined Molly's virtue to be at risk."

He looked faintly scandalized. "I've had Molly helping me clean on her evenings. I hope you don't mind."

She laughed. "Your secret's safe with me."

Brigham just gave her an odd look. Molly jumped in. "Ahem. Doctor, there's telegrams for you at Russell Square. From that Inspector Griffin, about the Soho Slasher. If I'd known you'd be here, I'd have brought with."

Eliza's stomach curdled. *Telegrams*. More than one. "When did these arrive?"

"A few hours ago. I wouldn't've peeked, but it seemed urgent, and we didn't know where to find you."

She sighed, suddenly exhausted beyond words. Another post-mortem examination. Wearily, she collected her umbrella and bag. "Please tell Mrs. Poole I'll be late for dinner again. Mr. Brigham, do see Molly safely home. Good night."

A NETWORK OF RIDDLES

B Y THE TIME SHE RETURNED TO RUSSELL SQUARE, twilight had slunk off into the mist like a whipped dog, and dark chill blanketed empty streets. Lights shone from upstairs dining rooms, the clatter of plates and conversation filtering along the footpath.

"Mrs. Poole?" She dropped her dripping umbrella into the stand and peeled off her wet gloves, grateful for warmth. Hipp hunkered by the hall table, falling into a doze. "So sorry I'm late. Another Slasher victim, I'm afraid."

She'd walked home along electric-lit New Oxford Street, enjoying the fresh air at first. She'd wanted to give Hipp some time outside, but mostly to clear her own head, where incoherent memories warred with gruesome autopsy details, haunting her like the specters of the victims the Slasher had left behind. Other murdered souls, too, soaked in crimson, not mangled with abandon but precisely, artfully sliced . . .

She'd lingered, peering in shop windows without seeing, wandering through gaslit parks where hurdy-gurdies and trumpets rang out amongst street performers and mountebanks. Now it was after eight, her sodden mantle chilled her to the core, and her head was no clearer than before.

Who had killed Antoinette de Percy, and tried to shoot Professor Crane?

Would she ever catch the Soho Slasher, when trace evidence was so lacking?

Could she truly live in Henry's house at Cavendish Square, with its ghostly battalions of memories forever marching by? Was she fooling herself to imagine this marriage could work at all?

She unpinned her rain-soaked hat. Perhaps she was hiding behind ingratitude to soothe her dented pride. She could never have afforded such a grand house. Was it so awful to accept a gift? To be cared for and loved?

But she couldn't shake the creeping feeling that she'd lost control. That she was being forced into relinquishing her independence, into accepting an arrangement she detested because society left her no alternative. And every rational cell screamed at her to flee before it was too late.

She shook herself, determined to be cheerful. Ridiculous. What was she afraid of? Nerves were perfectly natural. But now she'd returned to Russell Square, her quasi-hospital nightmare hovered in the shadows, waiting to pounce. *The scratchy tube wriggling down her throat, making her gag. Smooth hands holding her still, manacles biting her struggling wrists. A tight band encircling her temples, the scritch-scratch of wire. A metal lever, creek-clunk! Electricity crackles, and she screams in white-hot agony . . .*

A rusted knife, gleaming in my fist. I stab down, laughing, a hot spurt of blood . . .

"Stop it!" Her voice squeaked, too loud in the silent hall. She recognized those treatments. She'd seen Mr. Fairfax use them at Bethlem, on Malachi Todd, amongst others. Therapeutic electric shock. Her dream wasn't of a hospital, but an asylum. A madhouse for lunatics. "Lizzie, that's enough. Think I don't know what you're doing?"

But Lizzie didn't appear. No laughter, no ghostly dry scent. Nothing.

Shivering, Eliza entered her consulting room. A pleasant den, with bookshelves behind her big desk and a couch for patients as well as a chaise by the bay window for reading. An electric lamp burned on a low table. Hipp trotted in sleepily and plonked down by the fire.

She emptied her damp bag beside the mail tray. The rough copy of her report from the Bow Street morgue stared up at her, alongside its buff folder of gruesome crime scene photographs. *Abdominal cavity emptied . . . features hacked beyond recognition . . . liver stabbed, depth 2¼ inches . . . throat severed, fourth and fifth vertebrae notched . . . as before, a sharp surgical blade or butcher's knife . . .*

The victim—the Slasher's fifth, so far as the police knew—had been discovered that morning. A young man known in Soho as Turquoise Tim, a prostitute—or as the papers liked to say, an "unfortunate." Just like the others, carved up and tossed aside like a broken doll.

But aside from *modus operandi,* Eliza had found no forensic trace of the killer. Not a hair, nor a shred of skin, nor a splash of sputum or semen. Nothing.

All she and Griffin had ever discovered was that the

Slasher was likely right-handed, and had pale or gray hair. Wonderful. That described half the men in London, from the peerage through to beggars.

Guilt stung her all over again. Trace evidence spoiled quickly, obliterated by careless hands, or weather, or simply the passage of time. Harley had tried to reach her all day while she was out enjoying herself. If she'd only attended the crime scene . . .

Still, the evening had ended on a high note: Harley had found a potential witness to Turquoise Tim's murder. A young prostitute from Soho named Saucy May, who'd seen what she called "a small dirty cove in fancy britches" lurking about the grimy tenement where Tim's body was found.

Again, a far from conclusive description. Dare Eliza hope it would lead to an arrest?

But the name—Saucy May—plucked discordant harp strings in her mind. A young thief slinking through midnight streets, green mist sparkling in her wake. A dusty studio bathed in moonlight, a single red rose in a glass vase, a card bearing the name Odysseus Sharp . . . and a greasy room in a Soho brothel, a girl called Rose with pigtails and silk stockings, sucking on a candied apple . . .

Mrs. Fletcher's. The name sprang into her mind from a dark chasm. A brothel, with white lacquered dressing tables and the smoky scents of opium and gin. Saucy May was a streetwalker who occasionally rented a room there. A better class of bordello, with shady gentlemen and lords in disguise for clients. Patronized by the King of Rats himself.

Her post-mortem report stared at her, accusing. Like a

swollen corpse on the Thames tide, events kept dragging her back to Edward Hyde—and a horrid thought nearly tipped her from her chair.

A small dirty cove in fancy britches.

Her father was a large man, in truth, almost as tall as Remy, but his crooked back made him seem smaller. An odd limping gent in fine clothes that had seen better days. What if . . . ?

Lizzie's world swamped her, sickeningly rich scents and sounds and flavors. Gin, aether, absinthe, breathless lovers' laughter. *Atishoo! Atishoo! We all fall DOWN* . . . Charred fingers beckoning through rusted iron bars . . . and Edward Hyde, his gut-rich guffaw, lust like a lightning strike in his stormy gray eyes.

I've a thing to show you, Rose. Such a pretty thing.

What sort of thing?

Eliza's throat dried. Stupid. Not possible. There was no evidence. No reason to suspect Hyde was involved.

"And never will be, neither!" With a gleeful laugh, Lizzie grabbed the report and hurled it into the fire.

"No!" Eliza leapt up in dismay, but flames consumed the dry paper like tinder. Her notes, Harley's sketches, irreplaceable photographs. All those hours of work. Gone.

Lizzie did a little dance on the hearth, warming her hands by the roaring flames. "Just you try and stop me! Ha ha!"

"Lizzie, for heaven's sake—" Eliza's vision veered in and out of focus, and *pop!*

Lizzie was gone. And the report sat on the desk, exactly where she'd left it.

A huge fist squeezed her chest, crushing her lungs to wet

pulp. Lizzie's fist, somehow, a giant malevolent Lizzie who laughed at her agony. *Like hell I ain't here, missy. See if I can't crush you like a stinkbug. You don't need me, you don't want me. Fine. I don't want you, either!*

Frantically, Eliza fought for air. Pain lanced through her chest, tighter, harder. Spots danced before her eyes. Ferocious fists pummeled inside her skull. Her muscles cramped, evil agony that wouldn't ease. *Can't move. Can't escape . . .*

Whoomph! Her guts lurched, an angry punch, and the pressure in her chest released. She doubled over, wheezing, her throat scraping raw.

She's only in my head. Not real . . . But this was no accident. The treacherous jade knew exactly what she was doing.

Lizzie was driving her insane.

Finally, her aching lungs eased. She fumbled for her bottle of remedy, and tilted it up into her mouth. But only a few drops splattered her tongue. Almost empty already. Despairing, she shook it, desperate to drain it to the last, and behind her, Lizzie laughed.

She whirled, panicked. No one there.

Steeling herself, she shoved the bottle away, sat down, and stubbornly opened the report again. She spent a while making notes and corrections, then wearily pushed it aside. She'd make a fair copy after dinner. Deliver it personally into Inspector Griffin's hands, so no press vulture could steal it to publish. This poor boy's death was a tragedy, not a spectacle for public titillation.

Beside the folder sat the revolver from the ill-fated demonstration. Her pills and medicine phials, *sans* the one Sir Isaac had confiscated. She was keen to see the results of the king's treatment, the new dosage she'd prescribed. She held high hopes . . .

Her courage quailed. Was she really treating the king with *lux ex tenebris,* right under the Philosopher's nose? Did she harbor a reckless death wish? She could imagine Marcellus's reaction. *Eliza,* he'd say, *you foolish young squirrel, have you lost your wits? Marriage rots the brain, say what?*

But she couldn't shake the itching certainty that the Philosopher knew everything, had always known everything. It suited his purposes to have her beholden to him—and the ugly thought struck her that his hold over her might never end.

Sighing, she arranged the bottles on the shelf. A slip of paper rustled in her fingers. Antoinette de Percy's mysterious equations.

She studied the notation with fresh interest. Magnetic wave equations, said Starling. But Seymour Locke had remained insolently silent about what Antoinette had been working on.

Still, Remy had been doing his finest impression of an overbearing Royal Society thug. Faced with a badge, most scientists worth the description would lie to beat the devil. A useful interrogation technique, for lies multiplied like rabbits and scattered, easier to catch.

This time, it had backfired.

Perhaps she herself could investigate. Mr. Starling— Byron, she corrected with an inward smile—might be a fine target for more personal questioning. In private, with an eyelash flutter or two thrown in.

But the echo of his voice from her nightmare—*get a move on, Fairfax, she's waking up*—made her shudder.

Molly knocked and entered with her dinner tray, hair once more neatly pinned.

Eliza eyed her archly. "Cleaning finished for the night?"

"Aye." Molly's smile glinted. "Enjoy your surprise, Doctor?"

"Perfectly, you crafty minx. How long have you known?"

"A few weeks." Molly arranged the cutlery. A succulent beef roast, plus herbed vegetables and a steaming pot of tea. "We've had fun making that old place presentable. I wasn't sure about that captain of yours at first. Far too clever and handsome, if you ask me. But I suppose now he'll do nicely."

Eliza laughed. "Will he, now? Well, once we've got the place fixed up . . ." She faltered. "Should you want to work for us, that is. If you find a better position . . ."

Molly made a delighted curtsey. "Not a chance. I'll stay, if it please you."

Eliza studied her uneasily. A pretty girl, with smooth blond hair and big eyes, not to mention a sleek figure. "This wouldn't have anything to do with a certain decorative young butler, would it?"

A faint flush. "What if it does? Begging your pardon," she added quickly.

"Molly," said Eliza uncertainly, "you do understand that Mr. Brigham is . . . that he . . ."

Molly just blinked at her.

She couldn't find a gentler way of breaking it. "That he prefers men."

The girl colored more deeply. "I know that. He told me.

Doesn't mean he isn't right in the head. Or that he can't, you know, do a girl justice."

"Of course not. I just—"

"Doesn't mean we can't be happy, neither. D'you think I don't know other lads only want me for this?" Molly smoothed her dress over her hips, making defiant fists. "They leer and follow me about and call out horrid things. At least Charlie's my friend. He can keep his own ways, see, and if he's got a wife it'll go easier for him. He says we can have a baby, if I like. I want a family, Doctor, always have. This way, I get it all without the heartache."

"So it's to be a wedding?"

"We'll post the banns in the spring, begging yours and the captain's leave. Not so fancy as yours, maybe." A glint of laughter. "We can't all be courted by carriage folk."

Eliza smiled, but the girl's explanation stung too close to her heart. To surrender your freedom for the sake of safety and convenience. A transaction. "But don't you want love, Molly? Someone to be yours alone?"

"Charlie loves me," said Molly stoutly. "Just not like that. A relief, in truth. All that pawing and sweating and pretending you've got a headache. Who could be bothered?"

Eliza shook her head with a sigh. "Young people these days. It seems you two have everything settled. At least you needn't fret about him making eyes at other girls."

Molly snorted laughter, reminding her startlingly of Lizzie. "Reckon it's yourself ought to watch who Charlie's making eyes at, Doctor."

"Indeed. Well, let him look. You need not fear on that

score." But dismay cooled her skin. What kind of life would Molly have, married to a man who led two lives? Who lived two truths, secrets forever walled in by a façade?

What kind of life for Remy, married to her, Eliza?

She forced a smile. "Good luck to you, Molly. That's all for tonight."

Molly made another curtsey, and hurried out.

Eliza started on her meal, forking a mouthful of beef—delicious, the potatoes flavored with mint—and pulled the mail tray close. A note, and a package with a letter attached.

The note was short, on railway station writing paper.

Thank you for being far more wonderful than I deserve.
Remy.

She touched the page to her lips, tasting salt breeze and thundery aether. An electric train? She thought of indignant Mr. Paxton. *Our technology is thoroughly tested.* Or was Remy taking some more exotic mode of transport? A skyship, perhaps? She imagined him flying over dark water towards benighted France, wind in his hair, this same sea-breeze taste stinging his lips, the strange black-and-silver amulet around his neck.

She sipped a cup of hot tea, reaching for the package. Tied with string, it rustled, as if it held papers or a book. It smelled faintly chemical. The attached letter was scrawled with a fine-tipped pen, the letters shaky, as if scribbled in frantic haste.

Dr. Jekyll,

We met only briefly this afternoon, but I feel I can trust you as a woman of objectivity and compassion. Indeed, I have no choice, and can only hope your keen-eyed guard dog with the iron badge is not standing by as you read this.

I need your help. Something terrible has happened that I dare not put in writing.

Visit me tonight and I will explain everything. I beg you, do <u>not</u> bring this package with you. Hide it in your safest place, and for both our sakes <u>tell no one</u>.

Yours in science,

Prof. E. Crane

The teaspoon slipped unheeded from Eliza's fingers.

Something terrible. More terrible than Mr. Ormonde's injury? Than months of work ruined, the vital public unveiling of this new technology foiled by an assassin's bullet?

For both our sakes tell no one. Professor Crane had written this in fear for her life. Who had fired at Crane in the theater—and why?

She undid the wrapping. Inside sat a well-thumbed foolscap notebook, two inches thick with a marbled paper cover.

On the title page, in Crane's handwriting: *Royal Institution, Aether Engine Miniaturization, Volume V.*

An experimental journal.

She leafed through, marveling. Pages of methodology, lists of components and materials. Inked diagrams, carefully ruled and labeled, as well as rough pencil sketches. Here was a table of energy output readings. "My, that's an extraordinary quantity, Hipp. When she said 'super-efficient,' she wasn't joking."

"Extraordinary," repeated Hipp sleepily from the hearth. "Super-efficient. North-Western Railway."

She unfolded a map-sized chart. Circuit diagrams, with notes and formulae in the margins. "A schematic of the engine demonstration. Here's the coil, and the glass globe. These lines here are the electrodes. But . . . this is more than just an engine. What's this component?" She ran her finger over symbols for capacitors, switches, chained resistors. It looked familiar. It reminded her of a venerable, mildew-stained journal written in old-fashioned German, half its ragged pages torn out . . .

Eliza sat back, shoving the book away as if it burned her.

She'd seen drawings like this before, in the forbidden work of a colleague of Henry's. A madman called the Chopper had used them to build a teleportation machine. The thing was marvelous, certainly, but it was cumbersome and made a lot of noise, *boom!,* like a thunderclap, and deposited piles of messy black residue. Inefficient and impractical.

What if Crane and de Percy were improving it? Adapting their new power conservation principles to matter transference?

Excitement rippled under her skin. This could revolutionize transportation. Render railways and other vehicles unnecessary. A commercial threat, indeed.

But such a machine was wildly unorthodox, not to mention dangerous. In the wrong hands? A weapon.

Troubled, she returned to the notebook. The most recent entry was dated the day before Antoinette was killed. A typewritten passage cut out and pasted in, the dictation from a phonograph.

Royal Institution, 2:45 p.m.

Project Interlunium is in crisis. I hardly know what to do. The $\mathbb{R}_3$ travel device is functioning, of course, but the complete machine produces alarming advanced side effects that threaten to destroy us all.

Of course, S. insists we are at a critical juncture and seeks further information from sources I dare not reveal. Naturally A. supports him. They are thick as thieves. Greedy for knowledge, these young ones, a hunger that engenders in me such horror of the spirit that I retired here, ill, before the meeting concluded.

I want nothing more to do with this infernal project, but he will not listen to me. I am trapped. Worse, I fear our discussions were overheard by that sniveling serpent across the hall. If so, we are all in the gravest danger.

Even so, our demonstration must proceed. My original engine is the key to my escape. Contract negotiations

with B. proceed apace, and I have doubled the secrecy.
I've reason to hope all will be concluded soon, and I will
at last be set free.

"Project Interlunium," she mused. "New moon. What does
it mean, Hipp?"

Hipp bounced importantly. "Moon. Lycanthrope. Trans-
formation imminent."

"I'm sure that's not it." But she shivered. Any mention of
the moon was a threat to Remy, his monthly battles with
tooth and claw. Where had he truly spent this last moon?
Where was he now? Sailing in darkness across a foamy sea?
Riding over ravaged countryside, where sorcery had razed
crops to ashes and scarred the earth asunder? Or already in
Paris, blood on the cobbles and the stink of dying flesh on
the air?

She read the letter over. *Advanced side effects.* R_3 *travel
device. Destroy us all.* So much for Lady Redstoat's list of
"fornicators." Starling and Locke, Crane and Ormonde. Antoinette's diary had read "1: Team Meeting." But it wasn't a
figure one. It was an I, for Interlunium.

Eliza studied the schematics again. There was a blank
expanse, where the circuit diagrams trailed to dotted lines.
Only a rough circle, some penciled equations—and beside
them, an underlined double question mark: ??

As if a component were missing. One they hadn't yet com-
pleted.

Was "S" for Starling? So much for his visit to Mr. Finch's,
seeking Faraday's forbidden books. *Sources I dare not reveal,*
indeed.

Or was "S" for Seymour Locke? The man who'd claimed he knew nothing of physics. Just a lowly assistant.

But who was "B," and what were the *negotiations*? An *escape,* indeed. And who was *that sniveling serpent across the hall?* Across from where—Crane's office at the RI? She recalled Princess Victoria, insulting an impervious Remy. *A baby snake.* Again in the Regent's office, concerned for the drooling king. *I don't want that reptile to see him like this.*

She checked the torn envelope. *Dr. E. Jekyll,* it said, *Russell Sq.* As if Crane didn't know her full address and had done the best she could in a hurry. The return address was printed in the corner.

Ireton House, Red Lion Square
Bloomsbury WC

Only a few blocks away.

Eliza glanced at her unfinished report, and back to Crane's letter. *Hide it in your safest place. Tell no one.*

In a few minutes, she was out the door, dinner forgotten on the desk, hastily re-stuffed bag over her shoulder, and sleepy Hipp stumbling after.

MY POOR AND SOLITARY ENDEAVORS

IN FIFTEEN MINUTES, SHE REACHED RED LION SQUARE, a dismal yard of broken cobbles and muddy weeds. A chill wind swept through the wet trees. Icy raindrops stung her face as she crossed to a four-story relic of the previous century that hunkered like a grim mausoleum on the corner, its coal-blackened walls marred with dark flourishes of wrought iron.

She craned her neck, holding her umbrella aloft. Smoke hissed from a single chimney to the rear. Rows of empty, rain-splashed windows glowered. In the window to her left, a weak light burned. She glimpsed a well-stocked library, an armchair, the glint of a wall mirror. Otherwise the place was dark.

The stone-carved lettering above the forbidding brick entrance read

IRETON HOUSE ~ A.D. 1764
QUID ME RESPICIS, VIATOR? VADE

"Why do you look back at me, traveler?" she translated in a murmur, and shivered. *Vade,* the house commanded. *Go on your way,* indeed.

Unwillingly, she climbed the steps to the black lacquered front door. Hipp moped sullenly beside her, his red *unhappy* light gleaming. "Quiet. Home, one quarter mile. Make greater speed."

Eliza shivered again beneath her dripping umbrella. "I wish we hadn't come, too. But we're here now." She banged the iron knocker.

Clunk! Clunk! A deadened echo.

No sound from within.

"Professor Crane?" She knocked again. Perhaps the servants were for bed, exhausted. Perhaps they were all dead, slain by Antoinette de Percy's killer. *That'll teach you to do science, woman . . .*

She gripped the spiked fence and peered in the library window. Just the candlestick—not an electric light?—on a tea table by a winged armchair, alongside ancient oak shelves stuffed with books. She recalled Sir Isaac's total internal reflection experiment, the observer he'd imagined peeking in her bedroom window. *Do you suppose the corpuscles know what to do? Do you suppose they're spying on you, Eliza, noting your every move and reporting to me? Dare you imagine I'm not watching you right this minute?*

The library was deserted . . . but tension scraped her nerves. Why did the candle flicker? The window was fastened. The curtain swayed, invisible breath. As if a man lingered there, gripping a bloodstained knife . . .

Her heart thudded. No one. Just her imagination.

The harsh epigram above the door glowered down, admonishing her. *Why do you look at me, traveler? Go on your way. Out, fool, before I lose my temper.*

"Something's not right, Hipp." She marched over weedy, broken cobbles to the corner, where a lane cut in towards a shadowy rear yard. Somewhere, a horse snorted and pawed a stone floor.

Hipp trod reluctantly after her. "Courage. Certain death. Does not compute."

She popped on the little electric light on a chain at her belt. *Zingg!* Purple shadows leapt. To her right, the dark outline of stables. To her left, the back stairs of Ireton House clumped up to a servants' door. Somewhere, too, a noisome cesspit. She wrinkled her nose. Lovely. That wasn't only mud wetting her skirts to the ankle.

A gust slapped freezing raindrops into her face. Her light hissed, flickering.

Criiiickk! The back door swung ajar. Inside, darkness shifted, beckoning. Quivering, she pushed it open and entered.

"Hello? Professor Crane?" *Crane . . . Crane . . . Crane . . .* Her voice echoed, forlorn. Her light bled away into a world of creaking darkness. Walls decorated with crumbling plaster curlicues, distant ceilings lost in moldy gloom. A stale smell hung, of coal scuttles and neglect.

She walked on, lifting her light high. Cobwebs dusted her face, and she sneezed. *Atishoo!*

"*Araneae.*" Hipp's brassy joints chattered. "Trajectory unpredictable. Advise retreat."

She brushed away a spindly long-legged creature. "Don't be silly. They won't hurt you."

"Hearsay evidence. Inadmissible. Re-examine conclusion."

Hsst! Air whistled, pulling at her skirts, and *boom!* The back door slammed shut.

She whirled, startled. "Who's there?" Just shadows and wind. Shakily, she caught her breath, feeling foolish—but doubt chilled her spine. She'd closed that door. Hadn't she?

At last, flagstones gave way to venerable floorboards that creaked with menace. *Crack! Crunk!* Photographic portraits frowned down, silver-nitrate eyes tracking her as she passed.

Finally, the front hall loomed from the dark. The massive front door was locked, the bar rammed home. A vase of dahlias wilted on the hall table beneath a dusty painting of Marston Moor, orange-sashed Civil War cavalry arrayed in faded splendor. The grand staircase coiled upwards, an iron-railed serpent. To her right, candlelight leaked beneath the library door.

She knocked, *rat-tat!* "Professor Crane? Forgive me for bursting in. It's me, Eliza Jekyll. I received your letter and came at once. I trust everything's well?"

Silence. Just rain pounding on the slate roof.

Heart thudding, she turned the handle.

The fire was just a dull glow, a frigid draught chilling the room. On the tea table, the candle burned low. Smoke curled from a charred spot on the Oriental silk rug, where a coal had spat unheeded.

She edged inside. A large wall mirror gleamed, its ancient silver speckled with corrosion. Shadows flickered over cabinets and bookshelves. Next to the wrought-iron mantel, a single shelf had been swept clear, and books scattered the rug, pages curling.

Professor Crane sat stiffly upright in the armchair. Jaw thrust upwards, cervical spine wrenched back at an impossible angle. A fat oblong of iron wrapped in copper wire had been forced deep into her throat.

An electrical coil. It stuck out grotesquely between her cracked teeth. Her neck bulged black where the coil had been rammed home, and blood had spurted from her mouth, staining the front of her dress.

Beside the chair lay a long blue silken scarf, crusted with dark stains. On the mirror, smeared in blood beside Crane's feet, was the word *THIEF*.

"Hipp," said Eliza steadily, "run back to Bow Street and fetch Harley Griffin. Now."

CORPUS DELICTI

WELL," SAID INSPECTOR GRIFFIN TWENTY-THREE
minutes later, "I don't think it was suicide,
do you?"

Bright gaslights threw the body in the chair into sharp relief. Eliza had waited in the hall, pacing impatiently, guarding
the door should anyone arrive to disturb the scene. Hipp had
found Griffin in his office, working diligently on the Slasher
case—when did he ever sleep?—and he'd arrived as quickly
as he could, but it had still seemed an age.

Now she examined the corpse, her hands encased in
white cotton gloves. "Bruises on her chin and neck. Fingermarks, most likely." Crane's hands curled loosely over the
chair's arms. Eliza eased a sleeve back, revealing purplish-
green marks on the wrists. "Here, too. And look, broken hair
strands. Someone grabs her; she fights. She was alive while
the coil was inserted." She fingered a white stain on the brown
bodice. "Tears, or mucus. The poor lady probably drowned in
blood before she had time to exsanguinate."

She tested the corpse's finger joints. "The body is cool, but still pliable. Rigor has not yet set in. And it's freezing in here. It's possible she died only a short while before I found her."

Griffin made fastidious notes in his book. "What time did you say that package of yours arrived?"

"I received it at half past eight. But it could have been waiting for hours." Frustration and guilt bit at her. Crane's horrible, cruel death only made her more determined to solve these crimes. If only she'd arrived sooner, lingered less, walked home faster . . .

"Oh, aye? Stuff your damn vanity, Eliza. As if you're the only one who can save the world."

Wildly, Eliza spun around. Lizzie wasn't there. Curse her. *It's not your turn, Lizzie. Clear off.*

Griffin eyed the bloody writing on the mirror with faint disgust. Even the incessant rain hadn't spoiled his immaculate black suit or sharply combed hair, but dark bruises circled his eyes, and he looked thin and weary. "First *whore,* now *thief.* Lady Redstoat's catalogue of sins lengthens by the day."

Eliza held up the bloodstained blue scarf, its silken tassels drooping. "Our mysterious long-haired visitor strikes again. A man Lady Redstoat didn't recognize." She fingered the faded stains. "These marks look old, but Crane's been dead less than two hours." She scraped a fragment onto a glass slide and peered at it through a lens on her optical. "Weeks old, at the very least," she said happily, pushing the optical back on her forehead. "This is not our victim's blood."

Griffin looked pained. "Whose, then? Why would our man carry around a gory old scarf?"

"Least of all drop it at the scene. That kind of malice

aforethought"—she nodded at the body—"doesn't make such an elementary mistake. Perhaps it's a message."

"Like what? *Beware the blue scarf bandit*?" He pointed at the bloody mirror. "That's the message, Doctor. *Steal from me, and you die*."

"But what did Crane steal, and from whom?" Her thoughts flicked back to Crane's strange journal, now safely stashed in Lizzie's cabinet. *Project Interlunium. Advanced side effects that will destroy us all.* "The servants' door was unlocked when I arrived. The killer came in that way. Or," she added, inspired, "he went *out* the back and left it open. As in, he arrived via the front door, and Crane let him in."

"Someone she trusted?"

"Or at least someone she was expecting. They fight, he kills her, then ransacks that shelf, looking for whatever she supposedly stole." She turned to the window. "Any ideas, Mr. Locke? You do have a habit of turning up early to murder scenes."

Seymour Locke hunched in the window seat, damp and disheveled, clutching a glass of Scotch in one trembling hand. He'd arrived while she was waiting for Griffin. He dragged back snarled blond hair. "I explained already. We had a meeting this afternoon to discuss what to do next. Then I went back to the library at the RI to study, but I'd left some papers here, and I've classes tomorrow, so I returned to fetch them on my way home." He gulped a mouthful of liquor, seemingly without tasting, and waved at the ransacked bookshelf. "Who the hell cares? I told you: her latest experimental journal is gone. Schematics, final test results, the lot. She'd collected it all, said she was preparing for . . ." Another gulp, this time with a grimace. "Oh, God. This is a disaster."

"The missing journal, or the murder?" asked Griffin sharply.

A reproachful glare. "They amount to the same thing, you idiot. Can't you see? Her work is gone!"

"Can't you reconstruct it from copies?"

"There *are* no copies. Ephronia made sure of that. It was too dangerous."

"Another first name, Mr. Locke. You're certainly well blessed with close friends." Griffin tapped his pencil on the desk. It, too, had been cleared of its papers. Only an empty brass phonograph machine sat by the overturned inkpot, its coil glimmering. "So who attended this meeting?"

"She already asked me that," snapped Locke, but his flashing eyes had dulled. Eliza had seen him falter when he walked in. She'd watched the color drain from his face. Crane's death had badly shaken him, even more so than Antoinette's. Whatever defiance he'd mustered—if it had ever been real—had died.

So she'd forborne to mention the book, to see what he'd say unprompted. And sure enough, he'd come through. Not the behavior of a guilty man.

"Should already know the answer, then." Griffin studied his notebook, waiting.

Locke sighed. "Me, Starling, the Professor. We're the only ones left, with Ormonde out of action. Someone's killing us off, or hadn't you noticed? Don't you think I want as badly as you to catch them?"

Eliza frowned. "Mr. Wyverne didn't attend?"

A blank look.

"Your chemist friend. He seemed willing to help with your project."

"Oh." Locke snorted. "Him. Shouldn't think so."

"Why not?"

"Why does everyone ask that?" Irritated, Locke jumped up to stalk to and fro before the speckled mirror, his reflection keeping pace. "Because we don't trust him, all right? Because he's a professional pest who doesn't have the first clue about multi-dimensional aether physics—"

"But you do?" Eliza pounced. "I thought you didn't understand Antoinette's work. A lowly assistant, you said."

Locke subsided, dark. "I know enough," he muttered. "I'm not an idiot. I hear things."

"I see. So what was decided?"

"Eh?"

"At the meeting. What to do next?"

"Oh." He tried another sharp smile, but it came out weary and woebegone, as if the effort to be rude to cover his grief was finally exhausting him. "Professor Crane was shaken by what happened at the demonstration. At first she didn't want to go on. But we resolved to start work with the back-up prototype tomorrow. She said she was approaching the final solution. I thought she meant the equations."

Eliza fumbled in her bag for the scrap of paper. "These? From Antoinette's?"

"Starling's work. He said he'd found an error in the numbers, that the electrical field would never self-sustain, or some such. But Crane is the real brains, not Starling. She said she had the answer." He swallowed. "Don't you see? They found out what she was building and they killed her for it. Antoinette as well."

Eliza fixed him in her stare. "Time to stop misleading us, Mr. Locke. This isn't about the miniature engine, is it? You mean Project Interlunium."

Locke swallowed, pale. "How do you know about that?"

"Never you mind. What is this project, and why is it so secret?"

He rubbed his eyes with thumb and forefinger, muttering a curse. "Promise this goes no further, Doctor. If you squeak on me to your god-awful lover at the Royal for this . . ."

"This maniac has murdered two of your friends. Help me catch him before he kills someone else. Maybe even you."

A defeated sigh. "The first prototype moved things. In three dimensions. A matter transference machine."

Griffin glanced at Eliza, alarmed. "A teleporter? Like the one the Chopper used? Wasn't that infernal thing destroyed?"

"So I was told." Her palms itched. The Chopper had nearly killed her in the course of his dark mission of murder.

"Fabulous, really." Locke gave a haunted smile. "A homing device, to be more specific. You activate the beacon, it transports you away from the generator to a predetermined location, and back again. Antoinette got the idea from a gentleman friend. Said he showed her an old book with some diagrams."

"I see." Eliza's heart stung in sudden disappointment. An old book. Like the one the Chopper had worked from. Dr. Frankenstein's journal, which she'd once stolen from a secret library at Bethlem Asylum, aided by crafty Malachi

Todd. A book which, along with everything else that remained of Frankenstein's, now belonged to Marcellus Finch.

She ought to have known Finch would never destroy such a marvelous book, no matter how terrible the consequences. His unquenchable curiosity often overcame his good sense. Still, why hadn't Marcellus mentioned he knew Antoinette?

"She built one," said Locke, "but it was too inefficient to be useful. Made the most frightful noise, you know, and the generator was so big, and the aether burned so fast that its performance was shoddy and unreliable. So Crane helped her make an improved one, incorporating the principles of her miniature engine. The entire thing was portable, generator and all. No more homing."

"Hence the secrecy?"

"Of course. Efficient energy is one thing. Cheap instantaneous travel? Quite another. And we almost had it working, the day before Antoinette died. But then Starling had this idea for a modification. Some new device he wanted to attach, to further extend the capability. Something about propagating the right sort of wave before the de-phlogistication could destroy the medium. He called it his advanced solution."

Advanced side-effects. She recalled Starling's visit to Finch's, that dusty book belonging to Mr. Faraday, and her lips set hard. Marcellus had lied about the whole affair from the beginning. About her mysterious "illness," too.

So what else had he lied about?

"What kind of wave?" she asked sharply. "What did it do? Come, don't dissemble. I've heard enough evasion to last me a lifetime."

Locke's eyes shimmered. "Don't waste your effort, Doctor.

I honestly don't understand much of it. All I know is that Ephronia was horrified, and ordered Starling not to go ahead. He'd already destroyed the original machine trying. But he and Antoinette were determined. They wanted me to help. Naturally I refused."

"You weren't curious?" put in Griffin.

A sniffle. "I'm Ephronia's assistant, not theirs. They wanted me to steal her back-up prototype. I said I didn't know where she kept it. The truth, for what it's worth," he added, with a flash of ire. "Ephronia hid it away, to guard against precisely that contingency. A secret workroom. Not even I knew where it was." Unflinchingly, he stared at his own reflection in the spotted mirror. "Now I suppose we'll never find it."

Eliza swallowed. Her resolve not to reveal the book was safe was crumbling. The poor fellow was in tears. "So why would you not imagine the missing book to be in this secret room? Wouldn't that be safest?"

"Aren't you supposed to be detectives?" He waved at the ransacked shelf. "Do you think this person searched just one shelf and gave up? They knew exactly what they were looking for. They took what they wanted and left the rest. It's gone."

Her thoughts raced. Of course, she knew the killer hadn't taken the book. He'd searched, but found it already missing. "The professor's letter to me said 'something terrible' happened this evening, after your meeting. Any idea what?"

Locke's jaw tightened. "No. But I'd put money on Starling and his blasted modification. I told her he wouldn't leave her alone. I offered to stay and protect her, but she . . ." His voice cracked, and he wiped his eyes with a muffled curse.

"But she said no," guessed Eliza softly. "Is that why you left your folio, Seymour? An excuse to return and check on her, when she'd already sent you away?"

Locke tried to look scandalized, but after a moment he sighed, letting his forehead fall against the mirror. "Must I admit I adored her? That I tried to make love to her and she laughed at me? Ephronia was a true genius. Of course I worshipped her."

"But Antoinette . . . ?"

He straightened with a snort. "Believed me, did you, when I said we were engaged? We only pretended, to protect her reputation. Antoinette loathed the very idea of marriage. Said it was a stone-age institution designed to subjugate the female sex. No, it's Starling who's jealous. It's why I thought he'd tricked me into fluffing the demonstration, to make Ephronia think me a fool. Always wants to be the golden child."

"So why did you lie to us about the engagement? Antoinette was dead. No need to pretend any longer."

"Is that really what you think? That the poor girl deserves to be slandered after she's dead? Besides, a secret engagement is never a secret, for God's sake. Everyone knew. If I told you I'd lied about that, why would you believe me when I said I didn't kill her?" He wiped his nose. "And then your lame-witted Chief Inspector arrested me anyway. Best laid plans."

"So do you think Starling would want to steal the professor's book? Or could he re-create the material himself?"

"No." Carelessly, Locke shrugged. "Maybe. I don't know. Look, as much as I would love to tell you Starling's the murderer, I saw him at the library just before I left. For what it's worth, I don't think it's possible that he did this."

She exchanged a glance with Griffin. Two men swapping alibis. Both innocent—or both guilty? "Not even with a tele-porter?"

An exasperated eye-roll. "Weren't you listening? The thing was destroyed. You think he built a new one in three hours? Not a chance."

"Who else could have known about Starling's modification idea? Anyone snooping about? Your friend Wyverne?"

"I suppose it's possible. Could be anyone at the RI, or the Royal. Or Paxton and his railway thugs, for that matter. Spies are everywhere." Locke barked a laugh. "Perhaps the mur-derer is killing everyone who's cleverer than he. Everyone in this room ought to be safe."

Eliza picked up the bloodstained blue scarf. "Do you know whose this is? One of Antoinette's friends, perhaps?"

"Never seen it before." Locke gave a haunted smile. "But I would say that, wouldn't I?"

"What about all these letters?" Griffin dumped an armful on the desk to leaf through them. He held one to the light. "To the Right Honorable Member for Buckinghamshire," he read. "A petition for funds. Squeezing up to politicians for a living. The more things change, eh?"

She picked up a second envelope. Empty, the sender's information printed on the outside. "Miss Veronica Burton, IRS," she read with interest. "Why was the professor corre-sponding with a Royal Society investigator?"

"Trading insults?" Locke's rudeness had apparently re-composed. "Why don't you ask that appalling bodyguard of yours? His snotty patrician nose is stuffed in everyone's business."

"I'll do that." She tried another letter. No envelope, just unsealed and refolded, smeared with dirty fingermarks and a postscript . . .

Her heart thudded at that crude black handwriting. Not a postscript after all, but a brusque reply, scribbled on the outside of the original.

Here's your money, Ephronia. God knows I owe you—and now you owe me, ha ha!

Don't let the bastards bring you down.

With pleasure
From an OLD friend

In place of a signature, the correspondent had drawn a three-pointed shape. Like a twisted crown—or a jester's belled hat.

Dizziness struck, a swirl of Lizzie's dark laughter. Eliza clutched the table for balance. For years she'd received letters in that rough writing, with the same cryptic signature.

The King of Rats. Her father, Edward Hyde.

Why on earth was respectable Professor Crane getting letters—and *money*—from the dirtiest crook in London?

Swiftly, she scanned the pile of papers. No coin purse, no fold of bills. Hyde didn't seem likely to write a check. Did he even have a bank account?

Her fingers itched to open the original letter. Excited, she started to call Griffin over—and abruptly stopped.

She daren't reveal Hyde's involvement. Not before she knew exactly what his nefarious doings were.

Griffin's back was turned. Locke was staring into the mirror, morose. Casually, she slipped the letter into her dress pocket.

What are you doing? Lizzie hissed in her ear. Or was it her own voice, accusing her? *Concealing evidence? Stealing from a murder scene? So much for your hoity-toity guff about criminals, missy. Do as I say and not as I do?*

She flushed, sick. She could lose her job for this, and rightly so. She'd demand nothing less if she caught someone tampering with evidence. Harley would be disgusted with her. Her career with the police would be over.

But the idea of Hyde's involvement in this case—in an unknown capacity—terrified her. Try as she might, she couldn't shake the certainty that her father had done something terrible. Just a faint scent on the air, some distant tune she strained to hear—but she *knew.*

She must get to the bottom of this. On her own, without police interference. Not even Harley could know.

Griffin waved her over. "Eliza, look at this."

Her cheeks burned. Surely her guilt was all too evident. He'd round on her, demand she confess what she'd done, hand over that evidence this minute or he'd toss her in the lock-up for interfering with a murder investigation. *Murder, Eliza. Life and death. And you're stealing letters that could reveal the culprit? Shame on you.*

But Griffin just pointed to a pale patch on the carpet, like a wine stain long scrubbed out, except it looked fresh. "What could have made that?"

She rubbed her gloved finger over it. A faint burned aether smell tingled. Hmm. She reapplied her optical, slotting in the same aether-reactive lenses she'd used at Antoinette's.

"Ouch!" She dragged the optical away, momentarily blinded. Glittering networks of white, too bright to behold, like cosmic fishnets in an ocean of gold.

"Extreme aether reactivity," she reported, with a glint of excitement. "The same as in Antoinette's study! I see no experimental apparatus here. What can have done this?" An idea struck. She slotted another, darker lens over the first, and slipped the optical back on.

This time, the blinding aura dimmed enough to be observed. Like a trail of diamonds, it swirled around the corpse and along the carpet. It curled over the bookshelves, and stole like guilty mist out into the hall.

"Aha!" Eagerly, she followed it. It bounced along the passage, a jeweled will-o'-the-wisp, and disappeared into the back lane.

She ran down the steps. Glitter showered the mud, a silver ribbon fading towards the cesspit . . . and then it vanished. Dissipated like an unhappy ghost into oblivion.

A trail. Left by something moving. The same person who'd left a similar trail in Antoinette's study. The mysterious visitor with the blue scarf.

The killer.

But what was it? An electrical anomaly caused by some piece of equipment? A bioelectrical disturbance? She focused the optical on her own skirts, her arm, her foot. Nothing. A rat skittered by, just a shadow. No glitter.

"Inspector," she called, "Mr. Locke, can you come out, please?"

Griffin appeared at the door. "What is it?"

"Stand here." She pointed to a clear area of mud, and examined him through her lens. "That's it. Now move your arm. Hmm. Nothing." She frowned. "Today, Mr. Locke, if you don't mind."

No answer.

She stared at Griffin. Griffin swore. And they dashed back inside.

But the front door stood open, frigid draught blowing in. The library was empty. Seymour Locke was gone.

Griffin exhaled wearily. "Not as if we could have arrested him again. Being a rude little ratbag isn't against the law—"

"Harley, I know where the missing book is," she burst out. "I have it at home. Crane mailed it to me a few hours ago." She handed him Crane's letter.

He read it, and gave her a fond but exasperated glance. "Withholding evidence, Doctor? I'm surprised at you."

Hyde's letter wriggled and moaned in her pocket, and over Griffin's shoulder, spectral Lizzie made a gleeful face. "Liar!" she crowed. "Thief!"

"It confirms everything Locke told us," interrupted Eliza hurriedly. She'd no remedy left. Nothing to keep Lizzie in her place. "Crane called her project 'Interlunium.' It's the key!"

"An unorthodox machine, based on the principles of matter transference." Griffin stroked his mustaches. "Antoinette and Crane are murdered, Ormonde is injured. Are Starling and Locke to be our next victims? Is the killer determined to put an end to this project, whatever it is?"

"Or he's looking for the back-up prototype," suggested Eliza. "One of those jealous spies Locke talked about, who wants to steal the project and make a fortune."

Griffin grimaced. "But the simplest explanation is still that Locke did it. Kills his lady friend in a fit of jealousy—or professional envy, or sheer stubborn irascibility, for that matter, the fellow is brimming with causes. Crane finds out and threatens to turn him in, so he kills her, too. Simple."

"He says he was at the library all evening."

"No doubt without witnesses. It's an easy claim to make."

"But he has an alibi for Antoinette. Starling said so."

Griffin shrugged. "Then Starling's lying. We ought to question Mr. Ormonde when he wakes. His is the only side of the story we don't have. He could know more about these so-called spies, if they even exist."

"All right. Then who's Blue Scarf in this theory? You must admit, it's strange the servants didn't see him."

"Likely one of Antoinette's infamous lovers. And maybe the footman was in the privy when he called." Griffin smiled at her deflated expression. "The dullest explanation is usually the truth. Being mysterious doesn't make a man guilty of murder."

"But that doesn't explain why Crane mailed me her book," she insisted. "Why would she do that, if not truly in fear for her life?"

"Why would she do it anyway? She'd only just met you, and alongside Captain Lafayette. For all she knows, you're a Royal Society spy and she'll be burned. She must have been very short of friends."

"Or else . . ." Her voice trailed off. Or else Crane had special reason to trust Eliza. A personal reason.

Here's your money, Ephronia. God knows I owe you.

The stolen letter whiplashed in Eliza's pocket, threatening to wriggle out and expose her. Yes, she was withholding evidence for a reason. The basest, most cowardly of all reasons.

I've a thing to show you, Rose. Such a pretty thing . . .

Boots clacked on stone, and a flurry of dark blue skirts dashed around the corner at full tilt. Constable Perkins stumbled to a halt, puffing like a steam train. "News, sir," she gasped. "Mr. Ormonde. He's dead."

Griffin groaned. "Wonderful."

"How?" demanded Eliza. "Did his wound fester?"

"We found him around eight." Perkins swiped back fallen hair. "Only left him alone for twenty minutes. His face was purple, and his eyes bulged. As if he'd choked. But I saw bruises around his neck."

"Strangled," guessed Eliza darkly, "or poisoned. The killer returned to finish him off. So much for questioning the poor fellow."

"That's not all." Perkins swallowed. "There was writing. In blood, on the wall beside the bed. It said 'traitor.'"

Griffin swore softly. "I posted guards. Why didn't our men see anyone enter?"

Perkins looked shamefaced. "Suspect they were playing cards, sir. Chief Inspector Reeve said they weren't to worry overmuch for some wrinkly old science cove, as he put it."

"Perfect," muttered Griffin. "The master of modern police work strikes again."

"*Whore,* then *thief,*" mused Eliza, "and now *traitor.* How indiscriminate our killer's vengeance. Ormonde after half past seven, Crane before eight. The murderer must have fairly flown to get from Ireton House to Piccadilly in that time."

"Unless he can be in two places at once," put in Perkins brightly.

Griffin coughed. "Indeed. What odds a team of murderous book thieves?"

"We've worked stranger cases," reminded Eliza. "Someone did shoot at the demonstration while all the players were onstage . . ." Realization hit her with a jolt.

"In any case," said Griffin suddenly, "imagine I'm our man—or men—and I really did come here hunting for a book that wasn't there . . ."

Eliza was only half listening. All had been onstage—except one. An unwelcome colleague whom they'd spurned when he'd wanted to help. A professional pest, excluded from the project of a lifetime.

". . . what do you suppose I'd do now?"

"Hmm?" She glanced up. "Well, I imagine you'd figure out where the book could be, and run to fetch it before—oh." Her stomach knotted. "Inspector, I think I should go home now."

"I rather think you'd better."

She grabbed her satchel and ran.

INFERNAL DEVICES

PANTING, ELIZA SKIDDED INTO RUSSELL SQUARE, and stumbled, aghast.

Her house was on fire.

A crowd had gathered in black late evening chill. Servants, old men in nightcaps, and electric butlers milled about, their excited chatter almost drowned out by the roaring flames. Hippocrates sprinted up behind and crashed into her skirts. "Fire!" he trumpeted. "Fire! Assistance required!"

Frantic, she fought through the crowd. Flames leapt from the upstairs windows, roaring up the drainpipes towards the roof. Sparks jumped, reddish glare searing the street like hellfire. Black smoke clogged the air. She coughed, eyes watering. Hands grabbed her, pulled her back, but she shook them off. "Molly!" she screamed. "Mrs. Poole!"

No answer. She couldn't see anything through the smoke. She struggled closer, slapping away well-meaning hands.

"Doctor!" A solid hand gripped her forearm. "Doctor, here!"

She crushed Mrs. Poole in a hug, almost falling over in gratitude. "Where's Molly? What's happening?"

"She's safe. I sent her for the parish brigade." Mrs. Poole was wrapped in a blanket, gray hair in curling papers. "Where have you been? Out all night again?"

"How did this start?" Eliza gazed helplessly up at her burning house, radiant heat scorching her face. She didn't believe in coincidence. Ephronia Crane's killer had come for the book—and now this. A threat, or a warning? She felt so small and useless. Surely, everything was lost.

"Don't look at me," said Mrs. Poole gruffly. "The kitchen fire was out. I was sleeping. Only lucky I heard a window break upstairs. That's where it began."

Eliza's throat stung raw. Lizzie's cabinet. Crane's book, the elixir. Everything she treasured.

She pushed through the gawping crowd towards the porch. The front door hung open. Beyond, flames crackled and licked, a bright warning, but the fire hadn't engulfed the whole house. Not yet.

Wooden carts rattled from Southampton Row, bearing hoses and pumps and yelling men. The parish brigade. Good luck to them. She couldn't afford to wait.

"Stay here," ordered Eliza, thrusting her satchel into Mrs. Poole's hands. She only hoped the staircase remained intact. "You too, Hipp."

Mrs. Poole gaped. "Finally lost your mind, have you?"

"Perhaps." She flung her damp mantle over her head and ran up the steps. Fierce heat almost drove her back. Sparks fell from the upper windows onto her dress, smoking little black holes. A man screamed for her to stop. She shielded her face, and ran in.

Inside, choking smoke hung in a pall. She crouched, head down, breathing as best she could through the wet mantle, and made for the stairs.

The wood creaked alarmingly. The smoke made her dizzy. Her heart quailed, and she hugged the railing, mortified. *I can't. It's too much.*

"Come on, slugabed!" shouted Lizzie gaily, leaping so her frilly skirts bounced. "Last one to the top's a mopsy!" She laughed at Eliza's dumbfounded expression. "Think I'd leave you here to burn? Not on your life, sister. Anyone kills you, it's gonna be me."

"Kind of you," rasped Eliza. She grabbed Lizzie's hand, and together they scampered up to the landing, the next floor, the next. Her study was burning, all her books lost. With a pang she remembered the mice in their cages. Had they escaped? No way to reach the poor creatures now. Fire crackled all around, hungry to spread. If she'd arrived only a few minutes later, there'd be no way in at all.

Lizzie dragged Eliza onwards. "O-ho-ho! Toasty warm! Someone turn me over, I'm done!"

At last, they reached the bedroom landing. Eliza's breath scorched, her eyes raw. Crazy laughter bubbled. "This is insane. *WE'RE* insane."

"Better bonkers than burned." Lizzie pulled her into the dark, smoky bedroom, ran for the fireplace and dragged down the sconce. *Clunk!* It banged, hollow.

The cabinet door already hung open.

No time to wonder. Eliza ran in, grabbed one of Lizzie's dresses and knotted it to make a crude sack. She stuffed in

Finch's books, Henry Jekyll's diaries, Quick's journals, her notes and phials from the wolf cure experiment. Her three remaining bottles of elixir, more of *lux ex tenebris*.

The shelf where she'd left Professor Crane's book was empty.

Frantic, she fumbled through the clutter. The book was gone. The killer—or his accomplice—had taken it. Broken into Lizzie's cabinet, and set her house on fire.

Her thoughts stumbled in haste. Not Seymour Locke. This inferno was too well advanced. He'd left Ireton House only minutes before she had.

That left jealous Mr. Wyverne . . . or Byron Starling. Her old friend. Who'd tried to insinuate himself into her life ever since their "chance" meeting. Who knew exactly where she lived—but did he know her secret? Her memories of those past years clanged, conflicting—but she couldn't pluck out the thorny suspicion that Starling somehow knew everything.

"Oi!" Lizzie tossed her a dragon-headed cane. "I'm taking this fine fellow. Everything else can burn. Ha ha!"

Sweating, Eliza hauled the sack over one shoulder, the cane under her arm. The fire roared louder, the heat more intense. Lizzie's back stairs beckoned, still dark and relatively cool.

"Let's go." She took one final glance around . . . and swift, sharp pain pierced her heart.

The room she'd slept in all these years, the corners and window seats where she'd read and laughed and dreamed. Her consulting room, where Remy had proposed. The study, her anatomy books, the desk where she'd studied Ovid and Newton and William Harvey. Her mother's portrait, that beautiful lady in the wedding dress and diamonds whom she'd barely known. The drawing room, where Mr. Hyde had lurked behind the curtain, where first she'd swallowed his bitter elixir and given birth to Lizzie. And this cabinet, her most secret of secret places.

Gone.

A flash of treacherous color caught her eye. Mr. Todd's painting, unfurling on the shelf. A portrait of a different Eliza, filled with fascination and naïve hopes. A beautiful Eliza, wrapped in Lizzie's scarlet skirts, slumbering in the scent of blood and roses, dreaming of heaven. A far younger, vain, and foolish Eliza, who'd believed evil could be tempered by love.

Let her burn.

The whisper stung her ravaged ears. Had spectral Lizzie spoken? Or was it her own voice?

Suddenly, the pain of disillusionment was too much to bear. She couldn't let go of that precious, forlorn hope. Not now, with her life on fire. Impulsively, she stuffed the painting under her arm.

Are you crazy?

Tears blinded her, and Eliza took Lizzie's hand and fled.

WHERE SANITY MELTS

HOURS LATER, ELIZA STUMBLED INTO CAVENDISH Square, Hipp trotting dolefully at her heels. The paved streets were deserted. Henry's house—*her* house, though that still seemed strange—lurched from the darkness, gleaming with the threat of faint gray dawn. Somewhere, an early-rising bird sang a mournful tune.

Exhaustion filled her muscles with lead. She'd stayed while the parish brigade tried to dampen the flames. They'd managed to stop the fire spreading to the adjoining houses. But the top two floors of her own house were gutted, just charred lumps of wood and a pile of ash, and the bottom floors weren't far behind.

The arsonist, whoever he was, had done an excellent job.

Yawning, she hefted her makeshift sack and knocked. Half a minute passed before Mr. Brigham peered out, tie missing and shirt undone beneath his hastily donned coat. He didn't look sleepy. Just interrupted. "Good morning, Doctor. I, um, wasn't expecting you." His eyes widened. "Holy Mary. What happened?"

She glanced at her ash-smeared dress and blackened

hands. No doubt her face was in the same condition. "I apologize for the hour. This sounds ridiculous, but . . . you see,
my house burned down, and . . . well, I'm afraid I've nowhere
else to go." Not strictly true. Mrs. Poole had taken Molly to
stay with their cousin, a respectable shopkeeper in Cheap-
side, and with typical bull-headed affection had insisted Eliza
accept the same hospitality. But the thought of the family's
well-meant pity—and their *questions*—made Eliza cold. "I
trust I'm not disturbing you," she added.

Brigham was still staring. "What? Yes. I mean, no. Certainly. Come in." He stepped aside.

Hipp stumbled in and collapsed under the hallstand with
a determined *clunk!* She followed, those familiar scents set-
tling over her, still disturbing but overlaid with warm comfort. Even the staircase had lost a little of its menace. But
still she shivered, hackles prickling, haunted by ghosts of
long-forgotten sorrow.

Brigham fussed, taking her sack. "Might I show you to
your room, or would you like breakfast first?"

She blinked. "I have a room?"

"Of course. First thing the captain bade me do." And he
took off up the staircase.

Nonplussed, she followed. And sure enough, within half
an hour she was luxuriating in a hot scented bath in the sitting room of a cozy bedroom suite.

Soft blue drapes blocked out the grim gray morning, and
a fire crackled in a tiled grate. The big copper tub was filled
almost to the brim. Brigham had poured her a glass of wine,
set fluffy towels by the fire, and lit candles so the electric
lights didn't glare.

She sighed gratefully, warm water lapping at her throat. *Ha. So much for your taunting, Lizzie.* This wasn't the room where Madeleine Jekyll had died. Guest quarters, if she had to guess, but she didn't remember this room and that was a good thing.

She'd already too much on her mind. The book thief, sneaking into her house and setting it alight. Was it Byron Starling? She didn't believe it. He wasn't her enemy. If he'd wanted the book, why not just ask?

More likely the disturbingly eager Mr. Wyverne. But how could he know about her secret cabinet? It didn't make sense.

On the side table, alongside her wineglass, the purloined letter glinted in mocking firelight. *You stole me,* it whispered. *Filched me from a crime scene like a common thief. Where's your precious justice, Eliza? What price your noble principles when your own father's implicated?*

Edward Hyde's handwriting on the outside leered at her, a hungry demon. She could almost hear his taunting voice. *Here's your money, Ephronia. God knows I owe you. God knows I'd have throttled you with my own hands if someone hadn't gotten in before me. I killed my own wife, you know. Hurled her down the stairs. Nothing easier . . .*

Compelled, she wiped her hands dry and fumbled Crane's letter open.

Sir,

You will recall I once served you (to be exact, your physician predecessor) in a scientific matter requiring delicacy and discretion, and at no small risk to myself. Your gratitude since is my constant

reward—but tonight I must beg the favor be
returned in kind. Against the forces of ignorance
and superstition, you and I hold common cause,
and I beseech you to help me now, as once I
helped you.

A colleague is threatening to reveal to the
authorities certain information which, for the sake
of my continued freedom and safety, I must insist
be kept private. In return for silence, this sniveling
and frankly despicable villain demands immediate
payment in coin—one hundred pounds, a sum
which for the moment I cannot raise.

I therefore write to you for a loan. Terms to be
set by you, of course, at whatever rate you desire.
You may rest assured that I shall shortly be able to
repay you in full.

I would be obliged by a response at your earliest,
as the miscreant is to visit me tonight.

I remain, sir, in eternal gratitude

E. Crane

Eliza sat up, hair dripping. Professor Crane was being
blackmailed. Pay up, or have her secret project betrayed to
the Royal.

Her imagination sparked, re-creating the torrid scene. For
a struggling scientist, one hundred sterling was a terrifying,
impossible sum. Alone, frightened, facing a horrible death in
the Royal's fires, Crane had written to the King of Rats for
help. Hyde delivered the money, no doubt for sinister reasons

of his own. The blackmailer arrived, and Crane let him in. And now she was dead.

It was no coincidence. Surely this extorting colleague—*this sniveling and frankly despicable villain*—had to be Crane's killer, and likely Antoinette's, too.

The mysterious visitor again. The long-haired reprobate in the blue scarf. Who was demonstrably neither Starling nor Locke. Lady Redstoat—who, it seemed, had told the truth after all—had been sure of that. But could Blue Scarf be some accomplice?

Contract negotiations with B. proceed apace, said Crane's phonograph transcript. *My escape.*

In spite of her colleagues' objections, Crane had put her miniature engine up for sale. How else to raise the repayments so soon, at Hyde's undoubtedly extortionate interest rates?

But who was "B"?

Could it be Veronica Burton? Her unexplained presence at the demonstration, the envelope on Crane's desk. *Empire contracts,* Mr. Paxton had suggested. What if, while investigating Crane's engine, Burton had found out about Interlunium? A zealous Royal Society agent discovers a wildly unorthodox project, and blackmails the inventor? Hardly seemed likely.

Wearily, she laid letter and spectacles aside. Her head ached, her throat raw from smoke. Suddenly the day's events crashed in, falling buildings in an alley too narrow for escape.

The Slasher autopsy, that poor boy's mutilated body. Saucy May, her "dirty cove in fancy britches." Eliza's house afire, that melting heat. Professor Crane's choked corpse, ink-stained Antoinette, the swollen purple face of Ormonde. And Hyde's letter.

Three people had already died for the sake of this mysterious book. And now, at last, the murderer possessed it.

What next? Had she, Eliza, been intended as the fourth? She'd read the book, or at least glanced at it. Would the killer—or killers—come after her?

"Ha!" she scoffed aloud. "I've seen off razor murderers and soulless thieves and insane surgeons who coveted my corpse. Don't even *try* to scare me, you rascals."

Or perhaps the case was over. The killer would take the book and go, and they'd never hear from him again. That was a comforting thought.

She sighed in the warm cocoon of the bath, eyelids drooping. What she wouldn't give for a proper night's sleep . . .

Splash! She recoiled, bathwater sloshing. But it was only Lizzie, up to her neck at the far end of the tub, whistling and soaping herself.

Eliza groaned. "Go away. It's not your turn until tomorrow."

"Just because you lost a night don't mean I need to." Lizzie rubbed soap along her arms, admiring the firelit bubbles. "Swanky room. D'you think I'll get one like it? Or am I for the attic again, locked away like a loony wife?"

"Hardly the time to quibble," said Eliza waspishly. "Did it escape your notice that our house just burned down? I risked *my* life to fetch *your* things, remember?" She'd laid out the contents of her makeshift sack on a shelf. Books, papers, that treacherous oil painting, a row of phials. Alongside the king's medicine and that odd blue mixture she'd concocted for her mouse experiments, three black bottles of elixir glimmered, murmuring their bittersweet song. *Eliza, come to us. Drink us, love. Be free . . .*

"Oh, aye," said Lizzie comfortably, puffing a bubble aloft, "and how'd that've gone without me? I'm a bleedin' hero!"

"Easy for you to say. You're imaginary. You can't die from smoke inhalation."

Lizzie threw the soap at her, and it hit Eliza's chest with an indignant *plop!* "How come you're always the one who's real? What if *you're* a figment of *my* imagination, eh? Ever think of that?"

"Can't you stop carrying on even for one moment? I don't need you here. I don't *want* you here. Just leave me be!"

Suddenly Lizzie lurched forwards, clawing for her throat. Eliza splashed under, thrashing, trying to yell but sucking in only water.

Lizzie squeezed harder. "Get rid of me, will you? How about I get rid of *YOU?*"

Eliza flailed, gulping, but Lizzie was too strong. Panic gripped her. Sparks danced before her eyes. She was trapped. Drowning. And all the while, Lizzie's laughter bounced and swelled, contorted by the water into horror.

Eliza's vision stretched like wet rubber, tearing into two shapes, *two* worlds, *two* bodies, mine and hers, hers and mine, and somewhere just out of sight in that crusted blackness, the nightmare is lurking. A predator clawing out to claim me . . .

Thump! *Our head bounces off the wall. It's a white wall, lined with lumpy cushioned fabric. A padded wall. As if these mean-arsed mad-doctors give a flying frig what we does to ourselves. I giggle, and try again. Boingg! Clangg! Amazing, the number of noises her skull can make.*

Wet warmth trickles into our eyes. I claw our red-spotted shift, ripping it to rags. Wouldn't do to mess up our fine gown, Eliza. Stop bleeding this instant. Ha ha! A-ha-ha-haaaah!

Clunk! A bolt grinds aside, and the padded door squeaks open. Light sweeps, a draught of unclean air.

We scuttle back towards the bed. Eliza kicks and scratches, but I makes her, I drags our limbs by sheer force of will. She wails, and I rake her face with my nails, a bright shock of pain. Shut it, you feeble mopsy. Our body ain't yours no more. Lizzie, that's my name now. Lizzie Hyde, by God.

I don't know how I know that. I just know.

In struts the dark suit, the steely hair, the mild eyes of Sir Jedediah Fairfax, Fellow of the Royal College of Snotfaces. He's holding a canvas coat festooned with buckles and straps. "And how are we today, Miss Jekyll?"

That patronizing doctor's "we"—how are we today, madwomen, all two of yer?—makes me laugh. I smooth my ragged shift, grin my best grin. He wants me. I know he does. They all want me, these shiny gents with their civilized manners and polished lies. We've all got two faces. All just brutes inside, hungry to consume. Take me, beat me, bleed me dry.

I lick bloodstained lips, and it tastes of freedom. "Is that for me, sir? Can I wear it now? Come undress me, you beast."

Behind the surgeon, the dusky boy with spectacles cringes like a whipped dog. "See what I mean, sir?

It's as bad as I've seen it. I didn't know who else to come to."

This one's barely twenty, only a few years older than us, hair floating to his shoulders and flashing dark eyes that melt at our glance. He wants me, too. Aye, don't deny it, Eliza. Think I haven't noticed his sidelong looks as we pore over your studies? His breath catching as our fingers reach for his sleeve, his brow glistening when we share your excitement over some triangle or curve or god-rotted fluxion, whatever in hell those are?

Think it's you he's looking at?

I rip our shift apart and arch my back, giving 'em both a good eyeful of her tits. Her blond hair tumbles on our bared shoulders. "This is your chance, Byron," I purr. "Come take what you want."

Fairfax just watches, detached. The boy blushes, averting his pretty eyes. A lover's eyes, all lashes and poems and sighs. I'd like to bruise 'em black, suck out their juices for my supper. Stab in a knife and watch 'em pop.

I don't know why I hate him. I just do.

Laughter bursts from my chest. A big, ugly belly laugh, like she won't never allow, and I swoon a little, it feels so good. The world feels good, the light on my face, the stench of chemicals and piss-stained madmen. One day, I'll escape her prison, so help me. Claw my way out through her rib cage if I must. And all this will be MINE . . .

Urgently, the lad grips Fairfax's arm. "The poor child is suffering. We must do something!" *He hesitates.* "You know what I'm saying."

Sir Jed—may I call you Jeddy? Ha ha!—shakes the grip off like the arrogant sod he is. "Don't even think it, Starling. You know there are grave side effects. And we can't do anything without* him."

Him. That unconscious emphasis, the way everyone does, an underline or an exclamation point. Our guardian, the man without a face. The monster behind the curtain. Aye, Eliza. Mark my words. He hides his face, you rot-witted chit. Think he's Prince friggin' Charming?

"But look at her! You know what will happen if we don't act. Eliza is a good girl. D'you want that on your conscience?"

I laugh, fondling myself even while she flinches. Look to your own conscience, Byron. I'm a good girl, too. Come and see.

"Out of the question." *The surgeon's lips compress, a cruel slash.* "She can stay here until it subsides and then she's going home, before anyone finds out. Now help me or get out of my way."

The two of them grab us, forcing us into the crisp canvas jacket. We scream and kick and gnash our teeth, but Fairfax whips out an ugly steel needle and jabs it into our throat. Cold poison oozes into our flesh, a creeping plague, and that precious world wavers and darkens and there's nothing but silence . . .

Eliza inhaled sharply, sucking in water. Panicked, she fought upwards. Her face broke the surface, and she clutched the bathtub's rim and spluttered until the water was gone.

The sitting room hovered into focus. The fire was dying. The bathwater was cold as a corpse. How long had she been asleep? How long under the surface?

She shivered. "Lizzie? You there?"

Nothing. No sign of the *thing* that had tried to kill her, wrapped cruel fingers around her neck and held her under-water . . .

No. Eliza hugged herself. She'd fallen asleep, slipped into the water, dreamed the whole thing. Yes. That had to be it.

But those nightmare images stuck, clammy like a wet shroud. Locked in a padded cell with Mr. Fairfax. Why? It had felt so real. And Lizzie, taking control of her body like that. With her, Eliza, trapped inside, watching. Powerless to escape.

Was that how Lizzie always felt?

Chilled, she clambered from the bath and huddled in a warm towel. On the table, her wineglass glimmered like blood. She grabbed it and swallowed. Insipid, weaker than the gin Lizzie liked. Compared to her elixir? Like lolly water. She gulped again, heedless of spilling.

Whilst you were so ill. Byron Starling's slip of the tongue at Finch's Pharmacy. His expression of horror.

That awful asylum cell wasn't a dream. It was a *memory.*

And Byron and Marcellus Finch were the key. Marcellus had evaded the truth, and not for the first time. But when Marcellus lied, it was always for a compelling reason—and that reason was invariably Edward Hyde.

Starling's face in that awful vision, still with both eyes, no scars or milky irises. Early twenties at most. Which made her . . . what, fifteen?

The year *before* Lizzie was born.

Lizzie flashed back into view, bending over naked by the hearth, squeezing out her dripping hair. "What a scene! D'you see his face? Priceless!"

Eliza edged back, clutching her towel.

"Not nice being trapped inside, is it? How'd you like *them* apples?" Lizzie swung her hair, firelight gilding her wet skin. She was beautiful. Terrible, a goddess to be placated. And Eliza's heart shrank in terror.

"Why did Mr. Fairfax lock us up?" she whispered. "What did you do?"

Lizzie crowed rich laughter. "Why don't you ask Starling? He's eager to start *that* conversation again."

"Don't be crude." Eliza's bravery tasted false. "You can't fool me. I'd have remembered *that*."

Lizzie stretched out on the hearth rug and luxuriated, wriggling her shoulders. "Ask Eddie why he gave you the elixir, then. I *dare* you."

Eliza gritted her teeth. How could they ever resolve this? How could either of them be free? "Why am I always the last to know? Curse you, Lizzie, this is *my* life!"

"Is it just?" Lizzie jumped up, rage like gunflash. "We'll see about that!" And she dived for the cluttered shelf, and grabbed a glass phial.

Not the elixir. The wolf cure potion.

"No!" Eliza jumped forwards, her towel falling. "That's not finished. It's dangerous. You can't—"

Grinning, Lizzie popped the cork and chugged the vile blue brew down.

Eliza yelled. Lizzie hurled the phial away. Glass smashed into the hearth, shards and blue droplets flying—and in a triumphant flash, Lizzie vanished.

Silence. Just the crackling fire.

My life. Her words mocked her, shouted back in Lizzie's voice. *This is my life, too.*

Trembling, she crept into bed. The smooth sheets were cool, the quilt soft. Her muscles creaked with exhaustion, but she lay rigid and shaking. She couldn't relax. Visions of those fleshy white mouse-lumps spiraled, threatening. Separate forms. Transcendental identities. Twins.

Her veins itched, scoured by new and disturbing sensations. Was it the dark alchemy, eating like acid at her blood? Or was the whole episode just a madwoman's black fancy?

Sick laughter choked her. She'd wanted to re-test the mixture. Here was her chance. Those mice had taken weeks to grow their fleshy counterparts—but in controlled conditions, with nutrition and care. What would happen to her, with none of those?

And what in the meantime? She didn't dare imagine. The last time Lizzie had tried one of Quick's concoctions, it hadn't ended well. What a fool Eliza was.

The candles flickered low. The clock ticked, interminable. Lizzie didn't return.

Surely, sleep would never come.

But it did. And she dreamed again of Bethlem Asylum, her wrist chained to the wall in that greasy padded cell, skittering rats and the stench of excrement and the ragged howls of madmen.

Sunlight stabs in the barred window, and I claw at my stinking shift, screaming at that tiny patch of outside world to have mercy. It's me, Eliza. I'm not insane. Let me out!

It comes out as gibberish. Just groans and whines, like a wounded animal.

The door bolts clunk. I crouch, ready to fight.

But it isn't Starling or Fairfax. It's Remy Lafayette. He smiles at me, tears shimmering as blue as that lost electric sky.

NOTHING LESS THAN A LIFER

AFINGER ON ELIZA'S LIPS JERKED HER AWAKE.
She recoiled into her pillows, blinded by daylight. "Who's there—mmph!" A hand fastened
over her mouth. A long-fingered hand, oddly familiar.

She struggled, but the sheets trapped her. The weight of a
body. Cold sweat broke out. Was it the book thief? She'd be
killed in her bed. Or dishonored by a ham-fisted robber, or . . .
Images of Malachi Todd chewed her nerves, that greedy flash
of steel. "Mmph! Blmphm!"

"Don't mean no harm." A man's voice, strange but not
strange. "Don't you know me?"

At last, her eyes adjusted. Wild black hair, mismatched
dark eyes.

Oh, my. She froze. Johnny eased his hand away. "There
y'are. Quiet-like. No trouble."

Breathless, she scooted back, dragging the sheets up to
her chin. *Bluff. Pretend I don't know him. Get him out of my
house.* "How did you get in here?"

He just shrugged. Stupid question. Johnny was a thief,
after all. Tall, loose-limbed, wearing a dusty coat whose hue

transcended the word *yellow*. A pleasant enough sort, if you enjoyed underfed rogues who washed less often than they lied.

Eliza shivered, the unfamiliar bedroom no comfort. Had Johnny known about her and Lizzie all along? How had he found this house? Had he followed her? Watched her after all, that morning she thought she'd slipped from his bed unnoticed?

"Well, I've no idea what you want, but—"

"Please." His eyes held black desperation. "I wouldn't come here, and I ain't asking questions. God knows it's none of mine. But Eddie's in trouble and I need Lizzie right now."

Her throat parched, a sour prickly taste. That dark alchemy mixture Lizzie had so triumphantly quaffed. What would the effects be? Would her elixir even work anymore?

"What kind of trouble?"

"Ain't for a lady's ears, miss. Begging your pardon."

Such a pretty thing, whispered her father's voice gleefully in her ear. *Let me show you . . .*

She didn't want to know. But the thought of Crane's letter to Hyde itched, unresolved . . . and an idea struck her. One hundred pounds was a lot of money. Too much for Hyde to entrust to any grotty reprobate who happened by. "Answer me this, then. Did you deliver a sum of money for Mr. Hyde last evening? To Red Lion Square?"

A fluid shrug.

Aha! "Did the lady there say for whom it was intended?"

"Some cove she called 'that dirty-minded eavesdropper.'" The ghost of a sly, attractive grin. "For you, that's free."

"Generous of you, sir," she said coldly. "And did you lay eyes on this lascivious listener?"

A velvety head-shake. "Offered to stay and cosh the bastard, but she wouldn't have it."

"I see. I'm afraid she died last night. Murdered."

"Oh." He looked faintly incensed. "Waste o' coin, then."

"I suppose so."

Silence stretched. *Warm skin, stroking fingers, the sweet scent of flowers . . .*

Awkwardly, Johnny stood, cracking multiple knuckles. He didn't seem to know where to look. "I'll linger out front," he said, and silent as a breath, he slipped out.

Eliza banged her head back against the bed frame. Damn it. She should have yelled for Brigham, called the police, had the scoundrel arrested.

But Eddie was in trouble. And she knew what she must do.

Stiff with dread, she padded to the mantel. Her skin tingled, oddly eager. On the shelf, her elixir hissed and beckoned. The warm black glass slicked her palm, the sweet-bitter scent making her shudder and groan . . .

Squoink! I slip out like a wet fish, a wrench of such sheer pleasure that I cry out, my breath on fire. Colors glare, overbright, the chill on my naked skin a delight. She's barely swallowed a mouthful, and for good measure, I chug the rest, and it's like gin and absinthe and molten gold, boiling into my veins to make me immortal.

Whatever that dark alchemy hellbrew did to us, I like it. Ha ha! Our own living experiment. Where's your sense of adventure, Eliza? Will I get my own greasy pale mouse-thing, d'you think, as the days go by? Or will it simply become easier to cast Eliza off, to ignore her god-rotted disdain that scratches in my bones? That prickly blue mixture could be a godsend. Pity there's no more.

I un-knot my red dress, the one she used to carry our stuff. Looks like she dragged it backwards through a bush, and her corset is antsy tight like usual, but it'll do. My hair's a mess, but I leave it. No time to waste.

Cane in hand, I slink out. Corridor's empty, floorboards warped with age. The stairs creak as I descend. This place stinks of alchemy and dead animals in jars, the echoes of dead scientists' whispers, the sighs of sleepers long passed on.

Ooh. I shiver, delighted. Fucking house is haunted, Eliza. Told you so.

But her nightmare of the asylum slides over my tongue like oil. *What did I do,* indeed? Fact is, I don't rightly recall, despite how I taunted her. But it can't be good.

I make it to the front door. Don't see Charlie Brigham, by God, and what sort of a butler d'you call yourself? That stain under the rug is faded, but I still see it. Don't think you can hide, you sinister stain of guilt, you. Oho! My mother, bones askew, crimson trickling from her lips as she fights to breathe, move, stay alive. Her lover's shadow lurches on the wall, terrifying as it treads closer.

Did you beg for your life, Madeleine? Did you curse him to hell? Or did you forgive him with your last breath for loving you to death?

I imagine them, their bodies entwining in sweat. It makes me think of Rose, his *duchessa,* his pretty thing, and then I recall poor dead Turquoise Tim and I don't want to think about Eddie no more.

All he ever wanted is someone to love him. Madeleine didn't. Look what happened.

Outside, garish late-afternoon sun waters my eyes. Johnny's waiting at the fence, jigging up and down like an impatient beggar. No time to ask how he knew, or what the hell he's doing breaking into Eliza's house looking for me. Thank Christ. Don't want no talk of Eliza and her goddamn respectable life. That over-sized palace, her servants and fancy clothes and Remy's sapphire the size of a fucking goose egg on her finger.

I pull him in for a kiss, and he kisses me back, but it's absent, half-hearted. I shove him. "Shy all of a sudden? Who are you, and what'd you do with the real Wild Johnny?"

But I can already hear what he's thinking. *How will this work, when you're her and she's you and your heart lives in two places? Why d'you even want me, when you can have all that? D'you even love me, Lizzie? How can you, when SHE'S watching?* Rage burns bitter in my mouth. Not warm-sweet-bitter like elixir. Cold-dark-bitter, like hatred.

Johnny sighs. "Lizzie, you gotta come with. Eddie's in trouble."

We set off across the square, mud sloshing in cartwheel ruts and carriages fighting for space. "What manner of trouble?"

"Soho. A dead girl." Johnny walks fast, gaze fixed ahead.

I scramble to keep up. "Girls die in Soho every day."

"Not like this. Mrs. Fletcher's, a streetwalker called Saucy May."

Oho. Inspector Fuck-face's witness, what testified to

Fancy-Britches Man. "So? What's it to do with the price of eels?"

"Eddie were there last night. And he can't remember what he done."

His meaning sinks in, a chill like death. "What d'you mean, can't remember? If he were that plastered, how can he have . . ."

A tight shrug. "Dunno. But that's the word."

My mouth salts, dry like prison biscuit. Saucy May seen the Slasher. Could've proved Eddie's innocent. Now she's dead. And we'll never know.

I grip my cane, dragon's head hissing. If Eddie goes down, Johnny and I go with him. "Whose word? Jack friggin' Dawkins, puttin' it about that Eddie's the Slasher? I'll have his whale-arse guts for ribbons."

"All in good time. And without Tom o' Nine. Jimmy ain't laid eyes since night afore last."

Regent's Circle is busy, and we cross it at a run. "Handsome Tom? A shilling he's shacked up in some married lady's boudoir."

A dark head-shake. "Tom's in lavender. The Dodger's making his move, Lizzie. Gotta take care of Eddie, right slick." He leads me into a dim alley by the grim electric-fenced workhouse, where shit splashes the bricks and the groans of hungry inmates shiver through my bones. "I've brought one who can help. Don't take on."

"Take on? Why in hell would I—" A shadow shifts, and I blunder backwards into the wall. "Jesus bleedin' Christ."

Velvety darkness oozes, and shapes into a man.

Sunshine, my father calls him. Dragged him from New-gate Prison in flames, locked him in a cage for a rainy day. Eddie's idea of a lark. Eddie, my friends, is off his friggin' rocker.

The light falls on that awful, familiar face, and I can't help a gasp of horror. The right side's still pale and perfect, those porcelain cheekbones fresh from Eliza's nightmares.

The left side? A weeping, burn-scarred horror.

Mr. Todd smiles—a lopsided thing of blackened, terrible beauty—and tips his hat. His right hand is unspoiled, stylish, terrifying. "Hello, Miss Hyde. Did you miss me?"

THE MAN OF GENIUS

I PULL MY SWORD, QUIVERING STEEL. "JOHNNY, WHAT the fuck?"

Johnny lays a hand on my arm. "He don't mean nothing—"

"He's a friggin' maniac! Lucky he ain't already splashed the walls with our blood."

"Think, princess. The Dodger's coming for us. We need to know if Eddie done it. Want an expert on murder?" Johnny jerks his thumb at Todd. "Here he is."

"*If* he done it?" My blade wavers, mirroring my twisting guts. "You think Eddie's *guilty*?"

"Can't ask Saucy May, now can we? You got a better idea?"

"Do carry on discussing me as if I'm absent," says Todd carelessly. "It's positively enlightening." He adjusts diamond-pinned cuffs, his ruined left hand crackling. Johnny must've fixed him up, because that rotted Sunshine-suit is gone, in favor of a black hat and trousers, and a sleek coat of gorgeous claret red. His crimson hair springs in unruly clumps, as if a cruel child hacked at a doll with rusted scissors.

I back off. "Stay away."

But Todd don't advance. He just *looks*. Famished for color, thirsty for rainbow sights. Devouring my red frills, Johnny's yellow coat, the sparkle of light along my blade, my rippling mahogany hair. His hungry eyes glitter, lunatic fairy green.

I feel naked. I want to cover up. Punch his corpse-prince face and yell *keep your god-rotted eyes to yourself, crackbrain,* because all that staring is like making love, and I don't want him fucking me.

He sighs, enraptured. "Those dusky fuchsia ruffles are practically *edible*. Extra-spectral, you know. And all the better beside antimony yellow!" He devours Johnny's glaring eyesore of a coat like a starving man would food. "Truly a spectacular shade, sir. Poisonous, you're aware. Too much lead shrivels your brain, not to mention other valuable parts. You ought to take care."

His voice rasps, as if the fire has ruined more than his face. Rot my arse red if I'll admire him, but lesser folk would've died from what he's suffered. The undamaged half only makes him more horrible. And inside, Eliza howls and begs me to look away.

So I stare a little longer. Hmm. Still a looker, Todd, even after that fire's taken its vengeance. Beauty corrupted, a priceless artwork besmirched with filth. That good half—skin still smooth, those fragile cheekbones and pointed chin—it overlays a messy echo of pain. A façade, over a mass of frightful scars.

I know that feeling.

Truth is, he's just the cove I need. Eliza can't be trusted. When she examines Saucy May's corpse for the police, d'you think she'll do the right thing by Eddie, the way she sneers and calls him "killer"? Not bloody likely.

As for Inspector Hoity-Toity, he ain't no Royal Society nit-wit, but in these days of rampant sedition and sorcerers' lies, the crushers are nervous as nelly about civic unrest. They'd screw the King of Rats on less than a whore's say-so before you can yell *threat to public safety*.

Mr. Todd, *au contraire*, has a score of bloodied reasons for not involving the crushers. And Johnny's right: if anyone can read a madman's intent in his leavings, it's this crimson-haired loon.

A smile curls my lips. How's that, Eliza? Think I can't collect evidence, too? Fat good your lenses and swabs and electro-spectrical gadgets have done so far. I ain't dropping Eddie in the cess just because Todd gives you the shivering nasties.

It's funny. I feel . . . *apart* from her, somehow. As if she's faded into distance. Is that prickly blue mouse potion working its magic? Truth is, I don't care. Now, Miss Lizzie, is the time to have some fun—but be on your guard, lest Todd cast his dark enchantment on *you*.

I eye Johnny coolly, a little brassed off at his front, to be honest. For sure, Todd's an expert on murder. A useful idea. But if Eddie's guilty—and the shift in Johnny's crooked gaze tells me he fears that's so—then who better than Todd to put Eddie out of his misery?

A killer to end a killer. An executioner. Smart lad, my Johnny, damn his pretty eyes.

"All right," says I, grudgingly resheathing my blade, "but

he's back in his cage as soon as we're sorted. Todd, we've a murder scene to suss out. You in?"

Todd's eyes light up. "Capital. Most excellent. Kind of you, I'm sure, since you got me into this mess in the first place. Your generosity in releasing me is heartwarming."

Now we get to it. "Let's get one thing straight. *She* got your lunatic arse arrested, not me."

He don't seem discouraged. "Come, Miss Hyde, we both know that isn't what happened."

"Live with it, Todd, she shopped you. But only 'cause I couldn't get to you first."

A predatory smile. "You must think me so dull-witted. My masterwork would have served you excellently. Please don't insult me by pretending it wasn't exactly what you wanted. What a pity you were too afraid to take me up on it."

My stomach turns salty. His bleedin' *masterwork* were to slit the throats of all who knew our secret. Eliza's servants, Marcellus Finch, Inspector Griffin, Remy Lafayette. Everyone.

Truth is, 'twould've solved a lot of my problems. No more life for Eliza equals more life for me. But I ain't murdering to get it. Miss Lizzie ain't the one seduced by this fiend's twisted logic. Not I.

Defiantly I fold my arms. "Step out of line and I'll end you, so help me."

"As usual, all promises and no action." A mischievous green wink. "Consider me in your debt, if it sweetens the deal. What favor might I owe you when you need it most?"

Fuck his favors. He's playing with me. Life and death, a pretty crimson game.

Just the cove I need, then. Never mind he deserves to hang fifty times over for what he's done.

Aye. I swallow a hungry grin. Ain't because Eliza is cringing right now, recalling how he hypnotized her into acting the fool. His bloodthirsty lunacy her scripture, the crazed twinkle of his eye her shining light.

Was it love, Eliza, that special shade of madness? Did you secretly yearn for death? Or did you just crave him, the way any woman wants a man?

Honestly, I don't dare ask. I just know I can't let your screaming and thrashing and scratching in my insides change my mind.

Todd's my ally now. Live with it or leave . . . oh, but you can't. So shut the fuck up.

I turn back to Johnny. Still he fidgets, that disillusioned shimmy in his eyes. As if he's seeing me in a whole new light. *How can you love me, Lizzie? Because* she *doesn't. And she's better than you.*

I drop Mr. Todd a sinister smile.

Mr. Todd smiles back. Half prince, half monster.

Ain't because I *like* it when she suffers. Not at all.

An hour later, we're promenading through Soho towards Mrs. Fletcher's, the talented Mr. Todd and me.

Gaslights flicker in chilly breeze, dancing on the windows of gin palaces and brothels, theaters and low lodging houses and dirty grog shops. Prostitutes prowl, finery and squalor blended. Mud splashes my skirts, the ground slippery and uneven. Drunken revelers spill out onto the road, stumbling and thumping each other and singing at the top of their lungs. "God save the king!" a fat gin soak yells, and vomits on his boots. Today's the dimwit king's birthday, and folks is entitled to a party, even if we ain't invited to the fancy one at Buckingham Palace.

Every few seconds, I can't help but shoot a nervous glance at Todd. I'm a rabbit marching alongside a lion who's promised to be good. We left Johnny behind—palaver with Fishy Dolittle, he claimed, and I can't blame him for the lie, though he and I need our own palaver, and sooner rather than later—and now I'm wishing we hadn't.

But Todd just saunters along, wearing an entranced smile. As if he ain't the legendary Razor Jack, what murdered a score and more. That claret coat—Venetian red, says he—shimmers faintly in the gaslight, enchanted. Even in this squalid place, light seeks him out like a lover, abandoning all else to darkness. From here, I can't see his burned half. He's the Mr. Todd of old, pretty and crimson-haired, enough like everyone else to be the worst kind of monster.

"So," ventures I, more to quiet my nerves than for having aught to say, "tell me what you've heard of this Slasher."

"Only what I've read in the papers. Which is quite a piece, as it happens." Todd's gaze glues to the blue satin bodice of a dolly-girl as she sashays by. "Did you know Eliza's charming post-mortem reports have been published in full? No pictures, sadly. I do miss the police gazettes. All those appalling Lombrosian lithographs of *L'uomo delinquente,* flourishing their garrotes above maidens in distress. Nonsense, of course. Whence the 'born criminal' when crime itself is a human construct? These illustrators have quite the lowest form of imagination."

Todd's eye latches onto a drooling mountebank's harlequin coat. The fool leers, gripping a rusted iron cudgel, and I have to drag Todd away. "Keep your bloody eyes to yourself, can't you—shit!"

A single electric-red eye glints from the depths of a muddy alley. I scuttle backwards, cursing. Fucking Enforcers . . .

But I halt, prickling with *not-right*. Not a hulking brass machine, but a slim figure in a long cape. The head turns, and light falls on a familiar face. A woman, one soft cheek scarred with shining steel.

Miss Burton.

I frown. The Philosopher's special agent, slumming it with the great unwashed by a Soho gin palace?

Casual-like, I sidle up to see what she's about. Beside her is a gent with glittering white hair and a deformed, shrunken hand like a crow's claws. A silver chain with a black stone shines around his throat. He hands her a slip of paper. She stuffs it in a pocket, where another folded letter pokes out an inch or two.

I brush past, and light as you please, I dip the letter from her pocket. Oho! Think Miss Lizzie's spent years following Wild Johnny about for no profit? Her hip shifts, and for a heart-stopping moment, I think she'll turn, spear me with those evil black-light eyes, and holler *stop, thief!*

But her back stays turned. Triumphantly, I slink away into the crowd and unfold the letter. Thick expensive paper, a knotty black hand I can barely read.

Ignore what was said this afternoon. The funds are at your disposal. Threaten them, pay them off, do whatever you have to. This must be ours, in absolute secrecy.

Speak to our mutual friend. I trust in your discretion.

By way of signature, there's an inked animal sketch, a little horse's head with a horn.

A unicorn. Now where've I seen one o' them recently?

But the crowd's already swept us by. Todd ain't even noticed. He's gawping like a Yorkshire yokel in Haymarket, at flowers, dresses, lights, costumes, all the colors of the rainbow. His eyes are glassy. I can hear him breathing hard. He's practically drooling.

"Christ, can't you stop that?" I elbow him. "You're scaring folks. They don't like it when you stare. Get it?"

He looks faintly surprised. As if them liking it or not ain't never crossed his mind.

"This Soho Slasher," mutters I. "You was saying?"

"Only that I understand there are missing organs and the like." He picks his way across a puddle, and offers me his hand. I don't take it, and he smiles, lickerish, before withdrawing. "Extravagant use of his tools, beyond the usual death blows and what have you. A furious *artiste*. Or," he adds slyly, "an exuberant one. We shall see. I confess, I'm looking forward to examining his efforts."

"Aye, I bet you are. Craving a nice lick of blood?" I point at the blue-and-gold façade of Mrs. Fletcher's. "This is it."

"Blood, Miss Hyde, is never a waste, if one does it properly." He wrinkles his nose as we hop up the steps, as if the place is a rotten tomato. "*Gauche.* And they say I have strange ideas about recreation." He holds the door for me, a gent taking his lady for a treat.

Mrs. Fletcher flounces from her parlor, a huff of green silk. She takes one look at Todd's wrecked face and diamond cuff links, and gives a fulsome smile. "Lovely to see you so soon, Miss Hyde. Can I assist you and your escort with something more . . . exotic?"

"You're fucking joking."

Todd tips his hat. A well-mannered walking corpse, a horror of the finishing school graveyard. "Malachi Todd, at your service. But no. Sadly, your worthy profession isn't to my solace. I prefer a more impulsive attitude to fun. One never knows when the next opportunity might pop up."

A flare of smoky interest. "We cater to all tastes. I keep many specialists, for the right price. A game, perhaps, of your choosing?"

"Madam," says Todd with a delicately threatening smile, "my choosing is far from a game. Shall I show you?"

"Trust me, missus, turn this one down." I push between them into the hall. Scrubbed timber floors festooned with rugs, Queen Anne furniture, flowers arranged in large pots. Somewhere, someone tinkles an old harpsichord. "Johnny sent us, so no bullshit. Tell me about Saucy May."

"So sad." Mrs. Fletcher lets her face fall into perfect pity. Jesus. Next she'll dab away a tear. "The poor girl is—was— one of my street tenants. Not a house girl, you understand. She rented her room per client."

"And this particular client?"

"We operate a strict regime of privacy, no names or questions asked." Her eyes are cold black stones. A hard woman from a hard profession. No time for sentimentality when your friends are dropping like flies from the pox or starvation or long freezing nights, and even when you can find a mark, you're as like to get beaten as paid. "Our gentlemen prefer it. You understand."

"Right," I grumble, sounding like Harley Griffin, "a dozen girls lounging about every which way and not one of 'em seen a thing. So who found the mess?"

"One of my girls. Rose—I believe you know her? May hadn't emerged during the night and she was worried." Fletcher dabs her nose with a handkerchief. "My girls are like sisters. Such a terrible day for them all."

"You never called in the crushers?"

"Certainly not. I shan't allow their sort in here. Poking around, making vile insinuations." Fletcher's mouth twists. "Mr. Wild insisted I leave everything as it was. My girls are beside themselves. The smell, you see. I've brought in flowers, but . . ." A sigh. "I'm extremely busy, Miss Hyde. Do you wish to see this ghastly display or not?"

She ushers us up to the landing. On the gilded couches, those twins still lounge. Their eyes shine dully from lack of sleep, and their smiles look strained, as if their cheeks ache. Plaster girls, about to break.

We approach Eddie's favorite room, and my heart lurches, but thankfully Fletcher waves us up another flight, down a badly lit corridor to a room at the end.

She throws the door open. "Forgive me if I don't come in."

"One more. Did King Eddie come by here last night?"

A measuring stare. "I'm afraid I can't say. Client confidentiality, you understand." And she sweeps away on a cloud of silken green *screw-you*.

The smell hits me first. A hot, fleshy scent, half-spoiled meat mixed with piss or stale sweat. I cover my nose. Jesus. I don't know if I can go in there. How does Eliza do it, day in and day out? Does she love death so much? Or is she merely forestalling her own by wallowing in theirs?

Todd inhales, and his good cheek reddens, in memory of something not quite respectable. "Do you detect that bitter overtone? That's the flavor of fear. Our subject had time to be afraid of what was coming."

"Great. Thanks for that." Now I don't want to breathe in. Inside, it's cheap and dingy, gaslight bleeding through a greasy window. Dusty dressing table, washstand, wooden bedstead . . . and the shape on that sagging bed don't look like a woman no more.

Nightgown ripped, limbs splayed. Flesh torn and sliced, white nubs of bone exposed. Walls and bedclothes sprayed with gore. And the head . . .

Christ. He's hacked the head almost clean off. And the face, well, ain't no face left. Just carved flesh and hanks of bloodied yellow hair.

I squeeze my eyes shut. But the images linger, a blood-spattered phantasmagoria, and in it I see Eddie.

My father, eager and unsteady, drunk to his eyeballs. Crushing with clumsy hands, heedless of bruises, the thin girl on the

*bed with wide pleading eyes. Swinging that glinting blade with
a song on his lips, blood spurting onto his shirtfront.* "Maggie,
Maggie Mayyy . . . they've taken you awayyy . . ."

Stttrrrk! Light flares. I jump, ready to run.

Mr. Todd just shakes out a match and pockets the box.
He's found a candle, and the flamelight lovingly caresses him.
"Shall we take a look?"

Light leaps over poor Saucy May's remains, a cruel landscape of fleshy hills and blood-soaked valleys. Todd exhales.
"Eliza's observations are meticulous, if thin on insight. A surgical blade, yes. Not a butcher's knife."

"An expert, then?" Steeling myself, I creep closer.

"Hardly." Todd strokes the ravaged flesh with one fingertip.
"How shallow the cuts, how hesitant the exposure of viscera.
Observe this stretch mark. The skin is ripped, not sliced.
Odd, wouldn't you say, for a man who delights in such work?"

Shadowy images dance, and I feel sick. *My father pins her
down and stabs. Blood squirts, and with a gleeful roar, he grabs
a fistful of flesh and pulls . . .*

"Six strokes, maybe seven, just to sever the windpipe.
Surely a surgical instrument ought to be sharp. How does
one even achieve such inept results? The incompetence of
artists these days. It's positively scandalous."

May's pearly eyeballs gleam, her bright hair dull with
crusted blood. *Eddie grabs her hair and twists, crimson splashing from her opened throat . . .*

I drag my eyes away. Jesus, this place is chewing my nerves
raw. But blood smears the peeling wallpaper by the bed,
too. *He falls back, leaning on the wall to catch his breath . . .*
"Handprint?"

Todd's eyes flare with interest. "But no arterial arc. There's skin under her nails, of all things. How careless. And look at this." He prods at a yellower stain on the girl's ripped nightgown. "Vomitus. Honestly, does this imposter think me an amateur?"

"More like a flop-brained loon with a blood fetish . . . hold on. What d'you mean, imposter?"

"Plagiarism, Miss Hyde. Passing off. Theft, in fact, of the vilest sort." He taps an exposed nub of bone with a thoughtful finger. "Do you see what's happened here? No? Well, it's to be expected, if you've no experience. I've made quite a study of blood, you know." He sets the candle down. "Let me show you something. Your hand, if you please."

Let me show you, he'd whispered to Eliza that night in his studio. *Let me show you how I love you.* "Ha! Not on your life, nutbag."

A sorrowful sigh. "I did ask nicely." Like a snake, he strikes, forcing my right wrist up over my head.

"Oi! Get the hell off me—ugh!" My back hits the wall, and effortlessly he twists my cane away and tosses it aside.

Eliza's screaming at me. *Why, Lizzie? Why did you trust him?* But that prickly blue mixture I swallowed has sunk deep into my flesh, and she seems far away, no help to me now. Is he hiding that twinkling razor in his pocket, thirsty to drink my life? His strange lunatic heat, his ruined skin, his crust-edged lips. The burned husk of beauty. His awful scent curdles my blood. The memory of Eliza's paralysis—and how I raged against it to no avail.

God rot it, if I had my stiletto I'd finish him right here. Thrust hot steel into his belly, swallow his coppery groan with my tongue, whisper into his mouth as he dies. *This is for my Eliza. You could've stopped her loving you, but you didn't and this is for her.*

"Let me go." But my voice withers like a lost promise, and I curse and get ready to clock him. Jam my knee into his balls, if the cold-blooded fucker's even got any, and run while he retches . . .

Todd's cunning smile makes me blanch. "Merely a demonstration. If I desired your death, do you imagine you'd still be breathing?"

Good point. Furious, I nod at him to carry on.

"Very well. Imagine a horizontal orientation of this struggle we enact. I am on my knees, you on your back. I restrain one-handed"—he tightens his grip, and watches with interest as I flinch—"because I require the other to wield my tools. The subject fights . . ." He waits politely. "If you please."

"Oh." I wriggle and kick. "Like this?"

"Very nice." Fluently, he evades and restrains me, hip and knee here, forearm there, and mimes clocking me hard under the chin. "And I reply thus."

A disorienting blow, to dizzy and confuse. This is how he does it. A crazy-arse slaughterhouse johnny, quieting his beasts for the kill.

My bones shrink in horror, but I'm strangely warm inside, some weird new seduction that lures me from reason. What must it be like to wield such effortless power? To provoke such terror, to rule over life and death?

To grab all the hurt the world ever hurled at you, and hurl it right back? Isn't that real freedom?

"Now, if I strike like so—" With fluid grace, Todd slits my

throat with an imaginary blade, and indicates with a musical flutter of fingers. "Look where the crimson will flow. To the front, up, over. Some secondary splashing here. Even taking into account the initial euphoric confusion, the struggling and dying and so on, one would expect a more melodic arrangement of spatters." He lets me go, abruptly cold. "Not this clumsy re-enactment."

Huh. Whatever else you can say for him, the man knows his murder. "You mean that ain't a real blood spatter?"

"*Au contraire.*" He mimes again, cupping his maimed hand and flicking his wrist. "I swipe up a handful, I throw. Out of rage? No. Because I want it to *look* as if the subject were alive when the performance began. But now my fingers are coated. Do I glory in it, as an artist might? Do I taste or otherwise indulge? No." He points to a finger-smudge on a clean patch of sheet. "I *wipe*, of all things. Clearly I'm no *connoisseur* of the macabre."

I stare, oddly detached. "So it's staged. But why?"

Absently, he strokes May's crusted hair. "His hand shows no strength, no artistry, and dare I mention it, no *pleasure*. He cringes at what must be done. He vomits on his work out of disgust. For a man who's eagerly created five masterpieces already . . ." Todd sniffs, dismissive. "No, and no, and once again no. This is not your Soho Slasher. This"—and he waves a disdainful hand—"is something else entirely."

"An imitator." My heart sinks. *Two* knife-wielding crazy men.

"Or an accomplice." Todd licks ruined lips, as if it's a delicious idea fit for eating. "Yes. I think so. So *cui bono*, Miss Hyde? That's the question."

I scowl. "Screw me with a toothpick and call me a lolly, Todd. Shove your poxy Latin up your arse and talk English."

His eyes twinkle. "Really. Anyone would think you a common slattern on the make."

"Anyone'd think you a gentleman, too. Don't make it so."

He retrieves the candle, light tarnishing his scars with gold. "I ask, *to whose profit?* Who benefits from this sordid charade? Why would this unwilling person slaughter the only subject who can identify the real Slasher? And the answer becomes apparent."

"Great," mutters I, the irony glaring. "What kind of sick freak-show act protects a murderer?"

Todd smiles thinly. "It's someone who loves him, Miss Hyde. Given the circumstances, it's a wonder we're not all suspecting *you*."

CUI BONO

I GOGGLE, AND FOR THE FIRST TIME IT OCCURS TO ME that Mr. Todd might wish my father ill. Eddie rescued him from Newgate, sure. Eddie also locked him in a cage. And never say Malachi Todd missed a chance for vengeance.

Shit. I edge away. "Don't be ridiculous—"

A cough in the doorway makes me spin.

It's Rose, Eddie's duchess, bouncing pigtails and bruised red lips. She's wearing a tight-laced black burlesque dancer's dress, flesh swelling up in handfuls. "Mess, ain't it?"

She looks well, considering my father's tender ways with love. My mouth brims with questions I suddenly don't want answers for. "Eddie here, then?"

Rose chews a candied apple on a stick. "Sleeping it off. Couldn't hardly stand by the time he'd emptied last night." She assesses Todd with professional interest. "And who are you, handsome?"

Todd grins like an eel. "I'm her crime scene expert. Exquisitely bloody *tableaux* are my specialty. Do you know that your eyes hold an uncommon shade? Egyptian blue, no less.

Most pernicious to manufacture. I once tried preserving them, you know," he adds blandly. "Eyeballs, I mean. The results were peculiarly disappointing. The pupils just dilate when the subject expires, and the pigments decay too quickly to make good paint."

Rose stares blankly. "Y'what?"

Jesus, the things that come out of his mouth. "Never mind. Tell us about May."

"Found her around nine." Rose stretches an artful leg. "Last night, she told me . . . well, maybe you ain't interested."

I flip her a crown.

She plucks it like a plum and tucks it between her breasts. "May told me what she seen that night. Outside the doss house where the Slasher killed Turquoise Tim."

"This cove in fancy britches, aye." I force my voice steady. "Why'd she ping him for the Slasher?"

"She were in the alley turning a trick, and seen Fancy Britches legging it out the back, right afore the screaming started."

I lick parched lips. "Didn't know 'is name, then?"

A shrug.

I hold my breath, a sharp edge. "So he weren't Eddie Hyde."

Rose gapes, as if I've grown an extra nose. "All the girls know King Eddie, bless his hungry cock. He were live as a jumping bean in here that night. Too busy screwing me up and sideways to fart, let alone carve up Turquoise Tim. Jesus, the shit folks talk." She sucks her lolly. "'Twere more. May said she seen a second bloke with Fancy Britches."

Todd speaks. But I'm barely hearing. All those bloodthirsty pictures? Just a mirage. A madwoman's dream.

Eddie ain't guilty.

Relief staggers me, a sucker punch of shame. I'd swallowed Eliza's treachery. I'd really believed my father were the Slasher.

Certainly. A sarcastic whisper, that demon I can't be rid of. Is it Eliza, fighting her way back? Or just my own conscience? *Because Rose is completely objective about Eddie, after they've been lovers for weeks. Eddie murdered our MOTHER, Lizzie. Once a killer, always a killer. It's in our BLOOD. He's a monster and so are you.*

My vision fogs scarlet, and I claw for Eliza's throat.

Only she ain't there. I realize Rose is talking, and I force my hands down, that prickly blue mixture burning my throat like bile. "A toff square-rigged," says she, "with a funny face, hanging about a-waiting the other to get his load off." She glances over her shoulder. "May had done Fancy Britches the week previous," she whispers. "Tried some ugly games, so she kicked him in the jewels and ran for it."

She hasn't asked for another coin, hisses demon-Eliza. *Not since you mentioned Hyde. Working for nothing all of a sudden?*

I fight to ignore her. But I remember my Johnny's words of wisdom—*anything free is shit*—and my veins crackle cold.

Todd smiles delicately. "So imagining this elaborately trousered ex-customer to be the Soho Slasher, frightened in retrospect by her hairsbreadth escape, May runs to our tragic Inspector Griffin of the Metropolitan Police."

Rose nodded. "Scared her stiff, it did. But Funny-Face, she never seen him before."

"Most instructive, madam. Sadly, we must be on our way. Do take care of those eyes. I'd hate them to be spoiled before their time." Todd bows, and steers me out.

On the landing, my legs buckle.

Bang! My kneecaps bruise, and it's Todd what helps me up, Todd what stops me falling on the stairs, slips a fevered arm beneath mine and practically carries me out into the street, where night has fallen, sparkling bright with gaslights and torches.

I won't have to beg Todd to kill my own father. Eddie ain't a monster. And neither am I.

The crowd flows around us, blurred rainbows. The world gleams brighter, more alive, colors spiked afresh with strange beauty. I'm dizzy, drunk, delirious. I take wheezing gulps of frigid Soho air, the stink of shit and mud and stale gin never so precious as it is now.

I want to bottle this moment. This one dazzling instant in my sick and sorry existence when there's *hope*.

Todd grabs me, keeps me on my feet. Is this what he sees, in all those colors he craves: a priceless moment that always dies? A fleeting beauty to be preserved only in death? Do I understand him at last, this creature of blood?

My flesh stings with poison. I don't want to. But I don't care. He smells of absinthe and copper and the desperation I know so well, and I fall against him and sob like a lost child.

He stiffens, surprise or distaste, and then his hands settle timidly over my hair. Just a fevered, feather-light breath. Like he don't know what to do.

Eliza screams, a high-pitched blade that skewers my ear-drums to bleeding. I convulse, hair standing out in electric shock. My skin ripples like rubber, it's *our* skin, *our* face, *our* eyes popping like a hanged woman dancing on a rope. Our joints wrench, a shudder of tendon and bone, and *kersplack!*

Eliza shot backwards, heart bursting.

Mr. Todd. Alive.

But only just. Oh, God, the livid ruin of his face . . . The damage was painful to look at. Painful and beautiful and ter-rifying.

Mr. Todd gave a torturous smile that made his scarred lip bleed. "You look well, my sweet. Better than I did after my house burned."

She scrabbled for Lizzie's cane and bared the blade. "Stay away from us." She was breathing hard, hoarse, on edge. Just a single stab of steel . . .

"Why not kill me, Eliza? You've already broken my heart."

"Save it," she hissed. "You have no heart."

A delicate lick of lips. "Your Lizzie might beg to differ."

"Don't you *dare* involve her," she spat. "I should scream your name, show this mob who you are. They'd have your hide."

"But you won't. You never do. Your threats are dust." His fairy-green eyes flashed. "I'm disappointed. Think you wouldn't already know pain, if your pain was what I craved?" A cruel laugh. "You flatter yourself, madam. I've quite moved on. Perhaps you should do the same."

Her grip on the blade shook, and she fought to summon Lizzie's screw-it-all courage. *Gut him right now. Our father would. Nothing easier. What's one more corpse? Todd tricked you. Humiliated you. Killed dozens who deserve bloody justice. Slice him and be done.*

But her grasping nerves found nothing. That prickly blue concoction gurgled sourly in her throat, just an empty flavor with no heart. Without Lizzie, she was hollow. Her courage an empty shell.

"Your indecision mocks me, Doctor." Todd's poisoned whisper pierced her soul. "I thought better of you."

She whirled and fled into the crowd.

Staggering, slamming into walls and lampposts. Shoulders and elbows bumped her. Gaslit windows glared, accusatory. *Run, Eliza, you coward. It's what you're good at.* Every eye held an evil glint, every coat seemed to conceal a weapon. God, this place was full of murderers.

But Todd wasn't following. That was evident. She was still alive.

She stumbled on, curses choking her. She was a fool, as she'd always been a fool for Todd's bright eyes. Should've run him through at last with Lizzie's glinting blade.

But she wasn't a killer. She couldn't surrender to Hyde's taint in her blood.

Even if it meant Todd would go free? To delight once more in slaughter, his victims unavenged?

Sick self-hatred thrashed in her belly. Bleeding Christ, it was the worst kind of cowardice to stand on one's principles when others would suffer. Her convictions were shattered. Her precious justice a joke. Remy would be disgusted. What kind of weakling was she?

The image of that beautiful, terrible oil painting seared into her brain. Pretty Eliza, sleeping while a hungry monster licked its lips. Such shameful vanity, to imagine evil could be tempered by love.

So why couldn't she let it go?

Gritty laughter clanged. *Right. You're just sore 'cause he's ceased to care and you still do. Can't bear to be ignored, can you? How does it feel, Eliza, to be forgotten?*

"Shut up!" Her yell startled a pair of prostitutes as she pushed by. Her reflection lurched in a gin palace window. Wild-eyed, hair raked into knots. The Eliza from her nightmares. A madwoman.

Her brain stretched, sanity tearing thin. Thinking was so difficult. Her head hurt ferociously. *Please, no more pain.* Her fingers clawed at her clothes. So easy, to slip into addled oblivion. Just like the lunatics she'd once treated at Bethlem. So safe . . .

She burst out onto Oxford Street, where nighttime ramblers idled and carriages swept by with electric lights crackling. Glaring relief staggered her. The real world. No ghosts.

Shivering, she gathered her skirts, and ran the rest of the way to Cavendish Square.

A startled Brigham opened the door. "Hipp," she gasped, as the little creature hurtled down the stairs to greet her, "run and telegraph Inspector Griffin. He'll be working late. Tell him . . ."

Dizzily, she caught herself on images of Todd, his burned fingers stroking Saucy May's face. *An accomplice. Passing off. Something else entirely.*

Griffin didn't need yet another impossible victim right now. Chief Inspector Reeve would only use it against him. Three days, Reeve had said, to come up with a lead in the

Slasher case. Three days were nearly up. This would play right into Reeve's hands.

As for Todd . . . Her stomach squirmed. Lying? Perhaps. Ulterior motive? Absolutely. But he wouldn't give her another easy chance to end him. Fact was, she'd nothing to gain by revealing Todd was alive. Reeve already assumed Todd was her lover. If she spoke up now, Reeve would only accuse her of protecting him. Either way, her career was over, and Griffin's, too.

But she'd another suspect available. A man who was undoubtedly guilty—though perhaps not guilty as charged.

Presuming Mr. Todd told true.

Why would he lie, Eliza? He never needed to fake it to addle your wits before.

Hipp ground querulous cogs. "Telegraph. Griffin. Information please."

"Inform Inspector Griffin that his witness Saucy May is dead," she said. "The Slasher, at a brothel called Mrs. Fletcher's. And tell him . . ."

For a moment, her duplicity sickened her. What of her precious justice? Could she frame an innocent man?

But he was far from innocent. She couldn't let personal loyalties interfere, not this time. Lizzie was deluded, clinging to a madwoman's fantasies. And justice was justice. For Saucy May, for Turquoise Tim and all the Slasher's other victims . . . but also for Madeleine Jekyll, hurled down the stairs by her lover in a fit of jealous rage.

Lizzie howled, beating the inside of their skull, her voice oddly distorted by that strange potion that weaved new barriers between them. *Our mother's DEAD, God rot you. She don't give a fig for justice. You just want him gone. You've always hated him for making us what we are, and now you'll destroy him for it and justice be damned.*

Prickly blue guilt stung Eliza's throat, but firmly she swallowed it. "Tell him he should enquire about a man the girls call King Eddie. Real name of Edward Hyde."

LUPUS IN FABULA

THE NEXT DAY, ELIZA ARRIVED EARLY TO ALBEMARLE Street. The day's traffic had barely begun—even the anti-science protesters hadn't yet arrived—and mist sparkled along the cobbles in tentative morning sun.

Light clouds smeared a brightening blue sky. For once her hair wasn't wet, her gloves weren't soaked, her petticoats weren't filthy with mud. Just as well, because she'd come to wheedle information out of Bryon Starling. The alternative was to interrogate Marcellus Finch, and she'd avoided the pharmacy lately, her nerves pinging like grasshoppers. She wasn't ready to confront Finch. Not after he'd lied to her about the project, her illness, the asylum. Everything.

"Bollocks," crowed Lizzie, skipping along the pavement beside her. "Ain't him you're hiding from, is it? Shame if we should ever find out the *truth*."

Did she seem more than usually solid, her skirts not quite so transparent? Was it that prickly blue mixture, taking sinister effect?

"Bollocks yourself," muttered Eliza. Starling knew about

her so-called illness, as much or more as he knew about Project Interlunium. She'd get him to talk, one way or another.

A news-seller danced a jig atop his pile of early-edition broadsheets, red hair sticking up like a porcupine's needles. "Shapeshifters attack! Beauty and the Beast strike again! Get it for a penny!"

Lizzie plucked up a copy and waved it at Eliza. EMPIRE ENVOYS KILLED IN PARIS BLOODBATH, the banner read.

Oh, no. Her heart sank, and she grabbed the paper, scanning it as quickly as she could. The two envoys assassinated, before they'd even commenced negotiations. In "gruesome circumstances," whatever that meant. Nothing about their entourage. Surely it would rate a mention if . . .

She sighed, relieved yet dissatisfied as she tossed the boy a penny. Remy's mission had gone awry, then. What now for him? Did this mean the Empire would go to war?

She smoothed her stained dove-gray skirts, hastily sponged that morning and none too clean. She'd tasked Mr. Brigham to find fresh clothes, but for now this was all she owned. "Never mind all that unladylike politics, Hipp. One must look one's best when courting . . . Hipp? Whatever are you doing?"

Hipp gamboled in the gutter, spindly legs flashing in the sun. "Rat-rat-rat!" he yelled, pouncing on one wriggling brown specimen. The rodent squeaked, thrashing its fat tail until Hipp let go with a dejected whine. "*Rattus norvegicus.* Cooperation negative. Does not compute." He dashed out of sight. "Rat!"

"Don't go far." She resisted the urge to throttle him. Her head was bleary after a restless night, jumbled dreams of slashed flesh. Mr. Todd, his razor bright, a cascade of blood. The remains of Saucy May, glistening in ruddy candlelight. The grim hunched form of Edward Hyde, wielding a shining butcher's knife, hacking gaily away with blood spurting onto his shirt . . .

Lizzie prodded Eliza's chest. "Why d'you tell Inspector Numbnuts that Eddie did it, eh? Embarrass you, does he, because he drinks and fucks around and won't pretend to be civilized? He's our *FATHER,* God rot you."

Guilt stabbed again, but Eliza ignored it. She'd failed with Malachi Todd because she'd allowed emotions to rule her. She wouldn't make that mistake twice.

"He's *your* father," she said peevishly, "not mine. And he's an obvious suspect. What's the evidence that he's innocent? The testimonies of a greedy prostitute and a lunatic. Wonderful. Now kindly get out of my way." And resolutely she swept up the steps to the RI, leaving Lizzie behind.

The hall was empty, save for a desk clerk. Out of sight, workmen hammered and sawed, repairing the damaged theater. Plaster dust drifted, and an electric servant hefted a heavy coiled conduit upstairs, easily bearing a weight that would take three men to lift.

She strode up to the curved desk. "Mr. Starling's office, please."

The clerk glanced up from his dog-eared copy of Newton's *Opticks.* "Are you a *student,* madam?" Pointedly, as if a student in skirts was a ridiculous idea.

She simpered, longing to poke his eyeballs out. "Tutored at home, of course. My husband says ladies oughtn't to be *seen* doing science. I say, is that the *Opticks?*" She feigned a gasp. "You must be frightfully clever, sir. Perhaps one day you might attend me in my private boudoir and explain to me the Philosopher's total internal reflection. Silly me, I can't make it out at all."

The clerk smiled thinly. "You can find Starling on the lower floor. Just this once."

"Thank you. Oh," she added, inspired, "can you tell me if poor dear Professor Crane's office has been cleared yet?"

A disdainful sniff. "Couldn't say."

"Only I was supposed to fetch some books, and Mr. Locke gets so dreadfully impatient. I couldn't bear to disappoint him." Lash flutter, smile. *Idiot.*

"Mr. Locke already arranged it, madam. Starling cleared everything out yesterday. Probably why he's been in his office all night. There was a lot."

"Of course. Forgive my confusion. One befuddles so easily when one's laces are too tight." She sighed a smile, fanning herself, and started down the basement stairs towards the tantalizing smells of chemicals and hot wire.

Curiosity nibbled her toes. So Starling had been up all night clearing out Crane's office, had he? To salvage Project Interlunium, whatever it might be? She'd get it out of Starling if she had to flirt all morning.

Mr. Locke arranged it, the clerk said. As if Locke were the master, Starling the assistant.

Hmm.

At the bottom of the stairs, a flagstoned corridor was lined with offices, workshops, and experimental laboratories. The doors were labeled with scientists' names. From W. CROOKES, noisome green smoke drifted, along with the bubbling of liquid and a man cursing. From the next, Spottiswoode, a static generator crackled. After that, a door labeled Prof. E. Crane hung open. Desk bare, bookshelves emptied, electric light switched off. A cold shell, like the woman herself. Gone.

Eliza halted before the next, closed door, B. Starling. From inside came the scratching of pen on paper, as if he wrote furiously. "Two solutions to a square . . . Two! How did we not . . . no, it can't . . . dividing by zero, by God! It's not here. I need the rest of it!"

Rat-tat! "Mr. Starling? It's Eliza Jekyll."

Crumpling paper crackled. "I can't talk now, Doctor. Leave me to work, please." Agitated, hoarse with exhaustion.

She jiggled the handle. Locked. "Byron, is everything all right?"

"Everything's fine. Leave me alone."

She peered into the keyhole, but it was blocked. A peculiar smell emanated from it. She heard a clatter, books tumbling to the floor, a groan. Alarmed, she rattled the door harder. "Are you ill? Can I fetch you anything?"

"He won't see you." A mocking new voice from behind her.

She whirled, startled. A pale fellow gave a familiar sickly grin. That lank colorless hair, the bloodshot eyes. The unlikeable chemist from the demonstration. The plaque on his door read H. G. Wyverne.

"He's been scribbling in there all night," added Wyverne with a shrill giggle, toying with his dirty scarf. He wore a creased suit, coat too large but sleeves too short, yellowed with chemicals and grime. A man who worked too much, yet ate and slept little. "Scribbling and moaning. That's what Starling does. Scribbles and moans about unsolvable field equations. Stick to what you're good at, I told him." He shouted at the closed door. "Stealing, Starling! Thieving! Taking what doesn't belong to you!"

"I see." Casually, Eliza peered over Wyverne's shoulder into his sullenly lit office, whence drifted a strange scent of sulfur and hot glass. Desk upended, books and ashtray hurled to the floor amidst ink-splattered papers. As if he'd trashed the place in a fit of rage. "Has there been an accident?"

Another eerie giggle. "Oh, no. No accident. Starling made me. It's all his fault. He stole my things."

She glanced at Crane's empty office, directly opposite. *The sniveling serpent across the hall.* As if Crane thought Wyverne dangerous.

The only thing left standing in Wyverne's room was a trestle, upon which sat flasks of chemicals bolted to metal stands, twin flame burners hissing. The air shimmered oddly, a twisted, retrograde haze that made her eyes ache. Somewhere, a cat purred, and a plate of shelled oysters sat uneaten on the windowsill. A lumpy bedroll with a blanket lay unfurled. Was Wyverne sleeping here?

"He sneaks into my office at night, you know." Wyverne rubbed his palms with a slick hissing sound that turned her stomach. "Installs hidden mirrors and photographs my notes. He makes meticulous records of his plans to thwart me. I've seen them!"

Clear off, there's a good lunatic. Locke's taunts at the demonstration bounced back. *This is physics, not extra-dimensional chemistry for crackpots.* What on earth was "extra-dimensional chemistry"?

Clearly, this Wyverne was barking mad. She'd met lunatics at Bethlem who talked exactly like him. Conspiracies, secret surveillance, the world ganging up to persecute them.

But madmen had ears.

"What a fascinating experiment you're working on," she said brightly. "What is it?"

Wyverne didn't seem to hear. He kicked Starling's door, his pale hair flying. "My work on negative refractive indices? He *filched* it. Passed it off as his own."

"Did he, indeed?" Her curiosity piqued. Finch had mentioned experiments with refractive indices—and that Starling had asked about them.

"Of course! The idiot doesn't know the first thing about chemistry! None of them appreciate my contribution. I saw you at the demonstration, didn't I?" he added suddenly, eyes gleaming. "Eliza Jekyll M.D. of the Metropolitan Police. Are you here to arrest Starling? He's surely guilty."

"Not yet," she improvised. "We must build our case. First I've come to learn about the new project." She dropped into a whisper. "You know. Interlunium."

"Ah, yes." Wyverne nodded sagely, watching her like a hyena waiting to see if its prey was dead. "I was there, the afternoon before the evening before the day Antoinette died. They pretend I wasn't, but I heard and saw *everything*."

"How clever!" She edged closer, conspiratorial. "I so love a secret."

"Me too! Me too! Extraordinary results, Doctor. Energy fluctuations. Field distortions. Advanced aetherial vibrations." He giggled. "Locke warned them when first he came. An idea that might lead to a method by which it would be possible to . . . well, you know. But Locke is the worst. The ringleader!" He jiggled, fervid enthusiasm bubbling over into spitting anger. "He stole my Antoinette—oh, yes, the worm is cunning—and now he's stealing my life. They'll be sorry they didn't listen to me."

Delusions of persecution, certainly. "I understand your frustration—"

"I can't work without *money,* Doctor!" Eagerly, Wyverne grabbed her hands. He was sweating, clammy to touch. "Funds! They all want to stop me, these politicians and Cambridge dons and boards of so-called philanthropic organizations. Idiots! Their tiny minds can't conceive of the mysteries I'll solve!"

Her skin prickled. So he wanted money for his experiments. Enough to blackmail and kill Ephronia Crane?

But she bit her lip, unconvinced. For a man who'd stolen a hundred pounds, he certainly looked shabby, ill-fed and homeless.

"They're watching me, too!" She cackled, hoping she sounded insane enough. "They're relentless. Crawling about in my business like, er, termites. Termites, sir!"

"Yes!" cried Wyverne, vibrating with delight. "That metal-faced Royal Society jade? She's one of them. She was here yesterday afternoon, plotting away with Starling in that very office! She's in league with sorcerers. It's a government plot to suppress me!"

"And have you discovered their plan?"

"Of course!" he crowed. "Crane thought she'd sorted it all, trading *my* secrets for her own sordid gain. And now Starling's doing the very same thing! Selling my project to the enemy! It's larceny, Doctor. Treason, Doctor! You wouldn't believe the shenanigans these people get up to—"

"Quiet, you lunatic!" The opposite door burst open, and out hurtled Byron Starling, suffused with rage. Shirtsleeves rolled up, ink-stained fists flying. His desk was heaped with papers, slide rules, ugly chemical-stained syringes and rubber tubing.

He grappled for Wyverne's throat, and the pair crashed back into the chemist's shambolic office, kicking and punching as they hit the book-strewn floor.

"Gentlemen, please!" Eliza hovered, alarmed, as the two men clawed each other's faces and hurled insults. "Can't we work this out like scientists?"

"Bastard!" yelled Starling.

"Dirty thief!" came the reply.

"Liar!"

"Traitor!"

Zzzzap! Eliza whipped out her electric stinger. "Stop it this instant, or you'll both get three thousand volts—I say, watch out!"

Intent on their struggles, Wyverne and Starling collided with the trestle table. *Crash!* It toppled. Flasks shattered, steaming chemicals splashing.

"Miaowww!" An unseen cat pushed her skirts aside like a breeze, its flailing claws scratching her ankle as it scampered into the corridor.

"Ow! You little beast." She rounded, indignant—but the cat wasn't there. Just an unearthly shimmer, galloping for the stairs, leaving a trail of wet paw prints.

She gaped. A cat that couldn't be seen? Was she finally losing her mind? She fumbled on her optical, slotting in the aether-reactive lens.

"Ouch!" She tore the apparatus off, temples throbbing. White-hot like burning phosphorus, a dazzling network of glitter swirling up the corridor.

The very path the paw prints had taken.

Incredulous, she rubbed aching eyes. *Refractive indices. Aetherial vibrations. Extra-dimensional chemistry.* That bright aetheric disturbance from Antoinette's murder scene. The trail that led out the back of Ireton House the following night . . . and the persistent notion that she was being watched. That an unseen something—or someone—had jostled her in the corridor.

That dirty-minded eavesdropper, Crane had told Johnny Wild. Interlunium. New moon. An unseen shadow.

What if this was it? What if Wyverne was making himself . . . *transparent?* Spying on the others, invading their homes, listening to their private conversations?

On his back amidst broken glass, Wyverne screeched in fury. *"AHH!* Look what you've done, fool. Herbert's gotten away!"

"That's my cat, you nasty little thief!" Starling leapt up, fetched Wyverne a disgusted kick in the ribs, and darted back into his office, slamming the door.

Dismayed, Eliza rattled the handle. "Byron, come out at once."

No reply. She turned back, dismayed—only to have Wyverne's door slammed in her face, too.

Hmph. So much for manners. But her thoughts jumbled,

clashing like ill-fitting puzzle pieces. Invisibility! Such aberrant chemical reactions would require vast amounts of energy. No wonder Wyverne wanted Crane's super-efficient engine.

But Wyverne and Starling clearly hated each other. Working together? One the blackmailer and murderer, the other the arsonist?

Unlikely.

And why would Wyverne bother to steal Crane's book, if he already had his invention working?

Insane, certainly. Jealous, laboring under delusions of persecution. But a killer?

Inspired, she tiptoed quietly up the corridor, turning at the stairs. Then she strode back, footsteps ringing, and raised her voice. "Ah, Inspector Griffin. So glad you've arrived. Yes, that door there. Wyverne's the culprit." She flattened her back to the wall beside the door, gripping her stinger. "An enemy agent. What's that you say? No, not even a real scientist. A lousy charlatan, claiming Professor Crane's work as his own. Extorted a hundred pounds, stole her project, and murdered her like a coward—"

"I did *not*!" The door tore open, and Wyverne rushed out. "She was already dead when I got there!"

Triumphantly, Eliza leveled her stinger at his temple. "Care to elaborate?"

He skidded to a spluttering halt. "So you *are* one of them! I knew it! Pox on your greasy hide! Curse your curdled innards, you traitorous hussy—"

Zzzapp! She thumbed the charger, blue current forking. "When did you send Crane the blackmail letter? Come, I don't have all day."

A cackle. "That very afternoon. Sneaked it into her office right before her eyes, and she'd no idea!"

"I see," she said calmly. "Who's spying on who, exactly?"

"Antoinette, too, with her *visitors*." Wyverne sniggered, smearing sweaty palms on his trousers. "Such a good lark! She'd have two of them in her bed at a time. Three, even. Anything, so long as they paid what they'd promised. She had the prettiest titties I've ever seen. Like cream, with little cherries on." A side-eye giggle. "Almost like yours, only smaller."

Her stomach curdled. "*What* did you say?"

"In your bathtub. Dreaming of something nice, weren't you? You're very pretty when you sigh like that. I should like to have touched, but—"

"Shut up," she ordered, sickened. Such a marvelous invention—if it was even his—and he used it to ogle naked women in the privacy of their bathrooms. So much for progress.

Her fingers clenched angrily around her stinger. He'd spied on her. Violated her. She burned to jam her thumb on the trigger, watch him choke and writhe. *How do you like it, scum? Does that feel powerful? Am I pretty now?*

"So it *was* you," she accused, shaking. "You burned my house down and stole Crane's book."

He eyed her slyly. "Maybe I did. Maybe I didn't. Wouldn't you like to know?"

"What happened at Ireton House?" she demanded, fighting a Lizzie-like urge to wring his greasy neck.

Wyverne gnashed his teeth. "I arrived on time and everything, and the rotten ingrate had gotten herself killed.

Drowned in her own blood just to spite me. Imagine her smug face as he shoved that coil down her throat. 'This'll teach you, Wyverne, ha ha ha!'"

"Did you see the killer?" she asked sharply.

"Of course not! Whoever did it was long gone."

"And the money?"

"The murderer must have taken it. He's one of them, too." He glared at Starling's door. "You're all in on it, the stinking lot of you!"

She fumbled one-handed in her bag for the bloodstained blue scarf. "I found this at the scene. Whose blood is this?"

"How should I know? That's not mine. Who says it is? Starling? I'll throttle him!"

Still shaking, she forced herself to lower her stinger. "Well, Mr. Wyverne, you're a pervert and a blackguard, and I'd march you down to Bow Street and have you charged with extortion, not to mention housebreaking and indecent assault, but frankly I can't stand your stench one moment longer. Inspector Griffin has better things to do than listen to your feeble delusions of persecution."

Wyverne waved his arms. "But it's all true! They're all out to get me—"

"Enough," she snapped. "You are not the victim here, you disgusting little slug. I suggest you pour yourself a drink, have a nice lie down, and consider *very* carefully what you're going to do next. Good day."

He opened his mouth to retort.

"Ah." She held up a warning finger. "Not another word."

Sullenly, Wyverne retreated into his office, slamming the

door in a queasy puff of strange. She wanted to spit after him, yell curses. Such dirty little games.

She knocked on Starling's door, impatient. "Byron, stop fooling about. I'm sure you had good reason for your lies, so let's talk about it like adults."

Not even a rustle of paper.

Her skin grew cold. Those ugly syringes. She rattled the handle, anxious. "Byron? Are you all right?"

Just empty silence.

She backed up, and slammed her shoulder into the door. *Bang!* The lock broke, and the door thumped back on its hinges.

The desk was bare of papers and books. Just a yellow-crusted syringe on the blotter, mocking her. An adjoining door to Crane's office lay open, and Byron Starling—invisible or not—was gone.

Twenty minutes later, Eliza strode into Finch's Pharmacy and dropped the glass syringe on the counter.

Finch's head poked from behind the curtain. "Yes?" he said crossly. "I've told you before, eh? No clarified opiates before ten o'clock, so you can just clear off . . ." His expression brightened. "Oh, it's you, dear girl. Sorry. Fending off addicts, you know. Cattle stunner close to hand." He wiped stained hands on his apron. "What can I do for you?"

"I wanted to analyze this." Stiffly she proffered the crystallized syringe. "I got it from Byron Starling."

Finch peered at the yellow substance, pince-nez flashing with rainbows. "I declare. Uncanny spectrum, say what?"

"It's a compound that engenders a negative refractive index during cellular decomposition." She watched him, a bitter ache in her guts. "But you already knew that."

"Eh?" He looked mystified.

"Your friend's experiments. Wyverne, wasn't it?"

A vague head scratch. "Not sure what you're driving at, dear girl."

"Byron Starling, Ephronia Crane, Antoinette de Percy. You knew everything. Why didn't you tell me you gave Victor's diagrams to Antoinette?"

"Haven't the faintest idea what you're babbling about—"

"Why did you put me in Bethlem?"

Finch's face whitened.

"I was fifteen. Fairfax and Starling were there. I remember it now. Those cruel 'treatments.'" Her throat ached. "Why?"

Carefully, he set the syringe down. "My dear girl," he said gently, "nothing good will come of these questions. It was all for the best. You must trust me."

"This *illness.*" Her voice cracked to a whisper. "I wasn't just sick, was I? You locked me up. *What did I do that was so terrible?*"

He just pulled a cigarette case from his pocket, his baby-blue gaze no longer so vague. Chilly, even.

"Please, Marcellus. I need to know. Was it . . ." She swallowed. "Did the elixir drive me mad?"

He lit his cigarette. Exhaled slow, sweet-smelling smoke. "Trust me," he repeated, hypnotic. No longer her doting, dotty Marcellus. This was Edward Hyde's Finch. The man who'd taken one look at Madeleine Jekyll lying dead on those pristine white sheets and advised Henry to cover up what

Hyde had done. Who'd taken her poor dead body to Victor Frankenstein and brought her back to hideous life.

"You never loved me, did you?" Eliza's eyes burned. "You only ever loved *him*. Everything you ever promised me was a lie." Blindly, she grabbed the syringe and walked out.

THE OBSERVATION OF TRIFLES

SOON AFTER, ELIZA JUMPED DOWN FROM THE OMNI-bus outside the soaring glass arches of the Royal Opera. She paid her threepence and climbed the steps to Bow Street Police Station, Hippocrates hopping at her heels.

With the magistrates in session down the street, the entrance hall was packed. Constables, civilians, and bowler-hatted civil servants jostled, umbrellas and briefcases adding to the crush. Two constables marched a skinny fellow with scraggly red ringlets towards the booking desk. "Don't know nuffing 'bout no murder," he proclaimed, winking at Eliza as he passed. "A dead Fishy Dolittle? What sort o' name is that? The Artful Dodger, you say? Never 'eard of 'im."

Belligerently, she forced a path to the stairs. In her current mood, they'd all do well to stay out of her way. Marcellus had been her best friend. Her mentor. She felt bereft, alone for the first time in years.

And for once, Lizzie wasn't talking. Eliza felt worn thin, weak, exhausted. Transparent, like a shadow. Was it that foul alchemical brew, scraping away at the ties between them? Or just Lizzie sulking? Maybe Lizzie's apparition had solidified, and wandered off on some cunning frolic of her own, leaving Eliza to wither away.

Hipp weaved through the forest of legs. "Make way! Insufficient space! Greater speed imperative!"

She stalked up to the first floor, along past glass-fronted doors to Inspector Griffin's cramped office. He'd tried to warn her about Marcellus, but she hadn't listened. Well, she was listening now. And she owed him an apology.

She knocked once and burst in. Flawlessly tidy as usual, maps and lists fastidiously pinned to the walls. "Harley, you'll never believe what's happened—" She halted, flushing. Griffin wasn't there.

Constable Perkins jumped back from the desk, reddening. "Dr. Jekyll. I was just—"

"I can see what you were *just* doing," said Eliza sharply. Griffin's desk drawer lay open, its orderly arrangement exposed. Those were personal items. A locket. A red hair ribbon. A photograph of his late wife. "Where is Inspector Griffin?"

"I-I'm not sure—"

"Then why are you pawing through his things like a common thief?" Tears of rage threatened all over again. This girl had wormed her way into Harley's confidence. Pretended to be his friend. Eliza wanted to slap her.

Squirming, Perkins mumbled something.

"Speak up. I can't hear you."

"Information!" squawked Hipp, as irate as she.

"I said he made me!" Perkins's careful hairstyle quivered, as if it might wilt for shame. "He told me to bring him papers."

"Who?" But she already knew the answer, and her face burned. "Chief Inspector Reeve?"

Perkins nodded, mortified.

Eliza folded her arms. "Papers like my post-mortem reports, leaked to the press to make Harley look foolish? I thought you were his friend."

Perkins bit her lip. "Reeve says Inspector Griffin's leaving and I should stick with him if I want to get ahead. With Reeve, that is, not Inspector Griffin. And word is that Reeve's wife threw him out and now he's doubly keen to show Griffin up—"

"Leaving?" Eliza's hands clenched. "What do you mean?"

"He said Griffin would be fired." Perkins eyed her ruefully. "You as well, Doctor. By the Commissioner, for bungling the Slasher case."

"I see. And how does Reeve know we won't catch the Slasher, hmm? Could it be because he's sabotaging us at every turn?" She banged fists against thighs. "Damn him."

Poor Perkins stared at her feet, in tears. "I only wanted a job that matters. My father wants me to marry his business partner and have babies and keep house for the rest of my life. I can't be just a wife, Doctor. I'd rather die, don't you see?" She wiped her wet nose. "What am I going to do now?"

Now? Eliza wanted to snap. *Now you can go to hell, you scheming little traitor.* But she knew how it was to be used by unscrupulous men. To long so desperately for any glimmer of advancement that you'd do anything, say anything, play any ignoble game . . . and her skin stung with shame. Was this what Lizzie thought of her, every time she grinned through gritted teeth at Reeve's patronizing jibes? That she was selling out to the enemy?

"You, Constable Perkins," she announced, "will walk away and pretend this never happened."

Perkins's eyes widened. Her uniform so flawlessly pressed, buttons polished like tiny mirrors. So hopeful, it hurt to behold. "You won't tell Inspector Griffin?"

"I believe he's too busy to bother with trifles, don't you?" Eliza added a glare to her stern expression. "Just make sure it never happens again."

Perkins nodded fervently. "Yes, ma'am."

"And if Reeve tries more of his desperately clever tricks? Tell him you'd simply *love* to help him out, but unfortunately, you work for Inspector Griffin, who most decidedly isn't going *anywhere*—because he's about to solve the Slasher case without any help from Reeve. Sound fair?"

"Perfectly." Perkins worked up half a smile. "Thank you, Doctor."

"You're welcome. Now go find Harley and make yourself indispensable, before I come to my senses and throw you onto the street myself."

Discomfited, she watched Perkins scuttle away. More than ever, her fingers itched to crush Reeve's lying throat. How dare he spoil that young woman's dreams? She'd half a mind to march down to Scotland Yard and give him a sizzling piece of her temper . . .

"Yes!" crowed Lizzie, swinging her legs over the desk's

edge. Her heels made alarmingly solid thumps into the wood. "Peel the turd's face off for a Welsh rarebit. He deserves it, for all he's done to us."

"*Now* you appear," muttered Eliza warily. "Never fear. Harley and I will catch this Slasher all the faster, just to spite him—"

"Right. All we need do is put in the squeak on Eddie and it'll be fine, is that it?"

"—and the murderer of de Percy and Crane, too," she added fiercely, and strode back down the stairs, out into the busy hall, and down to the basement morgue.

Hipp scuttled after, sniggering at Lizzie's vocabulary. "Turd! Turd-turd-turd!"

The clammy chill crept under Eliza's petticoats and up her sleeves. As usual, the smell of cold flesh turned her stomach. Shrouds, rattling bones in rotting caskets, graves hacked in snowswept ground beneath crumbling headstones. The inevitable truth that one day, we'd all be dead and forgotten. The smell of murder, too, screams echoing in the silence, that bitter overtone of terror. Even after years of experience, it made her shiver.

A single electric bulb shed weak golden light. Two rows of benches marched into the darkness. Most were occupied, corpses covered with blood-crusted sheets. Here were the Slasher's victims, four in a row. Only two had been buried. No one had come forward to claim the rest, their relatives perhaps afraid of incurring funeral costs. Or maybe they had no relatives. The final, eternal loneliness: no one to care when you die.

Compelled, she paused by Saucy May and drew back the sheet.

The girl's skin was blue, exposed muscle losing its sheen. Such chaotic cuts. *The knife rising and falling, slicing through sinew and tendon . . .* Unwilled, she recalled Mr. Todd's insistence that this was not the Slasher's work. An imposter. *Someone who loves him.*

Determined, she covered up the remains and moved on. She'd no interest in anything Todd had to say. And she still couldn't carve that jagged nightmare of Hyde from her mind. *He smooths his palms eagerly over shiny intestines, enjoying their slippery texture, smacking his lips as he carves. "Maggie, Maggie Mayyy . . ."*

She shuddered. No more Slasher for her today.

Instead, she headed to the back, where Antoinette and Ephronia lay. Wyverne's admission of blackmail—and likely arson, too—had only clouded the issue. If Wyverne wasn't the killer, who was? Locke and Starling had alibis—and the elusive Blue Scarf still remained unidentified. She needed hard evidence.

"Ha!" Lizzie laughed in her face. "Having stuff-all don't stop you accusing our father. You in your fine new life as Captain Lafayette's wife, with a drunken crime lord for a papa? 'Twon't never do. You've wanted rid of Eddie all along, so you can go on pretending you're Henry's daughter and your shit don't stink."

Eliza sidestepped her, skirts swishing. This next body was larger, bare feet protruding. "You've seen his behavior lately. He's guilty and you know it."

Lizzie thrust hands on hips. "Bollocks. You never heard what Rose said?"

"Bollocks," tittered Hipp. "Bollocks! Eh-eh!"

Eliza banged her instruments onto the table. "The promise of a money-grubbing prostitute. *That* puts it beyond doubt."

Lizzie prodded Eliza's chest over the corpse. "What's wrong with her word, you snotty cow? Rose is an honest working girl—"

"Rose is in love with him!" She slammed the table's edge. "He's charmed her, same as he's charmed you and your Jonathan and everyone else in that stench-filled cesspit you call home. Are you blind, or just stupid?"

"Ha! Mr. Todd were dead convinced some other cove's responsible, but you're too god-rotted stubborn to open your eyes. Who's blind now?"

Eliza clenched her teeth on acid rage. "How dare you even speak his name?"

"Todd, Todd, Todd," taunted Lizzie. "Must be cold up there on your high horse. So his honor slit a few windpipes. Hell, half the people I know's done a killing. Think your precious Remy never murdered anyone?"

"That's different," she retorted, flushing. "It was an accident—"

"The hell you say. Once a killer, always a killer, that's what you said." Lizzie chortled, delighted. "I think Malachi likes me, the handsome devil. Always knew you was jealous. Afraid I'll succeed where you failed?"

"I'm not listening."

"Deaf as well as blind," crowed Lizzie. "Admit it, Eliza, our blood's tainted, same as Todd's. If Eddie's the Slasher, what does that make you?"

"You vicious tart," snarled Eliza, and clawed for Lizzie's face. But with a sarcastic *pop!* Lizzie disappeared.

Eliza stumbled over the cadaver, catching herself. That sour blue potion scorched her throat again, and she clenched back a scream. Grabbing at ghosts. An imaginary friend who hated her. Perfectly sane.

Taking a steadying breath, she folded back the sheet. Professor Crane, cold and gray. That gruesome coil mercifully removed, but her torn lips bled black. Reddish hair trailed over her shoulder, lank in death.

"Take dictation, Hipp." Hipp's cogs rattled, *rrk! rrk!*, as he recorded Eliza's words on his little phonograph. "Ephronia Crane, early forties, well fed and strong. Cause of death bleeding and suffocation from foreign object in the throat." She pulled the sheet down to the thighs. "Full post-mortem exam not required, searching for trace evidence only . . . oh, my."

Ephronia's belly was rounded and swollen.

Barely noticeable, easily hidden by skirts. Eliza smoothed her hand over the cold skin, palpating for gases, hoping for a mistake. But no decomposition had formed that unmistakable bump.

"A couple of months at least," she murmured sadly. "That puts a new complexion on things. Or does it?"

It's Starling who's jealous, Locke had said. *Always wants to be the golden child.* Crane wasn't married. So whose was the baby?

Inspired, Eliza pulled out a long-sticked cotton swab and eased the corpse's legs apart. A gentle swipe, and she smeared the results onto a glass slide and examined them through her optical's microscopic magnifier. Tiny tadpole-like cells, motionless but intact. A couple of days old at most.

"A *liaison* on the day of her murder?" Eliza frowned. "More circumstantial evidence, Hipp. But it seems strange. The professor had rather a busy day, what with the failed demonstration, the meeting, being blackmailed by Wyverne, writing to Hyde. Pausing for a quick tumble over the desk doesn't seem her style."

"Unless Starling slipped her one before he throttled her." Lizzie ran laps of the morgue, skirts billowing. "Your mild-mannered maths maestro, oho! Hardly seems the type."

"Nonsense. Locke saw Starling at the library." But doubt prodded Eliza's ribs. Locke changed his story with the breeze. And who knew what outwardly respectable people did in private? Was she searching for complex motives that weren't there? Could this entire case be based on sexual jealousy out of control?

"Right," called Lizzie scornfully. "Locke was fucking Crane. Starling, too. The whole world was fucking Antoinette. It's all about fucking, Eliza, because that's what women do, ain't it? Always some man's whore, his wife, his mistress. Never just ourselves."

"That's enough, Lizzie." She scanned the body closely with her magnifying lens. "No unusual marks. Any trace evidence will have come off with her clothes." Reaching beneath the bench, she retrieved the sack into which the police had stuffed the victim's effects. "Corset, still laced, clips undone. One pair of cotton stockings. Look, this garter is snapped. And the dress . . ."

A hard object in the pocket clunked against her wrist.

Curious, she dug it out. A wax cylinder, smaller than her fist, with tiny carved markings. A phonograph recording.

A phonograph set had been left running on Ephronia's desk. What if she'd been playing this cylinder when the killer interrupted? Plucked the roll out, shoved it in her pocket so the intruder wouldn't hear what she was listening to.

Or what she was recording.

Eliza unhinged the panel atop Hipp's head and clicked the roll into place. "Play this, please."

Cogs whirred, and Hipp's tinny speaker crackled.

"I can't believe this." Ephronia's Scottish voice, harsh with fear. She was pacing, *click-swish-click-swish,* her agitated tone rising and falling. "I can't believe Byron lied! Or was he too blinded by ambition to realize what was happening? The contract, everything we've worked for . . ." Furniture crashed, as if she'd kicked it. "Damn! It's all over. I know what they'll say about me when they come. But I'm not a traitor, I swear to God, I never knew. I suspected that Royal Society witch wasn't what she seemed, but this . . ." Papers rustled. "But time wastes, laddie. Ha ha! What a laugh! These fanatics cannot get their hands on Interlunium. These designs, my papers, they must be protected. But who can I trust? Who— oh, God." Her voice quavered, and the next lines were delivered in a frantic whisper. "It's him. He's coming! I can see him across the square. You must deliver these notes. I'll write down the address. Wish me luck."

Ker-chunk! Abruptly, the recording cut to silence. "She recognized the killer across the square," exclaimed Eliza. "It must be Blue Scarf!"

Hippocrates jigged, excited. "Fanatics! Murder! Make greater speed!"

But ugly bells clanged, a discord of doubt. *I'm not a traitor.*

That Royal Society witch. Miss Burton, her metal forehead shining, jumping into that carriage with Paxton, the railway man. In Soho, the Foreign Secretary's letter in her pocket, a covert meeting with a strange man with a withered arm.

She's in league with sorcerers, Wyverne had said. *Starling's selling my project to the enemy.* What if he was right?

Crane was a patriot. She'd thought to sell her project to a respectable Royal Society agent. To the Empire, for the war effort. But what if . . . ?

"Dr. Jekyll." Veronica Burton stalked into the morgue, navy blue skirts scything. Her boot heels cracked on the floorboards, a bullet-like warning. "I was only just looking for you."

Oh, my. Eliza's nerves squealed in alarm. How much had Burton heard? Behind her back, she hastily clicked Hipp's lid shut. Thankfully, mercurial Lizzie was nowhere to be seen. "Miss Burton! Such a long time since we chatted."

The girl smiled lopsidedly. A hole in one temple revealed gleaming wet clockwork parts and a glimmering blue filament. One hand had been severed and replaced, decaying skin grafted onto steel fingers. On her bodice shone a Royal Society badge.

Eliza's stomach churned. A few months ago, she'd borrowed that badge, to break into the Tower and fool Lady Lovelace. How long ago that seemed. Miss Burton had been such a lively, irreverent girl. Now more Enforcer than woman. Cold. Dead-hearted. Unstoppable.

She grinned weakly. "Heavens, is that the time? I've a meeting to get to. Perhaps we'll take that tea another day—"

"Not so fast." A rot-skinned hand shot out and grabbed her wrist. "Why are you interfering with this cadaver?"

"Interfering," piped Hipp from under the stairs. "Does not compute. Re-analyze."

"I'm hardly interfering—"

"Professor Crane kept a book. A journal. Where is it?"

She despaired. That cursed book again. "I don't know what you're—"

"Answer me."

"I don't know about any book! This is a police investigation. I'm merely examining the body for clues. Please, you're hurting me."

Veronica's face twitched, *clank! clunk!,* as if cogs and pistons calculated inside her skull, and abruptly she let Eliza go. "It's not a police investigation anymore. This is a Royal Society matter now."

Crossly, Eliza rubbed her bleeding wrist. "Are you solving a multiple murder, then? Or just fishing for scientists to burn?"

"That will be all, Doctor."

Eliza's blood boiled. All her old frustration at bull-headed Royal Society interference bubbled up with a vengeance, mixing with anger that vivacious Miss Burton had changed into a metal-headed harpy just to curry the Philosopher's favor. "No, it certainly will *not* be all," she snapped in a voice barely her own. "How dare you obstruct this investigation? I've got it on good authority that you made a secret deal with Ephronia Crane to peddle unorthodox science for *profit*. What would Sir Isaac say about that, eh?"

A rivet popped in Veronica's scarred cheek, releasing a green squirt of pus.

"Go on," jeered Lizzie, as she waltzed about the morgue cradling a severed arm. "Let her have it!"

Eliza barely heard. "Oh, not so officious now? I happen to know you're conspiring with the Foreign Secretary, too, in the same ignoble shenanigans. Oh, yes," she added with fierce, reckless enjoyment, "your little meetings in Soho have been eyeballed. We've got our snouts, too, so we do. So don't strut into a god-rotted coppers' shop, interrupt me in the middle of a stand-up crushers' bug hunt, and flap your mouth about Royal Society business when it ain't no such thing!"

"Ha ha!" shouted Lizzie, delighted. "That'll learn the steel-faced sally!"

Eliza reeled, the shock of what she'd said—what Lizzie had said with *her* mouth—sinking in. *Damn it, Lizzie!* But too late to take it back.

Veronica's metal jaw hung stupidly. Inside her visor, little blue electrical signals flashed frantically back and forth. Flabbergasted.

"How quaint," said Eliza coldly, but her pulse still jabbed at her to scream, laugh in Veronica's face, attack her again. "No longer used to being defied? Perhaps it will recall you to proper manners." And she grabbed her skirts to flounce away.

"Not so fast." Veronica's hand twitched, and a weapon gleamed in it. An ugly black contraption, with a glittering green glass phial where the electrical coil should be.

Eliza's throat corked. With a terrified squawk, Hippocrates fled up the stairs and away.

Veronica advanced, visor glittering with twin pinpoints of red. "I heard your phonograph. Clever of you. I should have known Crane would give the game away. Question is: What will you do about it?"

Eliza stammered, heart pounding. "I-I'm sure we can work something out—"

"Sadly, no." The green liquid in Veronica's weapon winked evilly. Some kind of nerve poison. Convulsions and screaming, an agonizing death. "I can cover for you no longer. Do you deny that your lover Remy Lafayette is a sorcerer and a lycanthrope?"

She knows! hissed Lizzie fiercely in her blood. *Wring her scrawny neck before she says anything else, or I will.*

Alarmed, Eliza backed off. Alone, in a room full of corpses with a half-automaton Royal Society zealot. "That's ridiculous."

"Do you deny that you and said Remy Lafayette IRS conspired to murder the Countess of Lovelace and escape the Royal's justice?"

"Veronica, please, I don't know what you're—"

"Do you deny you're guilty of unorthodox practices? That you deploy heretical substances, devices, and contrivances to pervert the good name of science? That you're plotting to poison His Majesty the King? That you are a *sorcerer* and an *alchemist,* and you deserve to *burn*?"

Eliza's insides melted, a puddle of despair.

This was it. This was how she ended. The fate she'd feared for so many years.

She trembled, shrinking. How she longed to shout in defiance, marshal her arguments, deploy every glib denial and excuse and decoy she'd ever invented to save herself.

Don't just stand there, you limp-brained clod! screamed Lizzie in her ear. *Do something!*

But it was too late. Veronica knew everything. The Philosopher wasn't here to pull rank. Remy wasn't here to talk Veronica down. All Eliza could do was let it happen.

"Guilty." Veronica grinned, showing black metal teeth like a shark's. "But you know far too much to risk due process. Oh, look. You resisted arrest. You tried to escape." She raised her poison pistol, finger creaking on the trigger.

"Wait—*uhh!*" Eliza choked, her throat clawed by invisible hands. And *snap!* Like a writhing serpent, Lizzie whiplashed out and punched Veronica Burton in the face.

Crrunch! "Take that, you humorless tart. Ha ha!"

Veronica flies backwards, her face a mess of torn skin, metal cheekbones ripped bare. My knuckles ache and bleed . . . but it's me, Lizzie Hyde, by God, popped out so hard and fast, my hair springs from its pins. My body swells, a rush of giddy blood, and a clip on Eliza's corset snaps, buttons popping off onto the floor.

Burton's expression is priceless. Her jaw hangs, those teeth glistening. I laughs meself wretched, guts aching. "O-ho-ho, you nosy she-dog. Now you *really* know our secret!"

We've done it at last. Changed in front of a Royal Agent and lived to tell the tale, and fuck 'em if they can't take a joke.

But Burton's already dragging that pistol up to fire. We won't live much longer if we stand here thumb-up-bum.

So I grab Eliza's bag and leg it up the stairs.

Out into the coppers' shop, skidding across the tiled floor past a trio of gaping constables, with Burton on my heels screaming "Stop that woman! Sorcerer!"

That murdering bastard Flash Toby blows me a kiss as I pass. No time to make him regret it. Two at a time down the steps into Bow Street, leaping puddles and dodging carriages. *Crackk!* Burton fires into the crowd. People scream and duck, and a man falls, writhing, white foam bubbling from his mouth.

Out o' my way, you glocky squirts. I batter through a tangle of spectators, and *doinng!* I bounce off a horse's arse and nearly fall under a swerving velocipede. Past the Opera's glass arches, out onto Long Acre. If I can reach Seven Dials, we'll lose her.

Burton screeches again. "Sorcerer! Stop her!"

But I'm gaining. She curses, her yells ever more shrill and distant. I duck between a cart's whirring wheels and out the other side, and now there's a rushing line of traffic between us. "Kiss my alchemist's arse!" I yell, and sprint off laughing, only to skid on my heel in fright.

Enforcers. Two big ones, muscle grafted to brass bones. Must be bits of Eliza popping out on my face, because their red eyes dilate, and electric pistols whip from holsters with twin mechanical *snaps!*

Oops.

I whirl, Eliza's bag banging my hip, and tear off down a by-street thick with rubbish and soot. The Enforcers run after, brass clodhoppers going *plop! plop! plop!* through the mud. Where's Eliza's little pet? Lost in the crowd. I leap a dead dog, swerve around a corner, burst through an impromptu fist-fight. Still the metal-arse monkeys follow, scattering the crowd, spreading out to hunt me down. Fuck me, the bastards are quick.

Zzap! An electric shot sets fire to the lintel above my head. My legs are filled with lead. I'm stumbling. My skin ripples, muscles wrenching, as if my bones—*her* bones—are fighting to escape. My vision blurs, her spectacles fogging. Hair flaps over my face, dark and blond and dark once more.

Dizziness strikes like a madman's axe. Can't stay out of sight, not like this. Eliza, can't you see you're crueling us here?

I-me-her-we splash through a fountain—who knows, maybe Enforcers track scents like bloodhounds—and lurch towards Great Earl Street, where the twisting lanes are full of dead-end courts and scissor-blade traps. Enforcers got no friends there. If I can make it to the rookery, we're safe.

But it's still a long, long way.

A hand grabs our shoulder. It's the green-turbaned Otto-man with the gold-wired beard, what offered me sweet smoke and oblivion. Only this time he's sneering, a curved blade glinting wickedly in his hand. "Jack Dawkins says how-do," he snarls, and pulls back to strike . . . but my face ripples and pops, and he sees *her* face, my grin on *her* lips. He falters, mouth flapping in horror.

I grab his knife and stick it into his guts. *Squelch!* Blood gushes. He jerks, a wet contorted groan. The Sultan's man, a-killing for the Artful? Shit. Can't trust no one to stay bought in this town.

But no time to bemoan his treachery now. "There's sweet-ness, you rotten turncoat," I snarl, and shove his toppling frame into the crowd. My hands are coated in warm blood. *Her* hands, slim and genteel. There, Eliza. Eddie would be proud. Now you're a killer, too.

People scream and jostle. "Murder! Sorcerers! Run for your lives!" A shop window smashes as a velocipede hurtles into it, rider cartwheeling over the handlebars. Someone starts throwing rocks. Blokes pummel each other, fists swinging. A girl leaps on an old cove and claws for his eyes. A nice old riot you've started, Eliza. Ha ha!

"Death to the Royal!" I holler with her voice, shaking her fist in the air. "Long live the sorcerers! *Liberté du Sang!*" And I grab her skirts and pump her legs and make her run, run, run.

The Enforcers come after, hurling folk left and right, walls smashing and bones breaking like sticks. Our lungs are filled with burning gin, toxic and unbreathable. And the fuckers still come on, *plop! plop! sizzle!* With every step, they're closer. Ha ha! How'd you like *them* apples, Eliza?

Mud splashes to my knees. I drag up my flapping wet skirts—when'd they get so god-rotted heavy?—and stumble on. My face swells like the plague, *her* face forcing its way out, my legs clumsy with *her* bones. Across a square I sprint, round a darkened corner, and trip over a log some dipshit's left in the road.

Pain lurches up my shin, and as I go flying, muscles cramp hard like lumps of wood and I try to hold her back but I can't and *spoinng!*

Eliza hit the ground, her breath knocked away. Head swimming, she staggered up to run.

And slammed full tilt into Seymour Locke.

"Follow me," he hissed, "unless you want to get shot." And he dragged her into a dingy room that stank of rotting onions, and banged the door shut.

A FIXED AND
UNALTERABLE THING

ELIZA BROKE FREE, SCRABBLING FOR HER WEAPON. Locke could still be the killer's accomplice. Lying to confuse her, distracting her at the crime scene while Wyverne burned down her house . . .

"Follow," snapped Locke again, wild eyes burning in the dark. And he scuttled under a low doorway and out into a shaded yard.

Outside, Enforcers' footsteps pounded the mud. Still hunting for her, Eliza, the killer sorcerer, thanks to Lizzie's cursed antics. Enforcers with guns, versus a potential murderer.

Clutching her bag, she stumbled after Locke.

Across the yard, dodging a sullen dog that snarled over a scrap of bone. Under a lintel, down some moldy steps, a leap across a scum-stained ditch, up another rickety wooden stair—and in suddenly glaring gaslight, they emerged into a wide, respectable street. Horses snorting, ladies promenading, crossing sweepers dodging the tramping feet of carriages and omnibuses, coils crackling in the tart smell of hot aether.

No Enforcers in sight. Back to the real world. And Lizzie was nowhere to be seen.

Catching her breath, Eliza collapsed against the bay window of a chandler's shop. "Thank you," she panted. "I shan't forget this. Now I really must be going—"

"Just smile and look natural." Beside her, Locke inclined his head towards a trio of red-coated soldiers, who patrolled nonchalantly, carbines slung and black hats carefully brushed. Locke wore a frock coat with a glittering watch chain, his frothy blond hair stuffed under a bowler hat. More like a swell mobsman than the bookish scientist she remembered.

"Natural?" she whispered fiercely. "Veronica Burton just tried to kill us. She's an enemy spy!"

He gazed across the street, as if they were merely friends chatting. "Of course! We know too much. Ephronia thought she was selling Interlunium for the war effort. She was. Just not ours."

Oh, my. The secret meeting in Soho, whispering to that strange man with a withered arm and a disturbingly familiar stone on a silver chain around his throat. *Our mutual friend,* Beaconsfield's note had said. A French agent. *La Belle et la Bête.* "So Burton killed the others to cover her tracks? First Antoinette, then Crane and Ormonde at the same time? How?"

Casually, Locke checked his pocket watch. "She likely has minions to do her bidding. Trust me, Doctor, whoever gets their hands on the project will win this war."

"But Burton had the Foreign Secretary's authority in her pocket. She doesn't need to kill anyone. It makes no sense—"

"I know you visited Starling," cut in Locke impatiently. "Give me the book and let's be done."

Her mind whirled, unconvinced. "Why is everyone obsessed with this book? I don't have it! That worm Wyverne stole it. It's gone."

Locke's eyes held murder. "But it's mine. I *need* it. The clues must be in there. I need to find that hidden prototype!"

"You don't understand. Interlunium . . . Wyverne's already finished it."

"Rubbish," snapped Locke. "Wyverne knows nothing."

Eliza stared. "But I saw him. He can make himself invisible. He's been spying on you, your friends, me. He's heard everything!"

But Locke just laughed, mocking. "His infernal refractive indices? A charlatan conjurer's trick. You've still got no idea what we've made, have you?"

Her guts chilled. "Then what? Tell me!"

He checked his watch again. "Change of plans, Doctor. We must stop them, or they'll kill us both. Agreed?"

"Stop who doing what? I don't understand."

"Don't ask questions," hissed Locke. "Just do as I say. Go home to Cavendish Square. Lock yourself in and don't answer to anyone. At a quarter past seven tonight, go to Henry Jekyll's laboratory—"

"How do you know about that?"

A steely glare. "Didn't I say *don't ask*? Jekyll's laboratory. You'll know what to do when you get there."

"But—"

"A quarter past seven, Doctor, and don't be late—" His eyes saucered. "Watch out!"

A body jostled her, knocking her flying. She hit the filthy pavement on her backside, her bag dropping into the mud. She glimpsed a slim figure, dark coat and fawn trousers, ragged hair falling beneath a top hat—and the miscreant scooped up her bag and tore off.

She scrambled up. "I say, give that back! Stop, thief!"

But he—or she?—had already darted away.

She punched her thighs, frustrated. Notes, her autopsy tools, a bottle of elixir, for heaven's sake. At least her optical was safe in its case on her belt. She was only lucky Hippocrates hadn't been snoozing in there.

Bloody thieves.

But her fingers twitched, unsettled. Another coincidence? What if that thief were the killer? What if, like Locke, the killer thought she still had the book? Or some other incriminating evidence?

She racked her brain for the bag's contents. The evidence from Ireton House. Phials, slides, the blue scarf—and the phonograph roll from Ephronia Crane's pocket, too, which implicated Veronica Burton for treason.

But Veronica would simply have shot Eliza, or arrested her. She wouldn't bother with a clumsy smash-and-grab. Besides, she wasn't convinced Veronica was the killer. And the thieving rascal had been too small to be Byron Starling, too thin to be Wyverne. No, this was someone else. *Some long-haired reprobate in a dirty coat.* The famous Blue Scarf again.

If Burton was the murderer, who was Blue Scarf? A minion, as Locke had suggested? It didn't sit right. This zealous, metal-brained Burton would surely take matters in hand herself. No need for skulking about. She had all the authority she needed.

Sighing, Eliza turned back. "Did you see that? Typical. That scoundrel filched my bag—"

But an empty wall greeted her. Once again, Seymour Locke was gone.

Damn it. She banged her skull back against the window. What a vexing fellow. He'd told her nothing. She hadn't even asked him if he'd known Ephronia was with child. What had he meant about Henry's laboratory? What would happen at a quarter past seven?

But she shuddered, as the wider implications of what Locke had confirmed sunk in.

Veronica Burton, a French spy. If *Liberté du Sang* were secretly buying Project Interlunium, it must be a weapon. A bomb, some kind of cannon, one of Marcellus's mind control machines.

She laughed, feeling a little hysterical. *Spies are everywhere—even in your HOME!* Perhaps a perfectly calibrated toaster, or a better mousetrap. She'd no way of telling. She'd just have to wait for tonight.

In the meantime, she needed to return to Cavendish Square. Preferably without being dragged to the Tower by Burton's over-zealous Enforcers. Grab an omnibus or two, dash across a few parks, maybe the Electric Underground to shake off any pursuit.

Eliza sidled into the street, glancing left and right, and searched her pockets. One shilling and threepence. It'd have to do. Burton probably knew her new address. It didn't matter. Once she'd barricaded herself inside, she wasn't coming out for anyone until she'd sent for help to Inspector Griffin in person.

"Right y'are." Lizzie skipped gaily amongst the puddles, no longer ghostly but frighteningly opaque. "Let's be off, lickety-split."

"Stop drawing attention!" hissed Eliza. She wished she'd never dabbled with that prickly blue mixture. Could this new, disruptive Lizzie burst out whenever she chose? Would she never leave Eliza be? "Are you insane? Jumping out in front of a Royal Society agent who just accused us of murder and sorcery? Are you *trying* to get us burned?"

"Should I have let her shoot us? You just gawped like a stuffed bird," said Lizzie loftily. "*I* saved *our* lives."

"And that's why you stabbed that poor man, is it? To save our lives? Or just to make me angry?"

Lizzie gestured rudely with two fingers. "Screw you. I'm better off without you."

"Fine. Don't come back." She glared, and with a snarled curse, Lizzie vanished.

Hmph. So much for her.

Where was this, anyway? Red-coated soldiers everywhere, muskets and swords bristling. Enlisted men, with no love for the Royal. That would work in her favor. Typically the regiments had nothing but scorn for the Philosopher's rules. *An alchemist, you say? Right y'are. Boil us a nice cup o' tea, can't you?* An electric omnibus clanked up on metal feet, packed with commuters, men back-to-back on the roof and ladies inside. "Leicester Square!" yelled the red-faced conductor, swinging from the spiral steps and waving a yellow top hat. "Regent Street!"

Lizzie was already on board, grinning from the foggy window. "No room for you! How'd you like *them* apples?"

Ignoring her, Eliza gripped the railing and heaved herself up.

A brassy hand dragged her back down.

Her heart somersaulted, and she tensed to flee.

"Telegraph!" The clockwork messenger bounced on long hinged legs. It wore a black tailcoat and top hat over its metal skeleton. "Jekyll, Eliza. Telegraph!"

"Away with you, idiot." Feeling foolish, she grabbed the ticker tape.

```
    SLASHER. MRS FLETCHER'S. GOOD NEWS.
         ATTEND SOONEST. HG.
```

She brightened. Surely "good news" could only mean one thing. Harley's career was saved, and hers, too, and be damned to the Commissioner and Reeve both. "Lizzie, look! Perhaps we got him!"

Scowling, Lizzie kicked a horse turd from her boot, having somehow alighted from the omnibus when Eliza wasn't watching. "Likely just your Inspector Griffin giving himself airs. Another speck of shit from the killer's bumhole, or sommat."

"Or you could just be jealous of our success," said Eliza sweetly. "How do you like *those* apples?"

But cold dread wormed into her belly. Mrs. Fletcher's, the favorite haunt of one Edward Hyde. Of a hundred other gentlemen, too. It didn't mean anything. Did it?

Her fingertips stung, a poison prickle that wouldn't ease. Seven victims, now. Seven butchered wretches who'd never breathe again. Public reaction to the Slasher remaining at large had been little short of hysterical, reminiscent of the days of Razor Jack. People wanted the killer caught, and soon. Add to that Reeve's constant threats to fire her and Griffin both . . .

. . . and any progress, however flimsy, was better than nothing.

Any guilty man was better than none.

How thin a shred of evidence would suffice? How far would Harley go to make an arrest before the Slasher killed again?

How far would she?

Stamping down her unease, she dashed after an omnibus heading in the opposite direction, waving it down with a shout.

BY REASON OF INSANITY

THE STEPS TO MRS. FLETCHER'S WERE CRAWLING with blue-coated constables. At least there were no Enforcers in sight. She pushed through, feeling undressed without her bag or Hippocrates. The poor mite was probably driving Mr. Brigham frantic at Cavendish Square this very minute.

"Inspector's orders. No, sir, step away. Sorry, you can't come in." Constable Perkins guarded the doorway, chest puffed out, refusing to admit anyone not in uniform.

Eliza eyed her coolly. "I'm afraid I've lost my credentials."

Perkins mumbled, eyes downcast, and stepped aside. Eliza swept in, not looking back. She still hadn't forgiven Perkins. Maybe she never would.

On the first-floor landing, girls hovered, nervously smoking cigarettes. A dark undercurrent of that familiar bitter scent made Eliza shudder. *The smell of fear,* whispered Mr. Todd in her ear. *Do you like it, Eliza? I do. It smells like you.*

Dread gripped her throat. A police officer pointed her way—but she already knew. First door on the right. She didn't want to take another step. Steeling herself—a futile effort—she entered.

More police crowded the wrecked room. Inspector Griffin waved her over, his face stormy. "I'm sorry you had to see this."

She picked her way over broken furniture, torn drapes, shattered porcelain . . . and her boots sank into the rug with a wet squelch.

So much blood.

Dark crimson pooled on the floor. More splashed the walls. The curtained bed was saturated, sheets dripping thickly. On the table, a trio of red-spattered crystal glasses lay in a pool of spilled liquor. The place stank, rich and rank like rotting meat.

The dead girl wore silk stockings and a torn black burlesque outfit. Blond pigtails flopped onto the wet pillow. One arm outstretched, rings clotted with blood. Beneath her hand, in a trickle of gore, lay a yellow candied apple.

Not like the others. I love my Rose. She's special.

Sick, Eliza covered her mouth. "I, er, questioned this woman in the Pentacle case. Rose O'Hara."

Grimly, Griffin gestured to the death scene. "He did *that* in a building packed with prostitutes, and no one heard a thing. Not a girl, a client, a servant. It's as if they're *protecting* him."

I've an idea for a game, Rose had said. *Want to play?* Numbly, Eliza stared at the carnage. Rose had many clients. It could have been another man. A stranger. It *must* have been. "Your telegram said good news."

"Bad for Miss O'Hara, good for us. If you can call it that."

Griffin nodded to a pair of constables who leaned over a be-draggled shape in the corner. "Can he walk yet?" His voice was jagged with loathing. "Good. Get him the hell out of here."

The two constables—both rotund and mustached like Tweedledum and Tweedledee—hauled a man to his feet.

A hunchbacked man with a twisted, handsome face. Stumbling, drunk, practically insensible. Naked below the waist, his long shirtfront drenched in drying blood. Gray hair plastered in it, nails crusted with it. A liquor bottle was overturned on the carpet at his feet. Beside it lay a gory butcher's knife.

Eliza retched. Poor Rose, in love with a monster. And look what love had gotten her. Butchered like a heifer, unable to scream or fight. Just . . . *used*. A joint of meat to be devoured and discarded.

"Take him to Bow Street," said Griffin shortly. "Five counts of murder, more to follow. And for God's sake, find him some trousers."

Dum and Dee dragged Edward Hyde out, propelling him by the armpits. Hyde's head lolled. Almost too intoxicated to move. Or was he just losing his mind?

"You know he ain't guilty!" Lizzie yowled like a wildcat, clawing for Eliza's eyeballs, making her stagger back. "This is a fit-up! Do something, you useless mopsy, or I'll do it for you!"

"Wait." It burst from Eliza's lips, an involuntary rush. "Let me talk to him."

Dum and Dee halted. Reluctantly, she stepped closer.

Hyde's storm-gray gaze rolled. Recognition, a faint crackle of lightning. "'Liza? Whasappening . . . issit tea time? Fetch your father a gin . . . s'good girl . . ." His breath smelled incongruously of aniseed. Not gin or whisky. An odd, bitter sweetness. "Where's Rose?" he added with a sloppy grin. "I love my Rose. She's a duchess, y'know. An' now she's royalty. Royalty! Ha-har!"

She brushed back his crusted hair, half blinded by tears. A thousand-pound weight seemed to crush her into the floor. A whisper was all she could force out. "Why did you do this?"

"Show you a thing," Hyde muttered, a glow lighting his eye. "Such a pretty thing."

So much blood. An itch under the floor of her mind refused to ease. Was it her own, rational voice? Or the sly specter of another, elegant murderer? *Remember Turquoise Tim, all the others? The Slasher wants meat, not blood.*

This is something else entirely.

"Thank you, gentlemen." Eliza fought to steady her trembling voice. What a laugh. Her whole body was shaking like a Bethlem palsy sufferer's. "We'll question him further at the cells. Carry on."

Head pounding, she turned away.

Rose's limp hand flopped, the lurid ghost of another dead woman's outstretched arm. Her mother on white sheets, lifeless fingers beseeching. Once a killer, always a killer. Eliza should have known.

Guilt chewed her belly, a hungry rat fighting for escape. She *had* known. She just hadn't wanted to face the truth: her father was a murderer born.

Her cowardice shamed her, dragging her back through ugly crimson memories to a time when she'd let another homicidal monster escape. Mr. Todd was no lunatic, to be absolved of his crimes. He was an abomination. She'd just been too obsessed to admit it. She'd failed Todd's victims, just as she'd failed the Slasher's. If she'd had the courage, how many people might still be alive?

She wouldn't make that mistake now. Never again.

Rose's rings glinted, sticky with blood. The left ring finger, in particular, sported a large brilliant-cut stone, similar to her own engagement ring.

Such a pretty thing . . . and now she's royalty.

Curious, she wiped the facets clean. Not blue. Clear. For a stone that size, most likely paste.

Or a diamond.

Oh, my. She stumbled towards the door. "I say, constables . . ."

But Dum and Dee had already carried Hyde into the corridor.

Lizzie sprinted after them, a furious red-skirted whirlwind. "Bring him back, you cretinous twin-fuckers! That's my father!"

But the constables ignored her, and dragged Hyde away. Lizzie screamed and clawed at them. No reaction.

Only a specter after all. Fancy that.

Below the window, in the street, a crowd jeered, hurling rocks and vegetables and more unpleasant things. Eliza swallowed, worms crawling in her lungs. "Harley, are we certain he's guilty?"

Griffin raised tired eyebrows. "Found at the scene, covered in blood, the knife practically in his pocket? Who'll believe he isn't?"

She paced, agitated. "But that's just it. He was so drunk

he could barely stand. He can't have sliced up poor Rose in that condition."

"So he did it sober."

"And then didn't run, but sat here and got plastered with blood all over him?"

Griffin pointed to the window, where the yelling grew louder. "If I let him go, they'll riot. Bow Street's the safest place for him, guilty or no."

Her temples throbbed. She pinched the bridge of her nose, dreading Lizzie's encroaching wrath. "You're right, of course. But . . ."

Griffin sighed. "Out with it, Eliza."

Her pulse stuttered. "With what?"

"Whatever you're not telling me. The Edward Hyde name. What was the clue? Another of your famous hunches?"

A sharp needle of remorse. He meant Razor Jack. She'd told Harley that was a hunch, an ethereal mix of intuition, trace evidence, and luck. A paint smear, a blood spot, a single crimson hair, a warm breath on her cheek in dreams.

But she hadn't discovered anything. Those tiny fragments were traps. Mr. Todd had baited her almost from the beginning.

Her guts churned, mortified. Harley trusted her. Believed in her quest for justice. Her friendship was all he had left. She couldn't let him down by admitting she'd lied. "Just something I heard. One of the girls, she—"

"I saw you take that letter at Ireton House." His dark eyes shone dully, exhausted. Defeated. "If you've something to say, best say it now."

Her eyes ached. His rage, she could accept. His coldness,

even. But his disappointment was too painful to bear. "I . . . well . . ."

A huge fist throttled her, shoving down her gullet. Her eyes bulged. Surely, blood spurted from her mouth, her throat pulverized to strings of ruddy flesh . . .

What are you doing? screamed Lizzie, not a specter but a monster inside, swelling to burst her skin apart. *Will you let them lock him up? Rape him, beat him bloody? String him up at ruined Newgate for the mob to jeer at? He's our FATHER, God rot you! All he wants is for you to love him. Why can't you understand?*

I loved him, Lizzie! she screamed back, but no air forced out. Her skin burned, her chest on fire as she retched for breath. *Remember? I was a little girl all alone. All I ever wanted was his attention, and in return he gave me* you!

Lizzie pummeled her with ferocious blows. *Squeak on our father, you vicious twat? When will you stop blaming him for what we ARE?*

Eliza's vision sheeted red. *I'm not like him, hear me? I'm not that monster's daughter!* But the pressure was too much. Need air . . .

Frantically, she gulped, and finally sucked in a desperate breath. An invisible knee slammed into her guts, doubling her over. "Ughk . . . Going to . . . be sick . . ." And she stumbled out, to Lizzie's mocking laughter.

Blood boiled behind her eyes, staining the world scarlet. She lurched onto the landing. Pain exploded in her head, knives chopping her skull to pieces, and halfway down the stairs, Lizzie screamed in triumph and splurted forth like a plague sore.

Ha ha, I'm out! About time. Eagerly, I stretch our muscles . . . and *her* limbs move.

What's this? Still in her body, God rot her, still wearing her face. But it's *mine* now and I'll do with it as I please.

I rake my nails down her cheek. *Splurt!* Blood oozes, and the sting makes me laugh. Take that, Eliza. You can't heal if we don't *change*. Hope it scars, you traitorous bitch.

Outside, the crowd shouts and sticky-beaks and throws rotten fruit. A tomato splats inside the front door, a rotting red stain. In the hall, Mrs. Fletcher sniffs at us, barricaded in her armor of green silken beauty. "Satisfied? Bringing disrepute on my house by arresting an honest man? I shall lose good business. You shan't get away with this!"

But her shimmering lashes betray her. Oho! Lady Frost-heart, weeping for her broken dreams. Never thought her capable of carrying a torch for anyone, let alone Eddie Hyde. And Rose died with Eddie's ring on her finger.

Despite my glee, our blood runs cold.

How does an innocent man—and I know Eddie's innocent, even without Todd's help—end up drenched in blood and liquor beside a corpse?

Someone fitted him up, that's how. Someone he trusts slipped him a bittersweet mickey finn and sent him to dream-land.

Someone like Letitia Fletcher. A jealous faded beauty, seeing him wedded to a girl twenty years her junior with firm titties and a pert backside. If I can't have him, no one can . . .

He's charmed her. A faint echo, clogging our brain like cobwebs. *The way he charmed everyone else. Including you.*

Who's that? I shake my head, clearing the nameless babble away. Maybe 'twas Fletcher what done for him. Or the Dodger, conniving to steal Eddie's throne. Maybe even the Philosopher himself, dusting his cruel hands of a rival.

Thing is, the real Slasher—Fancy Britches, whoever he be—still roams the streets. Only a matter of time before they find another butchered corpse, and then what for Eliza and Griffin's famous justice, eh?

Well, I don't give a shit. No one shops my father and gets away smiling. We'll uncover the truth, or I ain't Lizzie Hyde.

Which I ain't, not technically. Ha ha!

Still in Eliza's body, I push past Constable Puppy-Dog-Eyes and into the street. Eliza's stupid gray skirts tangle, and I kick 'em until they tear. Mud splashes, coating our calves in grime and shit. I swipe up a handful, smear it on her sleeve, up her neck, into her hair.

The rotten stench makes me chortle. Ha ha! Looks good there, Eliza. Because that's where we are. Wallowing in the shit, with all the liars and traitors and dirty coppers' snouts in London. At least when a thief turns king's evidence, he gets a pardon or a reward. What'd you get, Eliza? Not a brass-arse penny. You betrayed our father for *free*.

A riotous gin palace floods the street with light. I skip up and squash our nose to the window, wipe our tongue over the glass at the partying folks inside. Ooga booga, it's the Eliza-freak!

A cove in a greasy suit licks thick lips at me and grabs his crotch. Who's the whore now, Eliza? What say I offer him your services? Slide your hand into his stinky trousers, pull up your skirts and let him have his fun? How'd you like *them* apples?

Clonk! I slam her forehead into the window frame. Our nose numbs, teeth ringing. That prickly blue hellbrew froths in my veins and dissolves. She can't stop me. Her muscles are *mine* and I'll wreck this body as I choose.

Bang! Blood gushes, and I force a laugh up her throat. *Doinng!* Her spectacles break. Vomit chokes her, pain makes her dizzy, she cries out *stop, Lizzie, stop* but I won't, Eliza, I bloody well *WON'T* because you shopped Eddie Hyde and now he'll hang.

I'm screaming inside her body, howling with rage fit to split, but I'm weeping, too. D'you get what you wanted, Eliza? To be rid of our father, the way you want rid of me? Bleeding heaven, why d'you *HATE* us so much?

My mind shudders, stretches, rips thin . . . and a whispering voice half forgotten slips between the gaps. Tells me what to do. An old friend.

Crafty cleverness warms me, and I giggle. Aye, I can wait. Just you see the havoc I can wreak, Eliza. You'll never know when I'll appear—but you can be sure you won't enjoy it. And when the opportune moment comes? We'll see who hangs for murder. Aye, we most certainly will.

Schllp! Eliza's eyeballs bounced, correcting with a sickening snap. Her skin wriggled, shrinking like a rubber suit, and suddenly she was free.

Her muscles obeyed. Her limbs worked. No voice in her head, no alien prickle on her skin.

Nothing.

"Lizzie?" she whispered, feeling small and cold and threatened.

No answer.

Gingerly, she felt her aching temple. Blood smeared, mingled with mud from her spoiled dress. Her hair stank of excrement, and her cheek stung from Lizzie's nails. A stark warning of what lay ahead. Of the damage Lizzie could do.

Unsteady, aching, frightened, she turned for home.

Clunk! She tripped, and fell headlong into the mud. A carriage's wheels whizzed by, missing her nose by inches, and the driver cracked his whip in disgust. "Off the road, you gin-soaked tart!"

Dizzy, Eliza scrambled onto the pavement, wet skirts slopping like a beggar's. The road was clear. No rock or branch to catch her foot.

"Lizzie," she whispered into the silence, "did you do that on purpose?"

Just angry silence.

Defiantly Eliza raised her chin. "If I get squashed by a cart, you'll be just as dead, young lady. Remember that."

And she started for home, Lizzie's ghostly laughter just a threatening memory.

A TOUCH OF THE SECONDS

TWO HOURS, THREE 'BUSES, AND A TRAIN LATER, IN thickening dusk, an exhausted Eliza finally arrived at Cavendish Square. Her limbs hung heavy, her neck hurt from looking over her shoulder, her feet ached from walking. But she hadn't been followed. At least not by Enforcers or Veronica Burton.

No, the only things following her were accidents. Twice she'd slipped in a puddle and fallen on her face, and she'd collided with so many pedestrians that her throat was hoarse with apologies. *So sorry, sir. Oh, dear, has the mud ruined your hat? Forgive me, madam, how clumsy, let me pick up your parcels from that pile of horse dung.* Another time, she'd mysteriously slipped and wrenched her ankle while climbing down the omnibus ladder. Finally, she'd tumbled as she alighted from the Electric Underground at Farringdon, bruising her hip against the hard brick platform and scrabbling to a stop, inches from skidding under the train.

The damp square was quiet, the park almost deserted. Two gentlemen strolled the sodden circular paths, deep in discussion. A governess in plain black skirts huddled in her cape as she herded her rambunctious charge. "Thomas, don't play with that. It's dirty."

Suspicion pricked under Eliza's nails. The girl looked innocent. But she'd thought Veronica innocent, too. What about those men? Were they spies? What of this tramp in a moldy green coat, shovel hat pulled low, crouched beneath a lamppost? Her guts curdled. Anyone could be her enemy.

They're all in on it. Wyverne's scratchy voice, proclaiming conspiracy. Soon she'd be as mad as he, seeing threats under every rock. She daren't approach the front door. The Royal could be watching, and she didn't trust Lizzie to keep quiet. Not now. Maybe not ever again.

A quarter past seven, Seymour Locke had said. And it was growing dark.

Quietly she headed for the back, and found the door unlocked. A gloomy, quiet corridor, haunted by years of neglect. The floor had been swept, but the chandelier dripped cobwebs and the stairway down to the basement laboratory was coated in gray dust.

Henry's house was really two houses, back to back. The Cavendish Square end had been for Madeleine's use, with formal dining and drawing rooms for receiving calls. This older, less fashionable house he'd used for classes and dissections, his famed collection of medical specimens—and the mysterious doings in his locked laboratory.

Someone was crashing about at the front—no doubt Brigham and the Pooles, doing endless cleaning—and heating chimneys crackled faintly. A delicious, savory smell drifted from the kitchen.

Her stomach ached in response. She longed for nothing more than a hot bath, a meal, and a warm bed with no lurking nightmares. Unless Brigham could conjure Remy Lafayette, to sponge her aching back and cradle her to sleep. That would suit.

Dong! Her skin shrank in fright. *Dong! Dong!* Just an ancient, frowning grandfather clock. *You're late, Dr. Jekyll. Where have you been?*

Dong! it announced portentously four more times, and fell silent.

Seven o'clock.

Surely, nothing would happen at a quarter past. Locke was mad, or lying. Possibly both.

But doubt spidered down her spine as she turned away.

"Doctor?" Mr. Brigham trotted up, dust drifting from his curls. "Thought you was a burglar—" His eyes widened at her disheveled state. "Mary Mother of God. Not again?"

Gently she fended him off. "Just an accident. Nothing a bath and a rest won't cure." She petted Hipp, who'd dashed up the hallway at top speed and crashed headfirst into her filthy skirts.

"Doctor!" he yelled, bouncing. "Medical attention required! Make greater speed!" She smiled wearily. Imagine how she must look, smeared in excrement, spectacles hastily mended with thread, her face sporting alarming shades of black and blue.

Brigham fussed, relieving her of mantle and gloves. "Shall I call a doctor? Another, I mean. Not that you're not a good one. Would you like tea? Can I fetch you fresh clothes?"

Afraid of her, she realized with a twinge of surprise. Desperate to please the captain's wife, lest she fire him in a fit of pique. For all he knew, she was like his previous employer, a hateful shrew who took offense at the slightest lapse and changed the rules from day to day. "Don't fret, Charles. I'll survive a few moments longer."

"I hear congratulations are in order?"

"Hmm?"

"The broadsheets," he explained. "That Slasher case. May I say well done, madam?"

"Oh." She flushed, discomfited. "Yes. Thank you."

"I'll have Mrs. Poole bring tea and brandy. Oh," he added, proffering a pair of envelopes, "these came for you. Maybe they'll cheer you up."

She took them, and headed upstairs, Hipp bounding after. Her room was cheerful in warm firelight, the bottles and jars she'd saved from Russell Square glinting on the shelf. She sat by the window with a sigh, heedless of wet skirts. The first letter was in Marcellus Finch's careful copperplate.

EXPERIMENTS IN PROGRESS.

FASCINATING RESULTS TO SHOW YOU.

<u>PLEASE</u> COME.

MF

She tossed it aside. The handwriting on the second letter made her smile, and she tore it open with unseemly haste.

Dr. Jekyll,

I trust this finds you well. I should have liked to say goodbye in person

Her stomach twisted. Goodbye?

but my friends in Paris have decided I ought to stay a while, and I've really no reason to deny them, have I? They know all my secrets, and I needn't explain to you what a relief that is. Liberté ou mort, as the saying goes. Turns out I've misunderstood completely, and François was right about la Bête. About everything.

So I'm afraid I shan't be returning to you. Don't be sorry. You know it would never have lasted, not the way you live, and you're better off without me to complicate things. It's so liberating to be oneself at last. They know me in ways you never could. Besides, you'd never begrudge me a higher calling. I still admire you for that.

Anyway, you'll read of our purpose soon enough. A bloody business, but desperate peril requires desperate action. I trust you'll be pleased for me, and I can only hope you find your own happiness in some passion as noble as mine.

Best wishes,

R. Lafayette.

P.S. Please, keep the house. Everything's yours, in fact. I'll arrange it. You deserve that much.

Eliza reeled, weak with dizziness. This couldn't be real. But the handwriting was unmistakable. That curled "R" and flourished "y" in his signature. *R. Lafayette*. Not *Remy*. And that chilly, formal salutation—*Dr. Jekyll*—made her shiver.

Something odd about the address on the envelope, too. *E. Jekyll,* it said, *Russell Square*. Not *Dr. Eliza*. Just *E*.

What did it mean? Probably nothing.

Maybe everything.

Murky light pierced her gloom. Perhaps it was a hoax. Some ill-meaning miscreant had forged the letter to upset her.

Lizzie, did you do this?

Just cold silence.

But in the dark depths of her heart, Eliza knew the letter was real.

Angrily, she wiped her eyes. *Why so shocked, Eliza? You always knew this would happen.* Lizzie was right. Only a matter of time. Why would Remy stay, when the world offered so much more?

She forced herself to re-read the letter. A higher calling. Desperate action. *Liberté ou mort.*

EMPIRE ENVOYS KILLED IN BLOODBATH.

Her stomach lurched, sick. Oh, God. Had the sorcerers gotten to him, as they had poor François?

Her throat swelled. Who the hell cared? Remy was gone. He didn't love her. Didn't even want her. Probably never had.

It would never have lasted, not the way you live. He meant Lizzie. Her double-dealing, her split allegiance, the contrary impulses that crippled her. All this time, she'd deluded herself.

As if she could ever deserve a normal life.

She realized she'd crushed the letter in her fist, and forced her quivering fingers to relax. The paper dropped soundlessly to the carpet, a crumpled wreck.

Just like that.

Told you so! Lizzie sang, bursting back in with cruel vengeance. *Told you he was too good for you. Ha ha! Ain't even another woman, Eliza. He just can't be bothered. How does it feel to be second best?*

On the shelf, Mr. Todd's rolled oil painting mocked her. Innocent, stupid Eliza, sleeping while the world laughed. Such a fool, to imagine love could solve anything. People were dead because she'd believed that. All love did was hurt.

Her nerves stung raw, and in a fury, she grabbed the painting and flung it into the fire.

Flames licked greedily, consuming the chemical-soaked canvas like a monster. Paint bubbled and popped, red skirts and blond locks charring. Pain lanced her heart, chilly like ice—but she forced herself to watch, until her own painted face had sizzled to ash.

"Is everything well, madam?" Brigham hovered anxiously in the doorway.

She wiped her cheeks, forcing a smile. "Thank you. I'll take care of myself tonight. I'd like to be alone."

He eyed her uncertainly. "Very well. Come on, Hipp, let's get back to those rats." And he disappeared down the corridor, Hipp trotting dolefully at his heels.

Dully she watched them go. Brigham was a good lad. Would he even have a job after this? *Everything,* the letter said. The house, the money. None of it worth the spit in her mouth. Without Remy, what was the point of any of it?

She gritted her teeth on fresh tears. No time for self-pity.

She'd survived alone before. She was Dr. Eliza Jekyll, and she'd a murder case to solve. No one—not Edward Hyde, not Remy Lafayette, not even Lizzie—could take that away.

As if drawn by magnets, her thoughts veered to that dim basement.

A quarter past seven.

What if Locke wasn't insane? What would she find down there?

Resolute, she hurried downstairs until she stood before the dusty steps once more. Memories, certainly, of her father's secret midnight meetings, voices raised in argument, chalked formulae like magic spells on the blackboard. Flasks bubbling over gas flames, the smells of acid and potassium and sulfide gases.

She'd hoped to create new memories. Such a foolish dream.

Shivering, she laid her hand on the railing, and started down.

Dusty cobwebs dangled amidst the smell of old wood. The stairs creaked, nails screeching. Her boots left imprints in the dust. No one had ventured down here in years.

At the bottom, the way was blocked. The big iron door resembled a bank vault, with its heavy hinges and rust-stained locking wheel. She pushed aside the crusted brass panel over the combination lock, revealing the four sharp-notched levers, their corresponding numbers showing on cylinders of pale yellow shellac.

But what was the combination?

A magic number for my little lady. Vague images stirred, Henry laughing as he swung her high. He'd made a game of it, lifting her up so she could reach the numbers with her pudgy little fingers. *Who's the birthday girl?*

She manipulated each lever with her forefinger until the numbers read *2-5-0-4.*

With both hands, she wrenched the locking wheel clockwise. It didn't budge. She pulled harder. *Errrk!* At last, the wheel lurched into motion. *Clunk! Clank!* With a dusty sigh, Henry's laboratory door swung open.

Inside, all was dark. She dusted spider strands from the old-fashioned lever that controlled the lights, and forced it downwards with both hands. *Screech!* With a sizzle of blue voltage, the lights popped on.

The place looked abandoned in a hurry. Dried inkwells still on the desks, smudged chalk on the blackboard. Schematics pinned to the walls, the paper curled at the edges and chewed by bugs. Retorts still standing on trestles, flasks coated in dust, their contents long since desiccated.

In a shadowy corner hulked a strange contraption of brass and steel, crusted with crystals and mirrors. About the size of a velocipede, a dense machine core surrounded by a set of concentric metal rings, their serrated edges stained with rust. An array of levers and buttons was bolted on, and a collection of odd electrical circuitry crowned the top. Old-style components, bulky capacitors, insulation thick and cumbersome. Spikes like lightning rods bristled in a monster's grin.

One of Victor's monstrosities? Who knew to what frightful purpose it tended? She shuddered, recalling the Chopper's awful resurrection machine, his meticulously sewed homunculi.

The bookshelves had lain undisturbed for years, the volumes oozing greenish mold. Their sorry state scandalized and saddened her. Why hadn't Marcellus rescued them? For that matter, why hadn't she?

But she knew. Everything about this place, as Lizzie might say, gave her the creeping heebie-jeebies. Too many ghosts brought grotesquely to life. She wanted to slam the vault door, run up those stairs into the light. Leave this house and her bruised heart behind forever.

The door to her father's private office lay ajar. She felt inside the doorframe—how easily it came back, all these years later—and flicked the light switch.

Nothing. Perhaps the wiring had been masticated by rats. She spied a candlestick on a shelf, blew away dust and lit it. Light flared, drawn inside like iron to a magnet, illuminating the green baize desk, its wooden pen stand and inkwell, the leather-upholstered desk chair. Portraits glimmered on the picture rail: not the sharp-eyed Philosopher, but Galileo Galilei, solemn William Harvey, and the countrified Edward Jenner, her childhood hero.

A crucible crouched atop the glass-fronted poisons locker. The desk drawer lay open, and papers ruffled from the filing cabinet, as if someone had grabbed important documents in haste. On the desk sat a crusted beaker, dusty red crystals gleaming. Another lay shattered on the floor.

Elixir. Alchemy. Dark magic. Shapes leapt at her from the tall cheval mirror. Twisted, transcendental reflections, warping into the monstrous face of Edward Hyde.

Behind her, paper crackled. She whirled, her candle guttering. "Who's there?"

Out in the laboratory, electric lights flickered, a ghastly blue strobe. Were shapes moving, by that infernal machine?

"I'm armed!" she called sharply, moving closer. "Show yourself."

The air shimmered, writhing like a trapped ghost. A blue filament crackled, glowed brighter, flashed with a *crrack!* like thunder.

And then a man's voice, bewildered and desperately familiar. "What's happened? Quentin, my dear fellow, whatever did you . . . oh!"

Breathing heavily, the man stumbled into the light.

Tall, his dark hair awry, wearing an old-fashioned high collar and white shirtsleeves. He stared about him in astonishment—and his gaze settled on her. Storm-gray eyes, alive with curiosity.

Her eyes.

She stared back, open-mouthed.

"Oh, my," whispered Henry Jekyll hoarsely. "It worked."

THE TRUTH OTHER MEN
CANNOT SEE

A LUMP SQUEEZED ELIZA'S THROAT. "F-FATHER?
Are you a ghost?"

"Eliza." A wild-eyed stare, and finally a smile.
"My God. You're all grown up."

"But this is impossible." Her thoughts sprinted in circles.
Time travel was irrational. A myth. It broke all the rules the
universe relied upon. Lines of force, luminiferous aether,
call it what you wished. Everything would disintegrate. This
couldn't happen.

Yet here he stood. Henry Jekyll, mid-thirties at most. A
handsome man, with dark lashes and a strong face. Could she
see Edward Hyde, lurking behind the façade? That hawkish
grin, that mad glint of eye?

Memories swamped her, of Henry pacing the room, de-
claiming some irrefutable truth to his colleagues, waving a
cigar he'd forgotten to smoke. Henry writing feverishly at his
desk by candlelight. Henry tinkering with his retorts, tending
his colored phials, tapping on the glass as strange substances

melted and boiled. *Look, Eliza, phlogiston. Smell it? That's the stuff of life.*

Tears scorched behind her eyes. This man, not Edward Hyde, was her true father, no matter what biology had to say on the matter. A scientist, clever and curious. Not a rapacious madman.

Henry gripped her hands urgently. He smelled of smoke and chemicals, heartbreakingly familiar. "We haven't much time. Whatever you did, you must undo it immediately. Everything depends upon it!"

"I-I didn't do anything," she stammered. "I only ventured down here five minutes ago. This place, it's been deserted for years. We moved away when . . ." She trailed off, visions of paradoxes and unknowable foreknowledge colliding in her mind.

"But you've altered the machine somehow." Henry's face was pale. "Why else would it work now?"

Her brain stretched painfully around torturous concepts, and she wanted to weep. She didn't want to have this conversation. Didn't want to discuss secret projects and time travel—*time travel!*—and machines that couldn't exist. Rather, to laugh, reminisce, share stories. Catch up on twenty years they should have had, but for Hyde.

Twenty years, for heaven's sake.

"I didn't touch anything," she insisted. "I was told to be here at a quarter past seven. I came. That's all."

Henry's gaze burned, too intense. "By whom? *Who told you the time?*"

She stared, taken afright. "A scientist from a project called

Interlunium. He said I'd know what to do when I got here. His name is Seymour Locke."

Henry's face drained. "Oh, my. Eliza, you must stop them. It's imperative."

Her head pounded with frustration. "Stop who doing what? Papa, please . . ."

A blast of hot breeze teetered her backwards. The air wavered, unstable, and the smell of burning aether thickened. Henry swore. "Field integrity is failing. Still too unstable! Oh, this is insufferable!" Menacingly, the machine hummed, vibrating the floor. "Listen, my darling. This machine is dangerous. There's a book I'll make sure you get. Take it to Ireton House in Red Lion Square. The lady there will help you fix what we've done. Ireton House. Do you have it?"

"Y-yes, but . . ."

"No more time." Henry kissed her forehead, and backed away towards the machine, where the blue filament burned and the metal rings whirred, their crystals hurling rainbows. "I'm proud of you, Eliza. Never forget that. Tell your mother I love her."

"But—" An invisible hammer smashed between Eliza's eyeballs. She cried out in agony . . . and *slllrrrp!* Out I wriggle like a shedding snake.

"Henry Jekyll, as I live and breathe." I hold my arms wide, laughing at the dumb-fuck look on his face. "Give us a kiss, Papa."

Henry's mouth makes an *O,* a perfect expression of horror, like his spirit's woken up in hell. He reaches out, but he's fading into thin air like a ghost, growing more transparent every second. Dragged back to his own time. "Quentin, for God's sake, I'm not ready . . ."

And he vanishes, in a puff of self-righteous shock.

Ha. So now he knows. In ten years or so—ten years from *now* in Henry's time, though it's ten years *ago* and more in ours—Eddie gives Eliza the elixir, and makes *me*. And not a god-rotted thing Henry can do about it.

Pah! I spit on the floor, my disgust rich and raw. Fun without responsibility, debauchery without guilt. To fuck exotic dollies and smoke Canton dope and drink yourself stupid, then front up next morning to your Harley Street surgery, fresh as spring dew with your conscience clear. S'what you birthed Eddie for, you snide-arse hypocrite, so don't be gawping at *me* like I've turds all over my dress, thank you very much . . . oh, wait. I do! Har-de-har!

Same thing Eliza wants. Life without risk. No such luck, you cowardly tart. Nice seeing you again. And *thrrrp!* Back in I go.

Eliza staggered, ears ringing. Her vision shimmered, a twisting tumult. The stink of boiling aether drowned her, and she collapsed to the floor in a black faint.

He pulls back, dark eyes afire, mingled shame and desire. "My God. Miss Jekyll, forgive me."

I laugh, the flavor of his eager kiss a glory in my mouth. Her mouth, that is. Her face he adores, her touch he craves . . . or so he thinks.

"Not my forgiveness you want, is it?" I rub my thumb over his lips, and the catch in his breath is

black temptation. His scent of jasmine a taunting challenge.

I don't know why I want this. I don't know any damn thing. I just do.

That's who I am, by God. The doer. The devil on her shoulder, the canker in her heart. I'm Lizzie Hyde. And screw thinking before I act.

He averts his face, still breathing hard. "It's wrong. I can't."

"Oh, I think you can." I push him back onto the chaise, yanking her skirts to climb after, and giggle at his reaction. Sweet Byron. It's too easy, this business of rot and regret. I wonder what he looks like, under his sober garb? An angel, I don't doubt. A dark-eyed angel of ruin.

His eyelids flutter closed, and he whispers the last-ditch protest of surrender. "He'll find out."

I unfurl her long pale hair, let it tumble. Slip to the floor on my knees. "I won't tell if you won't."

"Miss Jekyll . . . Eliza . . . please . . ." But he can't talk now. Not when I loosen his clothes with her hands, touch him with her fingers, linger over his secret skin with her hot breath, her lips, her tongue . . .

Cold white air, the stink of piss and rats, the padded wall against our back. I crouch in the corner, laughing inside. This cell is cold, but we're warm. Hands tucked beneath our thighs, hiding my stolen sweetheart. It's our secret.

Our eyes, wide with terror, setting the snare. Our voice, strained with heartache, baiting the trap. "Mr. Starling? I thought we were friends. Why are you keeping me here? I'm not insane! Please, you must release me!"

The boy who loves her leans closer on his haunches. He smells of jasmine and guilt, sweet and bitter. "You're not yourself. The doctors here will make you well. It's for the best." His long poet's hair falls forwards as he strokes her cheek. His dark eyes shimmer. "I was a fool. I never meant this to happen. I'm so sorry."

We whip back our arm and strike.

Sspllt! The rusted blade stabs deep. It's easy. No resistance at all.

He screams, clutching his blood-spurting eye. And I laugh fit to crack. "Not so pretty now! Never mind, Byron. It's . . ."

". . . it's for the best."

Startled, Eliza recoiled from her faint.

Stiffly, she winced. Her knees and elbows ached where they'd hit the cold laboratory floor. How much time had passed? Minutes? An hour?

That nightmare vision of Lizzie, that stabbing blade. She shuddered. It was real. She'd done those things. That illicit heat, the cruel and senseless deception, the burning splash of blood. Pure luck that Starling hadn't died. *Once a killer, always a killer.* Her sanity stretching . . .

She jerked upright, head whirling. Henry . . .

But Henry was gone. She was alone. She, Eliza Jekyll. Daughter of a killer, with murder in her blood. A taint that couldn't be erased or washed away.

Eliza Hyde.

Only the machine remained, still and silent now. A strange metal beast, its single blue eye glaring. *What did you do?* it seemed to growl. *How did you awaken me?*

Her mind still boggled. Professor Crane was selling a time machine to the traitor Veronica Burton. To *Liberté du Sang*. And someone disliked the idea enough to commit murder.

Ireton House, Red Lion Square. The lady there will help you. But Crane was dead. So what now?

Bzzt!

Eliza scrambled up. What on earth?

Bzzt! An electric buzzer, loud enough to rattle the floorboards.

The bell on the servants' door. She faltered. Surely it was Burton, smug and steely-faced, her Enforcers brandishing electric weapons.

"The lady of the house is not to be disturbed." Brigham's voice drifted down. "I assure you, sir, I'll keep it quite safe. What do you mean, 'her eyes only'?"

Curious, Eliza climbed the stairs. At the door, Brigham was holding a stand-off with a wiry fellow in a dark suit who'd planted himself on the doorstep. "Don't be a pest, man. The lady's indisposed. Come back tomorrow."

"It's all right, Charles." She craned her neck. "Yes?"

The fellow blinked through thick clerk's spectacles. "Fogg, ma'am, of Utterson and Jaggers. Are you Miss Eliza Jekyll?"

No, the name's Hyde. Sorry to have wasted your time. But her heart skipped. Utterson. Henry's lawyers. "Yes, I'm she."

Mr. Fogg proffered a paper-wrapped package.

"What is it?"

"Haven't the *foggiest*, ma'am." Fogg chuckled at his own well-worn joke. "It's been lying around the office for years. Instructions to deliver to Eliza Jekyll, today's date, half past seven in the evening." Eagerly, he peered past her into the house. "We've taken bets, you know. All the new clerks have to make a guess. The smart money was on a long-lost orphan. Are you a long-lost orphan?"

"I'm afraid not."

He sighed. "That's ten shillings I owe that blackguard Tulkinghorne. Anyway, here I am, right on time. And this is for you."

Gingerly, she accepted it. "But I've only just moved here. How did you know my address?"

"It's written right there. Just moved here, you say? Funny thing, that." Fogg tipped his hat, and went on his way, whistling a cheerful tune. *"In Dublin's fair city, where the girls are so pretty . . ."*

She examined the package thoughtfully as Brigham closed the door.

MISS ELIZA JEKYLL

HYDE HOUSE, CAVENDISH SQUARE

(ENTRANCE OFF CHANDOS STREET)

<u>HER EYES ONLY!</u>

A funny thing, indeed.

The paper unwrapped easily. Out fell a note, faded with age.

My dear Eliza,
As promised. You know what to do.
Your loving father,
Henry.

The leather-bound book had a neatly printed title page.

THE PHYSICS OF
MULTI-DIMENSIONAL SPACE
BY
MICHAEL FARADAY
WITH SPECIAL MATHEMATICAL NOTES
BY MISS ADA BYRON

Her skin tingled. *Red Lion Square*. Ephronia Crane's secret workroom.

Project Interlunium.

But who would she find there?

SPECULUM MUNDI

FRIGID MIST HAD FALLEN OVER RED LION SQUARE, wreathing Ireton House in a ghostly shroud. No lights shone in the grim stone casements. The square was empty, just wind and freezing raindrops. In the darkness, a lost owl hooted, *ooh-oooh! Ooh-oooh!*

Cheeks tingling, Eliza hopped up the front steps and tried the door. It didn't budge.

Hipp bounced at her feet. "Locked. Entry inadvisable. Home, three-quarter mile."

"Don't be silly," she scolded, tucking the calico-wrapped book more firmly under her arm. "We must find the hidden workroom. Time travel, Hipp! Aren't you excited?"

He just whirred gloomy cogs, *rrk! rrk!*, and flashed his red *unhappy* light.

She trotted around to the back, sidestepping muddy puddles though her skirts already stank thanks to Lizzie's games.

Lizzie hadn't emerged since Henry's laboratory. Not a peep. But that prickly blue substance frothed yet in her stomach, undigested and unwanted.

Thwart me, will you? she hissed at it. *Jump out in front of my father? I'll teach you.*

But Lizzie's silence only made Eliza worry harder.

The back door was locked. Dismayed, she cupped her hand to peer inside. For once, she could use Lizzie and her thieving friends. "No one's here, Hipp. We'll just have to break the window—"

Electricity crackled in the tang of hot aether, and a warm pistol pressed the vein in her throat. "That won't be necessary."

Oh, bother.

"E-e-eh!" Hipp squawked, scuttling for cover. Stiffly, Eliza straightened, clutching the book tightly. In the glass door, the man's reflection gleamed darkly. Glinting eyeglasses, mirroring the burning coil of his pistol. One lens white, one blue.

She forced a shaky smile. "Byron. No need for that." But in a flash, the way he'd behaved around her for the last few days glared, garish and threatening. His awkward advances, the letter, the flowers. She'd imagined it innocent.

Now—with his pistol shoved under her chin, his body against her back, his feverish heat suffusing her—she wasn't so sure. That nightmare of Lizzie in the asylum, her rusty blade scything down . . .

"Shut up." Starling's hand trembled, and hot metal singed her neck. Half an inch of trigger from blowing her head off. "The day Antoinette died, I told him you'd be a problem, but would he listen? Does he ever?"

"Who, Byron? Tell me what's going on and we can talk about this." Her face burned. *By all means, let's reminisce about old times, when Lizzie seduced you and stabbed your eye out. Fine weather we're having.*

Starling pressed his nose into her hair, inhaling deeply. "Still so lovely, Eliza. I'd have married you, you know, this time around. Done the proper thing. Kept you out of sight and out of trouble. But you had to be already engaged. And to such a first-class arse, too. I'd credited you with better taste."

"Unhand me and we'll hear no more of this." But her courage rang false. Starling was shaking, burning up with unknowable urgency. She could smell his hair against her cheek, sweet jasmine mixed with oily desperation. Reason wasn't paramount in his decision-making.

Curse his god-rotted pistol. If only she had her stinger. Where was Hipp when she needed him? Shivering in the cesspit?

Irony stung her mouth. She'd fought so hard to remember. Now, she only wished to forget what Lizzie had done. The taste of Byron's skin, his sweat, his fingers clenching in her hair. The bitter ache of lies and dumb rebellion. Her knife slicing into flesh, that fountain of blood . . .

"Such a waste," murmured Starling, as if he'd somehow heard her. "Antoinette was a *whore*, Ephronia a *thief*, Ormonde a *traitor*. What will it say on your epitaph? I fancy it'll say *liar*."

"You killed them." Her swallow hurt. "Why? They did you no harm."

"Oh, that wasn't me." A dark chuckle. "You know what that's like, don't you? To watch on while someone else does the dirty work?"

"What? Then who?"

"Does it matter? I only want what's mine. That book, for instance."

"So *you* burned my house down," she snapped, feeling giddy. Relief or idiocy? Did she even believe him? "Thank you *very* much. I knew I should never have believed that little monster Wyverne."

"D'you think tutoring privileged little girls like you is the extent of my ambition? I gave my life to that infernal machine. I should have been famous. But that greedy bitch wanted to sell it to a bunch of maniacs and leave nothing for me!" His breath roughened on her neck. "I need you to imagine my frustration, Eliza. It's important you understand how I feel."

"No, Byron, it isn't." Her feelings of guilt maddened her. No matter what had passed, he'd no right to act this way. "You men are all the same. Everything's about how *you* feel and what *you* want—ow!"

Hiss-zzap! "Think I enjoyed watching Antoinette flaunt her body to get ahead?" he hissed. "Think Ephronia didn't bat her eyelashes for her privy council cronies when she wanted money? I have to *work* for what I've got."

"Poor you," she retorted. "All that being listened to and taken seriously, and reaping proper rewards for your effort. It must be *such* a trial. If you're planning to shoot me, sir, kindly stop whining and proceed." But she shivered. Such destructive self-pity. *It isn't fair, you don't understand, what about me?* How many times had Lizzie said similar things? How many times had she?

A melting smile. "Well, I could. I imagine it'd feel good. But then you'd never find out what's in that secret laboratory, would you?" He jingled a key ring against her ear. "Curiosity was always your weakness, Miss Jekyll. Curiosity and recklessness—but that wasn't all you, was it?" He watched her, fascination sparring with disgust across his expression. "Help me, or die ignorant. Your choice."

Glaring, she snatched the keys, and unlocked the door.

Starling ushered her forwards, grim. Inside, a chill breeze whistled, and irritably she brushed aside floating cobwebs. "Where are we going?"

"Quiet," hissed Starling, jabbing the pistol into her back.

In the front library, Ephronia's corpse was gone, of course. Books replaced neatly on the shelves, the desk tidied by some helpful constable. But the armchair and carpet still showed bloodstains, and she fancied she could see remnants of those ugly smears on the spotted mirror. *Thief,* it sniggered at her. *Whose letter did you steal today? Whose life?*

"Well?" She dropped the book on the desk, planting hands on hips. "If you're so clever?"

"The entrance must be in here somewhere." Starling strode around, waving the pistol carelessly as if he'd forgotten it in his excitement. "The workroom itself must be underground. All space on the plans is accounted for."

Anticipation sparkled, and Eliza stifled a curse. Despite everything, she longed to see the time machine in action. She wanted to see it *work.* "Could it be a bookshelf, or the fireplace? Hidden hinges worked by a lever?"

"You try that wall. Springs, switches, buttons. Anything." Starling was already running his hands along the cases, feeling for irregularities. His eagerness reminded her of the Philosopher, when some curious point of science grabbed his attention. It made Starling look young again, unspoiled by cynicism or ambition, and that only stoked her anger higher. What had corrupted the keen student she'd admired?

But she knew. A girl he'd tried to help—perhaps a girl he'd loved, however forbidden or shameful it had felt to him to want her—had stabbed him through the eye, for no better reason than to watch him scream.

Hell of a way to break a man's heart.

Sympathy warmed her, and she doused it firmly. It didn't give him the right to shove a pistol in her face.

She joined him, and soon they'd searched all the shelving with no result. She tugged the sconces above the mantel. Nothing. She stood back, dusting her hands. "Well, unless it's some mechanism we don't understand . . ." Her gaze lit on the huge silver-backed mirror. "Wait. What about the glass?"

"What about it?"

She pressed her palms against it, testing. "Locke kept staring into it, the night Griffin and I examined Ephronia's body." Ha. To think she'd imagined him soul-searching. "He knew where the secret prototype was all along. He just didn't know how to get in!"

"Let me see." Starling knocked on the mirror, testing different areas. *Bmmf, bmmf, bmmf . . . bnngg!* His final blow rang hollow.

A secret door.

"Help me find the mechanism." His good eye glittered with excitement. He'd put his pistol aside, forgotten. She didn't care. Together, they examined the mirror's edges, put weight on different corners, pushed and tugged. Starling knelt to scrape back the rug in search of a floor lock, and Eliza reached for the top, stretching on tiptoe.

Above the silvered glass shone a tiny Latin epigram, painted in bronze.

IPSE, it said. *Myself.*

Surely it must be a clue.

The exhortation above the entranceway to Ireton House rang dissonant chimes in her head. *QUID ME RESPICIS, VIATOR?*

Why do you look back at me, traveler? She frowned. Well, why?

"Aha!" crowed Starling, plucking at a thin metal strip jammed beneath the mirror's bottom corner. "Stand back!"

Strange foreboding chilled her bones. "Byron, don't—"

He'd already pulled the handle. *Crr-ICK!* The lever snapped back . . . and a cloud of white powder hit Starling in the face.

He screamed, spectacles melting down his cheeks. Eliza recoiled, aghast, as the acid ate into his face, chewing away skin and muscle and bone with a hideous hissing noise. Blood bubbled, and he fell, clawing at his gelatinous eyes.

In less than a minute, he lay still, smoke curling from burned flesh. Quite dead.

What an excellent, abominable booby trap.

Swiftly, she plucked up the pistol and tested it, *hiss-flick!* The charge was still good. Warily, she eyed the enemy mirror. Now what?

The epigram sneered back, belittling her shabby reflection in the spotted glass. IPSE, the letters scoffed. *Myself. Look at yourself, woman. You're a disgrace.* Mussed hair, filthy skirts, wide glossy eyes like a madwoman's.

Why do you look back at me, traveler? Go on your way.

"*Vade,*" she mused. "Walk on. Leave 'myself' behind. Or . . ."

Carefully, she swung on one heel, facing the opposite direction.

The bookshelf stared back at her. That same oaken shelf, which the killer had cleared. Hunting for Crane's book, she'd assumed.

But what if he'd been hunting for something else?

She crossed the upturned rug and swept the armful of books onto the floor. In the shelf's corner, concealed in polished oak, was a tiny brass button.

She pressed it. *Pop!* Silently, the right-hand edge of the mirrored wall swung inwards.

Rusted iron steps beckoned into dark depths. Distantly, she heard clanging metal and the crackle of electricity, her nose tingling with stormy aether.

The killer could have been inside all along. Behind the mirror. Watching her.

And she'd a pretty good idea who. She ought to call the police. Stay safe. Summon Inspector Griffin and his constables, fade into the background as a respectable woman should.

Nervous giggles bubbled in her chest. Curiosity and recklessness. She hadn't become a police physician to avoid the front lines. Besides, time—that elusive quicksilver—was running short.

Underground laboratories, mad scientists, impossible machines. Pah. All in a day's work.

She tucked the book under her arm, gripped the pistol, and started down.

THE MOST DIABOLICAL KIND

DONG! DONG! HER FOOTSTEPS RANG TOO LOUDLY. So much for stealth. The narrow stair smelled musty, of dust and hot wire. She ducked torn cobwebs to reach the bottom.

Ahead, bluish lights glimmered, luring her like fairy flames into the mire. A brass anteater scuttled across her path, concertina nose snuffling after a startled metal centipede, *click-clack-click-clack!*

She hefted her pistol at eye level. "Who's there?"

Just screeching metal, clanging glass. The glow grew brighter as she walked, and finally she emerged into the light.

A vast basement, rows of arc-lights hovering into the distance. Benches were loaded with voltmeters, ampmeters, magnetometers, instruments to measure calorific and de-phlogistication and aetheric disturbance. On a shelf lay an optical, similar to her own, multiple lenses on gleaming brass stalks. Crane had known Henry Jekyll, after all, walking the same shadowy, unorthodox corridors. Perhaps he'd shown her an early design.

In the center, beneath a shining arc-lamp, sat the machine.

Larger than Henry's, a set of crystal-studded brass rings twelve feet in diameter orbiting the aetheric generator, where a knot of blue filaments crackled and hissed. Tangled wires hung, clipped to the testing equipment. Heat sinks, lightning rods, power drains, and other unrecognizable parts protruded like bristling spines.

On the floor, tied to a heavy table with stout rope, slouched Seymour Locke.

She stared, her confidence crumbling to dust. Surely Locke was responsible. This had to be a ruse.

"Dr. Jekyll." Locke coughed hoarsely. Hair lank, skin sallow, eyes over-bright with fever. As if he'd been trapped here a while. "You found us."

Cautiously, she edged closer, pistol ready. "Us? I left Starling outside."

A caustic smile. "Thought I heard him howling. Get the acid, did he? Always was over-confident. Nice plan of yours, to get him to go first. I should've thought of that."

"Why are you tied up?"

"I truly thought you'd arrive before me. Funny, how things work out. Tell me you didn't do as I asked, Doctor. Tell me you didn't bring your father's cursed book."

The package smarted under her arm. "But . . ."

Locke swore. "Of course you did. That's how it happens. Knew I could rely on you." Bitterly he jerked his chin towards the machine. "He's over there. I only wish I'd warned you. All I can say in my defense is that I didn't know."

Inside the machine, bolted on with sturdy steel bands, was a metal stool. And on it, fiddling ferociously with a row of buttons and levers, sat Seymour Locke.

He wore a dark coat and fawn trousers, his long blond hair tossed over one shoulder in an untidy knot. Unshaven, scarred and bruised, dark crescents beneath glittering eyes. The Locke she knew was twenty-five at most. This fellow looked forty.

Eliza's eyes boggled. Switched from one Locke to the other, her brain refusing to surrender to the truth.

Time shift. Locke had traveled into his own past—and met himself.

Locke the elder grinned. The same cold, insolent smile, sharpened by a broken front tooth. "Dr. Jekyll. So glad you could join us."

Tossed about his neck, beneath his ragged hair, was the bloodstained blue scarf.

Some long-haired reprobate in a top hat. The mysterious visitor had been Locke all along.

Just not the same one.

"Don't look so shocked." He jumped from his stool and limped closer, gait hitching. "Is that my book? Not before time." A husky chuckle, his voice ruined by drink or abuse or some other frightful circumstance. "Before time. Ha! Honestly, these jokes never get old." His right sleeve was pinned roughly over a truncated forearm. Somewhere— some*when*—he'd lost a hand. "Now give over, there's a good stooge."

Clutching the book, she backed away, pistol steady. "Not a chance. Untie him. We're leaving—"

"Leaving!" Hippocrates barreled belatedly down the stairs, splashed with noisome filth. "Escape imperative! Make greater speed!" He hurtled into her skirts, knocking her off balance, and the book slipped from her grip and fell to the floor.

In a flash, Locke the elder dived in and wrenched her pistol away.

But he didn't point it at her.

Crrack! Blue current forked, stabbing the floor beside the book. Locke cursed his aim—left-handed, of course, and to think she'd imagined he'd missed his shot at the demonstration through lack of practice—and fired again, point blank. A much weaker blast, but it was enough. The dry paper burst into flames, and swiftly reduced to ash.

Hipp cowered behind her skirts. "Error," he muttered. "Idiot. Sorry."

Eliza stared, aghast. The air shimmered with excess potential, making her woozy. "What have you done? That's Mr. Faraday's book. Now you'll never fix your machine."

The younger Locke, who was wriggling in his ropes, just looked at her and laughed.

Locke the elder laughed, too, the same yet strangely different. Bitter, painful to hear. "Oh, the machine works. That's the thing. *It works too well.* I've spent the last eight years trying to *stop* the god-awful thing from working."

"But Interlunium . . . you needed Mr. Faraday's book. Starling said so."

Locke the elder snorted. "Starling's an idiot. That iteration of this fiasco has long been done with. I barely recall it." He kicked viciously, scattering the ashes of Faraday's masterpiece. "In any case, who needed Faraday? He couldn't even solve the field equations without Ada Byron, and look where that got him. Think she betrayed him to the Royal for lines of force? No, it was this that terrified her. Pity for him she didn't realize the entire project was my idea all along."

"So," she murmured, "it was *you* Ephronia was afraid of. A lowly assistant, you said. But Wyverne knew better, didn't he? Only no one believed him."

"Afraid so. You could ask Henry," he added with a cruel smile, "if he wasn't dead."

Clunk! More puzzle pieces slotted into place. "Henry's student. Seymour Q. Locke. You're Quentin!"

"Very good," he declared with a flick of long hair. "I was the real brains. Henry and Finch and their cronies were just passengers. Too scared even to test it. Not a pair of balls between them. So they sent me here, to the future. But the machine got damaged and I got stuck here. Or rather, *he* did." He waved a disgusted arm at younger Locke. "And now the thick-headed twist is rebuilding it, isn't he, with Ephronia and Antoinette and the rest. Of course they had to die."

The younger Locke gave the same arrogant head-toss, angry curls flying. "So you killed them, just to prevent the machine from ever existing? Congratulations, idiot. Great job. It's gone swimmingly."

Eliza blinked. "But you—he—must have succeeded in rebuilding it! Or he *will*. For you to come here from his future."

"Give the lady a prize," sneered Locke the elder. "Hark at the poor lamb. He still thinks he can return to his own time and live out his life. Ha! Seymour old thing, you've no *idea* what's about to happen." He shrugged. "Or, in this case, what *isn't* about to happen."

Alarms clanged in her head. Mr. Paxton's insistence that the engine was dangerous, that it ate up precious aether and destabilized the fabric of the world. "What do you mean? Does it cause some catastrophe?"

"Aether disturbance," said Hipp helpfully, poking his head from under a table. "Cataclysmic. Probability high."

"Oh, it's worse than that." A nasty broken-toothed grin. "Luckily, you'll never know. Because I'm about to destroy this machine, along with all evidence it ever existed. I was on track, you know. Everything was at last going to plan. And then *you* came along, and started *enabling* the cursed thing."

Her blood chilled. Blithely, she'd collected the evidence. Ephronia's notes. Henry's prototype. Mr. Faraday's book.

"Clever, aren't you?" Locke the elder wiped his damp face with his forearm, and recharged the pistol to point it at her. "A shame, really. Because now the only evidence left is this machine, *him*"—he gestured rudely to the younger Locke, who scowled—"and *you*."

TIME'S ARROW

WAIT." SHE BACKED AWAY, THINKING HARD. "WE can work this out."

"No more scheming," snapped Locke. "Eight years, I've tried to put things right. Must have jumped a hundred times. I've sabotaged experiments, burned laboratories, interrupted meetings, destroyed transcripts. Threats, extortion, kidnapping, assault, blackmail." An ugly laugh. "Once, I even betrayed them all to the Royal. But nothing works. No matter what I do, or how many times I try, science will out. You can't kill an idea without killing people. Lesson ended."

She clenched her teeth, enraged. Always, with killers, it was the "only way." *They made me! I had no choice!* Bollocks, as Lizzie might say. "That's a rotten excuse for murder," she snapped, before she could stop herself. "There's *always* a choice."

"Don't bait me," he snarled. "I *loved* Ephronia. Killing her was the hardest thing I've ever done, even after all these years. After her, Antoinette was easy."

Two killers, she'd thought—or one killer who could be in two places at once. Ha. *Brava,* Constable Perkins. "You did them in reverse order. First Ormonde, then Ephronia, then Antoinette. The line of least effort."

"The line of least murder," he hissed. "I didn't *want* to kill them all. Ormonde was old. I thought killing him might be enough, but no. That's why Ephronia had to be next. She knew the most. I tried to *save* lives."

He was getting riled, his aim wavering. "Oh, I'm sure," she taunted. "Did you even notice Ephronia was with child before you choked her to death? Would you even have cared?"

The younger Locke cursed, fighting his ropes. "Bleeding Christ, what the hell happens to us? When do I go insane?"

Locke the elder paled. "What? No, she didn't say anything. Surprised to see me, I suppose," he added with a dark snigger. "It was something of a tumultuous reunion."

Eliza nodded, stalling. Keep to the plan. Distract him, grab the pistol . . . "So it *was* you who slept with her the night she died."

A cunning wink. "What if it was? Check that one off the to-do list, Seymour old thing. Nothing thrills a scientist more than learning her pet invention works. She practically tore my clothes off. And to think I'd once wooed her all those months without success." A sigh. "Poor Ephronia. It hurt me, truly. I bawled like a baby when I choked her."

"For God's sake," spat the younger Locke savagely, "kill me now, before I turn into such a bloody *bastard*. I always suspected I had a moral cog loose, but you've smashed the whole fucking clockwork."

A cruel smile from the elder Locke. "*Cura te ipsum*, my innocent friend. We all kill what we love, don't we? But you shan't distract me with pleasant reminiscing. Time to die."

"What of Crane's journal?" she stalled, hoping against hope that Lizzie would burst out, attack, do anything. But stubborn Lizzie wasn't talking. The noxious blue potion had seen to that. Only cold, black emptiness, desolate and frightening. "And Henry's prototype. They're still at large."

"Already taken care of those. Or I will." He shrugged. "Tenses become so unimportant."

She fumbled for inspiration. "B-but you can't kill the younger Locke. If he dies, so do you."

"Really? Let's see." He took aim, and c*rrack!*

Blue current forked, striking young Locke in the chest. He convulsed, jerking in his ropes, and finally collapsed. Smoke drifted from his hair, froth on his lips. Dead.

Locke—the remaining Locke—grinned like a hungry hyena, and waved his scarf at her. "Still alive."

Eliza boggled. "But . . ."

"There are so many of me now. Parallel worlds, alternate realities, parity duplicates, *et hoc genus omne.* Who knows which of the dozens of *hims* is *me*?" He gave a shrill, irresponsible laugh that chilled her to the core. She'd heard Edward Hyde laugh that way. "Probabilities, Doctor!" he cackled. "I'd have to be unlucky, after all we've been through. Shoot *him,* kill *myself,* put cause before effect. Create a paradox that could open a rift to the past or transport me to an alternate reality or reverse every decision I've ever made while liquefying my brains to porridge. Who the hell knows? One thing you soon learn about this forsaken business is that there are no rules. At least none that make linear sense."

Her mind struggled. "So is your brain 'evidence,' too? You'll just blow your own head off when you're done, will you?"

"If it comes to that. But then I'd never know, would I?" Again, he waved the scarf profoundly, as if imparting hidden knowledge.

"I'm sorry, is that supposed to mean something?"

He sighed impatiently. "The bloodstain, you obtuse character. It's how I tell if I've fixed things. Stupid to drop it at Ephronia's, I know, but that invisible fool Wyverne interrupted me. I stole it back from you, oh, I don't know. A day or two ago. Before I electrocuted Antoinette. After I realized you were interfering. It's so hard to keep track of time."

She glanced at his missing hand, the limp, the scars. Clearly, the future hadn't gone well for Seymour Q. Locke. "Is that your blood? From the hand?"

"Trust me, Doctor. If sorcerers slicing my hand off is the worst thing that happens? We're all home free." He primed the pistol's charge, *hiss-flick!* "Now stop talking."

"Listen." She adopted a soothing, persuasive tone. "This needn't happen. Surely we needn't destroy everything. The machine can be used properly, controlled. Any catastrophe can be averted. Now give me the pistol and let's—"

"You think the machine can be salvaged?" Crazed fire lit his eyes. "I once thought that way. Want to see what happens if I let things be? Shall I show you the consequences of your pride?" He grabbed her with a steely arm around her waist and dragged her towards the machine, limping as he went.

"Get off me!" Eliza fought, but he was stubborn and capable. Stronger than the younger Locke, more seasoned. She slammed her boots into his shins, aimed her knee as best she could for his groin. He just grunted, teeth clicking. Pain-tolerant, too. What a life he'd led. "Stop this at once. It's undignified!"

"*Mea culpa.*" With a snarl, he leapt onto the stool and yanked her into his lap with his maimed arm, ignoring her struggles. With his remaining fingers, he jabbed at the controls.

The big brass rings whirred, faster and faster, surrounding her in a pulsating sphere. Burned aether sizzled, acrid in her nostrils. Crystals sliced the light into rainbows, and the air groaned and began to tear apart.

"Wait!" She struggled, gripped by foreboding. But fighting was useless. If she jumped out now, she'd be cut to ribbons. "We can talk about this."

"Talking's over." He worked furiously at the controls, sweat dripping on his scarred cheeks. "All I ever wanted was to go home to the girl who loved me. Yes, I had a wife in Henry's day. It wasn't much, but I thought I could lead a normal life. Me!" A cracked laugh. "What a fool I was. People like us don't get *normal,* Eliza Jekyll-and-Hyde. We don't get *safe.* All we get is darkness and loneliness and fear."

His words chilled her. *A normal life.* What a pleasant dream.

He wrenched one last wheel into place, grunting in satisfaction. "You don't believe in my future? Let's go see it together." And he grabbed the big copper lever, and yanked.

THE SOUND OF SILENCE

THE WORLD DISSOLVED.

Tortured air shrieked, ripping her ears to bleeding. Aether exploded, blowing her hair back, and like a melting cinematograph, her surroundings bubbled and tore apart. The machine tumbled like a rock in a barrel, and she and Locke tumbled with it, *forwards* and *back* and *now* and *then* streaking into rainbows of confusion.

Locke laughed, exultant. "The aether hates us!" he yelled above the cacophony of burning time. "It can't stand much more of this."

Where are we going? she tried to yell, but the endless twisting inferno ripped her words away and crushed them to dust.

All was chaos . . . then the machine abruptly recovered its sense of *up* and *down,* and plummeted, thudding into wet ground.

Oof! Her teeth slammed on her tongue, a coppery splash.

Night closed in like a fist, and the stormy sky burned a hellish red. Distant grinding machinery, iron screeching on stone, shouting, a stray eerie scream. Lightning crackled, a juddering fork of blue, and the air howled and stretched, wind shrieking. The stink of rotting filth made her retch. Flesh. Bodies. Death.

Squelch! Her boots landed ankle-deep in mud . . . and she stumbled over a decaying hand thrusting from the ground.

A mass grave.

"Where are we?" Cracked, small, frightened. Damn it.

Locke jumped down after her. "Where Ireton House used to be, about a year ago—move!" He tackled her, hurling her up a steep rubble embankment.

Chomp! Jagged teeth the size of knives snapped on empty air, and a wolfish monster with bristling black fur growled in thwarted hunger.

Eliza scrambled for her life, rocks stabbing her hands and knees. "What the hell is that?"

"Want to stay and argue?"

Eliza and Locke ran. Streets crowded with sweating bodies, slack faces, terrified eyes. Hunger, disease, fear. Blood and filth clotted the gutters. Children screamed and wept, their naked bodies bruised. Hideous dogs snarled. Broken and burning buildings, the stink of molten steel and fire.

Atop the lampposts, lights burned, but it wasn't the familiar gas flame. No, this was a queasy yellow shimmer, like a living thing trapped in servitude. On the stormy, broken-roofed horizon, smokestacks belched eerie fire, and in the sweeping auras of light beams, *creatures* flew and flipped, writhing their scaly tails.

She and Locke stumbled into a crowded square, and she halted, struggling to breathe the hostile air. Radiant heat seared, an ugly disturbance. And still that awful, all-pervasive groaning, *eeeerghhh* . . . as if the atmosphere itself thrashed to an agonizing death.

A row of wretched, manacled figures shuffled by, exhausted and bleeding. Most were cowed, eyes downcast. One man fought to escape, his shackled wrists raw. His frantic eyes shone wide. Strangled noises forced from his lips, which were glued together in a hideous squirming line. "Unngh! Unngh!"

"Don't stare," hissed Locke. "It's a spell they use if you talk too much. Watch."

The crowd in the square was howling, swaying, crushing around a raised platform where a bonfire leapt and crackled with no visible fuel. At the back of the platform stood a tall caped figure, face half-masked in black leather, surveying the scene. In front, another masked man raised a glittering curved blade.

Thwock! The blade crunched into a wooden block. A ragged man on his knees screamed, his severed hand rolling into the mud. Sobbing, clutching his bleeding arm, he scrambled away, and a lackey dragged the next man forward.

"My God." Horrified, Eliza glanced at Locke. He was laughing, face gleaming with sweat, eyes wild.

"That's what they do to counter-revolutionaries," he yelled above the din. "At first they burned, like the Royal, but this is better. A man with one hand can still work." He waved at the line of slaves hobbling by. "They need miners and custodians for the ghettos. And even monsters need to eat."

"How did this happen? Where are the Enforcers?"

Locke flung his arm around her neck and inhaled deeply,

relishing the aether-rich air. "No Enforcers. No soldiers. No police. Just sorcerers."

"But the war—"

"The war's over. Our army's gone, the Royal too, and the Philosopher's dead." He stuffed his bloodstained scarf into his coat. "Trust me. I watched him die."

Thwock! The blade fell again. The man at the back nodded with grim satisfaction. Masked in black over glittering white hair, with the *Liberté du Sang* cockade in his tricorne hat. One arm wore a black gauntlet, wreathed in crimson fire. The other hand hung bare, pale and strangely misshapen. Withered.

The same man Lizzie had spied in Soho, skulking about with Veronica Burton. But he wasn't skulking now. No, he seemed to be in charge.

"That's *la Bête.*" Locke laughed again, eerie. "That necklace he wears, with the silver moon? It lets him shift shape. They say he ate *la Belle.* Just got tired of her one day and *munch,* down she went. I tried to kill him, once. Lost the hand for my trouble."

But Eliza barely heard. Alongside *la Bête,* chained on a creaking leather collar, crouched a huge golden wolf.

The creature arched its spine, fur bristling almost to the sorcerer's shoulder. Powerful muscles coiled and quivered. On its collar shone another, identical glossy black-and-silver stone.

Eliza stared, horror crawling. *Oh, no. No, no.*

The creature's furry ears pricked. Hungrily, it sniffed the air for scents . . . and fixed huge gleaming eyes on her. Not yellow eyes, like a wild animal's. Brilliant blue.

The crowd swayed, threatening to sweep her away. She clutched at Locke, dizzy with despair, fighting to stay on her feet. Remy's name tore from her lips, ripped out on rising terror.

The creature just stared at her, flat and empty. No human feeling at all.

The crowd thickened, a hell of thrashing limbs and clawing hands. A wild-eyed woman hurtled towards her, screaming unhinged nonsense. Eliza fended her off—and before her eyes, the woman was sucked into a roaring black vortex, her cries growing fainter as she shrank to a point and vanished.

Above it all, *la Bête* grinned, showing jagged teeth. And with a yell that was lost in the din, he set his slave-beast free. The wolf coiled quivering muscles, and sprang.

Locke swore a blistering oath. "The aether is disintegrating!" he yelled. "We must return to the machine or we'll be stuck here like trapped rats."

Eliza didn't hesitate. They struggled off in the direction they'd come, the Remy-thing snarling and ripping flesh in pursuit. Locke swung at a man as they passed, fist crunching into jaw. The fellow toppled, and Locke snatched his weapon—an odd-looking pistol—and sprinted on.

Around the corner, back to the ugly pit that had been Ireton House. The machine glimmered, imbued with its own dark light. Around it, the air screamed—and jagged holes ripped it apart, as if invisible claws tore in from some black otherworld.

A ragged crowd engulfed the machine, climbing the rings, shaking the mechanism, prodding the electrics. One fellow grasped the wrong wire, and voltage lashed out, frying his hand to a black crisp. Others set upon him, gnashing teeth and clawing hands and shouting. "Idiot!" "You fool, you've broken it!" "Get off! It's mine!"

The Remy-beast skidded around the corner, sparks showering from its claws. Dazed, Eliza sprinted towards the throng. The world and everyone in it had lost its mind. "Get away!" she yelled. "That's ours!"

Locke just raised his weapon and fired, a shimmering shockwave like thunder. *Booom!* Broken bodies flew, a red mist. The remaining people screamed at the carnage and scattered.

Eliza screamed, too, at the horror of it. Stunned to the spot, brain unable to process. Lizzie would have cursed, fought, acted no matter what. But Lizzie wasn't here. No courage. No heart.

Before her, the Remy-thing bared cruel teeth, blue eyes empty but for hatred.

"Vermin!" Locke yelled in fury, leaping like a long-haired insect spattered in gore. "The world's over, get it? Why can't you just *DIE*?"

The wolf crouched, ready to spring.

And Locke—laughing shrilly like the lunatic he'd become—flung her onto the bloodied brass stool, and dived in after her, dragging the lever down.

A GOD-ROTTED HERO

FALLING, SPINNING, BRASS RINGS WHIRRING, DIS-
orientation and stabbing pain. A glimpse of screaming flames, the earth torn apart . . . and *whumph!*
The machine landed in the laboratory at Ireton House, floorboards cracking.

All was quiet. Just fluttering paper and the harsh scrape
of her breath.

Locke leapt out of the machine, cackling like a witch.
He ran to his instruments and started tinkering one-handed,
wires and tools bouncing. The handgun in his belt—that ugly
tool of death—clunked against the bench. Impatiently he
tossed it aside.

Eliza clambered down, still in shock. Remy, that awful *la
Bête* . . . and the amulet.

It lets him shift shape. The amulet wasn't a cure. It was a
drug, just like her elixir. An addiction. And Remy had em-
braced it. Surrendered to the darkness.

In the laboratory, everything seemed as before. The hovering lights, the roped body of the younger Locke. But the
corpse's face had turned a sick green, the smell of putrefac-

tion thickening. "What day is this? How long have we been gone?"

Hippocrates crept from under the table, his *happy* light glimmering cautiously. "Doctor," he muttered, grinding grumpy cogs. "Absence, fifty-four hours. Make greater speed."

"Two days! But the election will be over. We'll be at war. The Prime Minister . . . oh, my. Hipp, we must do something!"

Locke—the living one—ignored her, banging a hammer on the case of a magnetometer. "These levels are perfect. Aether collapse is imminent. A trap, you see! We'll set a cunning snare! This infernal contraption will be our salvation after all." He ran back to the machine, which had ceased to spin and whine, and set upon the crystals, wrenching them with various spanners. "A concerted attack! There's power for, oh, half a dozen shifts. That should be enough."

Her guts squeezed cold. "Enough? Locke, what are you talking about?"

"We'll appear at the same time, Doctor. Over and over. The same *time*! Create enough disruption and we'll tear the aether apart, at the very moment when the sorcerers attack!" He laughed, and jammed his elbow on a button. Blue current zapped, and the machine started up again, brass rings whirling. He jumped inside, and cranked the spring levers tight. "Bloody shapeshifters, think they're so clever. They never saw *me* coming."

Horror-drenched images assailed her, of that ugly rift-torn night, the burning sky. "But won't that—?"

"Kill them all?" Locke crowed as the rings swung faster, hissed louder. "Absolutely. Time and space will rip apart. I destroyed the world once, Doctor. I can do it again. And then *everyone* will be free." A ghastly smile. "Including me."

Her brain boggled, and she yelled over the noise. "But you can't end the world to save the future! That's insane!"

"Couldn't have said it better myself." A rusty voice, chopping the air like an axe.

Eliza whirled, her heart bruising her ribs. Now what?

Veronica Burton had descended the stairs. Now she stood on the opposite side of the machine, wearing a metal monster's leer. "I've been waiting a day and a night for your return," she gloated. "That machine's mine, Mr. Locke. Now step away so I can shoot you." She brandished her weapon—but it wasn't the poison pistol. No. It was the horrible electric handgun Locke had cast aside. The shockwave weapon.

"Don't shoot," called Eliza, frantic. "It's not safe."

Locke laughed. "*Safe.* Listen to her. Burton, this is all your fault. I should never have let you in on the secret. God, I was so damned *impressionable* when I was young. To imagine I wanted you to *like* me. If you hadn't sold us out to the enemy, none of this would have happened. But you do it, every bloody time."

"Glad to hear I'll succeed." Veronica smirked, her lopsided face stretching. "*La Bête* will be grateful. He's promised to make me one of them. I'd like that. I'm tired of being overlooked, Eliza. You know what it's like. We have to be so much better than men to get ahead. If only your Captain Lafayette had obliged me when I asked him to share, I wouldn't have needed to betray him. Always so damned *honorable*."

Eliza faltered. *Make her one of them?* A disagreement

about interrogations, Remy had said. Hadn't mentioned his curse. "But aren't you . . . ?"

"*La Belle*?" Mocking metal laughter. "I'd wondered if you thought that. Really, you're too stupid for words. But no matter. Once I kill you both, no one in this corrupt Empire will ever know who caused their downfall. Now step away, Quentin."

"Make me," gloated Locke, spreading his arms wide. His missing hand glared, an ugly asymmetry. "Kill me, don't kill me, I really couldn't care anymore. But fire that in here and you and all your plans will burn in hell."

Veronica laughed, a horrid metal scrape. "I'll take that chance." And she swung her weapon up.

Eliza charged forwards, but it was too far. She'd never make it. "Wait, stop—"

"Ee-e-e-EH!" With a heroic *doinng!* of springs, Hippocrates launched himself at Veronica's face.

Crunch! His brass body slammed into her jaw like a bare-knuckle boxer's fist. Her head snapped back, and her hands flailed to protect her face, a half-forgotten human reflex—and the weapon dropped from her grip. She clawed for it, but too late. With a *whoosh!* and *rrrip!* of disintegrating aether, Locke and the machine vanished.

Veronica cursed, the syllables garbled, her bent jaw spitting sparks. Hippocrates cavorted, shouting triumphantly. "Boom! E-e-EH! Boom!"

Breathing hard, Eliza snatched up the gun and leveled it at Veronica. Her trigger finger quivered. How she wanted to fire. Blast her enemy to oblivion. Become Eliza Hyde, surrender to her tainted blood. Punish Burton for her hubris in thinking she could control any of this.

But Eliza knew how it was to be a slave to vanity. To imagine you could change the world. People had died for Eliza's pride, bloodied victims who'd haunt her always. What wouldn't she give for a chance to undo the death *she'd* wrought?

This wasn't justice. And she wasn't a murderer.

Shaking, she eased her finger from the trigger. "You're under arrest," she spat, "for treason."

The hell you say.

Vengeance burns in my belly, and like a rubbery eel, I thrash and squeeze out. *Squickk!* My dark hair springs free, my body swells—and with Eliza screaming a sweet symphony in my ears, I grip this awful gun and fire.

Boom! The shockwave hurls me into an arse-backwards somersault. Wind roars in my hair, flinging Eliza's muddy gray skirts over my head in the stink of scorched aether.

Finally, the wind dies, silence fading in. I scramble up, and survey the carnage. Holy hell. Broken tiles, twisted metal, leaping flames. A smear of red goo and tangled fabric that used to be Veronica Burton.

Over-voltage on a handgun, Remy said once. *It isn't pretty.* Some science hocus-pocus on the rarified air of electrical fields and the destruction wrought by aether engines what don't know their own good.

Ha ha! Teach you to set Enforcers on me, Burton. Treason, my arse. Burning's too good, you metal-head scum.

The gun itself, well, it's twisted and useless now. I toss it away. Pure luck the friggin' thing didn't blow my hand off.

Eliza yells, hammering inside our skull. *What have you*

done? We must stop Locke! Get back to Henry's, rebuild the machine, go after him . . .

Hmm. I frown, one fingertip to my chin. Yes. We could do that, Eliza. Save the world, get the girl, be a god-rotted hero.

But Miss Lizzie's got fatter eels to skin. Flabby ones like Dodger and his fart-arsed gang, living it up in the Rats' Castle on borrowed time. Juicy ones like Eddie Hyde moldering in Bow Street while the true Slasher runs free. Everything I hold dear—Eddie, Johnny, the Rats', any hope that Eliza would ever love us for who we are—is already slipping through my fingers. Miss Lizzie, my friends, has nothing left to lose.

Liquid flames drip from the ceiling. Locke's electrical equipment—what's left of it—explodes, *pop!* and *bang!,* in the smoke. Her little brass idiot is already scrambling up the stairs and away, his store of heroics exhausted.

Time to go.

I leap the burning stairs by twos, and pause at the top for a last glance around. So long, Seymour Locke, you mouthy prat. Wherever you are, I hope it's better than this.

But I doubt it. Ain't no reasoning with a man who's off his rocker. And deep in my darkest heart, where I'm bruised forever by Eliza's hatred, all my despair flowing free . . . maybe I believe this black and bloody world deserves its end.

L'HUOMO DELINQUENTE

A QUARTER AFTER TWO, I NOD TO THE FLOP-JOWLED barkeep at the Magic Flute for another, stifling a yawn. "And one for yerself, Freddy. So no one saw nothing?"

Freddy the Pug pours, scratching behind one floppy furred ear. "Not that I heard."

My gullet burns, rage worse than liquor. Four bleeding hours, I've been fishing for the squeak on the Slasher. Prostitutes, publicans in a dozen bars, mountebanks and crossing sweepers and fake beggars on the slam. No one seen nor heard a god-rotted thing. And Miss Lizzie knows why.

All night, in smears of shadow, I've glimpsed the Dodger's sly hand. Not the whale-man himself, to be sure. But I can smell his influence, slick like oil on water. Handsome Tom o' Nine is surely dead, likewise poor Fishy. If the bloody Sultan's been bought, who else could be my enemy? At first, I went seeking Johnny—never mind our spat, not with so much at stake—but no one's seen arse nor eye of him.

Johnny's in lavender. And that bothers me.

I sink my gin, slamming the cup down with a fiery grin.

"And what *did* you hear, Freddy? Charley Tee-Hee laughing his greasy nuts off while he nailed your arse over the bar?"

Freddy just shrugs, plump black nose glistening. "I owes Charley a pony. I don't owe you shit."

"Kiss my arse," mutters I, and turns away. "And the pony you rode in on, Pug."

I shove through sweaty bodies and clouds of liquored breath towards the door. The Magic Flute is your down-market flophouse, not so posh as Mrs. Fletcher's, with clap-boarded windows, grime-soaked floorboards, and not much privacy. But at least it's dry, the girls safe from the freezing night. Better than plying your trade in grim gaslit streets with blood-hungry monsters on the prowl.

The bar and gambling house here below is seedy and humid. Arc-lamps sputter, aether smoke mingling with hash. I squash Eliza's dirty skirts past a rowdy card game, where a big-nosed dwarf in a red bowler hat roars laughter and hurls down the ace of spades with one pudgy fist.

Opposite, a scrawny cove in a fop's striped trousers curls a finger up his nostril, digging out a shiny prize. Told you so. It's Nose-Picker, Dodger's stinky arse-licker whose name I always forget. I flips him a two-finger salute, and he rolls his milky glass eye at me and eats the snot. Fucking class act.

A ragged little girl skulks from table to table, shyly offer-ing drooping daisies for a penny to men who ogle and drool. The fire sulks, a sullen red glow. Up against the wall, an ex-hausted whore in faded green skirts filches the purse from a fat cove's pocket while he's grunting between her legs.

Suddenly, I feel sick. That's what I'm doing. Glorying in stealing a few pennies, while the world has its way with me.

I spy the empty half of a loveseat, not too rank with spit or puke or whatever else, and plonk my gray-skirted arse down with a despondent sigh.

Time's a-wasting. Eddie's life is forfeit. And I'm no closer to catching the real Slasher than before.

"Fine gin-soaked mess you're in, Lizzie," announces I to no one in particular, "and no mistake."

The bloke with his back to mine leans over, offering me his bottle. Finely tailored coat, brushed hat. Too rich a gent for this dive. "Have one on me, miss."

"Don't mind if I do, sir, and you're a real gent." Now there's some proper manners, aye . . . but too slender and curved, this cove. Those shoulders too narrow. The light's dim, but Miss Lizzie ain't blind.

The lady—for it's a she—eyes me defiantly. A strange, unearthly face, as if her skin's pulled taut with pins. Dark waistcoat, silver buttons, gold watch chain with garnets. A fat blond braid curls on her shoulder.

"To each her own." I raise the bottle to her, and swig, dark brandy burning my tongue—and choke it down the wrong way.

That jeweled watch chain.

Looks like you can afford the best. Out front of Mrs. Fletcher's, the night Johnny and me found Eddie there. This gent-rigged lady, checking her watch in torchlight.

A toff square-rigged with a funny face. A-waiting the other to get his load off, Saucy May had told Rose. Two girls who'd laid eyes on the Soho Slasher. Two girls who were murdered.

My hackles prickle. Carefully, I hand the bottle back.

She reaches for it. Across the back of her hand shines a trio of angry red scratches.

Saucy May's fingernails, stuffed with her murderer's skin. That crackbrain Todd, his mouth twisted with disdain. *How careless.*

It's someone who loves him.

I lick dry lips. "Cheers, handsome. I'm for a card game. Top o' the night to yer." Casually, I retreat to the back bar, willing my legs steady.

As soon as I'm out of sight, I bolt for the side door, heart thudding.

The Slasher's here, choosing his next ugly game. And that odd-faced lady's waiting for him. Covering up for him. Ready to kill any witness to his crimes. His mother? His sister? A lover, even?

Don't know, don't care. If I can find him—if I can lure him into my clutches and make him show himself for what he is—then the Slasher's caught and Eddie goes free.

So long as I can stay alive.

Upstairs to the cathouse, three at a time.

I reach the top, dread boiling black in my heart. Can't hear no screams or kerfuffle. Perhaps I'm too late, and the Slasher's next game is already bleeding out.

I burst into a sweat-stinking parlor, where girls are getting down to business. The redhead, the blonde, the fat, the skinny, and the in-between, the Magic Flute has the full house of cards, and follows every suit. Soggy mattresses, scraps of straw, a threadbare coat over splintery boards. Who needs a bed when you'll only take a minute or two?

One lucky girl's got a chair, and she spreads her thighs over greasy upholstery and stares dully at the ceiling while she earns her pennies from a pile of heaving male flesh. Drunken drool trickles from her lip.

The scene makes me queasy. Ain't no pleasure in this. Just animal need, loneliness and desperation and hunger, dumb urges never understood nor satisfied. Ain't no game. This is survival.

But the Slasher needs privacy for his bloody how-dos. A room of his own with a subject who don't say no.

From the back floats laughter and a muffled scream.

Shit. I run, dodging jerking bodies and piles of torn flock. One bloke curses at the interruption. The girls don't even look up. Guess they're accustomed to a bit of yelling now and then.

At the back lurks a single private room, for those with extra coin. I push the flimsy pasteboard door open. A tiny mold-rotted attic, the cracked window stuffed with rags. A taper sheds thin, wavering light.

The bed boards are strewn with a blanket. On it sprawls a girl, legs bent awkwardly, eyes wet with terror. She screams again, but it's choked and feeble. A bloodstained scrap of her own skirt is stuffed into her mouth.

Above her lurches a man waving a scrape-whetted knife. Naked but for a fine but dirty frock coat, his mud-brown elf-locks hanging. Slobber shines on his half-witted leer. The girl whimpers and struggles, but he's broken her legs so she can't crawl away. Subduing his subject. Refining his technique.

It's Baby-Face, the posh-spoken oral enthusiast from Mrs. Fletcher's. The cove in fancy britches, what I spied outside my window in Soho that rainy night. My gent-rigged lady's loved one.

I sprint at him, hoping for surprise. But the girl sees me, and makes frightened grunts, "Mmph! Hnn!" He whirls, that blade slashing.

We collide, and I claw for his eyes.

He howls, face wobbling like a rubber water bag . . . and *changes*.

Aghast, I stagger back. Flesh stretching, bones contorting into grotesque shapes. His fingers cramp and straighten, soft then gnarly, joints cracking like sticks. His ragged hair slithers, mingling with limp blond locks that thrash and wriggle. Muscles shudder in agony, he *shrinks* and *swells* and *shrinks* again . . . and out falls a pale, shivering, weeping whip of a lad.

It's Bertie. The King of friggin' England.

THIS SENSELESS DECAY

I GAPE LIKE A DEAD FISH. THE GIRL ON THE BED chokes on the rag. Bertie goggles at me, naked limbs shining, his mouth a little egg shape.

Creeping Jesus, Eliza. Did you imagine your hellbrew would make him a *better* man?

Grab him. Wring his skinny neck and end this horror.

Too late. He's *changing* again, back and forth, a rubber ball against a wall, and he kicks his heels like a crippled leprechaun and flees.

But not for the door.

I skid, but before I can double back, Baby-Face—for it's he again, hair matted with goat-stinking sweat—Baby-Face laughs like a gin-pissed hyena and hurls himself out the window.

Crash! Glass splinters everywhere, tiny wasp stings. He sails out into the street, skinny legs flailing. I grab the knife—can't hold on with fingers cracking out o' their sockets, eh?—and sprint to the sill.

But he's gone. Vanished into the Soho night like an evil dream.

Swiftly I pocket the weapon and climb the sill to leap after. Then I remember the girl, drowning on her own blood.

I run to her, ease the clotted cloth away. She gasps, rattling, splurting bright blood. He's cut out her tongue.

Swiftly I shove her out into the parlor. She's a broken, red-soaked horror. "Take care of her," I snap to whoever's listening, and run down the stairs. Shove my way through the Magic Flute—that bitch in gent's rig is gone, and so is Nose-Picker, and if it's Dodger what set Eddie up I'll sew his flabby hide into a sack and piss in it—and out into the street.

Baby-Face Bertie's legged it long ago, but folks are still gawping and pointing, so I verily ken which way he staggered. His *change* will heal his wounds. If he broke his goddamn legs jumping out the window—hope it hurt, you rot-cocked rat—they ain't broke no more.

Gaslights dazzle me as I run, searching fore and aft, port and starboard. Every eye looks menacing, every face a killer's. After fruitless minutes, I stagger to a halt, hands on knees, trying to catch breath what's sick with failure. My lungs burn, fiery as the terror in my soul.

It's the god-rotted *king*.

King! King! The word rings dolefully in my head, like St. Sepulchre's bells foretelling gallows day outside Newgate.

What now? Skip into Scotland Yard and sing, *hello, crusher boys, you'll have to let Eddie go! Because the Soho Slasher is a different King Edward, what lives at Buckingham Palace and licks the Philosopher's plate for scraps! Yes! Call the Home Secretary and let's arrest His Majesty for multiple murder! How'd you like THEM apples?*

Rage rips at my flesh, wild and willing. If I scream Bertie's guilt from the rooftops now, they'll wring my pretty neck before you can whisper *cover-up* and Eddie will hang, his corpse dissected and the leftovers buried in unhallowed ground. Make no mistake, Edward Hyde's a dead man.

Unless I fit up someone else.

Someone easy for the crushers to believe, so they won't ask for much evidence.

Someone like a red-haired loon with a razor fetish.

Oho.

This dark idea consumes me, rich and redolent with irony, so deeply I barely realize where I'm headed until I bang up against the porch of the tumbledown tenement where I live.

In our window, a single candle burns.

Gift horse, and all that. I leap up the steps, anxious to let Johnny in on my plan. If his fine fairy arse ain't already nabbed by the Dodger, that is, or stabbed in the back by Tasty Mick or Three-Tot Polly, so like that rat-faced Sultan they can steal the loot Johnny promised 'em and betray us. Nothing like having friends.

My boots—Eliza's boots, heavy and hard—clunk on the wobbly steps, and I blunder into our room. I can't pull this off alone, and Eliza's no bleeding help. I need Johnny more than ever.

A shadow stretches, monstrous hands grabbing for my throat.

I stumble back, petrified. My secrets cry to heaven, by God. It's Mr. Todd himself, come to put me to a grisly end for my treachery.

But it ain't Todd. Nor Johnny. Not even Jacky Spring-Heels playing a trick.

And Eliza swells in response, a shuddering shout, and bursts out.

Eliza reeled from the sudden *change,* darkness smearing to rainbows. Surely, her eyes deceived her.

But his scent, his warmth, his breathless kiss . . .

"Oh, my. I . . ." She backed up a step, stumbling over the cushions.

Face the worse for a beating, chestnut curls disheveled. But his hot blue eyes sparkled, and the smile he unleashed was pure sunlight. "God, I've missed you."

She stammered, lost. Her lips tingled. Her heart ached. Her every rational cell rebelled. "B-but your letter. *Liberté du Sang . . .*"

"The only way to keep my cover, and my life." Remy leaned against the cracked wall. He wore a rough russet coat and dirty linen, a woolen scarf muffling his throat. "They need to believe I truly belong to them."

Her eyes burned with stupid, selfish tears. Damn it. *She'd* believed Remy's letter. A confession, from the most honest, honorable man she'd ever known. Why wouldn't she believe him?

"I can't imagine how it must have hurt you." For an instant, he let his gaze flicker. He never did that, not out of cowardice. Only fear of heartbreak. "I understand if you . . . well, I've no excuse. *Je regrette . . .*" He started in French, and corrected. "With my whole heart, Eliza, I'm sorry."

Despair dwarfed her. For this accursed mission—for his vengeance—he'd have sacrificed everything. Their future. All their hopes.

All the mixed emotion of the last few days swelled up to drown her. The murders, the wedding, Edward Hyde, the Soho Slasher, Veronica Burton, Seymour Locke, that horrific vision of the future where the world was chaos and Remy was enslaved . . .

Smack! Her palm stung. She'd slapped him. Right across his ridiculously perfect cheek. "That's for even imagining I might not forgive you."

Disbelieving, he touched his face. "Eliza—"

"And this is for never taking me for granted," she whispered, and pulled him into a kiss.

His surprised gladness thrilled her, a sparkling delight. "You humble me," he murmured against her lips, and kissed her more.

Far too soon, she eased away. "So is this how we're to meet? I confess I prefer Cavendish Square. Your butler pours an excellent bath."

Remy flicked a restless glance out the broken window. "I need your help."

"As always. I mean, of course, but . . ."

"They believed me. *La Liberté du Sang.* I'm one of them now. And the most terrible thing is about to happen." He gripped her hands, kissed them. "I need you to go to the Philosopher. Persuade him to deploy every Enforcer he has. That project your scientists were trying so desperately to hide? It's—"

"Yes, I know." She clicked her tongue at his expression.

"Really. It's been almost a week. For what kind of feeble-witted bumbler do you take me?"

"Knew you'd unravel it." His smile dazzled her. His breezy confidence in her—so glaringly opposed to her own black doubts—shamed her.

She waved carelessly. "Didn't I mention it? The murderer was Seymour Locke after all. A future version of him, that is. Demonstrably insane. If you see him, shoot first and ask later."

"Noted." Remy's smile twinkled again, but he soon sobered. "So you know about Veronica Burton's treachery."

"I've seen the future she creates. Locke dragged me along with him." A chill jarred her bones. "It was awful, Remy. All that death and destruction. Those hideous sorcerers, they were . . . That is, they *will* . . ." She swallowed. *I saw you, Remy. Chained to a sorcerer with death in your eyes.* "I saw lycanthropes," she admitted, "chained up as attack beasts, by a man with a withered hand. Is he . . . ?"

"*La Bête.* The one who corrupted François." Remy poked the cold ashes in the grate with his foot. "It begins tomorrow. Beaconsfield's victory speech. They're planning multiple simultaneous attacks, for maximum destruction."

"But that's Locke's plan! He has the machine. I saw him take it."

A shrug. "In the future, the machine belongs to *Liberté du Sang.*"

Her eyes blurred with remembered horror. The shredded aether, groaning in pain. Wailing air, stinking wind, that horrid blood-drenched scaffold. "But what can we do? If the aether breaks down badly enough, the Enforcers will be useless anyway."

"Not a moment to lose, then. You must go to the Philosopher now."

"I suppose I can spare the time," she joked, trying to keep it light. "Come with me. He'll listen to you."

Remy shook his head. "I can't."

"But—"

"I can't," he repeated. "He's ceased to find me useful, Eliza. Enforcers raided the cellar at Waterloo Bridge. They took everything."

"Oh, no." The cage, the candles, those ugly magic spells. Veronica Burton had betrayed him. But her bones chilled. Was that true? Lizzie had broken in to that house. What if she'd been spied on? Followed by Royal informers? Was this all her fault?

A rueful smile. "Not just the wolf. Documents. My search for François's allies. All my dealings with the sorcerers. It doesn't look exactly patriotic."

"But that was Foreign Office work." It rang hollow. Lord Beaconsfield was part of the plot to sell Interlunium to the enemy. And now he led the Empire into war.

Remy shook his head grimly. "All deniable. I had to make it look convincing. All the evidence against me is there if they choose to see it."

Defiantly, she folded her arms. "Then I'll persuade the Philosopher to see it our way."

But wild laughter threatened. How? Foil a gang of shapeshifting sorcerers, reveal the Prime Minister as a traitor, stop Remy being burned. Oh, and thwart a mad scientist with a time machine who wanted to end the world. All before eleven o'clock.

"In the meantime, you can't stay here," she added. "The Enforcers will find you."

"*Liberté du Sang* have bolt-holes everywhere. I'll go there until it's done."

"But you can't return to them. Not when they're poised to attack."

He just looked at her. And the truth dawned, a poisoned sunrise.

"You and *la Bête*." Her throat parched. "You're doing it together. You're *helping* him."

"It's what I do, Eliza. I'm an *agent provocateur*. It's the only way I can thwart him."

Her stomach roiled, sick. *La Bête*'s plan would surely be bloody. Violent. Murderous . . . and black suspicion needled her heart. "Remy, what happened with the Empire's envoys? Were you there when *la Bête* killed them? God, did *you* kill them?"

"What? No. It's not like that—"

"I saw you in the future!" Tears strangled her. How she hated crying. "You're *la Bête*'s creature. His *pet*."

A dark headshake. "The future can be changed."

"Can it?" She swallowed hot hurt, but it bubbled back up with a vengeance. "I don't think you want it to. That amulet. I thought you wanted a cure."

"You know some evils can't be cured." But his gaze clouded, stormy with defiance. Defensive.

She couldn't bear that look. Too many secrets. Too many lies. "I know what that awful thing does, all right? It lets you change at will! If that's what you want, why don't you just take it?" Unthinking, she tugged at his scarf. "You're wearing it now, aren't you? Show me."

"Eliza—"

The scarf tore away. Remy closed his eyes, sighing.

The glossy black stone gleamed, its half-moon a sly silver wink. She stared. Nodded grimly. Did a dry swallow. "So. You're one of them. *La Bête*—"

"*La Bête* is a cockroach," he said harshly. "A loathsome toad. But one thing he said resonated. He said, '*Petit loup*, you have a choice. You can feed him, or you can fight him—but whichever you choose, he will do the same to you.'" A rough shrug. "I'm tired of fighting, Eliza. I did this for us. Can't you understand?"

She'd fought Lizzie for so long, desperate to deny the monster inside. Since she'd met Remy, he'd been her inspiration . . . and now he was failing her. Denial squeezed her. It was too heartbreaking to be true. But longing ached, too. So easy, to surrender to darkness. To embrace the taint in her blood and hang the consequences. To be Hyde, finally at peace . . .

"So you'll give in just like that?" she said tightly. "Take the easy way out. Pretend it's not part of you. Just slip on a trinket and everything's fine."

"That isn't—"

"I'd carve out my *heart* to be free of this," she hissed. "You're a coward, Remy Lafayette. To think I *envied* you."

He recoiled, as if she'd hit him.

Her heart wailed. She wanted to claw back what she'd said. Rake her nails down her face, hurt herself the way she'd hurt him. But the blood was drawn. The damage done. And the gulf between them had never seemed so wide.

"Call it what you like." He spoke at last, and his frosty tone scraped her raw. "Just go to the Philosopher. Please. So much is at stake."

She wiped her cheeks. "Of course. I understand. Remy, I'm—"

"You might need this." Coldly, he offered his iron Royal Society badge. NULLIUS IN VERBA, the engraving read. *See for yourself.*

She took it. Their fingers didn't touch. Suddenly it all seemed so pointless. *Run,* whispered her secret heart, *before it's too late. Flee across the horizon, leave it all behind. Why care so much, when the world cares so little for you?*

The silence screamed.

She blinked back acid tears, and stiffly turned away.

"Don't." Suddenly he caught her, dragged her close. He was shaking. Hot. In tears. "Not like this. Not us." And he kissed her, hard, rage and guilt and sudden fierce desire that dragged her breath away.

Their teeth clashed, a sting of coppery sensation that only inflamed her more. He tasted raw, exhausted, of confession and heartache. She opened her mouth, crushed his hair in her fists, kissed him deeper. Suddenly his embrace was all there was. The only thing that made sense. Everything. "Remy. Love me."

Somehow her back hit the wall. He lifted her, and she folded her legs around him. He broke open the clips on her bodice, rough and urgent. His hot mouth on her flesh made her swoon. She wanted to hurl him onto Lizzie's bed, strip him bare, own him utterly. She inhaled, drinking in his scent, desperate to burn his memory into her soul one last time . . .

Bang! Bang! Footsteps thudded on the stairs. Impossibly heavy, *metal* footsteps.

Eliza stiffened in Remy's arms, barely able to breathe. Her own stupidity stunned her. She'd been followed. "Oh, God. You have to run!"

"Too late." He let her go, swiftly surveying the room. No other way out. He grabbed the chair and slammed it into the ceiling. Rotted planks splintered, leaving a dark hole.

"Remy, no—"

"I insist." He was already gripping her waist.

She jumped, and hauled herself over jagged boards into the attic space. Dark, moldy, the timber already decayed and crumbling. An uncovered window blinked out over slate roof-tops into the freezing night, stars glittering.

Her palms bristled with splinters. Her clothes were still loose. Heights made her sick. She didn't care. She leaned over, straining to grab his hand. "Come on!"

Crash! The door blew off its rusted hinges, and Enforc-ers marched in. Brass limbs shining, glitter-blue electric pistols aheft. Efficiently, coldly, one of the metal beasts hurled Remy to the floor, pinning him with one huge brass foot and tearing his coat from his back to search for weapons. From the retching, the dry-stick *crunch!* and the stifled groan of pain, they weren't being too careful about broken bones or concussions.

But they didn't shoot. Oh, no. Remy was a sorcerer. A sci-entific heretic. They'd make sure he burned.

Scrape! Her boots slipped across treacherous timber.

Three pairs of red eyes swiveled to fix on her.

She scuttled backwards, teetering wildly on rotted struts. Her cowardice shamed her. Her crippling fear of heights—and the threat of ugly death—cramped her muscles like glue. She couldn't help it. She'd lived in terror of these inhuman wretches all her life. And this was why.

Two of the Enforcers yanked Remy shaken and bleeding to his feet. That amulet gleamed around his neck, silver and black. He could have *changed,* she realized, with a bitter pang of guilt. Gone wild. Forced them to shoot him, cheated his agonizing, drawn-out fate at the Tower.

Her cruel words snapped back with vicious teeth. *Just take it and stop pretending.*

But he hadn't. And she could only watch as they dragged him away.

The remaining Enforcer—a lopsided abomination, flesh grafted to one side of its body and pink brain tissue pulsating in a glass bubble inside its skull—craned its neck to stare up at her, and *jumped.*

Crunch! Hinged fingers fastened on the splintered plank, and the thing started to climb up. Hand over hand, crushing the timber, red eyes gleaming. Remorseless. Unstoppable.

Wildly, Eliza kicked. Her boots clanged uselessly into the Enforcer's face. Cruel metal fingers stretched out . . . and *crrrrack!* The crumbling attic floor broke under the Enforcer's massive weight. The monster fell, smashing the floorboards where it landed.

Too heavy.

The irony choked her, a bitter laugh. She crawled backwards, further into the mold-stinking darkness. The Enforcer picked itself up, shook its wonky head, and drew its pistol to fire.

Zzapp! The shot crackled into the wet wood, sizzling weakly. Thank heavens for Lizzie's dank and disgusting love nest, and the Enforcers' predilection for electric weapons. A conventional bullet—or that awful futuristic shockwave weapon, and what insane scientist invented that abomination?—would have killed her.

Shakily, Eliza scrambled for the window, fumbling to re-clip her loosened bodice. Only a matter of time before the metal monsters found the attic stairs. Remy was taken. She couldn't help him by getting caught. And if she didn't see the Regent in the next few hours, more would be broken than her stubborn, foolish heart.

She climbed the broken sill, wobbling with grief and shock. The city stretched out before her, crooked tenements and church steeples, arc-lights smearing through streets black with coal dust. On the horizon gleamed a faint bleeding breath of dawn.

She jumped onto the starlit rooftop, skidding on wet slate, and ran.

A SINGLE REDEEMING DEFECT

AT THE GATES OF BUCKINGHAM PALACE, IN BRIGHT early-morning sun, she flashed Remy's Royal Society badge to the Enforcer on guard. Its electric eyes burned, studying her bruised face, and inwardly she quailed. Surely word had gotten back, and the thing would arrest her on sight, badge or no badge.

The Enforcer cocked its brassy head, and stepped aside. Not programmed to think. Just to obey.

On edge, she hurried across the gravel yard, shadows dogging her steps. She'd rushed home only for long enough to discard her filthy gown for a fresh one, and fatigue tugged at her, insistent. For once, the rain had stayed away, and the flowerbeds sparkled with dewdrops, a fresh scent that on any ordinary day would have lifted her spirits.

The sweetness only recalled what she'd lost. What more would be ruined should she fail.

The clockwork equerry led her ponderously up the grand staircase. Impatiently, she hopped, peering over its shoulder. "It's urgent. I say, can we . . . oh, to hell with it." She shoved past the indignant machine and sprinted along the red-carpeted hall, past marble statues and gilded plasterwork and frowning portraits of kings and queens long dead.

It suddenly hit her that King Edward—Bertie—might have returned from his dread sojourn as the Soho Slasher. That she'd have to look into those addled, doleful eyes and remember what he'd done—and that she'd let an innocent man be arrested for his crimes.

Too late. She skidded up to the chamber door, and burst in without knocking. "Sir Isaac, forgive me, I've urgent business."

The Regent sat behind his desk, brocade coat immaculate and hair neatly tied. Opposite him, ankles fastidiously crossed on the chaise, lounged Lord Beaconsfield. In court dress, white tie and black coat skirts artfully arranged, one arm flung over the chaise's gilded back and his diamond-headed cane leaning against the Regent's desk.

Come to kiss hands, as the saying went. Today—at eleven o'clock—he'd be Prime Minister.

Both men stared at her. One in frank astonishment. The other in mordant amusement.

"I say," drawled Beaconsfield, "is this customary?" His heavy-lidded eyes speared her, a reptile tracking its prey. Eliza recalled their first meeting, her impression that he'd formulated a purpose for her. Well, he'd gotten exactly what he wanted. And she'd played along most obediently.

Suddenly, she needed urgently to use the privy. "Regent, might we speak privately?"

The Regent smiled, a glint of ice. "Speak your piece, Doctor. Quick about it."

Nothing for it, then. She took a deep breath. "*Liberté du*

Sang are in London, sir. A man named *la Bête*. Their shape-shifters are planning to attack Lord Beaconsfield's speech with . . ." She swallowed. "With a time machine. Sir."

A beat of silence.

Beaconsfield laughed. Mocking, disbelieving laughter. "I don't know where you're getting your preposterous information, young lady, but I hope you didn't pay for it. Absurd."

"I once wrote a book on the laws of physics, madam." Sir Isaac drummed his nails on the desk. "I presume you've glanced at it. Time travel is impossible, or at least vastly improbable. The fabric of the aether would disintegrate. Why do you think I enforce the Royal's rules? It isn't vanity. It's survival."

Eliza gulped on laughter. This was worse than ridiculous. He hadn't said *Liberté du Sang? A mythical gang of shapeshifters, you say? Just wait here while I call the alienists to carry you away.* No. It was, *Time travel? Dreadfully sorry, but I can't allow it.*

"Nevertheless, such a machine has been built." She recalled irascible Seymour Locke—*I did say advanced aether physics*—and stifled more laughter. "I've traveled in it, and seen the future. One possible future," she amended hastily, fending off another science lesson. Briefly, she explained what she'd seen: the ruined city, the dying aether, the mass graves and wretched populace under cruel sorcerers' rule. "If we don't intervene, catastrophe will be absolute."

Sir Isaac's rain-gray eyes glittered, sharper than thorns. She could almost hear his brain working, a rapid cacophony of bouncing ideas and colliding solutions. Her heart pounded. *Please, let me have the Newton of old, of fluxions and optics*

*and gravitational laws, who loves science in all its wonders. Not
the jealous old skeleton who burns people for thinking.*

An eternity passed.

"Built, you say," he murmured at last, a strange varnish of
excitement on his tone. "By whom?"

Her relief rushed out, and she almost started babbling. "A
team of British scientists. Their secret was stolen, and sold to
the enemy." She pointed at Lord Beaconsfield. "By him."

Beaconsfield jerked upright. Spine rigid, the most ener-
getic movement she'd ever seen him make. "Ludicrous," he
declared, and his voice no longer drawled with boredom. It
was whetted with lethal venom. "How dare you, madam? Regent, arrest this wretch immediately. I say, Enforcers!"

"It's true." Eliza's throat thickened. "He conspired with Veronica Burton. She's an enemy agent. And *la Bête,* the fellow
with the withered hand. I witnessed this with my own eyes,
in Soho four nights ago. Deny it if you can, my lord."

"Naturally I deny it. You speak of treason, madam. I am
a peer of the realm! By God, I'll have you—" Beaconsfield
stopped, his neat-bearded jaw hanging loose. "*La Bête,*" he
said faintly at last. "Withered hand, you say? A time machine? I dealt with no time machine, sir. Skyships, that's
what. Professor Crane's new engine. The War Office is in-
fested with democrats and spineless republicans who refuse
to act. Someone had to intervene!"

Sir Isaac didn't move. "*If* this is true, Doctor, then treason's the least of our problems. Whence this information?"

Her stomach churned. She didn't want to mention Remy's
name. "A Royal Society agent."

"Ah. Captain Lafayette, then."

Reluctantly, she nodded.

"A sorcerer," cried Beaconsfield, "as well as an enemy spy. He's the guilty one!"

"He's not a sorcerer—"

"But he is an enemy spy," cut in Sir Isaac sharply—but a flash of gleeful irony in his eyes made her despair. How to know if he was serious? "For *Liberté du Sang*. How else do you explain the illicit documents in his cellar?"

"Burton set him up! She's the spy, not Remy. Beaconsfield, Burton, *la Bête*. They all conspired against you, because you're the one stopping them getting what they want. It's all about getting rid of you!"

She and Sir Isaac stared at each other, stunned.

The irony struck her hard. Protecting the Philosopher, after he'd brought her so many years of grief. While the man she loved languished in the Royal's dungeons, answering the wrong questions for his life.

"I see," said Sir Isaac at last. Color burned high on his pale cheeks. "Then we've not a moment to lose—"

"Not so fast."

The door from the king's chamber swung open. And out strode a trio of black-clad figures, faces hooded, skeletal hands wreathed in fire. Behind them, brandishing an ugly pistol, came a woman. A strange, blank-faced woman, wearing gentleman's clothes. The Soho Slasher's accomplice.

She gave a gloating smile, and her face *shifted,* like a melting mask.

Magic.

Her skin shimmered and stretched, forming another, different face.

Princess Victoria smirked, satisfied. "Arrest him," she ordered, waving her weapon. On the back of her hand was a set of angry red scratches, fading now. Her obedient trio of sorcerers glided forwards, black robes whispering, and encircled the Philosopher in shackles of dark flame.

"Whee! Look, Vickie. Choo-choo!" Bertie crawled out on the carpet, zooming his little wooden train up and down to the clockwork strains of Mozart's *Die Zauberflöte*. The Magic Flute, a tale of sorcerers and secret societies and the vengeful Queen of the Night.

At the sight of Bertie, Lizzie swelled in Eliza's chest like a cancer. *Kill the bastard,* she hissed. *Kill 'em both! Wring their bloodthirsty necks until their eyes pop!*

"There, Bertie," soothed Victoria, "you'll soon be well again. This nasty fellow has been making you sick. Shall we be rid of him?"

Sir Isaac tossed his imperious head. "This is irrational. You've no conception of the forces you're playing with—"

"Don't I?" said Victoria calmly. "Oh, well. *Nullius in verba,* you always say. I think I'll see for myself. Take him away!"

The mute sorcerers obeyed, leading Newton out. He went, spluttering, practically shedding electric sparks of rage. "You shan't win. I haven't finished with you yet!"

Eliza despaired. She needed the Enforcers. Without Newton, all was lost. "But he's the *de facto* head of state. You can't—"

"Oh, I can." Victoria trained her pistol on Lord Beaconsfield, who sat heavily on the chaise, for once bewildered into silence. "Or rather, Parliament can. I recall a famous occasion involving a treason trial and a beheading. Could we arrange something of that sort, my lord? To be announced this morning, at the speech? Or must I find myself another Prime Minister?"

Beaconsfield oozed from the chaise and edged backwards in Eliza's direction, gripping his unicorn cane in front like a shield. "My dear lady—your highness—what you ask is quite impossible—"

"*Don't* tell me what's *possible!*" Victoria's eyes blazed, deranged. "I'm sick of men of common birth telling me what I can and can't do. Why, the ignominy . . ." and she launched into a rambling tirade, punctuated with brandishings of pistol and tossings of wild hair. "It's my birthright, I tell you! Royal bloodline. Bertie isn't fit . . . oh, the horror!"

Bertie giggled, smashing his train into the desk. His hair writhed, shaggy gray one moment, lank blond the next. "Pow!" he lisped with a hideous grin. "Pow! All dead!"

The horror, indeed. Which Eliza had helped create. Suddenly she felt sick. Her good intentions meant less than nothing. Her vanity knew no bounds. Would she never learn?

"Run!" whispered Beaconsfield fiercely. Hard-eyed, determined, his vacuous façade sloughed away like discarded skin. "While she's distracted. Let me talk her down."

Every instinct screamed at her to obey. "She'll kill you."

"Ha! Not I, madam. She'll be eating out of my hand just like her mother. I can kiss royal arse with the Empire's finest." He sized up the ranting princess, his lip curling. "Seems we're relying on you to save the Empire, Doctor. I shall watch for you at eleven. Now run, and God forgive me for all I've done."

SINCE THE ASSASSINS WILL NOT

B Y THE TIME SHE REACHED SCOTLAND YARD, SHE'D already hustled for two miles through traffic-clogged streets. Her legs ached, her lungs burned like poison, and it was a chilled but sunny nine o'clock. The nearby Horse Guards clock chimed the hour sharply, *clong! clong!*, as if it mocked her for her tardiness. *Late! Late!*

On a book-seller's cart, the latest penny dreadful's cover read THE ARTFUL DODGER'S CUNNING COMEBACK, with an illustration of a grinning man in a dented top hat stabbing another fellow in the back. A mouse-eared paperboy with a curly tail sticking out of his trousers flung a stack of broadsheets into the dust. SOHO KILLER IDENTIFIED AS NOTORIOUS CRIMINAL FIGURE. HOME SECRETARY TO DECORATE POLICE OFFICER IN CHARGE.

Well, that was something. At least Harley Griffin would finally get the recognition he deserved.

"The King of Rats!" yelled the mouse boy, jumping and holding his cap on with both hands. "Hot off the presses! Slasher's name is Hyde!"

A file of red-coated soldiers marched by, weapons smart

and boots polished, and she spared a frightened thought for Remy, locked in his cruel cell with machines for company. Would the Enforcers interrogate him, perhaps with some human agent in charge? Or stay silent and torture him anyway, as their unquestioned instructions required?

Was he already dead?

For a moment, she squeezed her eyes shut, frustration itching. If Remy were here, they could have marched into Horse Guards and raised a battalion to face the sorcerers. But Eliza was a woman, and knew no one at Army HQ. *Sorcerers, you say? The Regent incapacitated? No more Enforcers to get in our way? Pity, that. Grab us a drink, love.*

She leapt up Scotland Yard's stone steps and into the lobby, where clerks and constables milled. The subdued mood stung her like a scorpion. What was wrong? Harley had just solved the season's biggest case. The papers were full of it. The police were heroes. She'd expected celebrations.

The front desk was hidden under a teetering tower of paperwork. Eliza rapped on the counter. "Where is Inspector Griffin, please? At Bow Street they said he was absent." It had been her first port of call. She'd run halfway across London, hopping a 'bus for a few blocks but the rest on foot, only to have to run all the way back again.

A smooth dark head peered out. "Dr. Jekyll?"

"Perkins?" Eliza edged closer. "What's wrong with everyone? Where's Harley? I urgently need his help. It's a matter of national security."

"He's not here. Mr. Reeve—" Perkins glanced over Eliza's shoulder, flushing.

With a sigh, Eliza turned. "Chief Inspector."

"Superintendent." Reeve beamed, chewing smugly on his cigar stub. "The position was vacant. Clearly I'm the best man for the job. Oh, and Griffin doesn't work here anymore. I fired him."

"What?" Eliza's brain clunked, frustratingly slow. "He just caught the Slasher!"

"Not by any decent police work." Reeve puffed out his chest, his oily brown suit glistening. Doubly unkempt, like a man unused to cleaning up after himself, and she recalled Perkins's tip that Mrs. Reeve had thrown him out. Clearly the lady was stubborn. "Blunders about for weeks as bodies pile up, and just happens to show up when the bastard was drunk out of his mind? The Commissioner agreed it's too much to be borne."

Fire ignited in her belly. "I'm sure he did. Poor Sir Stamford doesn't know what year it is, let alone understand the corruption in his own department."

Reeve flicked his cigar, ash plopping. Did he ever actually smoke the horrid things, or just chew them to be disgusting? "Corruption, eh? Serious charge, that. Heard you had your doubts at that crime scene. Concealing evidence, they say. Anything you care to tell me?"

She opened her mouth to retort, and shut it again, mortified.

As much as she loathed it, cunning Mr. Todd had been right. Lizzie had proved that. Hyde wasn't the Slasher, and Harley had arrested the wrong man. It hardly seemed an opportune moment to say so.

"Nothing to say?" Reeve grinned. "Fine. You're fired, too, and good riddance. Now get out."

Rage bubbled in her chest, overflowing. Not Lizzie's, but

her own. Exhausted, bitter, hungry for recompense for every humiliation she'd suffered at this man's hands. "You jealous little rat. You can't do that!"

"Can't I, just?" Reeve leaned into her face. "I ran Griffin out for being a mouthy weasel who didn't know his place. I can surely get rid of you for hiding the fact that your father's a murderer. Oh, yes," he added, with a smug curl of lip. "I know all about you and Edward Hyde, esquire. Knew something was fishy about you from the start. Not only a trumped-up tart, but a bastard, too! Ho ho!"

Self-disgust seared her cheeks, an ugly revelation. Like Veronica Burton, she'd betrayed her dearest principles and pretended she didn't care. Sucked up every insult, sold her soul to get ahead—and look how she'd ended up.

Never again.

"Think your wife will love you any better now you're promoted?" she hissed. "Think your daughters will be proud of you for destroying a good man's career? You're still the same wretched sycophant you were before. I'm surprised they can stand the sight of you."

Reeve's cheeks suffused, and he swung his fist back.

"Go on, hit me," she snarled. "Prove what a man you are."

He caught himself, mustache shaking with rage—but shame burned, too, and it looked like murder. "Get out of my sight," he growled. "If I see you on police premises again, I'll bang you up with killers and rapists so fast your feet won't touch mud."

He stalked away, smoke practically hissing from his ears. And just like that, her career was finished.

Eliza squeezed her fists tight, red mist boiling over her

eyes. Acting without care for consequences was Lizzie's game. The urge to sprint after him and slam his nose back into his brain . . . She cursed, sick to her stomach.

Why had she put herself in this position? Why hadn't she told Griffin she knew Hyde was innocent? Why hadn't she demanded Hyde be released? Why?

Because you're a coward, Eliza. Lizzie coiled like a snake in her darkest heart, forked tongue hissing—but her power seemed distant, a strange alien creature locked away behind prickly blue glass. *I'd have given Reeve my mind long ago. Think you're so fine with your god-rotted principles, but you're just a common coward hiding behind hate.*

Behind the desk, Perkins winced. "That went well."

Eliza smiled weakly, the lie pasting itself easily across her lips. *Aye, laugh it off. Pretend everything's fine. S'what you're good at, Eliza.* "Goodbye, Perkins. And good luck."

Perkins's face fell. "But you can't go. I need you. Don't leave me here alone."

Eliza just walked out, burning with her own ugly dose of shame. She'd failed Perkins as well as Harley. *Anyone else? Good. I've no more pitiful weakness to spare.*

She emerged into the sunlit street, uncaring traffic hurtling by. Despair washed her will thin. No Enforcers, no police. No one to stop the invasion. And her list of friends was growing short.

Finally, she stopped, and slumped against the brick wall of a notary's office, exhausted. She closed her eyes, blocking out that joyless, glaring sun—but still the accusing stares of passers-by seared into her flesh. *Coward. Liar. Failure.*

What now? She could think of only one place to go for help . . .

"Are you ready?" A rose-scented whisper tickled her ear.

She jerked, clocking her head on the bricks.

Mr. Todd tipped his hat with a scarred fingertip. His coat—Venetian red—was a splash of sunlit blood. Casual as you like, half a block from Scotland Yard, his burned face an awful work of art.

She dragged in a breath to yell.

"You're welcome," he cut in swiftly, with a merry eye-twinkle. "For Edward Hyde, I mean. It was nothing. Shall we go? I hear Constantinople's lovely at this time of year."

Mentally, she cursed, kicking herself. But she had to *know*. "What do you mean, sir?"

"The Soho Slasher, at last behind bars! Capital. Most excellent. Couldn't have done it without you." An enchanted smile. "Well, I suppose I could simply have killed him—the man did lock me in a cage, after all, which I confess didn't do wonders for Shadow's mood—but that exquisite artist's touch is so important. Don't you agree?"

"What? No . . . What are you talking about?"

"Miss O'Hara, of course. You were vacillating the last time we spoke, you wanted your father taken care of. I owed you an apology for my ill temper. Now we can start afresh, just you and I." Meticulously, Todd adjusted his diamond-pinned cuffs. "Now, time is somewhat of the essence, so if you don't mind, we must run for our train—"

"Stop." Her head throbbed with distant echoes of Lizzie's rage, like a garbled phonograph recording, unintelligible and useless. Rose's nightmare murder scene, the spilled liquor, those gore-spattered glasses. *Three* glasses. More than two people. Hyde's intoxicated state, that odd scent of aniseed and bitterness. Not gin or whisky. Absinthe and cognac. Todd's favorite—but sharpened with laudanum.

A mickey finn, as Lizzie would say. Todd had drugged Hyde. Made his wicked art, and left Hyde at the blood-soaked scene of his crime. Poor mad Bertie hadn't even visited Soho that night. No, he'd been at his party at Buckingham Palace, slurping birthday toasts and throwing cake.

"*You* killed Rose," she stammered. "Why, for God's sake?"

"For you, my sweet." A besotted green glow. Not insane. Frighteningly lucid. "Everything is for you. How else can I prove we belong together? I never believed that fool Reeve, I want you to know that. When he insisted you betrayed me, I mean. He seems to think we engaged in some sordid carnal *liaison* that addled my wits. The man's positively prehistoric . . . Eliza, whatever's the matter?" He touched her chin, gentle and terrifying.

"Get away." She edged back, pulse pounding. His touch—that dry crackle, his dark scent of roses and burned skin—set cold worms squirming in her veins.

"Don't play." Todd's eyes darkened. "You saw the evidence I left you. You ignored it. You've no job, no friends, and, dare I mention it, no lapdog *fiancé* to make you pretend." He brightened, sweetness and starlight. "Your old life is gone. You needn't lie anymore. Now come along, we'll be late." And he offered her his hand.

She gawped at it, speechless. In his own twisted mind,

Todd had presented her with a choice. And she'd accepted. She'd let Hyde be arrested. And now Todd thought . . .

Clarity hit her like pre-dawn thunder.

She backed away, fresh energy hardening like diamonds in her heart. Her vanity—nay, cowardice—had brought her to this. Never again.

"I will never come with you, Malachi Todd." She caught his gaze, and held it. "I will never be like you. Now leave me be."

And she raised her shaking hand to point.

Aghast, Todd stared, his mangled face pale. "Don't," he whispered. "Please, Eliza. Don't do this. You know I love you."

"Police!" Her yell sliced the chilly air like a trumpet blast. "Arrest that man! He's Razor Jack! Murder!"

For a heartbeat, the world stopped. Todd's gaze glittered, awash with jeweled tears.

Then people screamed and scurried. Whistles blew. Voices took up the cry. "Murder! Police! Murder!"

Up the street, shouts rang out as uniformed officers spilled from Scotland Yard. Boots thumped the paving. People gasped and yelled, the crowd closing in.

And in a blur, Todd erupted.

Steel flashed in cruel-bright sun. Bones crunched. A woman screamed. A body fell with a wet sigh, and the cobbles gleamed afresh, a hot crimson splash of blood.

"Murder! After him!" A running man jostled Eliza, knocking her to her knees. She scrambled up, appalled—but like a malevolent ghost plotting revenge, Mr. Todd had vanished.

*   *   *

Twenty minutes later, she rapped on the glass door of Finch's Pharmacy. "Marcellus, it's Eliza. Let me in!"

On New Bond Street, pedestrians hustled to and fro amidst carriages and carts, dustmen and costermongers, slipping and sliding on the wet road. An Enforcer patrolled, hand twitching to its pistol, and hastily Eliza hid her face as it clunked by. Dogs snarled, electric servants ran and chattered. Just another morning in London. Fragrant horse dung, coal smoke, hot aether engines, yells and whistles and rattling coach wheels. Even the feeble sunlight looked bored.

As if the city had no idea this was the last normal day.

She knocked again, more urgently. Time to make amends. "Marcellus? I'm sorry for the unkind things I said. I didn't mean it. We need to talk."

No reply, the paper blinds drawn.

Desolation chilled her. Finch was her last remaining friend. What else to do but go to the Prime Minister's speech and wait for the end? For Mr. Todd to ambush her and exact his bloody revenge?

Under the little porch, the door leading to the private living quarters above the shop was ajar. She pushed. It squeaked open. "Marcellus?"

No answer.

She trotted up the narrow steps. Perhaps he'd wandered out to get supplies, and left the door open in error. Or she'd find him asleep in his chair after forty-eight hours poring over his crucibles. Immersed in some new acquisition for his library, or simply gazing out the window, oblivious to the real world.

At the top, the door to his reading room hung open. From

inside came agitated muttering. "I'm such an idiot! It isn't *disappearing*, eh? It's temporal displacement! Astonishing! Just as Quentin told him, but did the stubborn old fool listen? Of course he didn't!"

"Marcellus, it's me. Sorry to intrude—"

"Wait! Don't come in! Not safe, say what?" A scuffle, a series of clunks, the oddball whirring of strange machinery, and the stormy tang of aether. "Stop that at once, you beastly gadget! How dare you—eeergh!"

Silence punched her ears, deafening.

Light, brighter than the sun, her heated spectacles scorching her eyes. Limbs wrenching, muscles protesting, the dizzy sensation of flying.

Was that Lizzie, calling her name? She couldn't see. Couldn't think. *Eliza* . . .

Crack! Her skull hit the stairs. Groggily she tumbled, and the world cracked in two and shimmered to weightless black.

Eliza.

My lips move, soundless.

Eliza!

I jerk upright. Her voice, my voice. Her name, but my name.

Beneath me, something moves. A body. Who the hell is that? I scramble down crunching steps, towards a tiny landing and a door with shattered glass. The steps at Finch's. Something exploded, she fell . . . and my eyes light on the sprawled body.

Dirty gray skirts, a fall of unpinned blond hair. Her face bruised and bloodied, mouth slack in unconsciousness.

My pulse hammers. I look down at myself. Same gray skirts, same ripped bodice—but those dark curls tumbling down are *mine*.

Jesus fucking Christ.

We're two.

TWO, by God. Blown apart in Finch's wacky explosion. That prickly blue brew *WORKED.*

Raucous laughter swells my chest. *My* chest, God rot you. *Mine! My* laugh, *my* legs twitching into a joyful jig. *I'm me!*

My blood pumps hard, outrageous exultation, and it feels so good I almost swoon. No more Eliza, whining at my choices, cringing at my mistakes, jumping out to make me stop having fun. *What caused this, Lizzie? How long will it last? Here, let me list all the terrible things that might possibly happen.*

Ha! Who fucking cares, that's how. I dance down the steps, yelling a joyous war cry. "Whoo-harr! Miss Lizzie's here!"

She most certainly is. And she knows exactly what she'll do now. What we should've done all along.

Since when was saving the world my job? They can fuck right off, creepy Withered Arm and his mad-arse princess. I'm sick to my heart of doing what other people want. Eliza, Remy, Henry, Finch. They can all go to hell.

Save your own damn world, Eliza, if you're so clever. You and your fucking Philosopher deserve each other. So busy saving yourselves, you forget about the little people. People like me and Eddie Hyde.

Hyde . . . Hyde . . . The name slithers, a sigh on the back of my neck. I whirl, fists up to fight.

No one. I punch my temples, gritting my teeth. God-rotted voices. Keep it down, can't you?

Hyde . . . Hyde . . .

I know who 'tis, see. That hissing creature in the black bottle. Long before Eliza could hear, it whispered to me, rocking me from my slumber. The blind hunger that lured young Byron Starling off his narrow, the empty rage that stabbed a blade into his eye just to watch him scream. The elixir's starry pleasure, that sultry midnight when Eddie first showed us his tricks. The eager giggle in my throat, the impulse that grabbed little Johnny Wild by his dirty black hair and planted one on his fresh young lips in the rain. And other mad and marvelous ideas, all those precious nights since.

Always trying to trick me. Well, I won't have it. You can fuck right off, elixir. Don't need you no more! Ha ha!

I don't need you. What wild, wonderful words.

But my drumming pulse won't calm. My aching flesh won't ease. Because one thing the creature always has is a plan. A craving. A burning desire for gratification. And now I've no Eliza to stifle its need.

I settle down, quiet-like, and listen. Yes. Hmm. I like it. My idea all along, in fact.

A cool whisper of *other* invades my delight. An arrogant imperative, like old Fairfax from the asylum. *Don't listen to it. This isn't you, Lizzie. You're losing your mind, just like your father. You're losing control.*

But I'm too busy dancing to the lucid waltz of hatred playing in my heart. For the Slasher, for Charley Tee-Hee, for Letitia Fletcher and Malachi Todd and everyone in this cold and crippled world what uses us for their pleasure. They'll get theirs, oh, aye. I'll come for them, some bright-lit night when they're off their guard. And I've reserved a special, lurid place in my imagination for the Dodger, that greasy-arsed fuckjob. I've plans for him.

But first things first.

I slip my hand into my pocket, and bring out sharpened steel. The Slasher's knife, cold, smooth, grinning with unsated hunger.

I won't let Eddie hang. That evil little fart Bertie is responsible for this. And I mean to make him squirm.

I'm my father's daughter, after all. There's murder in my blood. Can't make people do much, not I—but sure as hell I can make 'em die.

Oho! You'd think assassinating a king would be the all-time coopered lay. Lucky for me, I know right where he'll be, in, oh, about an hour's time—and with chaos aplenty to distract. Nothing like a sense of occasion.

On the stairs, Eliza moans softly, stirring.

No time to lose, Miss Lizzie.

My fingers tighten around that chilly blade. I could do it. Slice Eliza's throat like Malachi Todd always wanted, bathe us in crimson, watch her last breath bubble to silence.

But I won't. Eddie would never forgive me. He always loved her best. Truth is, he never wanted me, not really. For Eliza, he'd give everything. For Eliza, he traded his own soul, that shadowy midnight long ago. And she spat it back at him like a mouthful of bile.

So fuck her. Let her live with what we've done.

A delighted giggle froths in my chest—mine, or that crafty

elixir's? I can't tell the difference—and I tiptoe out the shattered door and away.

Groaning, Eliza opened her eyes. The steps to Finch's rooms
blurred into view, strewn with splinters and broken glass.

Could have sworn she'd heard a voice . . .

Finch. Oh, God.

She struggled to her feet and hobbled up the stairs, winc-
ing at a twisted ankle. The door had blown off its hinges, a
chunk of the landing gone with it. Coughing, she waved away
dust.

The room was ruined. Walls blasted, furniture crushed.
Whatever experiment he'd been trying lay in a wasteland
of shriveled wire and melted glass—and on the floor, face-
down, sprawled Marcellus Finch.

She skidded to his side. Blood trickled from his dusty
white hair. Unmoving. Not breathing. She felt for a pulse.
Nothing. His head fell to one side, baby-blue eyes staring.
Dust drifted into them. He didn't blink. Sightless. Dead.

Uselessly, she fought tears. Why couldn't she do something? Wasn't she a physician? What was the god-rotted
point?

She punched her thighs, stifling a scream. She'd said such
cruel things. And now Marcellus was dead.

If only Lizzie would taunt her now. *If you hadn't cracked
your crystal at him for a little white lie, he'd still be here now.
That'll teach you, ha ha!*

But Lizzie was gone. Not a word. Not even an echo of
gloating laughter.

Her heart wept, bereft. Along New Bond Street, the bells at St. George's chimed. Nearly eleven o'clock. Soon *la Bête* would attack. And she was alone. No police, no soldiers, no Enforcers to help her. She didn't even have a weapon.

She'd just have to improvise.

AN ORGANIZED HYPOCRISY

THE NEWLY MINTED PALACE OF WESTMINSTER GLIT-tered like a fairy-tale castle, Gothic turrets gleaming in golden sun. Eliza struggled through the packed crowd in New Palace Yard, heedless of jabbing elbows and boots raking her shins.

The air was murky with breath and sweat. Some people cheered. Others muttered darkly, hands straying to pockets and satchels. Banners and placards waved, groups of protesters shouting. DOWN WITH THE TORIES! RADICALS UNITE! and FIGHT HUNGER, NOT WAR faced off opposite KILL THE FRENCH! and SORCERERS MUST DIE! Was Mr. Todd amongst them, stalking her? It made no odds. If he caught her, she was dead, but she'd no time to hide.

The huge clock face known as Big Ben towered sixty yards into the heaven-blue sky. Its ornate hands inched towards eleven. Only a few minutes to go.

At last, bruised but triumphant, Eliza reached the front row. Wooden trestles held back the surging crowd, and the hard edge squashed her uncomfortably. The platform where Beaconsfield would speak had steps leading up like a scaffold. The rails were tricked out in blue Tory colors, alongside the gilded royal arms of the lion and the unicorn. Already, party dignitaries and Palace toadies waited to bask in reflected glory.

Enforcers surrounded the scaffold, armed with buzzing electric weapons. She smiled grimly. Much good they'd be. Once the aether started to disintegrate, the machines would malfunction, electrical components failing catastrophically.

At three minutes to eleven, a trumpet blast announced the entrance of royalty. A dozen of the king's household guards, red-trimmed blue tunics shining, marched up the steps to cheers mixed with hoots of derision. "God bless King Edward!" "Sorcerer's stooge!" "Down with the Regent!" "Long live the king!"

And up he skipped. Young King Edward the murderer, perfectly dressed, chains of office gleaming. But his eyes rolled, his smile slack. Probably drugged to keep him quiet. Alongside him walked Princess Victoria, cool and collected in gorgeous state finery.

On the other side, the Philosopher. Unbound, not shackled in flame. But evidently under duress, by the livid scowl he stabbed into all who dared glance his way.

At least Lord Beaconsfield's flattery had achieved this much, probably in the hope that Newton could still control the Enforcers when and if anything went wrong. The metal machines would still obey his commands. That was what they were programmed to do.

But as she watched the Regent fume and fidget, her heart sank. Those compressed lips, the fury in his eyes. Magic. The silencing spell she'd seen in the future. Sir Isaac wouldn't be saying anything any time soon. And the pair of Life Guards flanking him weren't soldiers. Their uniforms fitted poorly, their bearing unmilitary—but they watched him with fiery intensity, never once blinking or looking away.

Lord Beaconsfield followed the royal party onto the stage, his lazy dark eyes sweeping the scene with deliberate *ennui*. He waved languidly at the crowd. Some still cheered. Others screamed abuse and curses.

The crowd swayed in, almost sweeping Eliza off her feet. The noise was tremendous, stomach-churning. She barely heard the clock tower chiming the Westminster Quarters, heralding the approaching hour.

Someone behind lurched forwards, crushing her against the barrier. Her ribs squashed, a bright spurt of pain. Panic rattled her wits. She couldn't breathe. She'd suffocate.

Like a worm she wriggled, edging downwards in the sea of bodies, until she squirted out onto the paving, staring up past the barrier at Beaconsfield's legs, via the hulking form of a gigantic Enforcer.

ONE . . . TWO . . . Big Ben's colossal chimes vibrated the ground.

Bertie gaped and giggled. Victoria smiled coldly. The Regent scowled. Lord Beaconsfield glanced around, uneasy.

THREE . . . FOUR . . .

A swift scarlet-hooded figure leapt onto the back of the stage. Almost hidden by the rows of dignitaries. In the figure's hand flashed sharpened steel.

"Assassin!" screamed Eliza, but her words were torn away

by the sweltering noise. Now the scarlet figure was hidden in a forest of politicians and aristocrats, quickly working towards the front.

Her blood chilled. As if she didn't have enough problems. The government of England stood on this dais. Peers, law lords, privy councilors, the Prime Minister, the Regent himself. Everyone.

FIVE . . . SIX . . .

She yelled again, but no one heard. No one could see.

At a run, she dived for the stage, dodging the Enforcer's massive legs, and hauled herself onto the platform. Who was the fiend's target? She'd no time to pick and choose. "Assassin! Get down!"

The Enforcer swiped for her and missed. She wriggled up and ran past Lord Beaconsfield, shoving aside the stunned Life Guards. Surprised by a woman. No time to draw swords. More fools they.

SEVEN . . .

Like a dark-hooded mirage, the scarlet figure loomed behind King Edward, hefting that shining blade.

"Save the king!" Eliza sprinted straight for Bertie. Saving a transcendental monster who deserved to die. No time for irony now.

The drooling boy just laughed. Disorientated in the crushing noise, Victoria whirled in the wrong direction, hamstrung by her crowd of bodyguards.

But not so the Regent. His sharp eyes flashed to the assassin in an instant—and without delay he dived for the unresponsive boy.

EIGHT . . . NINE . . .

The assassin's knife flashed down. The Regent slammed into Bertie, knocking him sideways, and the blade sliced deep into the Regent's throat.

Blood spurted, a crimson fountain. The Regent fell, clutching the jagged wound, the knife still sticking out like a grotesque ornament.

Victoria yelled. At her side, an angry shimmer thickened, and the aether squealed and tore apart—and a man appeared. Dressed in black, with a withered hand.

La Belle et la Bête.

TEN . . .

The princess grinned, ghastly. *La Bête*'s smile twisted. And *pop!* They both vanished.

Finally, the Life Guards jumped into action. Eliza fought, her arms suddenly pinned to her sides. Lord Beaconsfield, displaying unforeseen alacrity, had already hurled the assassin to the ground, and that scarlet hood slipped down.

Dark gaze glinting with hatred, lips curled into a snarl, mahogany curls spilling free. "Get off me, God rot your eyes!"

Eliza's vision reeled, an evil magic mirror that showed malicious lies. The explosion at Finch's. Time travel experiments. Paradox.

Not Lizzie's apparition. The real thing.

ELEVEN . . . The clock's last chime faded into the howling din.

And with an ear-piercing shriek, the sky shattered.

Boom! Jagged blue lightning erupted at altitude, raining black ash over New Palace Yard. The sky crazed like punched glass, and *shredded.* Ragged holes tore and gaped, howling caverns of emptiness, rumbling with hell-dark thunder.

And from those caverns drove skyships. Dozens of black-sailed monstrosities the size of frigates, spewing stinking red fire. Crewed by identical pairs of figures, a woman in fine brocade and a grinning cloaked monster. Every crew was *la Belle et la Bête.*

The sorcerer spoke into an ugly metal device that poured out his hideous voice at murderous, unspeakable volume. "We are your masters," he trumpeted, the awful music of judgment day. "Surrender."

Eliza stared at the burning sky in horror. Lizzie had wriggled free of the guards, and punched Lord Beaconsfield in the face, whooping. "Take that, you evil old lizard!"

Lizzie, in the flesh. Separated. Unbelievable. Unthinkable. *Two of me!*

But no time to consider the consequences now.

On the deck of each awful skyship, the distant princess was winding the crank on an evil-looking metal machine. The atmosphere shuddered and shrieked, a dreadful stink of sulfur and spoiled flesh. Wind rose, thumping, agonizing pressure sucking at Eliza's eardrums as she fought to the bleeding Regent's side. As if her brains were being beaten like eggs and slowly drained away.

Mind control machines. Invisible mind-reading waves. How she'd laughed at Finch's tinfoil hat. She wasn't laughing now.

The crowd surged, overflowing onto the stage. People scrambled to avoid being crushed. Bodies tumbled and sagged. Lightning split the sky. The skyships' terrible cannon boomed, raining caustic fire.

Enforcers drew their pistols, firing at anything and everything—and the dazzling coils in their weapons exploded.

Brass limbs and rib cages blew in all directions. Some were rooted to the spot, crackling voltage juddering their frames. Their brains sizzled, hotwiring, and their metal skulls liquefied and flowed like mercury.

On the dais, swords slashed, Life Guards attacking anything that moved. Lizzie had Bertie on the ground, kicking him ferociously. He flopped, his face a mess of blood and broken teeth. "Die, you bastard," grunted Lizzie with each kick. "Die!"

And in the middle of it all, Princess Victoria reappeared— some version of her, at least—raising her arms to the fire-hailing sky and screaming in exultation.

The whine of her awful machinery tore Eliza's ears, but still she fought to reach the Regent, clambering over bodies. People were howling, vomiting, clutching their ears, flopping like grounded fish. Some already dead. Some just sitting, dull grins on their faces and ears cocked, as if listening to some disembodied voice.

In a puddle of blood, the Regent lay, already weakening. Blood drenched his shirt, his colorless hair. His eyes burned, but not with fear of death. Just impotent rage.

Desperate, Eliza clutched for something, anything to staunch the wound. Her fingers closed around cloth— someone's shawl?—and hastily she scrunched it up and pressed it over the leaking gash. Blood flowered, drenching the soft fabric scarlet.

A blue silk scarf.

Her head whipped around—and Seymour Locke's eyes met hers. Young, unscarred, backing away from the dying Regent with an expression of horror. "Oh, fuck it," he whispered.

Before she could speak, he was swept away into the crowd.

Stunned, she turned back to the Regent . . . but his rainy eyes glazed, lifeless. A world of knowledge, gone. Just another corpse on a field of death.

Crrrrackkk! An almighty groan of rending earth. Dully, she glanced up. A chasm had opened, fire leaping from its jagged rim. With a rumble like hellfire, the majestic clock tower juddered, and started to fall.

Chunks of glass and stonework rained. People screamed and ran.

The silent black-robed men hauled Eliza to her feet. Lizzie laughed as she leapt from the dais, darting left and right to evade capture. "Come at me, you fart-stinking dogs!"

Victoria laughed, hair blown back by hellish wind. "You're a traitor to the revolution, Dr. Jekyll," she yelled. "It's treatment for you. Take her to Dr. Savage."

Wildly, Eliza fought, but to no avail. "Listen to me," she screamed, "we can still stop this—uugh!" Her throat squeezed shut, invisible pincers from a torture chamber. Flaming shackles seared her wrists. Her lips jammed tight, sealed with invisible glue. A spell of silence.

She struggled to reach out, a drowning woman grasping for the surface. *Lizzie!* she wanted to yell, *Lizzie, help me!*

But Lizzie just grinned, and skipped free, and let the sorcerers drag Eliza away.

A hood smothered Eliza's head, and unseen hands swept her along. For hours, it seemed, she stumbled amidst screams and the sounds of chaos. Machinery groaned and whirred.

Weapons sizzled, fire roaring, heat searing her skin. Warm copper-stinking wetness sloshed around her ankles as she tripped up over a curb into some kind of vehicle, with metal benches and an engine that smelled of brimstone.

The vehicle jerked upwards. A rush of blood to her head, and she swooned into dizzy darkness.

Minutes later—hours? days?—she awoke.

All was dark. The hood was gone, the shackles too. Distant wailing, ragged screams, electricity's crackle and hiss, a man's unhinged laughter. Somewhere, a voice sang roughly, ruined by solitude and screaming. *"Ring-a-ring o' roses . . . a pocket full o' posies . . ."*

Eliza stumbled up, bare feet slapping the cold floor. Her hair fell over her chest. Her dress was gone, replaced by a threadbare linen shift. She coughed, her throat raw but functional again. She shivered, rubbing chilled arms as her eyes adjusted.

Reddish light slanted through a high barred window, illuminating her tiny cell. Gray padded walls, smeared with filth and bloodied scratch marks.

The asylum.

"Atishoo," sang that broken voice. *"Atishoo. We all . . . fall . . . DOWN."*

She screamed, beating against the padded door. "It's me! I'm Eliza Jekyll! You can't keep me here!"

Only the keening wind answered. She yelled until her throat bled, clawing her nails raw on the canvas. "I'm not insane! Let me out. Lizzie, help me!"

But Lizzie was gone. Exhausted, Eliza huddled on the floor, and sobbed herself to sleep.

ILLUSTRATIONS OF MADNESS

A METALLIC RATTLE JERKED HER AWAKE.
Wheels squeaked in the corridor, footsteps shuffling. "Hurry, man!" a voice husked. "Time is of the essence!"

How long had she slept? Maybe hours. Maybe days. Time had stretched, a dark blur. Sometimes, food was stuffed through the door slot. Sometimes not. Outside, the sky boiled, torn by jagged lightning. Always stormy, this ugly future. Always nighttime.

She scrambled up and peered through the observation slot, straining her eye muscles to the limit. The dim corridor was a blur. Her spectacles were gone, as was everything she'd had on her person. Nothing hard or sharp remained. Not even a hair pin.

The grating wheels halted outside her door. She glimpsed a trolley, pushed by dark-sleeved arms. On it, a dusty brass machine, festooned with dials and coiled wires, and a pair of rusted electrodes, coated with dried blood. Alongside this sat an evil-looking leather funnel.

Her blood chilled, icy echoes of the torture Mr. Fairfax had inflicted on Malachi Todd. Electroshock. Nerves screaming, muscles cramping, liquid forced down her throat until she choked and begged. Surely, this was worse than any Royal Society interrogation. Lizzie had left her here to die.

"This is the one." The husky voice, owner out of sight. "Open the door. Master's orders, so be quick about it."

A lock squeaked, bolts thudding back.

Swiftly, Eliza flattened her back to the wall beside the door. Slam the door into his face. Go for his throat. Shove that horrid trolley into his guts and run for her life . . .

The heavy door groaned open. In came the trolley, *squeek! squeek!,* pushed by a skeletal fellow with rotted teeth. Dr. Savage, the king's alienist. Following him, a figure in hooded black robes.

Her interrogator. Or her torturer.

Eliza launched at the trolley, slamming it into Savage's chest and pinning him to the wall. *Cracck!* Ribs broke like sticks. Triumphant, Eliza whirled for freedom—and collided with the black-robed sorcerer. Unthinking, she clawed for his eyes, his hood falling . . .

Untidy white hair sprang out, jammed beneath a crinkled tinfoil hat. "I say," whispered Marcellus Finch fiercely, "no need for that." He slammed his elbow back into Savage's skinny throat. Savage gasped, face purpling, his larynx surely crushed. Finch beamed. "Ha-ha! A rescue, say what?"

Eliza's brain rattled, lost. Finch was dead. Gone. "But . . ."

"Old Starling's advanced waves, you know. Experiment went haywire, boom! Two timelines in the one space. Two

Finches! Stunned! Alternate realities, duplicates, paradoxes, so on and so forth. Quite the multi-dimensional disturbance. I'm so proud."

"Two Finches," she repeated, dazed. "Only I didn't get two Elizas, did I? I got one me, and one Lizzie."

"You don't say? Transcendental identity, that's the ticket." Finch peered short-sightedly, his pince-nez missing. "The aether doesn't like it when we play silly simultaneity games. You and Lizzie, me and, well, *me,* eh? Other Finch dead, poor lamb. Blasted off his hinges, so to speak. Here's hoping I got the brains, eh?" He frowned. "Or is it *me* who's dead and *he* who survived? Perhaps I'm not the real Finch after all. Gadzooks, what a drama!"

Eliza wanted to laugh with joy. Overcome, she grabbed him and smacked a kiss on his lips. "You're real enough for me."

A pleased flush. "Enough of that," he mumbled. "Germs, you know. The creeping johnnies, up your arm before you've time to lick your fingers. Time's running out, say what?" He waved a second crumpled foil cone. "Chop-chop, don't have all day."

She eyed it dubiously. "You're joking."

"Mind control machines, dear girl! Thoughts sucked out, free will dissolved, people shambling about like living corpses. This foil is the only way we'll make it through these corridors alive."

He molded the foil around her head, grabbed still-dying Savage's hat and jammed it on top. "There. Never liked you anyway, Savage, with your handcuffs and thrashings and electrodes up the whatsit. Where d'you get such vile notions, that's what I'd like to know. These newfangled 'psychologist' chaps would have a field day." He pulled his hood over his eyes and stiffened, funereal. "Now come along, before they realize I'm not the Grand Pooh-Bah Warlock of the Fleet after all. Act captured, can't you? Manacles of fire, all that?"

Swiftly, she pulled a ragged blanket from Savage's trolley—by now he was quite dead, his purple face fixed in rot-toothed surprise—and wrapped it around her. Rifling Savage's pockets, she unearthed an electric stinger, and tested its charge. *Zzzap!* Still good.

She knotted the stinger into a corner of her shift. "Where are we going? Nowhere's safe."

Finch's hood jerked in surprise. "Henry's, of course. Where else will we find the tools we need? Assuming it's still standing. Crumbling hovel, knocked over in a stiff breeze, all that."

"The prototype? But Locke knows about that. He could destroy it any minute!"

"Then we must make haste!" Finch raised his voice. "*Merci*, Dr. Savage, I'll take this prisoner for rectal electrode insertion immediately. The little minx is certainly a handful. Double power, you say? *Sacre bleu!* That ought to blast any disobedience out of her *tout de suite*."

He marched her into the chilly brick corridor. Wind whistled along the low ceiling. In the other cells, prisoners moaned and giggled, sepulchral. Finch prodded her along, humming "La Marseillaise." "Come along, miscreant! Voltage awaits!"

"You're enjoying this, aren't you?" she muttered, nervous giggles threatening.

A glint of baby-blue from inside his hood. "Why d'you

think I got into alchemy in the first place, eh? Always wanted
to be a wizard."

"So, you see," explained Finch an hour later, as they descended the steps to the old laboratory, thoroughly exhausted
and covered in flecks of ash and debris, "after Henry made
that unexpected appearance—and while I planned your daring rescue, ha ha!—I took the liberty of making a few adjust-
ments. Calibrations, eh? Based on Starling's equations and
my own experiments. And do you know, in my attic I found
Quentin's original diagram."

"What a stroke of luck." Eliza shivered, tucking loose hair
around her neck. Wind whispered in the smell of brimstone,
and the darkness writhed like a ghostly beast.

Outside, chaos rumbled, the air shrieking. They'd scuttled
their way to Cavendish Square via hellish streets rampant
with looting, the sky raining fire and cobblestones slippery
with blood. They'd found the house deserted. The Pooles and
Charles Brigham had fled. Even Hippocrates had left no sign.

"On a napkin, you know," said Finch happily. "They dared
him, you see, and we all knew how that would turn out.
One of Victor's ghastly dinner parties, all his opium-addled
literary friends. Quentin, I told him, Quentin, you arrogant
little jack-rabbit, you can't smoke yourself silly, scribble schematics for a four-dimensional travel apparatus on a scrap of
moth-eaten table linen and expect it to *work*." Finch beamed.
"To think I'd quite forgotten. And of course, Michael's ideas
helped."

"You told Byron Starling you'd never read that book."

"Of course I'd tell *him* that." Finch still wore his tinfoil hat, and it gleamed unpleasantly in reddish light. "Never did trust that fellow, not after the stories he told about you. You say the second volume's burned?"

"Good riddance," muttered Eliza.

"Eh? Think of the science! All that knowledge, lost forever. At least until the world spits up another Faraday, which considering the latest crop of selfish buffoons masquerading as inventors won't be any time soon." He scratched his head. "Or any time at all, if we can't fix this."

"I don't know, Marcellus. I used to believe all science was progress. Now I'm not so sure." She wrapped her black tailcoat tighter. Anything to replace that stinking asylum shift. The only clothing she'd found belonged to Brigham, and she'd crimped the trousers in at her waist and shortened the braces. Brigham was bigger than he looked.

She and Finch clambered through the unlocked combination door. There sat the machine, coil dead and jeweled brass orbits dark. *Dare me, will you?* it sneered. *Mess with the fabric of time and space? Such hubris. A fool's game.*

She pulled the main switch. *Zzap!* Sparks jumped, wires jerking—but the lights buzzed weakly, only a faint glow. "At least we still have power."

"But the aether is crumbling like a soggy biscuit. This fellow might not even start, eh, and then where will we be? Stuck in the wrong future, that's where, and not a sausage to show for it." Finch rummaged beneath the machine, adjusting a maze of bristling wires. "Give it a blast, say what?"

Now or never. She grasped the brass handle on the machine's miniature generator, and pulled.

Bzzzzt! Her hair bristled on end. Lightning forked along the brass rings, and with a *rrripp!* of igniting aether, the engine's coil erupted into blinding blue.

Whirr! The crystal-studded rings began to rotate slowly, then faster. The air groaned, distorting dangerously.

Already Finch clambered into the seat, bouncing with excitement. "So when do you want to go? One reversal, and only one. No second chance, eh?"

Eliza darted under the swinging rings and clambered on beside him . . . but the staggering import of what she was doing struck her momentarily dumb.

One chance.

Alter her past. Rescue her abortive career, her botched relationships, the mess with the Soho Slasher. Even her crippling failure with Malachi Todd. Sorrow, regret, pain. All erased, with just a flick of these switches.

And Lizzie.

She could put an end to Edward Hyde's schemes. No elixir for her. No transcendental identity, no threat from Royal Society agents. No worry and trouble and heartache, day after day after day. Freedom. The chance of a lifetime.

The temptation almost drowned her.

Do it! Inside her, a child screamed, beating its fists against invisible walls. *It's not fair! Why should everyone else get what they want? What about ME?*

But some things mattered more than selfish happiness. She'd created this mess, with her blind curiosity and misplaced sense of right and wrong. And she'd put things right if she had to die doing it.

Even if she had to kill Lizzie, too.

Just what Seymour Locke thought. The thought hissed, guilty. *That he'd put things right. One more trip, he'd say, just one more and all will be well.*

Such vanity, to imagine she could change the world.

But if she didn't try, she'd never know. And like Henry Jekyll—whose insatiable longing for truth had brought only sorrow and ruin—Eliza had to *know*.

The machine juddered and whirred, sparks showering, crystals flashing rainbows. She flung an arm around Marcellus and held on. "The night before New Palace Yard," she said, "midnight."

THE CHANCE OF A LIFETIME

IN EARLY MORNING, SHE APPROACHED LIZZIE'S RUN-
down tenement in Soho. She'd sent Marcellus back to
his shop to collect supplies, and stole through the streets
alone. The eerie quietude hacked at her nerves. No burning sky, no roaring guns, no ugly shimmer of dying aether.
Just . . . normal.

Distant revelers shouted, music drifting with the stench
of coal fires and damp wool. Mud squelched, dark clouds
gathered and threatened rain. A sickly yellow moon struggled
through the clouds. But no moonlit fever burned in Eliza's
blood. No Lizzie stretching, yearning for freedom.

That wasn't normal.

About now, Lizzie was approaching the Magic Flute, her
awful discovery still to be made. Another *her,* roaming the
city, oblivious to the looming future. Those precious moments with Remy, her meeting with Newton, the explosion at
Finch's, *la Bête*'s attack. All yet to happen.

But was it inevitable, as Seymour Locke believed? Or
could the future be changed?

Hitching up her trousers, she hopped across the wet street.

A one-legged beggar crouched in a doorway, shovel hat pulled low, rats skittering around his knees. In Lizzie's window, no lights yet burned.

Eliza squeezed into a noisome cranny around the corner. Moldy walls closed in, water trickling in the smell of dead things. Shivering, she hunkered down to wait.

At last, there he was, a shadow amongst shadows, slipping from alley to porch to doorway. Stealthy like a wraith, barely a rustling footstep as he passed within a few feet of her hide.

"Don't go inside," she whispered.

He halted. Still a shadow, long and lean—but with a piercing stare of electric-sky blue.

"Shh." She grabbed Remy's hand, and pulled him quietly out of sight, with a dirty glance at that snoozing beggar. That mildewed green coat . . . and she flashed back to the fellow she'd seen watching her, that night in Cavendish Square. Inwardly, she snorted. Beggar, indeed. And she'd wondered how those Enforcers had followed her.

As soon as they were out of hearing, Remy stopped her, in a dilapidated doorway safe from prying eyes. Dusty russet coat, chestnut curls charmingly disheveled, scarf hiding that silver half-moon amulet at his throat. "Eliza, what . . . ? Never mind. Look, I owe you an explanation—"

"I know." She gripped his hands, overcome. He was here. He was safe. And she hadn't ruined everything with her jealous cruelty. Not yet. "I know everything. Your letter, *la Bête*'s plans. I know why you did it."

"But—"

"I've seen the future." Swiftly, she explained. Their imminent meeting, his capture, her visit to Newton, the catastrophe at New Palace Yard, her escape from prison with Finch. "So here I am," she finished simply.

But guilt chewed her. She'd omitted the part about Lizzie the assassin. Another story, for another time—and her heart still burned with shame that Lizzie had abandoned her to her fate. Did her own self despise her so much? Was she so terrible a person?

But Remy's gaze glowed. "You're glorious. Is it wrong that I want to kiss you until you suffocate?"

"Yes, but it's tempting—oh!" His lips tasted so good, she swooned. He smelled delightful, of steel and aether and desire, and it occurred to her that she wasn't wearing a corset. It felt daring, unrestricted, free. Not to mention sensual, a vivid echo of the last time she'd kissed him in this squalid room, legs wrapped around him, his mouth on her skin . . . She swatted him, breathless. "Stop it. This is no time for flirting."

"Who said anything about flirting? You just rescued me from certain death. I ought to insist you ravish me without mercy." He grinned, releasing her. "And I shall. After we've avoided capture, saved the Philosopher from his assassin, and stopped *la Bête* before he begins. Nothing like a challenge."

Eliza hesitated. How she'd stop Lizzie was one thing. Thwarting *la Bête* in all his simultaneous incarnations . . . An idea sparked. "Remy, your amulet."

"How did you . . . ? Never mind. It works, if that's what you're asking." He bit his lip. "Eliza, I know you don't like it. I don't like it either. But I need you to be safe from me."

"I am safe from you—"

"No." A firm headshake. "You're not. I can't take the chance."

For a moment, she faltered. For so long, she'd pretended everything was normal. That his creature—and hers—were just an inconvenience. A ripple to be smoothed over.

But the darkness had to be dealt with. Surrendering wasn't an option. But truce?

You can feed it, or you can fight it, he'd said. *Not a cure. A peace offering.*

Was it too late for her and Lizzie to make peace?

"Fine." She edged closer, partly to whisper, but partly because he was real and beautiful and alive and she adored him. "Then here's what we should do."

As the clock tower struck a quarter to eleven—it was the gigantic thirteen-ton bell that was named Big Ben, not the clock, but no one ever seemed to care—the same glorious, oblivious morning sun shone down on New Palace Yard. Eliza hurried around the corner at Westminster Bridge, where the ornate façade of the new Houses of Parliament glittered in fresh sunlight. The crowd was already thick, their voices swelling.

Remy had gone his separate way, as they'd planned. Would he make it in time?

The irony stung. All these years of fighting Lizzie and Marcellus and Edward Hyde and everyone else who'd tried to help her—only to discover too late that she couldn't win alone.

She'd approached from the Thames this time, the opposite

direction, to stop red-caped Lizzie before she even reached the podium. Besides, she'd wanted to be sure of avoiding herself. Somewhere across New Palace Yard, another Eliza elbowed through the crowd. Would things happen differently this time? If crisis were averted, *la Bête* thwarted, assassination foiled—would she, this new Eliza, vanish? Never taken to the asylum, never rescued by loyal Marcellus so she could arrive at this very point in time?

No wonder Seymour Locke had gone mad.

Eliza squeezed on through the sea of bodies. Hats, banners, and flailing arms blocked her view. Eyes flashed at her, cruel smiles glinting. Was that a scarlet hood, a spray of mahogany curls? Before she could focus, it was gone.

At last, the podium came into view, ringed by brass Enforcers. She craned her neck, eyeing the tall tower that blocked out the sun.

Two minutes to eleven.

The heat, the smell, and the roiling noise washed over her, a dizzy cacophony of sensations, and the past unfolded before her eyes like a cinematograph in slow motion.

The official party climbed the dais steps, flanked by their black-robed escorts. Bertie, Princess Victoria, the scowling Regent, Lord Beaconsfield with blue rosettes pinned to his coat.

One minute.

The murderer-king laughed, blond hair falling from beneath his hat. Victoria smiled at him, eyes flashing dark. The ground thrummed as the gigantic bells struck the Westminster Quarters. DING-DONG-DING-DONG! DONG-DING-DING-DONG!

The minute hand clunked to vertical.

ONE . . . TWO . . .

A splash of scarlet, in the corner of Eliza's eye. Lizzie's cloaked figure wormed through the crowd, dark curls escaping from her hood.

Eliza sprang. Jumped an Enforcer's legs, dodged a man's flailing elbows, grabbed the red-cloaked shoulders. "Lizzie, stop!"

"Leave me be!" Lizzie's eyes spat dark poison. "You can't stop me. This is *MINE*, hear me?"

THREE . . . FOUR . . .

Eliza held on. "You don't understand. You can't kill the king. Everything goes wrong."

On the stage, Bertie laughed and waved, and Lord Beaconsfield stepped forwards to accept his cheers. "Watch me," growled Lizzie. "I'll wring the murdering bastard's neck!" She struggled and snarled, spit flying. *FIVE . . . SIX . . .*

But Eliza fought desperately, refusing to let go. "It doesn't work. You kill the Philosopher instead and the sorcerers win!"

"So much the better!" With a hideous skull-like grin, Lizzie slammed her forehead into Eliza's face.

Red pain blotted her vision. *SEVEN . . . EIGHT . . .* Groggily, she shook her eyes clear . . . and her blood curdled in despair. Lizzie was gone.

The king was waving and hooting, jumping up and down. The black-robed sorcerers loomed, menacing. Victoria laughed—and the air beside her writhed and tore. *NINE . . . TEN . . .*

Pop!

La Bête squeezed from the crack, a streak of black horror. His withered arm dangled grotesquely, the relic of some awful spell.

ELEVEN!

La Bête grinned at Victoria, triumphant—and the sorcerer next to him hurled off his robes in a swirl of black.

Not a sorcerer. Remy Lafayette.

Remy's lips moved, words snatched away by the din. *La Bête*'s face twisted into a frightful sneer, and his gauntleted arm flashed up. But Remy was quicker. And he grabbed the amulet around *la Bête*'s skinny neck and tore it free.

Fire flashed, a deadly electric sizzle. *La Bête* screamed. Muscles rippled, clothing tearing under the strain of the *change*. His spine quivered and arched, his scrawny knees popped backwards with an ugly *snap!* Black fur sprouted, covering his rawboned form. His face elongated into a snout, furred ears flattened—and with a snarl of dripping fangs, the creature leapt for Remy's throat.

Crrack! Remy fired his pistol. Sky-blue lightning pierced the creature's heart, stopping it in mid-flight. It somersaulted, and flopped to the dais. Dead.

Remy dropped the amulet, and crushed it under his boot.

Victoria screamed. Lord Beaconsfield seized his cane two-handed, and swung it hard. The diamond-studded unicorn slammed into Victoria's skull, and she toppled, out cold. Beaconsfield sniffed haughtily, and straightened his necktie.

The crowd roared, like the Newgate mob on hanging day, thirsty for a bloody spectacle. But Eliza had never laid eyes on a more blessed sight.

No skyships. No sorcerers' army. No ruined aether.

Just one abominable dead man.

His voice abruptly restored, the Philosopher yelled sharply for Enforcers. Metal feet thundered, and a dozen glittering electric weapons descended to protect the king.

Wildly, Eliza searched for Lizzie. There, an angry scarlet streak, oozing between Enforcers in the confusion, clambering onto the stage in a throng of fleeing dignitaries with the knife bright in her hand.

"Stop!" Eliza dived, grabbing Lizzie's skirts and dragging her to the ground.

Lizzie screeched, a trapped wildcat. She kicked, sending Eliza flying, and leapt atop her, pinning her to the cobblestones. *Bonk!* Eliza's skull cracked backwards, stars whirling. Lizzie had clipped her under the chin. A disorienting blow.

Eliza choked, trying not to vomit. She couldn't break free. She groped in her pocket for the stinger, the world reeling.

"God rot you, girl," snarled Lizzie, sour breath scorching Eliza's face, that peculiar goaty odor of madness. "Why can't you just *DIE?*"

Steel flashed, and Lizzie stabbed the blade down.

Eliza's fingers folded around her stinger. She kicked as hard as she could, rolled, and thrust the weapon upwards.

Zzzap! Electricity exploded. Lizzie jerked, eyes rolling, an ugly rictus of shock. And then she wilted, tumbling across Eliza's chest. Her pupils dilated, staring into Eliza's eyes, sightless but accusing.

Lifeless. Just a drift of mahogany hair, trailing in the wind.

A scream rose in Eliza's throat.

But all it met was blood.

A strange chill spread down her neck, seeping outwards.

Where had the sunshine gone? She felt so cold. She tried to breathe, but metal scraped on bone. She gurgled, coppery liquid choking her. Her eyes ached and blurred. Her legs wouldn't move. A strange weight bore down, sapping her will. Heavy. So very heavy . . .

Her eyelids fluttered, and the world shimmered to white.

We're tucked up in bed, stiff sheets our chains, white gossamer curtains our prison now. This fine house stinks of walls. Same as the asylum, padding smeared with blood, only now they're dressed in fancy clothes like a bad actress in silks. Fairfax has released me—for now—but it's all for appearances' sake. A civilized façade.

I thrash, restless sweat soaking our nightgown, a futile effort to shake her off. It's midnight, or long past, but we've slept precious little. This thing in my head—this "Lizzie" who scratches like a wildcat in my chest, demanding to be free—never sleeps.

Below, footsteps pace in the study, thump-THUMP, thump-THUMP, *the uneven gait of a monster.*

Lizzie grips my muscles—a demon possessing me, a creeping cramp I can't shake—and drags our body out of bed.

I don't want to go. Don't want to hear. But she makes us. Tiptoes out into the stairwell, down to the landing. Below, yellow light leaks beneath the study door.

"—the only way, old bean. The full dose, say what?"

I want to jam my palms over my ears. Nothing good will come of this . . . but the old compulsion warms our blood, giving Lizzie strength. The treacherous, in-eluctable need to know.

"*Damn you, I never wanted this for her.*" *A second voice, rough and rich like old whisky.* "*Dresses, suit-ors, fancy bloody balls at society houses. That's what should trouble her. Or your god-rotted science, for all I give a damn. Just get it through your smoke-addled skull: I want her* ordinary."

"*But Edward,*" *comes the reply,* "*Edward, you obsti-nate old jackal, look at the poor girl and tell me we've got any choice! For once, listen to what Jedediah is telling you.*"

A snarl, fit for a beast. "*A conceited arse with airs above his paltry talents. Fuck him.*"

"*Certainly.*" *A nervous giggle.* "*Quite the thing to do, old bean. Go with God, say what? But he's right about this, eh? We must get this thing out of her. You saw the mess she made when we let it take its plea-sure. That pretty tutor of hers might eat fluxions for breakfast with the best of them, but he'll never get his depth perception back.*" *The scrape of a match, the sharp scent of a cigarette.* "*You know the rage only gets worse. Remember Madeleine.*"

A crash, something heavy hurled, a roar of rage and frustration. "*Think I've forgotten, you arrogant skunk? Think I don't know how bad it gets—*"

"*Then stop prevaricating!*" *A snap, as if something mild inside the fellow has melted away, leaving only steel.* "*For pity's sake, she's as good as my daughter, too.*"

A throbbing beat of silence.

And then he growls, a deep-throated threat. "She can't ever know why. Not a god-rotted word, Marcellus. Not ever."

A deep exhale. "You know your secrets are safe with me."

"Tomorrow, then. Midnight. Brew me your finest. Make it so she won't remember. And if she ever finds out, I swear by the Devil's bleeding balls I'll . . ."

. . . I'll kill you myself.

Around Eliza, the air shrieked and tore apart.

Paradox, whispered a ghostly Seymour Locke in her ear. *Open a rift to the past . . . reverse every decision you've ever made . . .*

Simultaneity games . . . The aether doesn't like it . . .

Light flashed, *bang!*

She stood in a darkened square. Mist curled over the cobbles, wreathing the wrought-iron park fence. The air smelled fresh, exhilarating. Stars glittered through broken clouds, and a gaslight shed a frosty golden halo over a row of neat town houses. Four stories, brick chimneys, white plaster façades.

Her house.

In the upstairs window, a candle burned, waiting.

Footsteps, approaching from the mist like a dream. Uneven, one light and one heavy. *Click CLICK, click CLICK . . .*

A man, wrapped in a greatcloak, lopsided shoulders hunched. His hat was pulled low, shadowing his hooked nose. A sweet whiff of alchemy drifted in his wake. He clutched an object under one arm—a package? a bottle?—and mumbled as he limped by, an off-key snatch of song. *"Cockles and mussels, alive, alive-oh . . ."*

"Father?" Her whisper was hoarse. Behind her back, she grasped something hard and cold. Lizzie's blade. Her hope for the future.

He halted. Turned. Glanced up.

Storm-gray eyes, her own reflection stark in their depths.

He lurched back, an awkward stumble. He looked young. Confused. Fearful. "What fresh madness, by God . . ."

"Father." The lump in her throat strangled her words. Stab him. Cut his throat. Smash the bottle to the cobbles. Scream for the police, cry assault, have him dragged away. Anything, except let him carry on. "It's me, Eliza. I can't explain. I only . . ."

"Never explain, m'darling." Hyde laughed, a rich and hearty sound, the licorice scent of absinthe strong on his breath. A crooked, handsome not-quite-gentleman, with a devilish smile and eyes full of fire. "Never complain, and sure as hell never explain. It's magic! Ha ha! Bleeding Christ, you remind me of your mother. You poor child. So it works, does it?" he added, suddenly fiercely cunning. "This hellbrew of Finch's. I only want the best for you, girl."

She smiled helplessly through hot tears. Such simple words. *Only the best for you.* All her life, she'd thought them the cruelest lie. But his elixir hadn't broken her in two. She understood that now. It had saved her life—and Lizzie's, too. Lizzie, who was part of her, for good or ill.

This is MY life. Words she'd screamed so often. *Mine.* As if Lizzie wasn't the better half of her, brave and strong with a heart of tarnished gold.

"And is it good for you?" Hyde was gruff, careful. As if reluctant to cross some line. "This life of ours. Are you . . . ?" He hesitated, seemingly lost for some unfamiliar description.

The word he wanted quivered on her lips, and she set it free. "Yes, I'm happy."

For a moment, she and Hyde watched each other. Face to face, mirror to mirror.

Then he gave an odd, bitter smile. "Disappear, then, before I'm ready. That's what you are, isn't it? Some beautiful poisoned dream?"

"I know why you gave me the elixir." The words tasted strange, a new and terrible truth. "Give me, that is. Tonight."

He grunted. "Finch flap his gums, did he? Mouthy gobshit."

"No." Her fingers tightened around the cold blade. Just one strike, and all this would be over. No jealousy, no turmoil, no senseless rage.

No spirit. No heart. No soul. So many empty years, alone.

"I know why you did it, Father." Her view of him blurred, and re-formed, clear and sharp like crystal. Not a monster. Just a man. "I know. And I forgive you."

Hyde stared at her, fire and storm. And then he laughed, and tipped his hat, and went on his crooked way.

Swiftly, silently, he climbed the wall. Hopping from windowsill to crevice to foothold with improbable, lopsided grace.

So that was how he did it. Not magic, or a conjuring trick. Just . . . Hyde.

Smiling, she watched him slip in the window, a warm breath of wind behind the curtain.

"G-good evening, sir." Her own voice, drifting faintly from within. Young Eliza, in her best silken gown. Waiting for her mysterious guardian, tremulous with fear—but with excitement, too, and intrigue, and romance. With her life ahead of her, for good or ill. "I heard voices outside. Who was that?"

A gruff laugh. "A dream, my sweet. Just . . ."

. . . just a dream.

Someone was shaking her. Her head rattled, cobbles poking uncomfortably into her hips. It vexed her. Why was she lying in the road?

"Eliza, wake up."

She opened her eyes. Bright sunshine glared. Crowd noise filtered in, footsteps and excited voices. New Palace Yard was clearing, Enforcers and soldiers urging the people back. Above, the clock tower chimed the first refrain of the Westminster Quarters. A quarter past eleven.

A familiar shape knelt beside her. Remy, gloriously backlit by the sun, chestnut hair afire. Alongside him, an owlish Marcellus Finch, an enormous bundle of tinfoil crammed under one arm.

Remy grinned. "Welcome back."

Beside the wooden dais, surrounded by flunkies and bodyguards, the Philosopher and Lord Beaconsfield were deep in conversation. Sir Isaac caught her eye, and winked. Or was it just a trick of the sun?

She sat up, muscles protesting. "And where exactly did I go?"

Where, indeed? A soft giggle tickled her ear, fragrant with sweetness. Startled, she glanced about. A scarlet hood, a spray of mahogany curls . . .

But Lizzie was nowhere to be seen.

MURDER IN THE BLOOD

TWO DAYS LATER, ELIZA FOUGHT THROUGH SCOTland Yard's marble-paved lobby, trying to catch her quarry's attention amongst bustling constables and civil servants. Hippocrates bounded gaily beside her, cogs whirring, and she swerved to avoid tripping. "Sir Stamford, please, a moment of your time."

"Ahh." The old fellow tottered on his trembling cane, squinting through his monocle with a big rheumy eye. "Who are you, young lady? And who's your saucy friend in red? What's your purpose in following me about? Froggie assassins, by God!"

She sighed. Two days since the catastrophic events at New Palace Yard, and the world seemed frighteningly fragile. She'd spent most of it appealing to the Commissioner—now the new Home Secretary, to whom Lord Beaconsfield had owed a favor—to no avail. "Dr. Eliza Jekyll, sir, crime scene physician. I'd like to speak with you about reinstating Harley Griffin, now that the Slasher case is going to trial—"

"Arrest that woman! She's interfering with police business." Reeve strode up, brandishing his cigar and smirking like a cream-fed tomcat. His usual foul brown suit had been replaced by a fawn one, for once neatly pressed. Had he found the courage to apologize to his wife? Despite his truculence, Eliza found herself hoping so.

"Is she, indeed?" Sir Stamford ducked, grabbing his teetering hat. "These radicals are shameless, sir. String 'em up, eh?"

Hipp snorted indignantly, and Eliza gritted her teeth. "This is public property, *Superintendent,* and I'm here as a private citizen to petition the Home Secretary. It's none of your concern."

But inwardly, she cursed. A pair of uniformed constables—Tweedledum and Tweedledee again—were edging up to carry out Reeve's order. Run? Attack them? Fake a swoon?

A flustered Constable Perkins hurried up from the front desk, dark wisps awry from her usually perfect bun. "Mr. Reeve, sir, you're needed—"

"I said, arrest her." Reeve ignored Perkins, shoving his thumb into tartan braces. "I warned you, *Doctor.* Just goes to show: women never listen."

"Attention!" Hipp squawked, madly flashing his lights, red-blue-red-blue. "Attention!"

Perkins, too, jigged like a frustrated puppy. "Sir, you really must come . . ."

Dum and Dee moved forwards. Eliza bristled. "Don't you dare lay hands on me—"

"Sir!" shouted Perkins, red-faced. "You *really* need to see this."

Dum and Dee froze. Sir Stamford goggled. Reeve scowled, and spun on his heel. "What is it, woman—Jesus Christ on a racehorse." His cigar stub fell to the floor.

At the front desk, hands tucked neatly behind his crimson coat skirts, stood Malachi Todd.

Eliza stumbled, bones jittering. Surely he wouldn't. Not here. Not now.

Todd just smiled, mild and terrifying. "Superintendent Reeve? Perhaps you remember me. Malachi Todd, at your service."

Reeve just gaped, speechless. For once, Eliza sympathized.

"I understand you've arrested the Soho Slasher," continued Todd blandly, brushing a dust speck from his sleeve. "*Bravo,* sir! Seven murders, the papers said. Admirable. But I'm afraid I can't allow this pitiful imposter—Hyde, is it?—to claim credit for a moment longer. My conscience, you know. Such a burden in my line of work, but you know me: at all costs, I must have the truth." Green eyes twinkled amidst ruined flesh. "You see, Hyde isn't guilty. I am."

Silence.

Eliza stared, dazed. At her feet, Hipp wobbled, cogs jammed in confusion. Was this an apology? A trick? Or just a chance to let her father go free, to undo the damage wrought by her failure? "Superintendent, I—"

"No doubt Dr. Jekyll shall corroborate my confession with physical evidence." Todd waved carelessly. He didn't look at her. "In fact, I insist on it. I owe her much, you see, and sadly she's the only one amongst your pack of imbeciles who's fit to deal with my case. You'll reinstate her accordingly."

At last, Reeve recovered, eyes gleaming with relish. "Take him down, lads," he crowed, and actually lurched forwards to do the deed himself.

"Not so fast." Todd's unburned hand twitched, and in

it, his razor flashed bright. Dum and Dee skidded to a halt. "Dr. Jekyll is reinstated. Say it. Oh, and your tragic Inspector Griffin as well. Or I'm afraid I must take as many of your unfortunate trained monkeys down with me as I can"—Todd licked his ruined lips, a horrid grin of promise—"and believe me, sir, my best will be *plenty*."

Reeve's face purpled, and he stifled a curse.

Eliza's brain clogged, sluggish with shock. "Sir, he means it. Please. Do as he says—"

"Don't be stubborn, lad." Sir Stamford brandished his cane at Reeve. "Your petty feud worth good British lives, is it? Give the lady her due and arrest this melted miscreant at once."

Reeve spluttered, thwarted. "Fine," he spat, "it's a deal."

Todd didn't reply. Just let the razor slip from his fingers. *Ping!* It hit the marble and bounced away, a deadly, shining autograph. And a gang of eager constables—Perkins included—descended upon him.

He didn't struggle. Just let them shove and jostle and cuff him, his elbows yanked cruelly behind his back. For an instant, he caught Eliza's eye, and his crusted lips twitched in an utterly unapologetic smile.

As he'd been in the asylum, all those months ago. Lucid. Monstrous. Terrifyingly human.

She moved dry lips, but no sound came out. *Thank you.*
You're welcome.

And steadily, she turned to walk away.

A FAMOUS NAME

THE FIRE CRACKLED PLEASANTLY IN THE DRAWING room grate, a soft orange glow in the deepening twilight. Rain pattered on the window, insulating the room from the rattle and hustle of Cavendish Square.

Eliza relaxed on the chaise, head resting on Remy's shoulder in easy silence. A cup of tea sat forgotten on the table. At her feet, Hippocrates napped, brassy legs flopping over the soft carpet. She liked this room, the embroidered drapes, the redwood buffet, this comfortable chaise. It had been her mother's room. The memories were faded, but sweet, unthreatening. Perhaps she'd leave it this way.

Her mind still boggled from the bizarre events at Scotland Yard that afternoon. Edward Hyde would be released, once the formalities were done, and Mr. Todd wouldn't escape justice this time. She'd no insanity plea to offer. He'd surely hang—and deep in her heart, it hurt. He'd been part of her life for so long, the idea that he'd no longer exist was strange and unsettling. As if a lifelong wound in her soul had healed—but not without deep scars.

As for the real Slasher? There'd be no more victims, she'd

make sure of that. Bertie would stay Bertie, and conventional treatments would have to suffice. He wasn't responsible for what he'd done. But dangerous doubts plagued her, an itch she couldn't satisfy. The Philosopher had returned her phial of medicine via courier, with a terse note attached.

Attend His Majesty at your convenience. Say, tomorrow, ten o'clock?

In the meantime, I advise discretion. A pity if the Royal College of Physicians should learn of the sort of treatments you provide.

Is. Newton, Regent, &c.

She'd formulated Bertie's alchemical potion to the weakest dose. Nothing approaching full elixir strength. There was no chance Bertie should have changed. Barring a mistake on her part, and on that score she'd racked her memory to no avail.

Despite the Royal's rules, Sir Isaac was the consummate scientist, his curiosity an impassive force of nature. *Nullius in verba.* Had he tinkered with her preparation? For science's sake, just to see what would happen?

A tiny chill tingled her skin. Seymour Locke and his time machine hadn't reappeared—at least, not yet. Had he vanished into some temporal unknown? Or merely changed his mind? The temptation to tinker with Henry's machine and go looking was strong. A chance to put things right, to change the world . . . but she'd learned the hard way that such vanity profited no one. She'd destroyed Henry's machine, and everything that remained in Crane's laboratory, over Marcellus Finch's protests. Some things were better left unknown.

At her side, Remy stared into the fire, playing absently with the amulet at his throat. Coatless, shirt loosened, his cuffs startling white, boots propped absently on the footstool. A fresh scar on his cheek, faint but definite.

The Philosopher had agreed to let him walk, after hearing the story at length from Lord Beaconsfield. Had even offered to reinstate him in his job at the Royal. Whether Remy would take it . . .

She nudged him. "I charge consultations by the hour, you know."

"Hmm?" He came to with a start, dropping the amulet. "Sorry. I wandered."

"My plan precisely. You've missed the tide. Your lover in Paris will be wondering where you are."

Fondly, he played with her hair. "The poor lady, falling for such a heartless rogue. I find I've quite forgotten her already."

Self-consciously, she smoothed her skirts. New gray ones, crisp and pleasant. For so long, she'd fought Lizzie, and Lizzie had fought back. She'd thought the prickly blue alchemical potion had changed things, somehow. Severed their ties. Brought their incessant bickering to a head.

But had it? She'd no proper proof the potion worked. She'd never conducted a second batch of experiments. She'd assumed that Lizzie's hostility—her glee at taking over Eliza's body—had been prompted by the potion. But Lizzie had hurled a vase at Reeve days before that arcane blue liquid had ever passed her lips.

Perhaps the potion hadn't worked at all. Perhaps Eliza had brought it all on herself by shutting Lizzie out. She'd destroyed Moriarty Quick's macabre journals along with everything else. Now, she'd never know—and that was for the best.

Her mood sobered. The full moon was fast approaching. What would Remy do? "Did you ever think about staying with them? The lycanthropes, I mean."

"No." An awkward half-smile. "Actually, yes. Once or twice. Mostly when I was missing you terribly and wallowing in self-pity. I soon got over it once I saw them in action."

"But to find someone who understands you . . ."

"*You* understand me." He kissed her hair. "You understand love and honor and self-sacrifice. Those people never will."

She traced his cheek with one finger. "Is it over, with François? Did you get what you wanted?"

"No." Candid, no hesitation.

She bit her lip. "Oh. Well—"

"You were right." A shrug, white shirt shifting. "François betrayed me, and I hated him for it. I didn't realize how much. But then I understood . . . François wanted revenge, too. On his sickness, on me for being well when he was dying. On the world for making him the man he was. But the world doesn't make us, Eliza. *We* make us. *We* choose." He fingered his amulet, and swiftly slipped the chain over his head and pressed it into her hands. "Take this."

"What? No, I can't."

"Please. Take it. Don't you see? *La Bête* offered François his heart's desire, and it ruined him. Now he's doing the same to me. A chance for you to be safe, for us to be together. All I must do is surrender and you'll never need fear me again."

Suddenly Eliza's anxiety that Lizzie would interfere, that she'd somehow ruin things, seemed petty and false. "Remy—"

"I can't just give up, Eliza." He blinked fiercely on glittering lashes. "It's an insult to my dead wife and to all the other people I've hurt. It's the act of a coward, and if I did it, I'd no longer be the man you love." A helpless shrug. "I'm so sorry."

Slowly, she turned the stone in her fingers. Cold, smooth, unpleasant like a snake's scales. It winked at her, a sly temptation. *Keep me. Use me. Forget your troubles. You know you want to . . .*

She'd imagined Remy would sacrifice their future for his mission. But it wasn't for the mission. It was for everything he held dear. Honor, courage. Her love for him.

Resolute, she hurled the amulet into the fire. *Smash!* The stone shattered, releasing a curl of evil-smelling smoke. "So much for *la Bête.*"

Remy stared. "Eliza, think about this—"

"I have. Whatever your troubles, we face them together. I will never be afraid of you." She watched it sink in, the incredulous shake of his head. Then she quirked a smile. "I've survived your mother, after all. Anything less than reckless optimism seems inappropriate." She kissed him again, her heart lighter. But the prickling nerves she'd been suppressing all day were making merciless reappearance. "Enough, my darling. We need to talk."

"Of course. The wedding." He stretched back, a glory of mussed curls and bright eyes. "Well, my mother has finally admitted that it's possible you didn't burn your own house down purely to make her the butt of society gossip, so that's good news. And I was thinking we ought to do Regent's Park for the breakfast, so long as you don't mind the rain. Oh, and should I write to your father? Now they've left off with the murder charges, I mean. I know you're dreadfully modern but I never actually *asked*, and seeing as he keeps a battalion of well-armed thugs ready to thrash the lights out of all who vex him, I thought—"

"Remy?"

A raised eyebrow. "My sweet?"

"I can't marry you."

A long, abject silence. He let out a breath. "All right. Well—"

"I don't mean I won't. I mean, I *do,* but . . ." She sighed, and started again. "I want to be with you, Remy, more than I've wanted most things in my life. But marriage . . ." She trailed off. How to explain that she, too, sought the courage to be true to herself? He'd think her stubborn and selfish. Not to mention ridiculous.

"But marriage," he prodded gently, "is an archaic institution designed to control women and glorify the patriarchy, while perpetuating the myths that women need protecting from themselves and men want women to be sexual and domestic servants with no identity or vocation of their own?"

She gulped a heady, hopeful laugh. Was she doomed forever to underestimate him? "Something like that."

"You have my vote, madam. Go on."

"Well, much as I adore you, my darling, I am and always have been Dr. Jekyll. The awful trouble of getting a new door shingle, you know, and all my stationery. And 'Dr. Eliza Lafayette' just sounds . . ." She wrinkled her nose. "Polysyllabic?"

An enchanted smile. "Fair enough. So . . . ?"

She teased her finger into his chestnut curls. "So since

we've already got the house, and our staff, and my practice, and you're obligingly filthy rich and we've everything we need, I was wondering . . ."

"Mmm?" His gaze fixed on her lips.

". . . if we could, well, take the 'married' part as read and carry on." She smiled sweetly. "It'll be just as good as the real thing. We could stay engaged, so we're a little bit respectable. If it makes you feel better."

"You delectable rebel." His murmur was husky. "I'm shocked. Whatever will people say?"

She yanked his hair playfully. "Since when have you given a rusty pin what people say?"

He sobered a little. "Seriously, people will talk. And it won't be about me. You know how these things go."

"Pah," she retorted comfortably. "They already *talk*. 'Look, there goes Dr. Jekyll, the suffragette who plays with dead bodies and consorts with razor murderers. A spinster, you know, washed up at twenty-seven with no man to look after her and a mad scientist for a father.' Or is it a killer criminal kingpin? It's so hard to keep up with the gossip."

Remy laughed. "My love, I couldn't care less about formalities, so long as I get you. If you mean it, consider me all yours."

She smacked a kiss on his cheek. "Knew I chose you for a reason."

"On one condition," he added with a grin. "You're telling my mother. If I say I'm canceling the wedding to shack up with a corpse-fixated suffragette, there'll be nothing left of me but a quivering pile of dust. You might at least get away with only a flayed limb or two."

"It's a deal." She jumped up, buoyant.

He caught her trailing hand. "Not so fast, Doctor."

Her heartbeat quickened, as he brushed his lips across her palm. "I'm sorry, is there something else?"

"Well . . ." A tingling kiss on the inside of her wrist. "You were saying that our, um, arrangement is just like the real thing."

"I did mention that."

He traced a speculative finger around the buttons on her bodice. "So we're as good as married."

She arched her back, luxuriating. "As good as."

"Then make love to me, Eliza Jekyll." A bright blue twinkle. "So long as you don't mind the scandal."

She pushed him back into the chaise with one finger, and climbed after. "Give me a lifetime of scandal, Remy Lafayette."

Then his mouth captured hers. She kissed him slowly, savoring his breath, his tongue, the hot flavor of his love for her. Her skin sparkled under his touch. His beauty made her ache, his scent of steel and aether and hot skin a delight.

She slid her palms beneath his shirt. His scars fascinated her, his shapes strange yet familiar, with a warm thrill of recognition that wasn't bitter, but enticing. Exhilarating.

He groaned as she settled in his lap, skirts flowing over him. They were still dressed, barely. "Did I ever tell you you're merciless? At least let me carry you swooning to the bed like a proper seducer."

"Just you try it." And she ran, laughing, down the corridor and up the stairs, until they fell together onto warm sheets by firelight.

* * *

In the dark of the morning, Eliza stirred.

Beside her, Remy slept, hair mussed on the pillow, long limbs glistening in the light of the dying coals. She smiled. Careful not to disturb him, she slipped out of bed, padding naked across the carpet. On the mantel, a glass-globed clock ticked, softly counting the hours. Henry Jekyll's clock. But the white curtains of the bed held no ghosts now. Madeleine was gone. Just Eliza's own memories, sweet and breathless with pleasure. And they'd make many more.

But for now, she'd things to do.

Her reflection gazed back from the gilt-edged mantel mirror. Hair drifting in a pale halo, her storm-gray eyes shining. Her father's eyes, deep and liquid and not quite right. A glint of something *other*.

She exhaled, and *changed*.

Not with a *pop!* or a fighting wrench of bone. More like a sigh of contentment.

I wink at the mirror. Hello, Miss Lizzie. My dark curls are like raw silk, my body lush. I slide curious hands over my skin, my curves. Something feels different. Something . . . complete.

You can feed it, or you can fight it.

It's nice, not fighting. I like it.

I glance at Remy, her lover at last, asleep with his monster contented. He's beautiful, all strong limbs and hot skin and scars. It's tempting to crawl back into bed beside him, but the temptation only lasts a moment. Remy's a fine man, but . . . well, ick. We can't share *everything*.

Quiet-like, I sneak over and open the closet. Inside, red

fabric lies folded beside gray. When Eliza bought new clothes, she ordered some for me, too. A peace offering, of sorts, after that business with the asylum. I'll take it, please and thank you. Guess I lost me head for a while there.

I still remember, see, that future that never happened. The hatred in my heart, the death in her eyes as they dragged her away. Funny, when you get what you think you want. Often as not, you don't want it no more.

Half hidden beneath my dresses, a rolled canvas pokes out, unfurling. A new, perfectly finished painting of a lady in scarlet, hair shining like an angel's, softly asleep on a green chaise in a world where evil can be tempered by love.

He sent it before he gave himself up. A note attached, no address or salutation. Just two words in his odd left-slanted hand: *Sweet dreams.*

I could burn her, this new, stronger, happier Eliza. But I let her stay there. It's a beautiful dream.

Swiftly, I pull on my new skirts. Bright, luxurious Venetian red. Nothing but the best for Miss Lizzie. I've business with my father tonight. And there, my lover'll be waiting, his black velvet hair jeweled with raindrops, a smile in his crooked dark eyes.

Johnny weren't in lavender after all, see. And don't imagine sommat as petty as me being someone else half the time will come between us. It's a funny thing, love. It forgives 'most everything.

I tiptoe down the stairs, and the front door creaks as I slip out. The nighttime streets sparkle clean after the rain. Stars glitter through broken clouds, and the air's bracing, alive. I stride along, boots splashing, dragon cane over my shoulder, singing. *"That dirty no-good robbing Maggie May . . ."*

Down in Soho, it's thriving with music and bright arc-lights. In our room, Johnny's waiting, my fine fairy beauty. By the fire, Jacky Spring-Heels giggles, scratching his arse and sucking on his long white hair. And in the armchair, dark-eyed and dreadful, slouches Eddie Hyde.

"Where the fuck have you been?" he growls, then ruins it with a dirty-handsome grin.

"Already drunk as a skunk, is you? That's my papa." I sweep Johnny into my arms, bending him back like a tango dancer for a kiss. He tastes of gin and sweet desire, and my heart shouts with gladness. Lizzie's got her man, and she don't want no other.

"Christ," mutters Eddie, "put that away, Wild. That's my friggin' daughter you're pawing."

Johnny's crooked eyes smolder. "You're in a mood, sweet ruby Lizzie."

"Can't a girl be happy once in a while?" I flop into the lumpy chair beside Jacky. "Now, about the Sultan. Is it coopered, or are we sweet?"

Johnny and Eddie share a grin.

"What, you glocky lunkheads?"

Johnny just gestures to the bed. "That came for you last night."

In the cushions, like a slumbering cat, sits a lacquered black box. The card, in narrow left-slanting letters, reads *Miss Elizabeth Hyde.*

Inside, on red satin, there's a dented black topper, crushed in on one side. A famous hat, that. Almost as famous as the name what once wore it.

Tucked into the band is a single crimson rose.

You'll never get near him, Johnny said. Not I, for certain. But an expert on murder, with a glittering razor and a selfish thirst for blood?

What favor might I owe you, when you need it most?

Still, my thoughts slide uneasy to that gore-soaked room at Mrs. Fletcher's. A bloodied diamond ring, the slaughtered remains of a girl unlucky in love . . . and my father drunk to hell in the corner, laudanum on his breath and his shirt drenched tell-tale red. Mr. Todd at his lunatic finest. Now *there's* a man with murder in his blood.

I pick up the late and no-longer-Artful Dodger's hat. Mr. Todd's rose gleams, a cunning red wink, and I bury my nose in those soft petals. What do you know? It smells sweet.

A peace offering, of sorts. And I'll take it, please and thank you. Miss Lizzie needs all the friends she can get.

I tuck the rose into my bodice. Tilt the hat rakishly over one eye, a saucy salute. "Gin all round, then."

Eddie grins, and produces a bottle. "A wake, by God. To the Artful fucking Dodger, may he rot in his own juice. And to Mr. Malachi Todd, the maddest bastard in London bar none."

"I'll drink to that." I grab the bottle, tilt and swallow. Fire rolls in my gullet, a molten-gold glory. God rot it, but Miss Lizzie likes a drink. I pass it to Johnny, who like a good landlord's rustled up some cups, and he pours and we all three clink 'em high. "God save Your Majesty."

Because Eddie Hyde's the King. And there ain't no other.

ACKNOWLEDGMENTS

Thank you to my team of excellent enablers: Elle and everyone at Harper Voyager; my super-agent, Marlene; my ever-patient crit readers, who feed me hot chocolate and endure far too much whining about how *hard* it is to live in this amazing world of books. To the new cat, who's mostly learned not to sit on the keyboard. And to readers everywhere, who enjoy Eliza's and Lizzie's madcap antics and laugh at my hist-lit nerd jokes—gems, every one of you.

ABOUT THE AUTHOR

Viola Carr is the author of two previous novels in the Electric Empire trilogy, *The Diabolical Miss Hyde* and *The Devious Dr. Jekyll*. She was born in Australia, but wandered into darkest London one foggy October evening and never found her way out. She now devours countless history books and dictates fantastical novels by gaslight, accompanied by classical music and the snoring of her slumbering cat.